LIBERTY AND TRUTH
PEACE AND PROSPERITY

RYK BROWN

The Frontiers Saga Part 3: Fringe Worlds
Episode #3: Liberty and Truth Peace and Prosperity
Copyright © 2022 by Ryk Brown All rights reserved.

No part of this book may be reproduced, scanned, or distributed in any printed or electronic form without permission. Please do not participate in or encourage piracy of copyrighted materials in violation of the author's rights. Thank you for respecting the hard work of this author.

This is a work of fiction. Names, characters, places, and incidents either are the product of the author's imagination or are used fictitiously, and any resemblance to locales, events, business establishments, or actual persons—living or dead—is entirely coincidental.

CHAPTER ONE

"*Nathan?*" Cameron called over comm-sets. "*I hate to be the one to say this, but...*"

"She's right," Jessica said, keeping her voice low enough for only Nathan to hear.

Nathan was torn. The man before him looked exactly like Casimir Ta'Akar, but twenty years younger. Every fiber of his being wanted to believe that it was indeed the man who had fought by his side and singlehandedly enabled him to liberate Earth and her core worlds so many years ago. But that man was long dead. Executed by other house leaders of Takara.

He wanted to believe that it *was* Abby, Doctor Chen, and Vladimir, but only Doctor Chen looked the same as she had the last time they had seen her. Both Abby and Vlad looked a bit younger than before. Not as much as Jakome, but younger.

"You undoubtedly find all of this difficult to believe," Jakome stated. "Were I in your shoes, I would keep us isolated until our identities can be proven. Preferably, someplace warmer than this?"

A wave of relief washed over Nathan. It was so like the Tug he remembered to practically read his mind. "Thank you for understanding," he told Jakome. "Jess, you and the Ghatazhak escort them to medical. Have Master Sergeant Baris check their DNA against records."

"Yes, sir," Jessica replied.

"It would be best if I notified my ship that we are going inside...willingly," Jakome suggested. "They have strict orders to disable this ship and all aboard—including the four of us—if we are taken captive."

"Of course," Nathan agreed.

Jakome tapped the side of his neck, just below his left ear. "Captain Elias, we are going inside. Maintain position and condition until further notice. All other standing orders remain in effect."

"*Understood, my lord,*" the Bonaventura's captain confirmed.

Jakome turned to Jessica. "Lead the way, Jess," he said, addressing her in an oddly familiar fashion.

Jessica took a breath, exchanging glances with Nathan. "Follow me."

"Nathan, it is me," Vladimir assured him.

"I know," Nathan replied. "Just humor me though."

Vladimir nodded his understanding, following Jakome and Jessica.

"We won't have any genetic records for Doctor Sorenson or Casimir," Doctor Chen told Nathan as she followed them out.

"I know." Nathan looked to Abby, still holding onto her son. "Abby, it's not that I'm not happy to see you..."

"I understand," Abby replied, letting go of her son.

"Captain, it's her, I know it," Nikolas insisted.

"Stand down, Ensign," Loki instructed.

"It's all right," Abby told him, touching his face. "He *has* to do this. He has no choice." She followed Doctor Chen. "It's good to see you as well, Nathan," she said as she passed.

Kit and the other three Ghatazhak followed them out. Kit paused near Nathan, asking, "Orders?"

Nathan sighed. "I honestly don't know."

* * *

"We verified Doctor Chen and Commander Kamenetskiy," Master Sergeant Baris reported. "But we don't have genetic data for Doctor Sorenson or Jakome for comparison."

"What about cloning markers?" Nathan wondered.

"Cloning technology has advanced considerably over the centuries," Abby told him. "I doubt you'd be able to detect a clone with your technology."

"It is difficult to do so even with *current* technology," Jakome added.

"I'm afraid you'll have to take my word for their identities," Doctor Chen told Nathan. "I've spent the last two days with Jakome, and as best I can tell, he is Tug."

"Perhaps I should explain," Jakome offered.

"To say the least," Nathan agreed.

"After the war, Takara was a fractured world. Deliza was a leader in appearance only, with the nobles making all the decisions. Both the war and the reformation of the Alliance that followed brought great profit to the houses of Takara. Deliza's own child, Prince Toren, had not turned out to be the man she had hoped, and she felt uncomfortable leaving him in charge of House Ta'Akar upon her passing. So she created me."

"Why didn't she just clone herself?" Nathan wondered.

"Cloning does not work for everyone. In Deliza's case, the first two times she was cloned went fine, but the third time resulted in an abnormality known as "Hurrun's Syndrome". To clone herself again would have meant certain death, so she chose to live out her life, hoping for a cure to Hurrun's. Unfortunately, that cure never came. In fact, Hurrun's became more common, and it was one of the major reasons the Alliance banned cloning."

"How did you manage to be created then?" Jessica asked.

"I was born just prior to the ban."

"But wasn't that a few hundred years ago?" Nathan said.

"One of Deliza's projects was to resurrect and to *improve* upon the anti-aging serum that was lost when Caius fell." He looked at Jessica. "I believe *you* were the one who took him out."

"A twofer," Jessica remarked nonchalantly.

"So you've been alive for three hundred plus years?" Nathan surmised.

"Approximately, yes," Jakome replied. "And I expect to be alive for another three hundred, perhaps more."

"But you don't have any of Tug's memories, right?" Nathan asked.

"It's more like *feelings*," Jakome explained. "I liken it to the phenomenon of déjà vu. It is the result of genetic memory."

"I thought that was debunked," Nathan said.

"So did I," Doctor Chen agreed.

"In the sense that the term was originally used, yes. But science later discovered that it was something entirely different. You probably assume that you get your natural leadership qualities and your ability to negotiate with others from your father, and that would be correct. Not, however, in the way that you would assume. Our experiences change our DNA, and those changes are passed on. You got your flight instincts from your grandfather's experience, passed on to you through your father. If you were to father a child now, that child would inherit those same natural abilities. However, if *after* fathering that child, you learned to play the violin, the *inclination* for that skill would not be passed to your child because they were encoded into your DNA *after* your child was conceived."

"So how do Tug's experiences translate to you?"

"I was created using a sample of his DNA that was taken *after he* retook the throne of Takara. When I see you or Jessica or Vlad...even Doctor Chen, I instinctively trust you *because* of my father's experiences *with* you."

"Your father," Nathan commented. "If you're a *clone* of Casimir, then…"

"It is a term I chose to use for the one whose DNA I was created from. It is also why I chose to be known as Jakome rather than Casimir. Without his memories, I am *not* the same man. I do, however, have the same *potential* as my genetic donor, perhaps even more so since I was created from DNA that was altered by his life experiences."

Nathan shook his head. "It's all pretty mind-boggling."

"As I'm sure it was when you first discovered you were a clone," Jakome commented.

"How did you know I was a clone?" Nathan wondered. "That was never really made public."

"Deliza told me everything about each of you, as well as about my father. I have also studied all of your histories in great detail, as well as that of the original Aurora. I know everything there is to know about each of you."

Nathan looked uncomfortable. "Why?"

"Perhaps I can help with that," Abby suggested. "I took it hard when I lost Nikolas, and the fact that there was never any evidence of the Aurora's destruction made it even more difficult. I spent years analyzing everything possible, and I concluded that it was at least possible that you were *not* destroyed. But I could not get anyone to listen to me. No one *except* Deliza. She provided the support I needed to continue my research, while I continued my work on the gate network for the Alliance. Together, we determined that your survival was not only possible but *probable.* But by that time, we were deep into the war, and resources were limited. That, and the fact that we had no way to determine where or *when* you had ended up, put a damper on things."

"We heard about what the Alliance did to you," Cameron told her.

"The rogue gravity well side effect has no grounding in science," Abby insisted. "Except maybe *political* science. It was just a way for the Alliance to take control of all interstellar traffic, and therefore have control over humanity. I tried to argue the Science Academy's findings, but they destroyed my reputation and ended my career, just as they did for anyone else who did not support their findings. Had it not been for Deliza..."

"What about your family?" Nathan wondered.

"I'm afraid my obsession with Nikolas and the Aurora destroyed my marriage and alienated my daughter," Abby explained. "I lived out the remainder of what was my third life with Deliza. I passed shortly after her, just after scanning and storing my consciousness for long-term storage."

"Long-term storage for what?" Nathan wondered.

"For the day that you were found," Abby replied.

"Deliza Ta'Akar left detailed instructions for myself and my kin to continually watch for signs of the Aurora's reappearance and to provide assistance to her as needed. She once told me that all that we were was only possible *because* of the Aurora and her crew. In a way, she was ensuring the legacy of her father by ensuring that House Ta'Akar would forever support the Aurora, her captain, and her crew. *That is why I am here.*"

* * *

"I apologize for the two days of suffering you had to experience," Jakome explained as everyone took their seats at the conference table in the command briefing room. "Two days was the shortest time that we could safely create a replacement body for Commander Kamenetskiy, and Doctor Chen did not know your location. Even Vladimir did not know. Fortunately, he knew enough *about* this world that we were able to determine its location. Ironically, had your Ghatazhak arrived a few minutes earlier, we might have met two days sooner."

"How would you have known who they were?" Nathan wondered.

"I would have recognized them from historical records. I assume that was whom you sent in to retrieve the commander and Doctor Chen?"

"It was," Nathan admitted, taking his seat. "The purpose of this briefing is to discuss the state of the Alliance and how we will proceed from this point forward."

"Captain, if I may ask Jakome a question?" Kit asked.

"Of course, Lieutenant."

Kit looked at Jakome. "Do you know what happened to the Ghatazhak?"

"The official record states that they died in the Great War," Jakome replied.

"All at once?" Jessica asked in disbelief.

"The historical records of battle are limited, but it appears they were killed in an ambush on their way to a covert op that would have shortened the war."

"That doesn't make sense," Kit argued. "General Telles would never have put *all* the Ghatazhak at risk of ambush."

"Like I said, the details are limited. Because of this, many theories have arisen over the years. My belief is that the Alliance set them up. General Telles was opposed to many of the changes the Alliance was making for the war effort. I believe he realized that the war was just an excuse to increase their control over member worlds and to grow the size of their fleet."

"Was there any evidence of their deaths?" Jessica asked.

"I'm afraid there was," Jakome answered. "Debris from their transports was found. Among the debris were bits of human tissue that were identified as belonging to several of the Ghatazhak."

"Was Telles among them?" Nathan questioned.

"He was."

"Why would Telles go on an op?" Jessica wondered.

"If the op was important enough, he might," Kit stated. "That's the kind of leader he was."

"There were many conspiracy theories, most of which died out over the centuries," Jakome continued. "But all the available evidence supports that they died in that ambush."

"If the Alliance *wanted* the war, why would they send the Ghatazhak on a mission that would shorten it?" Nathan asked.

"I believe that originally, the Alliance only intended to start a war with the Ilyan, whom they could have defeated within a few years. But the Ilyan

Protectorate was not equipped to fight a real war, and the Alliance was winning faster than they liked. Fortunately, the Jung suddenly decided to side with the Ilyan, ironically with the very ship that the Alliance had returned to them. The Jar-Benakh."

"Well that can't be a coincidence," Jessica muttered.

"It wasn't," Vladimir said. "The Benakh was fitted with a remote command code override before it was returned to the Jung. I designed it myself."

"And they didn't discover it?" Jessica challenged.

"I did a very good job of hiding it," Vladimir bragged. "I made it from Jung equipment and aged it so that it appeared to be original issue. I even altered the manuals to include the item and created false service logs to make it appear to have been in use long before the ship fell into Alliance hands."

"You're sneaky," Jessica noted, impressed.

"Why didn't we know about this?" Cameron wondered.

"The order came directly from Miri," Nathan stated. "She, Vlad, and I were the only ones who knew."

"Op sec, baby," Jessica said. "The fewer who know, the safer the secret."

"Then it *was* the Alliance that caused the Jung to side with the Ilyan," Jakome realized. He looked at Nathan. "This also confirms the theory that the Aurora was *set up*."

"How so?" Nathan wondered.

"Because *two* of the only three people who *knew* about that device were *on* this ship," Jessica surmised.

"But how did they *know*?" Kit asked.

Nathan's head fell back against his chair. "Miri's headaches."

"What?" Jessica asked.

"About two years ago, she started getting migraines. They did all sorts of tests and imaging but couldn't figure it out. They eventually injected her with some kind of experimental nanites designed specifically to diagnosis and repair brain tissue."

"I've never heard of any such nanites," Doctor Chen chimed in.

"Apparently, they were top secret. They seemed to do the trick, as she got better almost immediately. What if those nanites were actually designed to capture her memories and deliver them to someone else?"

"That's not possible," Doctor Chen argued. "But they could have been designed to specifically repair the damage done by a Jung memory reader."

"I'm afraid your sister died suddenly of a brain aneurysm only a few months into the war," Jakome stated. "*Before* the Jung sided with the Ilyan."

"That can't be a coincidence either," Jessica stated.

"That *is* one of the many conspiracy theories I spoke of," Jakome said.

Nathan was silent for a moment. He had accepted the fact that he had no real family left. In fact, it had not bothered him as much as he had expected. But he had imagined his sister living out a normal life, watching her children grow into adults, doting over grandchildren and perhaps even great-grandchildren. All from the comfort of the family estate in Vancouver. This was different.

"What about her children?" Nathan finally asked Jakome.

"Historical records show they lived long, normal lives after their mother's passing. Both married and had children of their own, and so on. In fact, the Scott family estate is currently occupied by their descendants."

Nathan felt a wave of relief wash over him. There was comfort in the knowledge that his niece and nephew had survived, and that his family line had continued, even if not under the Scott name. After gathering himself, Nathan asked. "What exactly has the Alliance become?"

"In simplest terms, the Alliance has become an interstellar oligarchy disguised as representative democracy. Over time, the changes that were made to the constitution led to the centralization of powers, putting them under the control of the Central Alliance Council. Member states no longer have autonomy to rule themselves. This was a requirement for interstellarization to be successful. With so many different member states, interaction between worlds was fraught with loopholes and arguments over interpretations of law that crippled any expansion of the Alliance, as well as its markets. *Especially* the latter. In fact, many now believe that the entire *purpose* of the Alliance *is* the profit of its markets, evidenced by the fact that every seat on the CAC is filled by politicians bought and paid for by the largest corporations in the Alliance. In fact, half of the council members are believed to be controlled by SilTek, one of the original founders of the Alliance, and the only one that was a corporate-owned world."

Nathan felt his stomach turn with guilt.

"You couldn't have seen this coming," Cameron assured him, noticing his change in expression from the opposite end of the table.

"You did."

"No I didn't," Cameron objected. "If I had, I wouldn't have allowed it to happen. I only worried about their motives at the time."

"Without SilTek, the Alliance never would have survived," Jakome told them. "For all its faults—and there *are* many—the Alliance *has* provided a quality of life for quadrillions of people that would not have been possible. Some even argue that an oligarchy is the *only* structure that can do so, other than a dictatorship."

"Then why do so many people choose to leave the Alliance and settle in places like the fringe and even the badlands?" Nathan asked.

"Every person must choose which freedoms they are willing to sacrifice in exchange for the level of peace and security they require to be happy," Jakome stated. "One of the things the Alliance has done that I agree with is the provision of assistance to those who wish to settle *outside* Alliance space."

"Historically, socialism can only survive when *everyone* being ruled by it agrees with its principles," Nathan stated. "In early pre-plague history, leaders simply executed or jailed the opposition. Later, they used propaganda to force believers to mock and ridicule those who publicly opposed them, causing the rest to keep their opposition silent in order to survive."

"Precisely," Jakome agreed. "The Alliance found a way around that, at least on the surface."

"On the surface?" Cameron asked.

"Since the Alliance controls the flow of goods via the gate network, they can prevent worlds beyond their borders from ever achieving the same quality of life for their citizens."

"Thus preventing any other worlds from becoming true competition for them," Nathan surmised.

"Over time, border worlds slowly adopt Alliance ways to the point where they are not much different than their neighbors on the Alliance side of the border. Sooner or later, border worlds join the Alliance in order to obtain their own jump gate, which *gives* them the quality of life their citizens are lacking. This results in a gradual expansion of Alliance boundaries."

"Which is exactly what drives people from fringe worlds out into the badlands," Dominic added. "Take your Doctor Symyri, for example."

"Is he the same Doctor Symyri?" Nathan asked Jakome.

"He is. Nikolori Symyri began cloning himself every twenty years not long after your disappearance. He had become enthralled with the idea of immortality through cloning and ran one of the leading cloning clinics for several centuries. In fact, he *invented* the method of rapid clone growth, as well as the ability to grow a clone to a precise age. His process led to an unprecedented boom in cloning, with the wealthy cloning themselves regularly in order to stay young. This boom was one of the reasons the Alliance was able to grow so quickly. New worlds had to be settled to accommodate such a rapid growth in population."

"It's also one of the reasons the Alliance put restrictions on cloning, eventually making it illegal," Dominic added.

"But if growth and profit were the goals, why limit your population?" Cameron wondered.

"Too many wanted new worlds to be created *within* Alliance space. There were only so many hospitable worlds available, and only so many worlds that could be terraformed. Terraforming takes decades. Banning cloning forced people to move to the fringe, slowing the demand for more hospitable worlds *within* Alliance space."

"The biggest killer of business is too much success," Nathan mused. "The Alliance is thinking long term."

"The Alliance *always* thinks long term," Jakome said.

"Few humans are able to do that," Nathan pointed out.

"That's because humans generally think in terms of their *own* lifespans which, without cloning, is currently around three hundred years *if* one has the financial resources. This is why the Central Alliance Council relies on artificial intelligence to analyze all matters, make recommendations, and project the outcomes of all possible solutions. In essence, artificial intelligence *is* controlling humanity. And not just at the upper levels of government, but at every level, right down to the individual. AI is so ubiquitous in Alliance society that human consciousness is *shaped* by its influences. The majority of people let their AIs make their decisions for them, freeing themselves of both responsibility *and* accountability for their actions. And the AI system is quite adept at hiding this dependence from its citizens, just as it hides the central control of all AIs from them."

"You're saying *all* AIs are centrally controlled?" Cameron asked.

"I never did like AIs," Jessica grumbled.

"Not *all* and not *directly*," Jakome explained. "But they are all created by SilTek and therefore produce similar results."

"Why would people give up their freedom like that?" Aiden wondered.

"How many bad decisions have you made in your life?" Jakome asked Aiden. "Dated the wrong person, chosen the wrong meal at a restaurant, taken the wrong job? Personal AIs are always with their owners. They experience everything their owner experiences. All the senses, all the emotions. They monitor your vital signs. They even control your health nanites. They know *everything* about you, inside and out."

"That's insane," Nathan commented.

"Again, why would anyone *want* that?" Aiden repeated.

"Personal AIs learn so much about you so quickly that they can list your options, predict the likely results of each option, and recommend the best choice. The idea is that by eliminating bad choices, their owner experiences a better life."

"Sounds to me like they become slaves to the AI," Jessica argued.

"More like slaves to the Alliance," Jakome corrected. "Humans are like cattle to the Alliance. We exist to continually create wealth and power for the corporations and the government pawns they control."

"But people can choose *not* to follow the advice of their AIs, right?" Cameron asked.

"Yes, but when those choices result in outcomes that have a negative impact on society, the individual is held accountable for those choices. Sometimes with criminal charges."

"Seems a bit extreme," Jessica commented.

"It depends on how you look at it," Jakome replied. "Some believe that personal AIs are what keeps humanity from making the poor choices which contribute to the problems that generally plague civilizations. Others believe that they remove the very reason for life itself. Our knowledge, experience, and perspective are gained by the mistakes we make. Without them, we do not mature as a species.

"Where do you sit on the issue?" Nathan wondered.

"I believe that AIs have their use, but those uses are limited. Humans thrive on adversity. Fear of failure is what drives us. It is why we prepare, study, train, and plan. Wandering through life following the recommendations of an AI, regardless of how beneficial those recommendations may be, is not living. It is just existing."

Nathan exchanged glances with both Cameron and Jessica. "Well I think it's safe to say we're not going to be making contact with the Alliance any time soon."

"If they started the war and used us to do so, they'd hunt us down and kill us," Jessica surmised. "They'd have to."

"Yes and no," Jakome told her. "While I am certain that they would *prefer* you all dead, by now they have such complete control of their population that they could convince them of anything. I would expect any move they made to be covert."

"Well if *you* became aware of us, then the Alliance probably did as well," Kit surmised.

"Actually, my contact took care of the alert generated by the facial recognition of your people. They were all marked as false matches. Fortunately, it happens often enough that the matches will likely go unnoticed."

"Then they don't yet *know* that we survived?" Jessica asked.

"I do not believe so," Jakome assured her.

"We are in your debt," Nathan said.

"Not at all," Jakome replied. "As Deliza said, we are all in *your* debt. Again, that is why we are here. To help you."

"Help us with what?" Cameron asked.

"Perhaps we should start with repairing your ship?"

Vladimir's eyes lit up. "You can help us with that?"

Nathan looked at Vlad. "You haven't already talked to him about this?"

"I just woke up an hour ago," Vladimir defended.

"Yes, we can help you repair the Aurora. In fact, we can provide you with whatever you need. The challenge will be doing so without raising suspicion. The Alliance monitors all transactions. It would be best if we had a cover story to explain our activities. Especially for the sudden increase in exporting items out of Alliance space."

"How about establishing a new settlement?" Robert suggested to Jakome. "Perhaps someplace *beyond* the reach of the Alliance?"

Jakome seemed intrigued. "That might work. There is no limitation to settlements beyond Alliance space, and Ranni Enterprises would just be one of many corporations that have done so."

Nathan looked to Robert, smiling. "Looks like you just got your own world to settle."

"I should warn you that we will have to be discreet about the movement of materials and supplies from Takara to here. The Alliance monitors the movement of all vessels, even in the fringe. We would have to, how do you say, 'cover our tracks?'"

"But it can be done?" Nathan asked.

"Yes," Jakome confirmed. "For now, the

Bonaventura will remain in orbit to provide support and protection until the Aurora is space-worthy once again. I can also transfer some of her crew to your command to assist with repairs."

"We could use some troops if you have them," Kit suggested.

Jakome looked curious.

"We've created a bit of a situation," Nathan explained.

Jakome grinned. "Why am I not surprised?"

"We've recently run a load of medical supplies into the Vernay region."

"The Vernay region is in the badlands," Jakome cautioned.

"We are aware. On the way in, we ran off some pirates. Shortly after, they sent a couple shuttles looking for us, and our Dragons had to take them out. We're currently providing security for the six worlds there, using half of our Dragons and half of our Ghatazhak. But we fear it's only a matter of time until the pirates come in force."

"If you don't mind my asking, why did you feel the need to run cargo into the badlands?"

"We ran up some debt getting Vladimir to Pyru, and that's how we're repaying it," Nathan explained.

"Debt to whom?"

"A trader named Chiqua Kimbro," Nathan replied.

"I can pay that debt for you."

"It's a big debt," Nathan warned.

"I'm sure I can afford it," Jakome assured him.

"That would be great, but we can't just abandon those worlds," Nathan argued. "We've made promises to them."

"Of course." Jakome took a deep breath, letting it out in measured form. "I would recommend that you commit all of your forces to protecting the Vernay worlds while the Bonaventura provides security for the Aurora."

"Why not just send the Bonaventura to the Vernay region?" Jessica suggested.

"A ship the size of the Bonaventura would draw considerable attention. If we use your Ghatazhak and your Dragon fighters, you would appear to be mercenaries, or better yet, a rival pirate gang looking to take over new territories. This is common in the badlands, and the Alliance rarely gets involved in such matters."

"The best way to ensure your own security is to keep those around you unstable," Nathan stated.

"I see you haven't forgotten history," Jakome commented.

"Perhaps I should bring the Bonaventura's chief engineer down to get a better understanding of your needs?" Jakome suggested.

"I can help with that," Dominic offered.

Jakome glanced at Dominic, unfamiliar with him.

"My apologies," Nathan said. "Jakome, this is Dominic. He is an engineer from the current time and has been helping us during Vladimir's absence."

"An honor to meet you, sir," Jakome greeted.

"I've got a pretty good idea of this ship's repair needs, as well as how we might be able to integrate current technology into this ship."

"I would advise against that," Jakome insisted.

"Why?" Nathan wondered.

"One of the Aurora's strengths will be that she is *not* using current technology. Particularly those that require an AI to function. This makes her immune to the type of cyber attacks that opposing forces would likely attempt."

"Like when we first battled Caius's forces," Jessica said. "Their shields were designed to protect against energy weapons, not kinetic weapons like the original Aurora's rail guns."

"Your jump range will also be a big advantage," Jakome added. "Not even the Alliance has ships that can jump that far."

"Just how far can this ship jump?" Dominic wondered.

"You don't know?" Nathan asked, surprised by the engineer's question.

"Such specifications were never made public knowledge," Jakome explained.

"Single-jump, one thousand light years," Vladimir bragged. "One-minute range of two thousand. *And* she can be fitted with additional energy banks to double that."

"*My God*," Dominic exclaimed. "You could travel across the galaxy in a matter of weeks."

"Days actually," Vladimir boasted. "She recharges in only two hours."

"Which makes this ship a threat to the Alliance as long as it is *not* under their control," Jakome added.

Nathan considered that for a moment. "It's only a matter of time before they know about this ship."

"I don't know that it's the *ship* they're likely to be concerned about," Jakome told him.

"Meaning it's *me* they would be worried about," Nathan surmised.

"You *and* your senior staff," Jakome replied. "The Aurora is not the only Expedition-class ship that was lost without a trace. Four others disappeared. There are also three of them on display on Alliance worlds."

"Like museum exhibits?" Vladimir asked.

"The Expedition-class ships won the war and started the expansion of the Alliance."

Vladimir looked quite pleased with himself. "Imagine that."

"We'll have to cross all these bridges when we come to them," Nathan decided. "For now, I'd just like to focus on getting this ship back into space. We'll figure out what to do with her after that."

"As you wish," Jakome agreed. "If you will provide me with a list of your immediate needs, I will send one of my shuttles back to Takara to get things started. "I only ask that you keep the list small for the moment, preferably limited to items that are difficult to acquire in the fringe. It will take time to put together a legitimate deep-space settlement mission."

"I can provide you that list," Dominic told him.

"Vlad, do you feel up to reviewing that list?" Nathan asked.

"I feel fine," Vladimir assured him.

"Great. Dominic, you and Commander Kamenetskiy review the list and submit it to Jakome as soon as possible."

"It would be my honor," Dominic replied.

"Cam, you, Jess, and Kit see to getting more forces up and operating on Kataoka," Nathan continued. "Abby, I'd suggest you spend some time with your son before he departs."

"I plan to," Abby agreed. "But I would also like to help you as much as possible."

"Trust me, I plan to utilize your expertise in any way I can," Nathan assured her. "Robert, you and Aiden put your heads together and begin preparing for a scouting mission. I want a destination for our new settlement as soon as possible."

"Will do," Robert replied.

"Doc, I'm sure you've got patients that have missed your expertise," Nathan said.

"Captain, the Bonaventura's CMO has offered to install some of their advanced diagnostic equipment in our medical department."

"Can they spare it?"

"We can make do without it," Jakome insisted. "We will include replacements with the first shipments from Takara."

"Very well. Let's get to work everyone." Nathan stood along with everyone else. "Jakome, may we speak alone?"

"Of course, Captain."

* * *

Jakome followed Nathan into the ready room, taking a seat as Nathan closed the door and perched on the corner of his desk.

"I get the feeling that something is on your mind," Jakome stated, feeling the tension in the room.

"Despite your familiarity, we've only just met. We know very little about the state of the Alliance, but we know even *less* about *you*. And that frightens me."

"I have offered to get your ship back in the air and to support you in whatever endeavor you undertake," Jakome reminded him. "Why would that frighten you?"

"Because it is *exactly* what the Alliance would do to gain our trust and get control of us...all without firing a shot."

Jakome nodded, surprised and impressed by Nathan's logic. "I see your point, Captain."

"I apologize if I have offended you."

"Not at all. On the contrary, I am thankful that you *are* so cautious." Jakome thought for a moment.

"Perhaps this will put your mind at ease. If the Alliance discovers that I *know* that you and the Aurora exist, and I *know* where you are located and do *not* inform them, I will be charged and convicted of treason. I will be executed, and House Ta'Akar and all of its assets will be seized."

"What about your family?" Nathan wondered.

"I have no family," Jakome assured him.

"Why not?"

"Same reason as you, I suppose. Duty came first. The things I must do and the decisions I must make would put a family in danger. Had Deliza not survived, I would not be here. My house would not exist. I was created to ensure the survival of my house. But rather than fathering heirs who may or may not have been suited to lead, it was decided to keep *me* alive...*forever.*"

"I thought cloning was illegal in the Alliance?"

"House Ta'Akar does not intend on *staying* within the Alliance. Neither does Ranni Enterprises."

Suddenly, it all made sense to Nathan. "You're not helping us because of a promise you made to Deliza. You *need* us to help settle a new world for yourself, far beyond the Alliance's reach."

"It is not for *myself*," Jakome corrected. "It is for everyone. It is to show that you don't need an *Alliance* to create a peaceful, prosperous world." Jakome paused, considering his words. "You have only been in this time for a few days, correct?"

"Seven I believe."

"Then perhaps I should explain a few things for you."

"Please do," Nathan invited.

"It is not a coincidence that worlds beyond Alliance borders are so slow to thrive, just as it is not a coincidence that organized pirate gangs control the badlands."

"You're suggesting that the Alliance is *responsible* for the two?"

"All of humanity is dependent upon the Alliance. Their manufacturing base, their gate network, and their short-range shipping fleet create that dependency."

"But the fringe worlds, and to some extent the badlands, are served by privateers," Nathan pointed out.

"Yes, but only to a limited extent. Very little is produced by the fringe worlds. Most don't have the industrial capacity to compete with Alliance worlds. Humans are inherently lazy. If there is a way to make their lives easier, they want it. This desire keeps the goods flowing from the Alliance to the fringe worlds. It also gives the Alliance some measure of control over the fringe worlds. The more they want, the more control they give up."

"But sooner or later, worlds grow, and when they do, they industrialize," Nathan stated.

"And when they start to, the Alliance grants them a gate, but only one that connects with a border world. The goods flow even faster, and at less cost to the consumer, furthering their dependency. Eventually, that world is invited into the Alliance, and ninety percent of the time, they accept."

"But don't people go to the fringe to *escape* Alliance oppression?" Nathan wondered.

"When drawn in slowly in this manner, they don't see themselves as being oppressed. They just see their lives getting better, easier, and safer. In many ways, it is similar to a drug addiction."

"And the Alliance is the dealer."

"I'm afraid it gets worse," Jakome warned. "Doctor Sorenson's claims have always intrigued me, and I have been conducting covert research of my own for decades."

"I didn't realize you were a physicist," Nathan mused.

"Perhaps 'sponsoring' would have been a better choice of words."

"And what have you concluded?"

"That the claim that long-range, high-burst-energy jump drives damage the inter-dimensional barriers and cause rogue gravity wells is entirely false."

"And you have found proof?"

"Not so much proof as a coincidence which cannot be ignored. You see, my people have found *devices* that *create* the rogue gravity wells. We call them 'gravity mines', and I believe the Alliance is responsible for them."

This had not been what Nathan had expected, but it made sense, and in a disturbing way. "I am not committing this ship and her crew to a war against the Alliance," Nathan told him.

"I am not asking you to," Jakome replied. "The majority of Alliance citizens are perfectly happy as things are. They don't care what the truth is. They only care about their own realities, and there is nothing *wrong* with that. What I object to is how the Alliance uses these lies to exert control beyond its borders, and on the very people who left because they did not *want* to be controlled."

"How do you intend to prove what the Alliance is doing?" Nathan wondered.

"I have no intention of doing so," Jakome insisted. "Instead, I intend to offer an alternative. I will start a *new* Alliance. One composed of newly established worlds, all built from the ground up and governed by their founders in whatever way they see fit. Just as the original Alliance constitution had intended."

Nathan rose from his position on the edge of his desk, moving around to his chair behind it. "If it failed once, what makes you think it won't fail again?"

"It would have worked had it not been for the war. It could even work now with the *existing* Alliance. But convincing a population as vast as that of the Alliance would be nearly impossible."

"Lazy humans."

"Precisely," Jakome agreed.

Nathan sighed. "Have you ever marveled at how some of us are fine with a paradise made up of lies, while others would rather live in a world of truth, despite all of its hardships?"

"I have from time to time," Jakome admitted. "In fact, I find that I must constantly remind myself that just because I disagree with another's perception of reality, it does not make it any less valid. This is why I chose to show my reality to others by example. They can see it if they choose, or they can ignore it. Either way, I will be doing something of *value* for humanity rather than just increasing the wealth and power of my house. I'm hoping that we can do this *together*."

Nathan studied Jakome for a moment. "Why?"

"I'm sorry?"

"*Why* are you doing this?" Nathan repeated. "You control the lives of hundreds of thousands. You have the wealth and power to make the reality that you control whatever you wish it to be. Why risk all of that on such an endeavor?"

"Because it is what Deliza would have done,"

Jakome replied without hesitation. "And I believe it is what *Tug* would have done."

Nathan smiled. Although Jakome seemed a lot like Tug, he was definitely his own man.

* * *

"I cannot tell you how excited I am to be working with you, Commander," Dominic said eagerly as Vladimir inspected the ZPED status display.

"And I cannot tell you how happy I am that you got this reactor back to full power," Vladimir replied. "Now I can purge the forward weapons bay and get rid of those things that bit me."

"I'm afraid I already beat you to it," Dominic stated. "I hope you don't mind."

Vladimir grinned. "Why would I mind?"

"In my experience, most senior engineers take offense when someone does their work for them."

"I am not most senior engineers," Vladimir laughed. "I am '*super* engineer'."

Dominic looked pleased at his mentor's comment. "I have studied all your work," he admitted. "You have always been one of my inspirations."

"You have excellent taste," Vladimir chuckled. "What else have you done?"

"Well, obviously, we got the fabricators working. I've also identified how we can get the ship level again."

"Really? How?"

"It will involve draining the bog and digging out the mud underneath the ship's gear doors so that we can fuse it into solid soil that can support our weight."

"Being level would help a lot," Vladimir agreed. "What made you think of this above everything else?"

"It came to me when we were looking for ways to

reduce power usage. The gravity generators use a lot of energy. Leveling the ship would allow us to shut them down completely."

"Good thinking," Vladimir agreed. "You have gotten this ZPED to run far more stably than it was designed to. How did you manage it?"

"Your containment field emitters were all oriented the same way. It was discovered centuries ago that offsetting them by ten-degree increments from emitter to emitter, then altering the direction of those increments from ring to ring, less power was lost due to flow resistance between emitter rings."

"That's incredible!" Vladimir exclaimed. "And so simple."

"Most great solutions are."

Vladimir sighed. "There is so much for me to learn. It is just like my time at the academy. There was so much technology coming out of the Data Ark, I felt like we were far behind in our abilities."

"It must have been an amazing time," Dominic said. "To have so many advances in science and technology revealed to you all at once."

"I enjoyed the challenge," Vladimir admitted. "However, it did lead to some long nights of studying when I would have preferred to be out drinking and chasing women with my friends."

"I would be more than happy to help you catch up," Dominic offered, hoping the offer would not offend the legendary engineer.

"I would appreciate that," Vladimir replied. "If it is not too much trouble."

"It would be my honor, Commander."

Vladimir slapped the older man on the back, causing him to stumble forward a step. "Wonderful! But please, you must call me Vlad."

"Of course."

"Now show me that list."

* * *

"I was hoping I'd find you," Nathan stated as he sat down across from Abby in the mess hall.

"I'm waiting for Cameron to assign me a cabin," Abby replied.

"I trust you got to spend time with Nikolas before he left?"

"I did," Abby replied. "Not nearly enough though."

"I doubt it ever will be," Nathan said as he began eating. "He's a fine pilot by the way."

"He told me he nearly died," Abby stated.

"Not because of anything he did wrong," Nathan assured her.

"I know. I didn't mean to…"

"It's okay, Abby. I'm just glad to see you. And I'm certain Nikolas is too."

"You know, I have dreamed of this day my entire life…ever since the day you all vanished."

"I'm glad you did," Nathan stated. "Had you not, Jakome would not be here offering invaluable assistance. You managed to save us once again." He smiled at her.

"It seems that no matter how hard I might fight it, I will always be connected to a ship named Aurora."

"A lot of us feel that way," Nathan agreed. "I need to ask you something."

"Go ahead."

"How long have you known Jakome?"

"I knew him for a few months before I passed."

"Passed?"

"I eventually lost my desire to live," Abby admitted.

"I'm surprised to hear that."

"It's not that I wanted to die. I just didn't want to

live through however many years it took until you reappeared. I was only living for *that* purpose, to see my son once again. It just made more sense to live out my life and die of natural causes. After being scanned of course."

"So your consciousness has been stored all this time?"

"A few hundred years, yes."

"Wow. I didn't realize they could do that."

"A lot has changed."

"So when were you reborn?"

"Same time as Vlad," She replied. "We actually woke up next to each other."

"Then you don't know Jakome that well."

"Not really," Abby admitted. "All I can tell you is that he *is* who he claims to be." Abby looked at Nathan for a moment. "Is there a problem?"

"No, it's just difficult to put so much trust in him so quickly," Nathan explained. "Even if he does look and sound like Tug."

"Is that *you* talking or Jessica?"

"A little of both, I suppose," Nathan admitted. "I *want* to believe it's him, but it just seems so impossible. And the convenient timing doesn't help."

"I suspect you're going to find a lot of things in this century that seem impossible. As to the convenient timing, that's because of the safeguards Deliza put in place. She made sure that *when*, not *if*, you returned, you would quickly get the help you would most likely need. Her foresight is the reason we are here. As for Jakome, it is his sense of honor and duty to Deliza—whom he saw as his sister, daughter, and mother—that brought him here. And that's because he *is* Tug, at least at his core."

Nathan sighed. "I hope so, I truly do. Because we're betting everything on him."

Abby patted him on the hand. "You've bet on much worse odds in the past."

Nathan smiled at his old friend. "It is good to have you back, Abby."

"It is good to be back."

"What are you going to do?"

"I'm going to help Vlad get this ship running again and help him take advantage of all the technologies that have been developed since you disappeared."

Nathan shook his head. "It's so weird. For us, it was all just a week ago, but for you it has been a lifetime."

"*Three* lifetimes," Abby corrected. "This is my fourth body."

Nathan smiled. "It is nice to no longer be the only clone aboard," he said as he rose to depart.

CHAPTER TWO

Being the world nearest the Vernay passage, it was not abnormal for Kataoka to be visited on occasion by ships. Most times it was a cargo ship already relieved of half its load by pirates patrolling the passage. But a *passenger* ship was rare, usually only appearing every few years.

When they did come, they contained the usual passenger types. Those seeking adventure in the badlands; the down-trodden with no better options; or those whom worlds within the fringe had rejected. Rarely did strikingly beautiful women step off onto Kataokan soil.

Because of that, Gia and her three friends concealed themselves as best they could. Head wraps, bulky clothing, and dirty faces helped blend them in with the other passengers. Other than the interest generated simply by the occasional arrivals, no one gave them any undue attention.

Gia found the nearest local who did not look threatening. "What's the best tavern here?" she asked an old man.

"The New Old House," the old man answered.

"Unusual name."

"Center of town. Can't miss it," the old man told her, continuing about his business.

"Ladies," Gia said to her three fellow travelers, heading toward town.

* * *

"Are you insane?" Jessica asked as they waited for the Seiiki's cargo ramp to deploy.

"I may be willing to risk *our* lives trusting her, but

not his," Nathan replied, pointing at Jakome to his right. "He's the Aurora's ace in the hole."

"Does Cam know about this?" Jessica asked.

"It was her idea," Jakome assured her.

"Captain," Chiqua greeted from the bottom of the ramp, two of her men beside her. "I wasn't sure you were going to make it."

"We had a bit of a delay," Nathan explained as the three of them came down the ramp.

Chiqua looked at Jakome, noticing the difference in both his appearance and his gait. He carried himself differently than Captain Scott and the rest of the Seiiki's crew, and he appeared even more out of place in the fringe than they did. "Is *this* our fortunate turn of events?" Chiqua asked, nodding in Jakome's direction.

"Chiqua Kimbro...uh...Tug Redmond."

Jakome exchanged a surprised glance with Nathan then turned back toward Chiqua. "A pleasure."

"First time in the fringe?" Chiqua asked.

"Is it that obvious?"

"Time is short," Nathan told her. "What are we hauling?"

"More medical supplies, food, drink, assorted tools and gadgets," Chiqua explained. "I arranged them on pallets so they'll be quicker to offload at each stop."

"What are you asking for them?" Nathan wondered.

"I'm not," Chiqua replied as she headed up the ramp. "I'm going to negotiate each trade myself."

"We're not planning on going to all six Vernay worlds," Nathan warned. "We're dropping it all on Kataoka and then returning."

"How are we supposed to get all this stuff to the other five worlds?" Chiqua demanded.

"That's what the Acuna is for."

"But we had a deal," Chiqua argued.

"Our *deal* was to get your cargo safely in and out of the badlands. I never promised to use *this* particular ship."

"Then you're paying the Acuna out of *your* shares," Chiqua insisted.

"I plan to," Nathan assured her.

"What if the *Acuna* gets raided?"

"She'll be protected same as we would be."

"Not sure how I feel about those terms," Chiqua admitted.

"I don't care," Nathan told her, his expression unchanged.

Chiqua stared at him for a moment. "Very well. Let's get this operation rolling," she said walking past them and up into the Seiiki.

"Charming woman," Jakome commented.

"Yeah, not one of my better choices of partners," Nathan admitted.

"Tug, huh?" Jakome added.

"Couldn't think of anything else at the moment."

"It works."

"Unless she knows that name," Jessica warned.

"The name does not appear in historical records, at least not in relation to House Ta'Akar," Jakome insisted.

"Let's hope," Jessica said as they continued to inspect the incoming pallets of cargo.

"Why eight pallets?" Jakome wondered.

"In case you get raided," one of Chiqua's men told them as he passed. "The last one loaded is for the pirates. Makes it easier that way."

"Sounds like an interesting place, these badlands," Jakome commented.

* * *

"I have to confess, I know very little about these old Expedition-class ships," the Bonaventura's chief engineer admitted as he, Vladimir, and Dominic reviewed the Aurora's list of needs. "I do, however, know what resources I can safely part with in order to assist with your repairs."

"Well you've seen the list," Dominic said. "What do you think?"

"I have already reassigned as many engineers as I can safely spare to your ship and still make it back to Takara if the need arises."

"What we need most are raw materials and more fabricator time," Vladimir told him.

"Well, while we cannot help you with the raw materials, we can certainly help with fabrication. The Bonaventura carries a standard compliment of three fabricators. Micro, standard, and large format."

"Large format?" Vladimir asked, unfamiliar with the term.

"It is primarily used to create large panels and structural members for repairing bulkheads, frames, and hull panels," Chief Gansa explained.

"You can fabricate *hull panels?*" Vladimir asked.

"Of course."

"I would suggest that you save all your damaged items for recycling," Chief Gansa added.

"You have an elemental recycler on board?" Dominic realized, suddenly becoming excited.

Chief Gansa looked at Dominic, puzzled at his surprise. "Of course."

"What is that?" Vladimir wondered.

"Cutting-edge tech," Dominic explained. "It takes scrap and reduces it to its most basic elements, and then stores them as solid pellets, liquids, or gases, to be used for fabrication."

"You knew such a thing existed and you didn't tell me?" Vladimir scolded Dominic.

"Last I heard they were still in their prototyping phase," Dominic defended. "I had no idea they were in production."

"They are not," Chief Gansa confirmed. "It is a beta unit. We are testing it."

Dominic looked confused. "How did you get it?"

"We invented it," Chief Gansa told him. "Or, I should say, Ranni Enterprises did."

Dominic was dumbfounded. He looked at Vladimir. "You people really do have the most incredible luck."

A broad grin came across Vladimir's face. "Dead for centuries, and Deliza is still rescuing us; and in more ways than one." He put his hand on Chief Gansa's shoulder. "Mister Gansa, we are going to give that device some serious testing."

"Excellent," the chief replied. "And please call me Gyandev."

"Gyandev? Is that Russian?" Vladimir asked, letting his accent become a little more pronounced.

"Russian?" the chief asked, unfamiliar with the term.

"Let's just assume that it is, my friend," Vladimir said, putting his arm around the Takaran engineer's shoulder. "Let's take a look at that thing."

"Do you have some scrap ready to feed it?" the chief wondered.

"I'm sure we can find something," Vladimir assured him.

* * *

Nathan made his way through the Seiiki's packed cargo bay, heading for the exit.

"All this shit gets unloaded?" Marcus asked as Nathan passed.

"The first two pallets go to one side to be traded with the Kataokans; the rest go to the Acuna," Nathan replied, pointing to the cargo ship parked about ten meters off their stern to the right.

"Are we hauling them over there?"

"I don't know. Just stack them outside for now. I want to be ready to leave as soon as possible. I'm headed over to the Acuna now. I'll ask."

Nathan headed down the ramp, joining the others already at the bottom of the ramp, moving out of the way of the Kataokans coming up to assist with the offload.

"Two deliveries in just as many days is unheard of," Darren declared as he approached. "I assume this load is not free however."

"You bet it ain't," Chiqua was quick to state. "What have you got for me?" she asked the young man, directing him off to the side to negotiate beyond the earshot of Nathan and the others.

"Do you want us to keep tabs on her?" Jessica asked.

"No need. The one thing we can trust Chiqua to do is be greedy," Nathan replied. "Let's go talk to Alex."

Nathan, Jessica, and Jakome headed toward the Acuna, closing the short distance quickly.

"Not exactly an awe-inspiring sight, visually speaking," Jakome commented, looking the vessel over as they approached.

"Don't expect to have your opinion changed when you see the interior," Jessica warned.

"Alex, Josi, and Shane came down the Acuna's

port cargo bay ramp to meet Nathan and the others as they approached.

"Captain Tuplo," Alex greeted.

Jakome shot a look at Nathan.

"Long story," Nathan told him under his breath.

"I promised we would give you more business," Nathan said. "Are you ready for your first run?"

"Depends. Where are you headed?"

"Not me," Nathan corrected. "The stuff I'm carrying. One pallet to each of the other five Vernay worlds."

"What's on the pallets?"

"Miscellaneous stuff," Nathan replied. "Nothing hazardous."

"I assume I'm hauling stuff back?"

"Most likely. Chiqua will be going with you to do the trading."

"I'm going to require a deposit," Alex insisted. "We have expenses after all."

"Like what?"

"Like propellant, which ain't cheap in the badlands."

Jakome pulled an Alliance credit chip out of his pocket and tossed it to her. "Will this cover it?"

Alex caught the chip, studying it. Her eyes widened when she realized its value. "I like your friend."

"Tug, this is Alex, captain of the Acuna Dera," Nathan introduced. "This is her chief engineer, Josi, and their brother Shane."

"A pleasure," Jakome greeted.

"Where are the return goods going?" Alex asked.

"Back here for now," Nathan stated. "Our sister ship, the Mirai, will take them on to Hadria."

"You have a sister ship?" Josi asked, surprised.

"We can fly it to Hadria for you," Alex offered. "For a price of course."

"How much?" Jakome asked.

"To Hadria?"

"No," Jakome corrected. "For the whole ship."

Alex laughed. "Funny."

"It wasn't meant to be."

"Uh, Tug..." Nathan said.

Jakome gestured to Nathan not to worry. "How much?"

"The Acuna is not for sale," Alex stated.

"Perhaps I should clarify," Jakome began. "I do not wish to *own* your ship. I only wish for it to be at our disposal, to haul what we want, where we want, when we want."

"You want to lease the *Acuna*?" Josi realized.

"Believe me, it would not be my first choice," Jakome assured her. "However, I suppose its very *appearance* might draw less attention."

"Fifty thousand per month," Alex stated, certain that a protracted bartering session would follow.

Jakome pulled yet another credit chip out and tossed it to her.

This time, Alex's eyes nearly popped out of her head.

"That should cover the first six months," Jakome stated confidently.

Alex looked at him. "Who *are* you people?"

"We will require some upgrades to your vessel," Jakome warned.

"What kind of upgrades?" Josi asked, still not trusting them.

"Shields to start with," Nathan suggested.

Jakome nodded agreement.

"And maybe a few point-defense turrets?" Jessica added.

"We don't have the power for all that," Josi warned.

"You will," Jakome assured her. "My people will get to work on your ship as soon as you return."

"What about *this* run?" Shane asked. "Are you going to protect us?"

Nathan pointed to the six Dragon fighters parked in the nearby clearing. "*They'll* protect you."

"You bought *them* too?" Alex asked.

"In a manner of speaking," Nathan confirmed.

"I thought they were protecting the Vernay worlds?" Josi challenged, hoping to catch him in a lie.

"There are five more coming, as well as some..." Nathan looked at Jessica. "What do we call them?"

"Special operators," Jessica replied.

"Yes," Nathan agreed. "Two of our *special operators* will accompany you on all flights, to provide security."

"Should I ask what kind of *special operating* they do?" Alex asked.

"It would take too long to explain," Nathan replied. "Rest assured they can handle anything that comes up."

"And what do you expect...to *come up?*" Josi asked.

"Hopefully nothing," Nathan replied. "But this *is* the badlands."

"Do we have an arrangement then?" Jakome asked Alex.

Alex looked at Josi, who didn't seem convinced. On the other hand, Shane looked overjoyed. "We do."

"Excellent," Nathan said. "We will work out

the particulars of communications and chain of command later."

"Right," Alex agreed, looking down at the two credit chips in her hand and smiling.

Nathan, Jessica, and Jakome turned and walked back toward the Seiiki, which was already in the process of being offloaded.

"How much are those chips?" Shane asked, trying to peek in Alex's hand.

"Enough to get through our entire fix-it list five times over," Alex assured him.

"I don't like it," Josi insisted.

"They just handed us half a million credits, Jo," Alex said. "I fucking *love* them."

"Why us?" Josi argued. "With that kind of money, they could hire *anyone.* Why don't they use their own shuttles for that matter?"

"Who cares?" Alex insisted. "We can hire crew, build a hangar, fix Pop's house. Hell, we might even be able to afford his procedure and get him back in the game."

"These people aren't telling us everything," Josi insisted.

"They're providing *fighter escorts*," Shane reminded Josi.

"And shields, and guns, and new reactors," Alex added.

"I don't *trust* them," Josi told them. "Why the hell do you think they paid us so much up front? So we wouldn't ask too many questions, that's why."

"So what?" Alex replied. "We're in the badlands, remember. It's not like we have to worry about breaking any laws. And we already can't fly into Alliance space."

"What about the Korsan?" Josi challenged.

"Fighter escorts," Shane reminded, pointing at the Dragon fighters again.

"This money is going to save Pop's life and *change* ours," Alex insisted. "We might even be able to move *out* of the badlands and start plying the fringe instead."

Josi sighed. The idea of getting the Acuna in perfect working order was beyond comprehension, as was the idea of getting out of the badlands. "Just promise me you'll be careful, and don't let them talk you into anything dangerous."

"More dangerous than flying cargo through the badlands?" Alex asked, trying to coax her little sister into smiling.

* * *

"This ship is amazing," Vladimir declared as they entered the Bonaventura's fabrication compartment. "Do you have many of them?"

"The Bonaventura is one of a kind," Chief Gansa stated. "She is Prince Jakome's private vessel."

"Takara doesn't have her own ships?" Vladimir wondered.

"Of course. We have many types of ships. Cargo ships. Passenger ships. Cruise ships. Private yachts..."

"I meant *war* ships," Vladimir said.

"No worlds are allowed to have warships," the chief said, as if it were common knowledge.

"How do you protect yourselves?" Vladimir wondered.

"From whom?"

"Other worlds?"

"They don't have warships either."

"What about from worlds *outside* the Alliance?"

"No one would attack an Alliance world," Chief Gansa chuckled.

"Then the *Alliance* has warships," Vladimir surmised.

"Yes, but not as many as you might think."

"The Alliance only maintains a small fleet of about forty heavy cruisers," Dominic explained. "They are mostly just for show. The Alliance hasn't fired a shot in anger in several centuries."

"What about the pirates?" Vladimir wondered.

"They don't have the firepower to challenge the Alliance," Dominic explained.

"What about this *Korsan* that everyone talks about?" Vladimir wondered.

"Their ships are too small to challenge the Alliance," Chief Gansa assured him. "They couldn't even challenge this ship, and all our weapons are defensive. Alliance cruisers are five times our size, and they have *offensive* weapons as well."

"But aren't the badlands *huge*?" Vladimir said. "How do they maintain control?"

"The Korsan is just one of *many* pirate gangs. They just happen to be the largest, most powerful gang in *this* area," Dominic explained.

"This is the elemental recycler," Chief Gansa said, gesturing toward the large machine along the far wall of the compartment. "Mister Cavuto?" the chief called to a nearby technician.

The technician and his assistant picked up a large piece of debris bought up from the Aurora and placed it inside the recycler's chamber. After closing the door, Mister Cavuto pressed a button. A few seconds later, pellets began falling into a line of small bins along the wall to the left.

"Amazing," Vladimir exclaimed.

"It sure is," Dominic agreed.

"The eventual goal is for the device to be able to recreate the item, or even repair it, all with just the press of a button."

"Like a fabricator and recycler in one?" Vladimir surmised.

"Something like that."

"Any chance we can get one of these installed on the Aurora?" Vladimir asked.

"I'm afraid you'd have to talk to the Ranni people about that."

Vladimir leaned toward Dominic. "Add that to the list."

"Definitely."

* * *

"*Uh...Alex?*" Shane called over the intercom.

"What's up, Shane?" Alex replied from her seat in the Acuna's cockpit.

"*There are four guys outside. They say they've been assigned to us?*"

"Tell them to get lost," Alex instructed.

"*I don't think they're going to listen.*"

"Jesus, Shane," Alex cursed as she rose from her seat and headed aft.

The Acuna was built around the core frame of an old pod jumper designed to straddle a standard cargo pod then jump it to another location. Alex's great-grandfather had originally purchased it from a friend and fixed it up. He used it to support his family, jumping cargo pods from large carriers in orbit to the surface, back on Soro before it became an Alliance border world and independents like him were pushed out into the fringe. Later, her grandfather had modified a cargo pod to serve as living quarters and such, giving the Acuna the ability to not only make longer journeys, but also to attach a cargo pod on either side rather than just a single, underslung pod.

Other than updating systems here and there, and adding some external sensors and comm-systems, the Acuna had been pretty much the same for the last fifty years. It was an ugly ship, but it was *theirs*, and that was enough.

After passing through the galley into the central intersection, Alex hung a right, stepping through the hatch into the port cargo pod. "Can I help you?" she said to the four men standing just inside their outer hatch.

"Are you Captain Foruria?" Loki asked.

"Who wants to know?"

"I'm Loki Sheehan, and this is Nikolas Sorenson. We'll be flying escort for you."

"Okay." Alex looked at the other two. "And who are you?"

"I'm Kit, and this is Mori," Kit replied. "We're here to provide security."

"Tuplo didn't say anything about security."

"My idea," Kit admitted. "I'm in charge of the Vernay quick-response forces. I think it would be best if we kept two of us on board during your deliveries."

"If we've got escort fighters, who are *you* going to protect me from?"

"Hopefully no one," Kit admitted.

"No thanks," Alex stated. "We can protect ourselves."

"I wasn't offering you a choice, ma'am," Kit warned.

"Who are you calling *ma'am*?"

"Terms of the agreement stipulate that Mister

Redmond has the right to provide security as he sees fit," Kit explained. "He sees fit to provide *us*."

Alex scoffed. "The two of you are going to protect us from pirates?"

"What, you think we should bring more men?" Kit asked.

"The Korsan usually board in groups of four to eight," Alex warned.

Kit looked at Mori. "Maybe you should stay here then. Sounds like this is a one-man job."

"I'm already here, and Kataoka *is* kind of boring."

Alex shook her head. "Whatever." She looked back at Nikolas, who was carrying a device. "What's that for?"

"A TDL," Nikolas replied.

"A what?"

"Tactical data link," Loki explained. "We thought it would be a good idea if you could see our tactical sensor data, and we could track your jump calcs so we don't lose you in a firefight."

"We have data comms," Josi defended, just entering the compartment.

"I'm sure you do," Loki replied. "But they may not integrate well with our systems. They're pretty old."

"I beg your pardon?" Josi snapped.

"I meant *our* systems are much older than *yours*."

"Can you make that thing work with our systems?" Alex asked Josi.

"Shouldn't be a problem," Josi assured her, taking the device from Nikolas and looking it over.

"I can help," Nikolas offered, smiling at Josi.

"Suit yourself," Josi replied, not giving him a second look. "Just don't touch anything."

"How long until we depart?" Kit asked.

"As soon as Josi installs your TDL, I'm guessing,"

Alex answered, turning around and heading back inside.

"She seems nice," Kit commented.

"She's not so bad once you get to know her," Shane told them. "Make yourselves comfortable I guess."

Kit looked around. "Not sure that's possible."

* * *

"I don't understand why you didn't want me to pay off your debt to Chiqua," Jakome said as he and Nathan headed up the Seiiki's ramp. "Would it not be better to be finished with her and concentrate all your efforts on the repair of your ship?"

"I'm not the one repairing my ship," Nathan joked as he activated the ramp controls to close up the back of the ship. "Besides, I made a promise to these people, and I intend to keep it."

"So is that what you plan to do with the Aurora once she is repaired?" Jakome asked as they headed forward. "Protect the defenseless from those who prey upon them? You certainly won't run out of customers."

"To be honest, until now I was kind of lost about what to do with the Aurora," Nathan admitted as they headed forward through the port corridor. "Then something occurred to me."

"And that was?"

"Have you studied much Earth history?" Nathan asked as they headed up the ladder to the flight deck. "Pre-plague stuff?"

"I'm afraid I haven't," Jakome admitted.

"In the mid twenty-first century, after a significant effort at globalization, the Earth suffered a period of geo-political instability. Nations would attack their neighbors for one reason or another, and the world would do nothing. Everyone was afraid of escalation into nuclear war. Do you know how they solved the problem? A privately operated military, sponsored by a handful of the wealthiest corporations on the planet. They called them the Ghost Force."

"So corporate military?"

"No, and that's the key," Nathan explained as they entered the cockpit. "They weren't *owned* or *controlled* by the corporations. The corporations just provided financial support. But the key was that none of the corporations could tell these guys what to do."

"Why would corporations pay for a service they could not control?"

"War created economic instability, which was bad for business."

"I thought business boomed during wars?"

"Only for the companies making weapons," Nathan corrected as he began powering up the Seiiki's flight systems. "So when some country got out of line and threatened the stability of the planet, these guys went into action. They simply prevented nations from settling differences with violence."

"By *inflicting* violence," Jakome realized. "An interesting solution. But I am surprised that this was allowed."

"That was the beauty of it," Nathan explained. "These guys were from all over. No one even knew who they were or where their gear was kept. But when a skirmish broke out, they would swoop in with superior airpower and highly-trained troops, and put an end to it."

"How could you possibly hide such a large organization?" Jakome asked as he buckled himself into the copilot's seat.

"They weren't that large actually. In fact, there wasn't a single action where they used more than a hundred air units and maybe a few hundred combatants."

"And yet they were able to defeat much larger forces?" Jakome wondered. "They couldn't possibly have been *that* good."

"They weren't," Nathan confirmed. "I mean, they *were* good. Damned good. The trick was in their timing. Because they were independent, they could swing into action much earlier, *before* the conflicts got beyond their ability to put down."

"Similar to the Ghatazhak Quick Response Force?"

"Bigger but the same idea."

"And such an organization could stand up to any nation?"

"Well not the bigger nations, but they weren't the ones attacking their neighbors. For the most part, it worked."

"What ever happened to them?" Jakome wondered.

"Nobody knows. Eventually, the conflicts became fewer and fewer, and the need faded away, as did the Ghost Force."

"How do you know all of this?"

"I thought you knew everything about me."

"Yes, but your degree wasn't in pre-plague history, it was in modern history."

Nathan smiled. "Yeah, I saw it in an episode of 'History Files from the Ark'. It was popular when I was a kid. I loved that show." Nathan activated the auto-launch system, and the Seiiki began to rise from the surface of Kataoka.

"Why are you telling me all of this?" Jakome wondered.

"Cuz he's a Boy Scout," Jessica remarked as she entered.

Jakome looked puzzled. "I am not familiar with that term."

"It's someone who always has to do the right thing," Jessica explained, taking a seat behind them.

"It has recently occurred to me that, for the first time, I have a ship with considerable abilities for good that is not bound to any government body," Nathan explained.

"Only because we stole it," Jessica mused.

"We didn't *steal* it," Nathan insisted. "They tried to *destroy* us, remember?"

"That has yet to be proven," Jakome reminded him.

"We weren't bound to any government during the Dusahn war," Jessica reminded him.

"We were bound to the Sol-Takaran Alliance," Nathan argued.

"Splitting hairs, aren't you?" Jessica replied.

"My oath was to defend and support the *ideals* of the constitution. Just because the Alliance is no longer honoring them doesn't mean that we shouldn't."

"See? Boy Scout," Jessica joked.

"Then what *are* your plans?" Jakome wondered. "Other than *not* supporting the Alliance."

"To continue doing what the *new* Aurora was designed to do," Nathan explained. "To protect and support the peaceful coexistence of worlds. *Especially* in the badlands."

"Sweet!" Jessica exclaimed. "We're going to be pirate hunters!"

"Not exactly," Nathan corrected as the Seiiki began to accelerate toward the sky.

"You intend on single-handedly stopping all piracy in the badlands?" Jakome asked.

"Well not *all* of it," Nathan admitted. "Maybe just the worst of them. I don't know. It just seems like a good use of a great ship."

"It might be better to come up with some set criteria for when you get involved," Jakome suggested. "For example, when they kill women and children."

"Something like that," Nathan agreed. "I haven't completely thought this through. We've only been here for a week after all."

Jakome smiled. "Deliza was right about you."

* * *

"Mom!" Alex yelled as she entered. She tossed her coat onto a side chair and headed into the family home. "Mom!"

"Stop yelling," her mother replied, entering from the other room. "What are you doing home? I thought you were on Kataoka?"

"We were, and we're headed back soon."

"Where are Josi and Shane?"

"They're back at the ship, running the load in. I don't have much time. Listen, Mom, contact that regen doc and make an appointment for Pop as soon as possible."

"We've talked about this, Alex. We can't afford it…"

"We can now," Alex insisted, handing her mother the two credit chips her new employer had given her.

Her mother stared at the chips in disbelief. "Oh my God, Alex. What did you do?"

"Some rich dude leased us for *six months*," Alex explained. "Can you believe that? And he *way* overpaid."

"But you should fix up the ship first."

"There's more than enough there to do both, Mom. Just transmit those chips to our accounts ASAP before someone tries to steal them."

"Who would lease the Acuna for so long?" her mother questioned. "What are they asking you to haul? What about the Korsan?"

Alex put her hands on her mother's shoulders. "I've got everything covered, Mom. Just transmit those chips, okay? Now where's Pop?"

"He's tinkering with that old skimmer in the barn, for all the good it will do."

"Don't tell him how much I just gave you," Alex instructed. "He'll worry."

"You mean like me?"

"Look, Mom, we're just hauling run-of-the-mill stuff between the Vernay worlds and Hadria. We've got a fighter escort and security, and our employer is even planning on upgrading our shields."

"For run-of-the-mill stuff?"

"Yeah, I don't get it either," Alex admitted. "But they've got the credits, so..."

"I don't like it."

"I'm going to get us *out* of the badlands, Mom."

"Just be careful," her mother insisted.

"I always am," she replied, kissing her mother on the cheek before heading out. "I'll call you!"

Her mother gazed at the two credit chips again, staring in disbelief.

* * *

Nathan, Jessica, and Jakome came down the Seiiki's ramp, once again parked in the Aurora's shuttle hangar bay.

"Welcome back, Cap'n," Marcus greeted.

"I want to get back in the air as soon as possible," Nathan instructed.

"The Bonaventura boys got everything lined up and ready to load," Marcus said, pointing at the pile of gear sitting to the side. "We'll have you ready to go in half an hour."

"Excellent."

"Mister Payan," Jakome greeted his assistant as he approached.

"Your shuttle is ready, my lord."

"We have the list?"

"We do," Mister Payan replied. "And it is quite lengthy."

"And the funds?" Jakome asked.

"Two million credits, as you requested."

"Two million credits?" Nathan asked.

"I took the liberty of leaving you with some funds, should you need them," Jakome explained. "It will probably take a week or more to fill this list and ship it back to you without drawing undue attention. In the meantime, the funds should be more than enough to handle any issues that may come up during my absence."

"But *two million*?" Nathan exclaimed. "That seems generous."

"It won't buy as much as you might think."

"I'll try not to spend it all in one place," Nathan joked.

"Until we meet again, Captain," Jakome said, offering his hand.

Nathan took his hand. "You really need to start calling me Nathan...especially since I'm going to start calling you Tug."

Jakome nodded respectfully then turned to Jessica. "Jessica."

"See ya soon, Tug," she said with a wink.

The two of them watched as Jakome and his

assistant headed to their shuttle parked on the flight deck beyond the shuttle bay entrance.

Jessica noticed the look on Nathan's face. "Still hard to believe, huh?"

"The absolute *last* person I expected to see, let alone come to our rescue," Nathan admitted.

"Kind of apropos, though, don't you think?"

Nathan looked at her. "I suppose it is."

"First thing we buy are updated guns," Jessica insisted, walking away.

* * *

"*How much longer is this going to take?*" Nikolas complained over comms.

"Once they finish here, we go back to Kataoka," Loki replied.

"*I lost feeling in my butt hours ago.*"

"You could turn down your gravity, you know," Loki suggested.

"*Zero-G makes me nauseated.*"

"Just dial it down enough to give your butt some relief."

"*Now why didn't I think of that?*"

"Because you think too much."

"*Now you sound like Josh.*"

"Yeah, I hate it when that happens."

An alert beeped, drawing Loki's attention to his sensor screen. "Two contacts just jumped in to the west of the settlement."

"*I don't have them,*" Nikolas said.

"I just lost them," Loki reported. "Follow me down. We need to find them."

CHAPTER THREE

"*Kit, Loki.*"

Kit tapped his comm-set. "What's up?"

"*Two brief contacts west of you. Jumped in then disappeared a few seconds later.*"

"ID?"

"*Not enough time. Best guess based on size would be pirate shuttle.*"

The screech of a jump sounded from outside the Acuna's open cargo bay door.

"*Korsan!*" someone yelled.

Kit stepped up to the hatch, peering at the horizon. "Looks like you guessed right. Two shuttles just jumped in and are headed for our position."

"Shall we jump down and engage?" Loki inquired.

"Negative. Hold top cover. Engage anyone else that shows up. And activate the QRF on Kataoka. I'll keep comms open so you can monitor."

"*Copy that.*"

Alex came running up the ramp. "We've got a problem."

"Let us deal with it," Kit told her.

"Just don't use your blasters…"

"I know. Vissian gas." He peeked outside again as the two shuttles landed and men began to disembark. "They know about the gas too, right?"

"Oh yeah," Shane said. "One of them learned the hard way a while back. One shot and he went up like a fireball."

"How do you people live here with all this gas floating around waiting to blow up?" Mori wondered.

"It only ignites when it comes into contact with plasma energy," Josi explained.

Kit shared a glance with Mori. "This should be fun."

* * *

Chief Anson and his three squad members sat comfortably alongside the Ghatazhak QRF shuttle, watching the movement of Kataokans around the settlement at the edge of the airfield.

"Finally," Corporal Teece moaned, spotting Jokay and Abdur coming out from between two buildings with a bundle that they hoped was their lunch.

"What the hell took you so long?" Sergeant Tuncay asked.

"Abs had to stop and talk to a working girl."

"Seriously?"

"Hey," Abdur defended. "I haven't gotten any action in over five hundred years, remember?"

"None of us have gotten any action in over five hundred years," Specialist Roose commented.

"Waste of time," the chief stated. "We don't have any credits."

"Not to mention backup bodies," Jokay joked. "You never know what new venereal diseases have developed over the last five centuries."

"That's what nanites are for," Abdur said.

"I can see it now," Jokay chuckled. "Hey, Doc, can I get a booster shoot…down there?"

"*Attention,*" the shuttle's AI voice called over the main bay's loudspeaker. "*Flash traffic. Lieutenant Vasya requests immediate QRF response to Estabrook. Message sent via Dragon One. Message age: three minutes, twenty-four seconds.*"

"Looks like the entertainment will have to wait," Chief Anson commented as he and the others rose to climb back into their shuttle. "Pilot, spin up for quick-launch to Estabrook."

"Too bad," Abdur complained as the shuttle's grav-lift systems began spinning up. "Those girls were *cute*."

"Listen up, people," Chief Anson barked as the shuttle's side clamshell doors closed up, sealing them inside. "Estabrook's got vissian gas leaks all over the place, so RGs only."

"How about blades?" Specialist Roose asked as he stepped up onto his auto-suit platform.

"How about you just put a slug in them so we can get Abs back to his girls," the chief said as the shuttle began to rise.

"Departure jump in twenty seconds," the shuttle's AI announced.

* * *

"*I am receiving flash traffic from Lieutenant Commander Sheehan,*" Talisha's AI called over her comm-set.

"What is it?"

"The QRF has been activated. He requests that you put all four Dragons on Kataoka on alert-ready status."

Talisha rolled out from her comfortable position lying on the grass underneath her fighter, jumping to her feet as the Ghatazhak QRF shuttle began lifting off the ground in the distance. "Mount up!" she barked at the other three pilots.

"*What's up?*" Allet asked over comm-sets.

"QRF is taking off," Talisha replied as she climbed up the access ladder built into the side of her Dragon fighter. "Boss has put us on alert-ready status. Get your birds hot and ready to launch."

* * *

Kit and Mori strolled confidently down the Acuna's port ramp, Alex following close behind. About thirty meters away, the two pirate shuttles touched down, their hatches opening a moment later. As expected, four men piled out of each shuttle.

"They're taking up support positions," Mori observed as four of the men spread out, maintaining a safe distance from the Acuna.

"Shit tactics," Kit commented. "Half in, half out."

"You expected better?"

"I was hoping for a challenge," Kit chuckled.

Alex cast both of them a sidelong glance. Either these men were incredibly brave or just plain stupid. "These are Brodek, you know?"

"What's a Brodek?" Kit asked as he eyed the four men who were walking toward them.

"Two blades and a blaster each," Mori observed.

"Brodek is the clan that works this area on behalf of the Korsan," Alex explained. "They took over a few years ago, after killing off the Tourons."

"Another clan?" Kit surmised.

"Yup."

"That kind of thing happen often?"

"It does in the badlands," Alex replied.

All six Ghatazhak were now in full combat gear, standing at their stations inside the QRF shuttle.

"*We have arrived at Estabrook,*" the shuttle's AI announced over their helmet comms. "*Entering orbit.*"

"Dragon One, QRF," Chief Anson called over comms. "On station. Sit-rep?"

"*QRF, Dragon One,*" Loki replied. "*Looks like two shuttles touched down about thirty meters off the Acuna's port side. I show eight combatants, four close in, probably talking with Kit now. The other four are spread out in a half circle about fifteen meters out. Setting up tactical link now.*"

"Any other contacts?"

"*Negative. Just the two so far. Kit ordered us to hold cover in case any others showed up though.*"

"Copy that," the chief acknowledged. "We'll head down now to back them up." He waited a moment for the tactical display on the inside of his helmet visor to light up, showing the positions of everyone on the surface in the engagement area. "Pilot, prepare an insertion jump. Five clicks west of target, angels eight, stealth mode."

"*Understood.*"

The four men approached, each of them sizing up the two unfamiliar faces standing on either side of Alex.

"Middle one's Vodar," Alex said under her breath. "A real slimy bastard."

"Alex," Vodar greeted.

"Vodar."

"Going somewhere?"

"Soon as we finish our business here."

"You hauling out?" Vodar asked.

"How is that any of your business?" Kit asked.

Vodar looked Kit over, not feeling terribly intimidated by the considerably smaller man. "Who's your mouthy friend?"

"I'm not her friend," Kit corrected.

"Then what are you?"

"Security."

Vodar let out a hearty laugh. "You know who we are?"

"Don't care to," Kit replied.

"We're *Brodek*," Vodar told him, menace in his tone.

"Is that the name of your little boys' club?"

Vodar looked at his second-in-command. "Can you believe this guy?" He turned back to Kit. "You sure you wanna do this, boy?"

"Well, most of the time, *want* has nothing to do with it. But in your case...I might have to make an exception."

The QRF shuttle suddenly appeared in Estabrook's atmosphere, but without any jump flash or clap of thunder. A second later, the doors on either side opened, and six Ghatazhak stepped out, starting their free fall toward the surface.

"Kit, Derel," the chief called over comms as he dove toward the surface. "On approach. Insertion in thirty seconds."

The six Ghatazhak began spreading out as they dove toward the surface, maneuvering into their insertion positions based on the locations of the combatants on the surface a few thousand meters below and about a kilometer downrange of them.

The chief studied his tactical display, pulling his own chute release once his display flashed green. His parachute deployed, his system automatically steering him onto the proper course for his insertion.

"I'm gonna assume that you and your friend here are new to this part of the badlands," Vodar stated. He then turned to Alex. "I'm also gonna assume that these two idiots aren't speakin' for you. Cuz if they were, I'd already have cut a piece off ya, just like I did your old man."

Kit smiled. "You know what one of the biggest

advantages of being average-sized is?" he asked Vodar.

"For the life of me, I can't think of even one," Vodar replied.

"It's that dumbasses like you are always underestimating me."

Chief Anson's AI counted down, displaying the time to his insertion jump in the upper corner of his helmet visor. At two seconds to go, his parachute disconnected, and he started his free fall once again. When his jump fields formed, he instantly transitioned to a new position a meter from the surface and ten meters behind one of the combatants forming a half circle around the Acuna.

Meanwhile, the other five members of the QRF team landed in similar positions. All six men drew their rail gun rifles and took aim at their respective targets as they dropped to one knee to reduce their target profiles.

Although there were no jump flashes or thunderous cracks, the sudden appearance of six men in full combat armor, kneeling in firing positions with their weapons trained on the pirates, did not go unnoticed.

Vodar casually turned to reassess the situation, spotting one of the newly arrived combatants out of the corner of his eye.

"Vodar?" one of his men questioned, becoming anxious at their new reality.

Vodar turned back to Kit, taking another step forward and looking him in the eyes in the hopes of intimidating him. "You will stand down your dogs, and you will allow us to collect our payment from this ship."

"Not going to happen," Kit replied confidently.

"Whether you win or lose, the Brodek will rain hell on this settlement as retribution."

"Also not going to happen," Kit replied. "So I suggest you and your men depart *peacefully* while you still can."

"You have been warned," Vodar said as he turned away.

Kit kept his eyes locked on Vodar as the man turned away and was not surprised when the man spun back around with a half-meter long blade in his right hand. In a flash, Kit drew his own knife, twirling it twice as he leaned back just enough so that the tip of his attacker's weapon just missed Kit's throat. Kit then stepped forward, plunging his knife into Vodar's left side, quickly withdrawing it. Unfortunately, the big man wasn't going down quickly. Kit spun around to his right, changing to an overhand grip on his knife, bringing it around to drive it into the side of Vodar's neck.

All six Ghatazhak fired their rail gun rifles at once. With one shot each, they dropped all four of the perimeter guards and two of the three men backing up Vodar.

The third man was Mori's responsibility. He blocked the man's attacking arm with his left hand, driving his combat knife into the man's chest and pulling upward, ripping him open.

Kit pulled his knife out of Vodar's neck, stepping aside as the man fell to the ground, clutching the gushing wound in his neck. Now on his back, the man stared up at Kit in complete disbelief. In all of

Vodar's years in the Brodek clan, no one had ever taken arms against him.

Kit knelt down next to Vodar, pulling his med-pack out of his thigh pocket. "Don't look so frightened," he told the bleeding man. "You're not going to die."

Alex was stunned. She had seen her share of blood, but it had always been at the brutal hands of the pirates. What she had just witnessed had been nothing short of miraculous. A perfectly timed, precision execution of eight men, all performed without any signs of emotion.

She watched Kit as he bandaged Vodar's neck wound and then injected him with something. "What are you doing?"

"Saving his dumb ass."

"Why?"

"He's worth more to us alive."

"He nearly killed our father!" Alex protested. "Let him die!"

"Not until he's properly interrogated," Kit insisted.

"Fuck that!" Alex insisted, pulling her own knife and lunging toward Vodar on the ground.

Kit blocked her attack, pushing her firmly over. "Mori!"

Mori stepped over, taking the knife from Alex's hand and then pulling her back up onto her feet. "Get inside and get this ship ready to launch."

"Chiqua, this is Kit," Kit called over his comm-set as he finished injecting nanites into Vodar's neck. "Wrap it up and get your ass back to the Acuna. It's time to go."

"*Why? What's happening?*"

"Just do it," Kit insisted. "Derel, secure the perimeter. As soon as we lift off, return to Kataoka."

"*Copy that,*" Chief Anson acknowledged.

"Loki, stay on station. Any more pirate shuttles show up, you take them out. As soon as we get back to Kataoka, I'll send you backup. We're going to full alert status in the Vernay until further notice."

"*Understood.*"

Kit continued patching up Vodar, getting the man's bleeding under control.

"Maybe you shouldn't have stabbed him twice?" Mori suggested.

"This fucker wasn't going down with just one," Kit insisted.

"You think he's going to make it?"

"Yeah, I didn't hit anything major," Kit replied. "But he will be getting his meals intravenously for a while."

Vodar continued to stare up at Kit in fear and confusion.

"I hope you're worth the effort," Kit told him as he injected another dose of nanites near the big man's belly wound.

* * *

"I still don't get why we can't jump directly from Dencke *to* Kataoka instead of using this *passage*," Jessica commented from the copilot's seat of the Seiiki.

"If you're expecting an explanation from me, you're barking up the wrong tree," Nathan admitted. "Hopefully Abby will be able to figure it all out."

"It's weird having her back," Jessica said.

"Really? I don't find it weird."

"I don't mean it the way you think. I had just gotten used to the idea that everyone we knew was long dead. Family, friends..."

Nathan looked at Jessica. "I'm sure she led a long

and happy life," he told her, taking her hand. "She had plenty of uncles to take care of her."

Jessica nodded. "I know. It just sucks."

An alarm beeped.

Jessica glanced at the sensor display. "Four contacts."

"*You got this, Cap'n?*" Josh asked over comms.

"Four, bearing three two, up fifteen relative," Nathan reported. "Twenty clicks and closing."

"*I count six,*" Josh corrected.

The sensor display changed, showing six icons instead of four. "Correction, six," Nathan updated. "Not the shuttles like before."

"I'm not getting any ID data on them," Jessica warned. "But I am picking up weapons. Shields, plasma cannons, and missiles."

"I guess they were expecting a fight this time," Nathan decided. "Seiiki, shields and weapons, please."

"*Shields coming up, weapons deploying and charging,*" the shuttle's AI reported.

"Josh, don't fire unless fired upon," Nathan instructed over comms.

"*I had a feeling you'd say that,*" Josh complained.

"*What are we doing?*" Mick asked over comms.

"Just having a little fun," Josh replied as he turned his Dragon fighter toward the rapidly approaching pirate fighters.

"*You call turning into their gun sights fun?*"

"You don't?"

"*They warned me about you.*"

"They were right," Josh chuckled as he dialed up a micro-jump. "Hold on. I'm slaving your controls to mine for a moment."

"*I don't like the sound of that.*"

"Trust me."

"*That's what people typically say right before they screw up.*"

Josh smiled as he pressed the jump button. Suddenly, the six approaching pirate fighters were less than a hundred meters in front of them and closing fast.

"*Shit!*" Mick exclaimed.

There was very little spacing between the enemy fighters, maybe not enough. Josh snap-rolled his fighter ninety degrees over, causing his wingman's ship to do the same. A split second later, both ships barely squeezed between the two middle pirates, causing them to break formation haphazardly.

"Yee-haw!" Josh yelled. "Bet they just shit themselves!"

"*I know I did,*" Mick replied. "*Can I have control back now?*"

"*That's* fucking with their heads," Jessica cheered.

"*Make a run for it,*" Josh suggested over comms. "*If they go after you, we'll know what their intentions are.*"

"I'm pretty sure I know what their intentions are," Nathan replied as he pushed his throttles all the way forward.

"*Unknown ship. Kill your engines and call off your escorts, or we will destroy you.*"

Jessica quickly punched the transmit button. "Go fuck yourself!"

Nathan looked over at her. "Was that really necessary?"

"Yes. Yes, it was."

Three bolts of plasma streaked over them, barely missing their dorsal shields.

"Is that the best you've got?" Jessica called over comms.

Nathan reached over and deselected Jessica's comm-set on the comm-panel. The next three bolts did not miss, rocking the ship.

"Can I fire now?" Josh asked as he brought his ship around and locked his missiles on three of the targets.

"*Please*," Nathan confirmed.

"I've got the left three," Josh announced.

"*I've got the right,*" Mick acknowledged.

"Launch, jump, shoot," Josh instructed, pressing the missile launch button.

A long door on the underside of Josh's Dragon fighter opened, and three missiles dropped out, their engines lighting to accelerate them away as they cleared the bay.

Josh pitched up slightly then jumped just beyond the targets he was attacking. He then killed his engines and pitched over one hundred and eighty degrees, bringing his nose onto the three pirate fighters that were now trailing him. A quick press of his firing button, and the three pirate ships began jinking to avoid his plasma cannon fire. The problem was, they weren't trying to evade the missiles that had jumped in behind them a split second *after* Josh had.

Three explosions erupted as all three missiles slammed into their targets and detonated.

"Damn! You guys suck at this!" Josh exclaimed.

"I got three!" Josh reported as he flipped his nose back over and jammed his throttles to full power again. "How you doin', Mick?"

"*I got two!*" Mick replied.

"*Last one's buggin' out,*" Nathan announced.

"Nice work, guys," Nathan congratulated over comms. "Form back up on me and let's get out of here." He glanced at Jessica. "That's certainly going to piss off their leader."

"Pirate hunting is fun," Jessica exclaimed.

"We're not *pirate hunting.*"

"Could've fooled me."

"*On your six, Cap'n,*" Josh reported.

"Syncing up jump systems," Nathan announced.

"*Those guys were complete amateurs,*" Josh boasted.

"You know, it's not going to be as easy next time," Nathan warned.

"*God I hope not. That was hardly even a challenge!*"

"*It was enough of a challenge for me,*" Mick admitted.

* * *

"We have completed a detailed ground scan," Laza reported. "The depth of the mud is only sixty-three centimeters on average and is currently frozen."

Vladimir peered up at the sky, which was finally beginning to lighten after the long night. "How long will it stay frozen?"

"About a week."

"The main gear can only extend to one hundred centimeters," Chief Avelles reminded them. "That's not going to leave enough clearance to do the repairs underneath."

"And it will sink as the mud thaws," Laza added.

"Just fuse it," Dominic suggested.

Vladimir looked at him doubtfully.

"You had fused soil in your day."

"Yes, but..."

"Ah, yes. Fused piers came along later," Dominic remembered. "We can fuse the soil under the ship's gear and then excavate around them to get clearance for the ventral hull repairs."

"You can fuse *just* the soil underneath the gear?" Vladimir questioned.

"In a pyramid shape, as deep as seventy meters. We just have to do the math to make sure the pads will hold the ship's weight."

"How long will that take?" Vladimir asked.

Dominic thought for a moment, looking up and to the left as he considered the question. "I'll just use the ship's max design weight, and... Done."

"What?" Vladimir asked.

"I made the calculations."

"In your head?" Laza asked in disbelief. She immediately pulled out her data pad and began running the calculations herself.

Dominic looked at Vladimir, smiling. "Bio-neural interface," he explained, holding up his left wrist, which had the small computer interface attached to it.

"I have to get one of those," Vladimir decided.

"All four gear systems passed diagnostics," Chief Avelles stated.

Vladimir took a deep breath, tapping his comm-set. "Cam, extend the gear."

Cameron stepped up to the tactical console, calling up the landing gear controls on the multipurpose display at its center. "Are you sure about this?"

"*Better now, while the mud is still frozen. Otherwise, it will just rush into the gear bays and muck everything up,*" Vladimir explained.

Cameron took a breath then pressed the button to start the landing gear extension cycle. "Gear bay doors are opening. Slowly, but they *are* opening," she reported over her comm-set. After a beat, she added, "Gear bay doors are open. Gear coming down."

The four of them watched silently. There was a *crunch* from deep underground, then a moaning. The ice around the ship began to crack. A tiny fissure exploded into a web of cracks that soon sent bits of mud-ice flying.

The ship began to rise. Slowly at first, as if it were meeting considerable resistance, but then more freely, lifting majestically from the frozen bog in which it had rested for nearly two weeks. In less than a minute, the mighty ship reached its maximum gear height, and its stern dropped slightly, leveling the ship.

Vladimir carefully studied the ship which he had spent the last five years designing and building. It was his child, far more so than her predecessor had been. Every scratch, every gouge, every damaged hull panel caused him anguish. "My poor girl."

"At least most of the frozen mud seems to be falling away," Chief Avelles commented, hoping it would ease Vladimir's pain.

"How are we going to start the excavation if we can't get the ramps down?" Laza wondered.

"We lift the excavators to the flight deck and use a shuttle to ferry them down," Vladimir explained as he examined the damage to her ventral surfaces. "We have a *lot* of work to do," he sighed. "We might as well get started."

* * *

Nathan, Jessica, and a band of technicians and loaders approached the Acuna. "How was your trip?" he asked Chiqua as she, Kit, and Alex descended the ramp to meet them.

"We have a prisoner who needs immediate medical attention," Kit reported.

"Prisoner?" Nathan questioned.

"We had a bit of a standoff against the pirates," Kit explained. "On Estabrook, just as we were about to leave."

"How many?"

"Eight."

"And only one survived?"

"We gave them the opportunity to walk away," Kit assured him.

"But of course, they didn't take it."

"They're not very bright," Alex commented.

"Not very good in a firefight either," Kit added.

"How bad?"

"I stabilized him and gave him a couple shots of nanites, but he lost a lot of blood, and we don't have any trans-heme."

Nathan turned to the lead Takaran technician they had brought along to supervise the upgrades to the Acuna. "Can you do the upgrades while she's loaded?"

"Most of it, yes, but we'll probably need to unload at least part of her cargo to access some of her internal systems."

"What are you thinking?" Jessica asked Nathan.

"I'm thinking we abort running this cargo back to Hadria and get the prisoner to Doc Chen."

"We could use the intel," Jessica admitted.

"How long before the Acuna is ready to fly again?" he asked the lead Takaran tech.

"At least a few days."

Nathan looked to Chiqua next. "Can't be helped."

"The hell it can't," Chiqua argued. "I've got trades already lined up for half of this cargo."

"If you want to have regular access to the Vernay worlds, we need more intel on the pirates." Nathan looked to Kit. "Move the prisoner to the Seiiki. We'll take off immediately."

"What about my cargo?" Chiqua demanded. "You can't just leave it lying around here. Half of it will get stolen!"

"No one's stealing anything," Kit assured her. "Not as long as we're here."

"No way," Chiqua insisted. "I'm not standing for this."

"I wasn't asking your permission," Nathan declared.

"We had a *deal*."

"How we get *your* cargo in and out of the badlands is *my* call, not yours. So I suggest you start adding some wiggle room into your trade schedules to accommodate a changing tactical environment."

"I can't run a business this way!" Chiqua objected.

"It will only take us a few hours to get back to Dencke. I promise we'll come back and move your cargo to Hadria afterward."

Nathan turned and headed back to the Seiiki without another word, with Jessica hot on his heels.

"This is just great," Chiqua complained.

"Let's get him to the Seiiki," Kit said to Mori.

Jessica jogged a few steps to catch up to Nathan as they head back to their ship. "I love it when you use phrases like 'tactical environment'," she teased. "It makes me all hot."

Nathan rolled his eyes. Her attempt to ease his tension had succeeded as usual.

* * *

"Captain Taylor?" Laza called from the entrance to the captain's ready room.

"Yes?"

"I've finished my preliminary route analysis between Hadria and the Vernay worlds."

"And what did you find?"

"I believe the mappings of recurring gravity wells are inaccurate."

"How so?" Cameron asked, intrigued by her science officer's claim.

"Gravity wells, regardless of their size or duration, send out ripples that affect the orbits of other objects. The effect is small, almost immeasurable in most cases, but they *are* there *if* you look for them."

"And you're saying they're not?"

"Some are there, but many *are* missing...when they should *not* be missing."

"Is it possible that the effects of one gravity well might have affected those of another?" Cameron suggested. "Somehow canceling them out?"

"There would be an effect, but even *that* would be measurable."

"So there are *no* gravity wells?"

"Oh no, there are many of them. Some fixed and some that seem to appear and disappear at random intervals and locations. And *that's* the problem."

"You mean, that's why we have to use the Vernay corridor?" Cameron assumed.

"No, I mean the randomness of the patterns of the rogue gravity wells *isn't* random at all. It just *appears* to be random."

"Are you certain?"

"No, not without about a thousand times more data, but I am starting to see patterns...patterns that should not exist in naturally occurring rogue gravity wells."

"Any chance this *pattern* that you're sensing is the result of the damage they claim the long-range jump drives cause?"

Laza sighed. "I'm afraid that's beyond my understanding of interdimensional physics."

"Then it's a good thing we have someone aboard who *does* understand it," Cameron said, tapping her intercom. "Abby, Cameron."

"*Yes, Cameron?*" Abby replied.

"Can you come to the captain's ready room? We have some data that needs your unique perspective."

"*I'm on my way.*"

"I want you to spend all your time working with Doctor Sorenson on this," Cameron instructed Laza.

"Yes, sir."

* * *

Darren routinely ended his day like everyone else, at the tavern on Kataoka. Other than a few eateries along the main boulevard, there was little else to do on their dusty world for entertainment.

Within a few minutes of taking a seat at the bar, a surprising turn of events occurred. An attractive woman, not much older than himself, took the stool next to him.

"Buy me a drink?"

Darren looked over at the woman, captivated by her beauty. "Uh...sure."

"I'm Shya," she introduced.

"Darren, son of Rod."

"It's so *cute* how you all introduce yourselves that way."

"What way?" Darren wondered.

"By stating the name of your father. Do the women introduce themselves the same way?"

"No, they state the name of their mother," Darren explained, paying the bartender for both of their drinks with the simple coinage of their world. "Are you new to Kataoka?"

"Why do you ask?" Shya wondered.

"I've never seen you before."

"Maybe you just never noticed me?"

"I would've noticed *you*," he insisted.

"Are you blushing?" she cooed. "That's so adorable."

Embarrassed, Darren looked around for the first time since coming in and noticed three other attractive women working the room. That's when he realized. "Uh...I don't really have much money," he told Shya. "I mean, if you're..." He found himself drawn to her cleavage longer than might be appropriate, even for a working girl, and quickly brought his gaze back up to her eyes.

"Relax, sweetie. This one's on me," she told him, taking his hand and leading him away.

Darren's smile broadened, unable to believe his luck.

* * *

The med-techs floated the patient down the Seiiki's ramp and across the hangar bay deck toward the forward exit, with Nathan and Jessica following them.

"I see you got the ship raised and leveled," Nathan

commented as he met Cameron at the bottom of the ramp. "It looks pretty bad."

"Yeah, Vlad practically cried when he saw the underside," Cameron replied. "Who's the casualty?"

"One of the pirates who attacked the Acuna while on Estabrook."

"Is he going to make it?" Cameron wondered.

"Hopefully," Nathan replied. "We could sure use the intel."

"How can you be sure he'll talk?" Cameron asked.

"Oh, he'll talk," Jessica assured her as she passed.

"Any friendly casualties?" Cameron asked.

"Negative," Nathan replied as they headed back toward the exit together.

"I wasn't expecting you back so soon."

"We decided to bring the prisoner back first," Nathan explained. "We'll be returning to Kataoka shortly."

"You might want to talk with Laza and Abby," Cameron suggested.

"Maybe when we get back," Nathan replied. "Chiqua was a little pissed by the delay." Nathan turned to Marcus as he reached the exit. "Get her fueled up and ready for departure," he instructed. "And tell Josh we take off again as soon as everyone's re-upped."

"For a ship crashed in the middle of nowhere, we sure do a lot of flyin'," Marcus grumbled.

CHAPTER FOUR

Nathan headed down the central corridor toward the entrance into the Aurora's shuttle hangar bay at the aft end.

Jessica came jogging up behind him. "Doc says pirate-guy will live."

"Yeah, I heard."

"He probably wouldn't have if we'd loaded up the cargo first," she said. "Kit's knife punctured the guy's abdominal aorta. No way the nanites could close that up fast enough."

"Even with the double-dose he gave him?"

"That slowed it down enough to keep him from dying. I'm going to have to talk to that boy about his aim."

Nathan and Jessica reached the entrance to the shuttle bay just as the elevator door to their right opened and Abby and Laza stepped out.

"Nathan," Abby called after him.

Nathan paused at the entrance. "I know Cam said I needed to talk to you, but I'm a little short on time right now."

"That's *why* we need to talk," Abby insisted.

Nathan turned to Jessica. "Get the ship spun up."

"Sure thing. How do I do that?"

"Just tell the AI to spin up for departure."

"Right," Jessica confirmed, continuing into the shuttle bay.

"Make it quick," Nathan told Abby.

"Okay. You can single-jump straight to Kataoka. You don't need to multi-jump your way through the Vernay passage."

"Okay, maybe not that quick."

"Laza has conducted extensive surveys of the direct route between Dencke and the Vernay worlds. Her findings confirm my original suspicions."

"That long jumps *don't* damage the interdimensional barrier?" Nathan surmised.

"Not that suspicion."

"There's another?"

Abby sighed. "I never really told anyone, because it was more a feeling than a theory, but after studying her data, I'm beginning to think I was right all along."

"Cut to the chase, Abby."

"If the rogue gravity wells were being caused by damage to the interdimensional barrier, they would be truly random," Laza explained. "The gravity wells *I* detected were not."

"What do you mean, they were *not*? Not random?"

"Precisely," Laza confirmed.

Nathan looked at them both. "How is that possible?"

"I'm not even certain they are *actually* gravity wells," Laza added.

"Are you suggesting they are *artificially* created?" Nathan asked, dumbfounded.

"I cannot speak to the cause. All I know is that there *is* a repeating pattern," Laza explained. "It's almost imperceptible, but it's there. I'm certain of it."

Nathan shook his head. "This is getting weird."

"The claim was that long jumps caused tears in the barrier, and since we jump through the dimension in which *time* does not exist, a tear can occur anywhere," Abby told him.

"Then why don't the jump gates cause damage?" Nathan wondered. "They're long jumps."

"Because they aren't in motion when the energy

spike is applied. Only the object being transported is. Or at least, that's their explanation."

"I'm confused. Are these gravity wells real or not?"

"We'll need a *lot* more data to make that determination," Abby admitted. "But Laza has enough data to predict *when* and *where* the anomalies will occur."

"And to be honest, they don't occur that often," Laza added. "At least not along the direct route from Dencke to the Vernay worlds."

Nathan thought for a moment. "How is it that no one has figured this out?"

"The Alliance Science Academy is considered above reproach," Abby explained. "Everyone simply accepts it, and no one really has the resources to prove them wrong. Besides, contradicting the ASA is the quickest way to ruin a scientist's career. Trust me, I know."

"Captain, the gravity ripples I've detected from the so-called gravity wells appear to be far weaker than one would expect," Laza added. "I suspect most people just assume they decay over time, which they do. But the effect they *should* have on other celestial objects would *not* fade. And those effects are simply not there."

"*We're ready for departure,*" Jessica reported over Nathan's comm-set.

"Bottom-line this for me, Abby," Nathan requested.

"There is no reason you cannot single-jump *directly* to the Vernay worlds...*from* Dencke."

"What about Hadria?" Nathan wondered.

"I would have to conduct more scans to answer that," Laza replied. "I'd prefer to continue studying the Dencke-Vernay route, though. Just to validate my findings."

"And you're sure about this?" Nathan asked Abby.

"I'd bet my life on it," Abby replied.

* * *

Josh eased the grav-lift power collective upward, causing his Dragon fighter to rise from the Aurora's flight deck. As his ship rose, he reached over and raised a lever, causing the landing gear to retract. A quick glance to his right to ensure his wingman was also lifting off, and Josh moved his hand to his throttle, easing it forward just enough to give his fighter some forward thrust.

"Aurora, Hotdog. We're wheels up and climbing."

"*Copy that, Hotdog,*" Ensign Dass answered.

"*Seiiki's rolling out now,*" Nathan announced.

"We'll circle at one click until you're up and then fall into escort position," Josh reported.

"*Sounds good.*"

Josh glanced at his tactical display, noting that the icon representing his wingman was right where it should be, aft and to starboard. "Let's have a little fun while we can, Mick," he suggested, pushing his throttle all the way forward.

His fighter lunged forward, accelerating rapidly. Josh loved flying fast. The only thing he liked better was flying faster.

"*Do you ever fly like a normal person?*" Mick wondered.

"I thought I was," Josh laughed.

"Only Josh would circle at Mach two," Nathan commented as he pulled the Seiiki's grav-lift collective upward. The ship began to slowly rise from the Aurora's deck, the backside of her forward hull section sliding down their forward windows and disappearing as the ship climbed.

"*Shall I raise the gear?*" the Seiiki's AI asked.

"Yes, please," Nathan replied.

"You can't raise the gear yourself?" Jessica teased.

"She offered," Nathan defended as he keyed in their departure route.

Jessica noticed the new course plot. "You're not using the Vernay passage?"

"Nope."

Jessica continued watching, curious as to what route he planned to take. Her eyes widened when she saw the final jump plot. "You're going direct?"

"Yup."

"What about the rogue gravity wells?"

"Abby and Laza said there's nothing to worry about."

"You're single-jumping, direct."

"It's only fifty-seven light years."

"I thought anything over ten caused damage to the whatchamacallit."

"It's all a lie."

"According to Laza?"

"No, according to Abby. Laza just confirmed it... sort of."

"Sort of. Great. We get to play guinea pigs again."

"You should be used to it by now."

"It's been a while."

"*Uh, Cap'n?*" Josh called over comms. "*Am I reading this right? Are we single-jumping...direct?*"

Jessica keyed up her mic. "What's the matter, Josh? Ya chicken?"

"*Hell no. I just wanted to make sure it was Nathan flying and not you.*"

"It's me," Nathan confirmed over comms.

"*Not to question you, Cap'n, but are you sure this is a good idea?*"

"Abby says it's safe."

"*Abby also said you can't jump through solid matter, and Loki jumped through the tip of a mountain.*"

"Well someone's got to validate her theory," Nathan said as he pushed his throttles forward and pitched up toward the sky.

"*Theory?*" Mick didn't sound happy about the idea.

"*Let's do it!*" Josh exclaimed.

"*I'd rather talk about it a bit more,*" Mick insisted.

"Form up on me," Nathan instructed as he guided his shuttle toward the sky.

Two Dragon fighters fell in behind the Seiiki as they climbed skyward, taking escort positions to either side. The three-ship formation climbed rapidly through the atmosphere of Dencke, quickly leaving the planet behind and transitioning into the vacuum of space.

"I'm taking jump control," Nathan announced. "Sit back and enjoy the ride."

"*Hands free, baby!*" Josh replied.

"*Great, nothing like letting someone else jump you to your death,*" Mick commented.

"What's wrong, Mick?" Jessica teased.

"*Oh, nothing. There's nothing at all crazy about doing exactly what everyone in the galaxy says you shouldn't do.*"

"Everyone except the one person who *should* know," Nathan corrected. "Here we go, boys." Nathan pressed the jump sequencer. The ship's auto-flight system made final adjustments to course and speed, then initiated the jump. A second later, the jump flashed, and the planet Kataoka appeared before them, filling their windows.

"*Are we dead?*" Mick asked, joking.

"*Yee-haw!*" Josh exclaimed. "*No more Vernay passage! Although I am gonna miss shootin' pirates. They were such easy targets!*"

Nathan looked over at Jessica and smiled. "I'm getting that feeling again."

"What feeling is that?" Jessica asked, almost fearing the answer.

"That feeling that we're about to change everything."

* * *

Kit and Mori were standing guard over the cargo stacked on the ground on Kataoka, a few meters from the Acuna. A handful of Takaran technicians had been at work since they had arrived less than two hours ago.

Kit couldn't help but eye the Takarans, which Mori found odd.

"They are *our* people," Mori reminded Kit.

"Just because they're from what was once *our* homeworld doesn't make them *our* people," Kit argued.

"More so than anyone else we've dealt with since this mission started."

Kit chuckled. "Longest QRF mission in Ghatazhak history, no doubt."

"No doubt."

A distant crack of thunder caught their attention.

"We expecting anyone?" Kit asked.

"Not that I know of."

Chiqua strode down the Acuna's ramp, having heard the sound from inside. "Pirates?"

"I don't think so," Kit replied as he squinted to

make out the shape of the distant approaching vessel. "Single ship...small..." His expression changed to one of surprise. "It's one of our shuttles."

"Well it can't be the Seiiki," Mori insisted. "They've only been gone about ninety minutes, and the Vernay passage takes at least an hour *each* way."

"Maybe it's the Mirai?" Kit suggested. "Bringing more gear and technicians perhaps?" Kit continued examining the object, now able to better see its shape. "It's definitely a Navarro-class."

"What's going on?" Alex asked as she came down the ramp to join them. She looked up, immediately recognizing the familiar shape. "Is that...?"

"It's got to be the Mirai," Mori decided.

Alex looked at them. "How many shuttles do you people have?"

"Just two."

"Just two. Hell, *two* of those shuttles can haul as much as my entire ship. What the hell do you need us for?"

"It's complicated," Kit told her.

"Everything with you people is complicated," Alex muttered.

"You don't like the money?" Chiqua asked her.

"Oh, I love it. I just wish I knew what exactly it was that I was being paid to do."

The shuttle began its final approach, reducing speed as it descended, its grav-lift generators humming loudly.

"That's the Seiiki," Mori realized.

"That's impossible," Chiqua insisted.

Two more cracks of thunder were heard, even closer than before. Two small black objects could be seen just above the distant horizon, no apparent motion noticeable.

"Dragons?" Mori suggested.

A few seconds later, two Dragon fighters streaked overhead at twice the speed of sound for Kataoka, less than fifty meters off the deck.

"Gotta be Josh," Kit said, smiling.

The Seiiki settled onto its gear, its grav-lift generators immediately winding down as the ship landed. Its aft cargo door opened, lowering to the deck, and Jessica sauntered down the ramp, followed by Nathan.

"What happened?" Kit asked as they approached. "You get turned around in the passage?"

"Not exactly," Nathan replied, smiling.

"We found a shortcut," Jessica joked.

* * *

Thirty minutes later, the Acuna's cargo was aboard the Seiiki and ready for departure.

"You ready, Josh?" Nathan called over comms as he prepared his ship for takeoff.

"*About time,*" Josh complained. "*We've been circling forever.*"

"You could have waited in orbit."

"*That's even more boring than circling.*"

"Ship's all buttoned up and ready to go," Jessica announced as she entered the Seiiki's cockpit and headed for the copilot's seat to Nathan's right.

"So what's this shortcut you were talking about?" Chiqua asked as she entered the cockpit.

"You'll see," Nathan replied, activating the liftoff sequence.

The ship rose gently from the deck, climbing smoothly skyward as it began to accelerate. Nathan glanced at the sensor display, verifying that Josh and Mick had already fallen into escort positions to either side.

"We probably don't need the escorts any longer," Jessica noted.

"Josh needs something to do, and the trainees need the practice."

"Trainees?" Chiqua wondered, concerned.

"They're all fully qualified pilots," Nathan assured her. "They just don't have a lot of time in type."

"And why is that?"

"Well, the Dragon fighters we arrived with were the very first ones off the assembly line," Nathan reminded Chiqua. "*No one* had any time in them when we left."

"I keep forgetting about the five-hundred-year thing," Chiqua admitted.

The sky outside quickly darkened as they climbed out of Kataoka's atmosphere and turned toward their destination.

"You taking control again?" Josh asked over comms.

"A-firm," Nathan replied as he prepared for the jump.

"So how much time does this shortcut save us?" Chiqua inquired. "I still might make my trade connections if it's fast enough."

The jump flash washed over them, and Dencke appeared outside their forward windows, a few hundred kilometers ahead.

"Josh, you guys go ahead and put down. We'll head on to Hadria. Let Cam know that Abby and Laza were right. We'll see you in a few hours."

"You got it, Cap'n," Josh replied as the two Dragon fighters accelerated away from them, turning toward the planet.

"Wait a minute," Chiqua said, unsure of what was happening. "Is that…*Dencke?*"

"Yup."

"You jumped all the way to Dencke...*directly*? Are you insane?"

"My science officer conducted a detailed study of the direct route between Dencke and the Vernay worlds and found no danger to jump traffic," Nathan explained as he prepared the next jump.

"But all the nav charts..."

"They are wrong," Nathan said.

"But how is that possible?"

"I don't know," Nathan admitted, "but I do have a few theories. The point is, we can jump directly in and out of the Vernay region."

"What about Hadria?" Chiqua wondered. "Can we jump directly between Hadria and Kataoka?"

"We don't know yet," Nathan admitted. "But even using Dencke as a waypoint saves us nearly two hours of travel time."

"More importantly, it means we can respond to any crisis in the Vernay region in a few minutes," Jessica added. "Any pirates show up, and we'll be all over them."

"If the rogue gravity well charts are a lie..."

"I didn't say that," Nathan corrected as he activated the next jump. "I only said the charts are wrong about the direct route between Dencke and the Vernay worlds."

The jump flash washed over them again, and Hadria appeared in their forward windows, rising toward them.

"Now let's get you and your cargo to the surface so you can complete your trades."

* * *

Loki walked up to the Acuna's port side near its forward gear, spotting a pair of feet in brown boots dangling from the gear bay. As he approached, the boots disappeared, rising up into the bay. A moment later, he heard a familiar, female voice cursing angrily. "Everything okay?" he asked.

"*What?*" the voice replied.

"I asked if everything was okay?" Loki repeated.

Alex's head came down out of the gear bay, upside down, her usually well-tied-back hair dangling in the dirt. "No," she told him. Her head went right back up, and a moment later, she dropped down out of the bay, feet first. "Fucking auto-lube system is stuck open, and the shit is oozing everywhere."

"When did that start?" Loki asked, trying to make conversation.

"About five months ago."

"Five months?"

"Cheaper to refill it every couple of weeks and wipe up the goo than it is to fix it," Alex explained.

"So why are you fixing it now?" Loki wondered.

"Cuz we've got the time, and we've got the money." She looked at him. "Why so many questions?"

"Because I'm bored," Loki admitted. "Not much to do here but sit around and contemplate life."

"Aren't you supposed to be on patrol or something? You know, protecting us from pirates?"

"We patrol in shifts. I'm not up for another four hours."

"Shouldn't you take a nap or something?"

"I don't sleep much."

Alex looked Loki over then handed him her wrench. "Then make yourself useful."

Loki took the slimy wrench, as well as the rag handed to him. After wiping the wrench off, he crouched down to get under the ship then stood up in the gear bay and looked around. "What am I supposed to do?"

"You see that gray box with four conduits connected to it? On the overhead, toward the back of the bay?"

Loki turned aft, spotting the box. "I see it."

"See the big bolt head in the middle of it?"

"Yes."

"I need to replace that, and I can't get it loose."

"Okay, I'll see what I can do." Loki repositioned himself and reached up, putting the wrench onto the bolt head and attempting to turn it.

"*Righty-tighty, lefty-loosey,*" Alex told him.

Loki smiled. Some expressions seemed to last forever. He struggled, unable to loosen it. "Man, it really is stuck. You don't have a power wrench?"

"*No such luxury. I can ask your tech-goons if they have one.*"

"Let me try it again," Loki suggested, repositioning himself for better leverage. Once in position, he pushed with all of his might. The bolt head suddenly let go, sending his hand forward into the wall, cutting open his knuckles and drawing blood. "Damn it!"

"*What's wrong?*" Alex asked. "You didn't break it, did you?"

"No, it's loose," Loki replied, examining his bleeding knuckles. He reached up and unscrewed the bolt head, pulling the valve assembly out once it was free. "Is this what you wanted out?" Loki asked as he crouched back down, handing her the valve.

"That's it," she replied, taking it and handing him a replacement. "As long as you're there, can you put this one in its place?"

Loki took the replacement valve and inserted it into the hole, screwing it in by hand.

"*Don't tighten it down too tightly,*" Alex suggested.

Loki used the wrench to snug the valve assembly down then crouched back down again, duckwalking out from under the ship. "That should do it," he said, handing her back the wrench.

"Thanks," Alex said. "Shane probably overtightened it, like he does everything else."

"Why didn't you have *him* fix it?" Loki wondered.

"Because you came along first. Besides, he's getting *serviced* at the tavern."

"*Serviced?*" Loki wondered.

"Apparently they have a new batch of beauties working."

"Ah, yes. I heard."

"I should probably clean up your hand," Alex offered.

"I'm okay."

"Just shut up and follow me," Alex insisted, heading toward the port cargo ramp.

"You're the captain, Captain."

Alex led him up the ramp into the empty port cargo bay, passing by two Takaran technicians as they exited.

"So how are the upgrades going?" Loki asked.

"I have no idea," Alex admitted as she opened the locker and pulled out the med-kit.

"They don't keep you updated?"

"They keep Josi updated, and she tries to explain it to me, but it's all blah-blah-blah. All I want to know is which button to push to make the stuff work."

"A good pilot understands how all their ship's systems work," Loki recited.

"They teach you that in *pilot school*?"

"Something like that."

"Well I never went to *pilot school*."

"How'd you learn to fly?"

"Who says I know how?" Alex said as she began cleaning up his tattered knuckles.

Loki was surprised. "You seem to fly this thing around fairly well."

"It's mostly automated," Alex admitted. "My father taught me the minimum I needed to get this thing from place to place, but that's about it."

"Does your crew know?"

"That I don't know how to fly? Of course."

"And they're okay with that?"

"It's not like we have a choice," Alex admitted. "This ship is the only way we have to support ourselves and our parents." She looked at him a moment. "You're not going to tell them, are you?"

"Tell whom?"

"Your boss or that money guy who leased us."

"Well, technically, I really should..."

"We *need* this gig. It's the only way we can get my father the care that he needs. *He* knows how to fly this ship."

"Then why did you tell me?"

"I don't know," she admitted. "Josi's always telling me I talk too much." Alex finished cleaning up his wounds, spraying some heal-aid on his now-clean knuckles. "That should do it."

"Thanks," Loki said, looking over his knuckles. "What was that you sprayed on it?"

"You never heard of heal-aid?"

"Nope."

She looked at him quizzically but shook it off.

"I'll make a deal with you," Loki offered. "I won't reveal your secret, but only under two conditions. First, you have to promise that you won't try to do anything you're not certain you can do...piloting-wise. I can't allow my people to be put at undue risk because of your lack of flight training."

"What if they ask me to do something I can't do?"

"I'll see to it that you always have a pilot on board to help you out."

"What's the second condition?" she asked.

"You let *me* teach you the basics."

Alex breathed a sigh of relief. "For a moment, I thought you were going to have that blond-haired guy teach me."

Loki chuckled to himself. "I wouldn't wish that on anyone."

* * *

"How's our guest doing?" Nathan asked Doctor Chen as he entered Vodar's room in the Aurora's medical section.

"We had to go in and manually repair his abdominal aorta, but he should recover."

"When can we ask him some questions?" Nathan wondered.

"You can ask him now," the doctor said.

Nathan eyed Vodar, who appeared to still be unconscious.

"He's faking," Doctor Chen told him.

"Open your eyes, asshole," Jessica demanded.

Nathan cast a disapproving glance at Jessica.

Vodar opened his eyes, spotting Jessica then Nathan. "Where am I?"

"Aboard our ship," Nathan replied.

Vodar looked at Nathan. "Who the fuck are you?"

"I'm the one asking the questions here."

Vodar looked straight ahead again, resolute in his defiance. "I will tell you nothing."

"Oh, but you will," Jessica threatened.

Vodar glared at her, letting a single chuckle out. "You will all suffer for your defiance," he snarled.

"From what I hear, you're the one who's going to suffer," Nathan argued. "It's my understanding that your leaders have very little patience for failure."

Vodar said nothing.

"I'm going to make you a very simple offer," Nathan told him. "Cooperate, and we'll release you and allow you to take one of the shuttles you came in. Refuse, and we'll use pharmaceuticals to make you talk then return you to your clan."

"Either way, your pirate days are over," Jessica stated.

"Oh, I almost forgot," Nathan said. "There's also option three."

Vodar looked at him.

"I can turn you over to the Foruria family and let them decide your fate."

Despite Vodar's best efforts to hide it, Nathan could see that option three was not the man's first choice.

"What's it going to be, tough guy?" Jessica asked.

"Your drugs will not work on me," Vodar claimed. "All Korsan have been inoculated against the latest truth serums."

"Not against ours," Doctor Chen added from the back of the room.

Nathan turned to look at the doctor, surprised by her involvement in the conversation.

Vodar studied the doctor's face a moment, trying to discern if she was being truthful.

"What's it going to be?" Nathan asked.

Vodar glared at Nathan. "Go fuck yourself."

Nathan sighed. "You'd think they would've come up with a snappier retort over the centuries."

"Sometimes the classics are still the best," Jessica commented.

"So I guess it's safe to assume that option one is out," Nathan said, turning to the doctor. "Doc, if you please?"

* * *

Darren pulled his trousers back on then sat back down on the edge of Shya's bed to don his boots.

"You don't have to leave so quickly, love," Shya cooed.

"I feel guilty taking too much of your time," Darren admitted. "I know how busy you must be. I mean, everyone's talking about you and your friends."

"You'd think this world never had any pros."

"None like you," Darren said, turning back to look at her.

"Is that why you come every day?" she asked, smiling at him.

"You have to let me pay you *something*," Darren insisted.

"Maybe you already have."

Darren looked confused. Shya sat up, moving closer to him, the bedsheets wrapped around her naked body. "With most it's work, but with some..." She leaned in closer and kissed him. "If I took money from you, then you'd be like all the others. A girl in my line of work needs guys like you to remind her what's good in life."

Darren blushed. "I did bring you something," he told her.

"You did?"

Darren reached for his jacket on the side chair, reaching into the pocket and pulling out a small, red box, handing it to her.

Shya opened the box, finding four chocolates inside.

"Ambrosia truffles," Darren announced proudly. "I know you don't eat enough, and one of these has all the nutrients you need for a full day...in a *candy*."

Shya was genuinely excited. "Where did you get these?" she exclaimed. "They must have cost a fortune!"

"I'd like to say they did, but truth be told, I got them for free. Sort of a thank you for a deal."

"That must have been some deal," she said. "These had to come all the way from an Alliance world. Stuff like this almost never makes it into the badlands."

"Well there's going to be a lot of new things available out here pretty soon."

Shya took a nibble, savoring the delicate chocolate. "Mmmm. I'm surprised the pirates didn't take these."

"Pirates won't be bothering us anymore."

"What are you talking about?"

"We've got a new guardian angel," Darren bragged, as if he was solely responsible for making it happen.

"Who?"

"Some guy named Tuplo. He's got a couple of mint-condition Navarro-class shuttles and a bunch of Dragon fighters. I'm pretty sure he has a base somewhere as well. Or maybe even a larger ship. I'm not sure. But he's helping a trader named Chiqua run trade between Hadria and the Vernay worlds."

"Aren't you worried about retribution?" Shya wondered. "I heard the Korsan are ruthless."

"They already came once," Darren told her. "Dragons took care of them."

Shya looked worried.

"What's wrong?" Darren asked.

"You should steer clear of this Tuplo guy," she told him. "He's going to bring you nothing but trouble."

"I don't know," Darren objected. "He seems pretty confident."

"He doesn't know the Korsan like we do," Shya insisted. "I've seen them skin people alive just for fun. The best thing any world can do is pay them their cut and hope for the best."

"Maybe…but I have a feeling things are about to change."

Shya reached out and put her hand on his cheek. "Just promise me you'll be careful," she asked, looking into his eyes. "I couldn't bear to see you get hurt."

* * *

"So far, all readings support my original hypothesis," Laza insisted. "The anomalies are *not* actual gravity wells, and they are *definitely* not random."

By the looks on the faces of all those sitting around the command briefing room's conference table, the Jung scientist's statement was difficult to believe.

"You're suggesting these anomalies are *created?*" Melei realized. "By whom?"

"By the Alliance," Abby stated confidently.

"But why?"

"The Alliance maintains control of its member worlds by keeping them dependent on the gate network," Dominic explained.

"There is simply no scientific basis to support the claim that long-range jump drives damage the interdimensional barrier, nor that they cause rogue gravity wells," Abby insisted. "Even their *theories* are full of nonsensical logic."

"Then why does everyone believe it?" Aiden wondered.

"Easy," Jessica opined. "Propaganda."

"You're talking about *trillions* of people spread over *hundreds* of worlds," Aiden argued. "How do you control and coordinate *that much* propaganda?"

"Fifteen hundred and thirty-seven worlds *within* Alliance space," Dominic corrected. "And at least four times that number *outside* of their territorial boundaries."

"Jesus," Nathan exclaimed. "I had no idea humanity had spread out that much."

"And that's a conservative estimate," Dominic added. "Many believe there are at least a thousand uncharted settlements *beyond* the badlands. But as to Lieutenant Commander Walsh's question, the Alliance has a complex network of interstellar communications that utilize active interdimensional conduit communications, also known as AICC. This allows real-time communications and data connectivity between all Alliance worlds."

"*Real-time?*" Nathan asked in disbelief. He looked at Abby. "Is that one of *your* inventions?"

"I'm afraid so," Abby admitted. "It uses low-power, continuously active conduits into subspace."

"Subspace?" Vladimir asked, unfamiliar with the term.

"I thought that only existed in science fiction," Nathan commented.

"The correct term is 'interdimensional space'," Abby explained. "Subspace is just the popular name. Just like how the term 'jump drive' became the common name instead of the superluminal transition system. It refers to the space *between* dimensions. You see, there is no actual *barrier* between dimensions, just a very thin space. The jump drive allows a physical object to cross that space and enter the dimension we refer to as D3, or the dimension without time. After the deployment of the first few jump gates, we discovered that a low-power conduit could be used to create a constantly active connection to the space separating D3 and D4, but not actually *entering* D4, as the jump drive does. But since that space is *nondimensional*, signals sent into it can be received anywhere in the universe, instantaneously."

"It's like the original internet, only on a much larger scale," Nathan realized.

"That is *incredible*," Vladimir exclaimed. "Why has no one told us about this until now?"

"It's only in common use in Alliance space," Dominic explained. "Just like the gates, it is proprietary technology."

"It requires an AICC node station," Abby added. "It acts as a relay between subspace and our four-dimensional space."

"The AICC and the gates are what make the Alliance so strong," Dominic explained. "It's also what makes their propaganda so effective."

"How so?" Nathan asked.

"Without them, the quality of life drops significantly. You lose contact with the rest of the galaxy. You can no longer order whatever you need on the net and have it arrive a week later from halfway across the galaxy. In essence, you are limited to only what is available from your *own* world or from worlds that might reside within a few short-range jumps. The existence of the gates and the AICC is what makes a high quality of life affordable for trillions of Alliance citizens. Most people would rather accept the propaganda as reality than disrupt their comfortable existence."

"It's a common theme throughout human history," Nathan stated. "The lie is often easier to live with than the truth."

"Any chance we can get one of those AICC nodes?" Cameron wondered.

"They are only Alliance-issued, and they are very expensive," Dominic warned.

"There are dark-net nodes," Abby told them. "Or at least they were starting to pop up by the time I went into long-term SA."

Nathan looked to Dominic.

"I have heard of a few," Dominic confirmed.

"Can we build one?" Nathan wondered.

"We would need plans," Dominic replied.

"I could probably engineer one myself," Abby said, "but plans would be a lot faster."

Jessica looked to Nathan. "Didn't Vodar say something about the Korsan having interstellar comms?"

"He did," Nathan confirmed. "I just assumed he was referring to some sort of jump comm-drone network."

"What if he was talking about these AICC nodes?" Jessica suggested. "I doubt he even knows *how* the pirates communicate between systems."

"Most pirates are completely unaware of what is happening outside of their own sphere of control," Dominic confirmed.

"Vodar claimed the Brodek clan was in constant communication with the Korsan," Jessica explained. "The moment a capture is inventoried, the Korsan know about it. That's how they know what to move where, in order to keep all their clans equally supported."

"I had no idea the Korsan were *that* technically sophisticated," Dominic admitted.

"You've got to have *some* level of technological sophistication to jump around and raid other ships and such," Jessica argued.

"Not as much as you might think," Dominic corrected. "Most of their ships are flown by AI. They just tell the AI where to go or what to do. They rarely fly them manually. I doubt that most pirates even know how."

"Are *all* ships flown by AI these days?" Nathan wondered.

"Alliance ships don't even *have* manual flight capabilities," Dominic told them. "And half the ships outside of Alliance space don't either. Only the really old ships still use AIs as assistants rather than as their primary pilots."

"Not surprising," Nathan said. "It was already heading in that direction back in our day."

"It would be a huge tactical advantage to have one of those nodes," Jessica stated. "Not only would we be connected to the galactic network, we'd be able to contact Tug directly."

"I was thinking the same thing," Nathan agreed. "We need to find out if the pirates *are* using AICC nodes, and if so, how we might get our hands on one."

"Or at least get the engineering plans," Abby added.

"I might be able to help with that," Dominic offered. "But I would need access to the dark-net."

"So, again, we need access to one of those nodes," Jessica reiterated.

"Not necessarily," Dominic told her. "If we can find a fringe world where a dark-net node is known to exist, all we have to do is find out how to buy a connection to it."

"How does that help us?" Nathan asked.

"On the dark-net, I should be able to find someone selling the engineering specs on an AICC node."

"Any idea how we find out what worlds have dark-net nodes?" Nathan asked Dominic.

"I can make a few inquiries, but it will take some time."

"Well I'd like to avoid trying to get onto a pirate-controlled node," Nathan said. "But getting back to Laza's original point, it seems clear that traveling directly between Dencke and the Vernay worlds is safe."

"I believe you *missed* my point," Laza corrected.

"I understood your implication, but I'm not ready to risk unlimited long-range jump travel based on a few days' worth of data collection and analysis."

"Long-range jump travel *is* safe," Abby insisted.

"I don't doubt that," Nathan told her. "My concern is over the nature and capabilities of whatever device the Alliance is using to *create* these anomalies, and what effect they may or may *not* have on the safety of jump travel. All we know for certain is that the anomalies between us and the Vernay worlds are *not* true gravity wells and are *not* random. And while this does not justify jumping willy-nilly in any direction, it *does* warrant further investigation. In the meantime, we need to decide how to best use this safe corridor to our advantage."

"Well, to begin with, it gives us an instant transition corridor," Jessica stated. "We could bring the Ghatazhak back to the Aurora and let them respond from here."

"We would have to reprogram the comm-drones stationed in all six Vernay systems," Robert pointed out.

"We should keep one shuttle equipped as an emergency response ship," Doctor Chen suggested.

"We could bring the Dragons back to the Aurora as well," Robert added. "That would make ongoing training easier, and I'd be able to start pairing trainees with more experienced pilots for patrol duties. Assuming you wish to maintain a presence in the Vernay region."

"I think we should," Nathan agreed. "Probably a two-ship patrol element would suffice."

"I'd fly at least three," Robert suggested. "Senior, cadet, and trainee. Just in case."

"It's your wing," Nathan said.

"It is?" Robert replied, a bit surprised.

"It is. I received a communiqué from Loki an hour ago," Nathan explained. "He is requesting to be temporarily assigned to the Acuna. Something about making sure her crew knows how to use their new tech, how to fly evasive patterns, and how to hide their jump trail. Apparently, their ship is mostly AI flown, and Alex has very little manual flight experience."

"He'll have to send his fighter back," Robert stated.

"I've ordered him to escort the Acuna here as soon as her upgrades are completed," Nathan told him.

"You're bringing the Acuna *here*?" Cameron questioned. "Are you sure that's a good idea?"

"They don't even know about the Aurora," Jessica said, adding her objections.

"And it's time they did," Nathan replied. "We may be asking a lot of them in the future. It would be a lot easier if they knew exactly what they were getting themselves into."

"This is a bad idea," Cameron argued.

"They have a ship that no one will bat an eye at, while we're jumping around in mint-condition classics that everyone drools over," Nathan pointed out. "Not exactly covert."

"We can always scuff them up," Jessica suggested. "Make them look as if they're falling apart."

"Don't even think about this," Vladimir snarled.

"We *need* the Acuna and her crew," Nathan insisted. "They know this region of space, and they have contacts. They can come and go without raising suspicion."

"The only thing we *need* them for is to fulfill our obligation to Chiqua," Jessica pointed out. "Which we wouldn't have to do if you had let Tug pay off our debt."

"We need Chiqua as well," Nathan argued. "She also has connections. If it weren't for her, we wouldn't have found Dominic. Who knows how else she might be able to help?"

"The more people who know about us, the more chance there is that the Alliance will eventually know," Jessica reminded him.

"Assuming they don't already," Nathan countered. "And if they do, we're going to need all the help we can get to put this ship back into space *before* the Alliance finds us."

"You suck at lying low, you know that?" Jessica told him.

"I never claimed otherwise," Nathan chuckled.

* * *

Loki listened while the lead Takaran tech finished reviewing the operational procedures for the Acuna's upgrades. He could tell by the look in Alex's eyes that she wasn't going to remember much of what was pouring out of this guy's mouth.

The problem was the same today as it was back in Loki's time. Techs spoke a different language than pilots. To make matters worse, Alex wasn't really a pilot. True, she was able to direct her ship from departure point to destination with ease. To the untrained eye, she even looked as if she knew what she was doing. But as the complexities of her new systems were explained, her eyes were glassing over.

In a way, Loki felt bad for her. It was her chance to secure her family's future and restore her father to health. All she had to do was continue faking it for a few more months, and her father would be back in the pilot's seat where he belonged; she would be in the right seat again, doing exactly what he told her to do.

In fact, Loki was quite impressed with the young woman. As petite in stature as she was, she had a personality that demanded respect. He was pretty sure it was mostly all an act, that it was a persona she had been forced to take on after her father's injuries, just to survive. But it was convincing.

"Are you sure you understand all that?" the technician asked, uncertain of her ability to operate the new tech properly.

"Yeah, I got it."

"Are you sure?" he asked again. "If you get things out of order, you can cause severe problems."

"It's all hooked into the AI, right?"

"Yes, but..."

"And there are procedure manuals in the ship's database, right?"

"Yes, but…"

"But nothing. I can fucking read. Now get the fuck off my ship so I can get back into space. I'm tired of this rock."

The technician turned and headed for the exit. "Lieutenant Commander," he said, nodding to Loki as he passed.

"I'll keep an eye on her," Loki murmured in a low voice to the tech as he passed.

"I heard that," Alex snapped.

"You were supposed to," Loki told her. "Before this, I used to train fighter pilots. The first thing I told a new student was that in order to learn, you first have to realize what you don't know."

Alex just looked at him. "Huh?"

"Where's your ship's center of gravity when empty?"

"Uh, in the center?"

"Doubtful. It's in your manuals, probably in the performance specifications section. I assume you've read it?"

"Only the parts regarding flight ops," Alex admitted.

"There is far more to being a pilot than knowing which button to push or what command to give your AI."

"It's worked so far," Alex said, mostly to herself.

"I've gotten permission to act as your 'copilot', but if this is going to work, you're going to have to trust me and do what I say."

"You *told* Tuplo that I don't know how to fly?" Alex asked, enraged at his betrayal.

"No. I told him that I felt it would be better for

mission safety if you had a copilot helping you out while you got used to the new tech we just added. He told me to take as long as I thought was necessary."

"He *trusts* you?"

"We've been through a lot together."

"Like what?"

"A *very* long story," Loki assured her. "But for now, we need to get off the ground."

"Where are we going?" Alex wondered.

"To our base of operations in the fringe. All you have to do is get this ship into space then accept the AI link with my fighter, and I'll do the rest."

"What about when we arrive?" she asked. "What are the approach procedures?"

Loki smiled. "There is some pilot in you, after all. I'll transmit touchdown coordinates to your AI before I disconnect. Just let the AI take her in."

"What if it fails?"

"You do know how to land manually, right?"

"Yes, but I've only done it a few times, and it has been a while."

"Good."

"Good?"

"Good that you're being honest. I'm sure your AI will do fine, but if there is a problem, I'll be on comms with you."

Alex surveyed her cockpit, observing the extra systems that were just installed. "I'd feel better if you were in the right seat for this. Can't your fighter's AI fly itself back to base?"

"Yes, but it can't operate its weapons without me," Loki explained. "Besides, it's better that you do this on your own."

"But I'm not *really* doing it on my own. My AI is doing it."

"Baby steps," Loki told her. "When we get to base, we'll program a VR sim for you to practice in. I'll have you able to operate this ship *better* than your father in a few weeks' time."

"Fat chance," she insisted. "He was flying it for decades."

"Trust me," Loki reminded her. "Now let's review the AI linkup procedures before we go."

* * *

Shya relished the time between customers. It was hers and hers alone. It was her opportunity to wash off the stink of her occupation and start fresh again. It was a ritual that she repeated every single time. It was what grounded her and kept her sane in an otherwise insane world.

The truth was her life had always been this way. She had started like most, getting sucked into it at an early age, quickly becoming accustomed to the nicer things she was able to afford in this profession. While other women looked down on her, she knew they envied the conditions in which she lived. Cleaner attire, better accommodations, better food and drink, and a certain level of respect that she demanded of the men desiring her services.

Most men in the badlands were simple creatures. They worked hard to survive and had little time for the trials of courtship. Sooner or later, they all settled down, found themselves a young bride and started a family. But that took money and resources, which took time to acquire. She filled the emotional and physical gaps that existed during that time.

However, Shya was no different than any of the women in the badlands. She, too, longed for someone to call her own. She just didn't want to be completely dependent on him, as most women in the badlands seemed to be. She had been saving her earnings for years. Someday, she would go somewhere far away from the chaos of the badlands, and create her own little homestead with, or without, a mate. The day she finally entered into a relationship, it would be on her terms, not her mate's.

The thing that most girls in her line of work didn't realize was that the real money to be made was not in prostitution, since the house always took such a large cut. The real profit was in *information*. Men talked in the company of a woman with whom they were about to have relations. They bragged about the people they knew, and the things they had seen. Knowledge was power, and her profession gave her a lot of it.

Shya returned to the main floor at exactly seventeen hundred local time as planned. Sitting at the bar was her handler, the man who pretended to be her regular customer once a week on the same day. To the people of Kataoka, he was a small trader plying the Vernay worlds, paying his cut to the Brodek clan whenever asked. There were a handful of men like him. All with small jump shuttles only capable of carrying a thousand kilograms or so of goods. No one paid him much attention and no one noticed when, after gathering intel from all his girls on the Vernay worlds, he jumped back to Crowden to deliver what he'd learned to the Brodek. To them, he was just a horny, old man who engaged a professional at every port.

The funny thing was, he never touched the girls in his network, and for that, Shya was thankful.

* * *

"How are we looking?" Alex asked over the Acuna's intercom.

"*Everyone's off,*" Shane reported. "*We're buttoned up and ready to go back here.*"

"What about our security team? They aboard?"

"*We're here,*" Kit replied.

"Jo, you ready?"

"*More ready than we've ever been,*" Josi replied from the Acuna's engineering compartment.

"Are you going to ride back there the entire way?" Alex asked.

"*I just want to be sure everything is working right,*" her younger sister replied. "*Besides, it's only for a few hours, right?*"

"I have no idea," Alex replied. "I don't even know where we're going yet. I'm just following the Dragons."

"*That sounds rather ominous,*" Josi decided.

"Acuna, Dragon Leader," Loki called over comms. "Are you ready for departure?"

Alex glanced at her systems status display. "Ready for takeoff," she replied.

"You have the departure rally point?"

"I do," Alex assured him.

"Then we'll see you up there. Leader out."

"Okay," Alex muttered to herself. "Let's see if this shit still works." Alex pressed the departure sequence button then the activate button. The Acuna's grav-lift system began to hum, and the ship rose smoothly from the surface of Kataoka. She monitored the displays as her AI retracted their landing gear and automatically began to accelerate forward, bringing the ship's nose up slightly. The ship then rolled gently to starboard, pitching up even more as their main propulsion levels increased, sending them rocketing into the sky. So far, everything was operating the same as any other departure.

"How are things looking?" Alex asked over the intercom.

"*Humming along fine back here,*" Josi replied. It was the first time in a while that her sister didn't respond with some complaint that included a string of expletives. It was a bad habit that all three of them had picked up from their father, despite their mother's best efforts to prevent it.

A few minutes later, the blue skies over Kataoka yielded to the inky blackness of space. The ship turned toward the jump rally point Loki had provided. "Dragon Leader, Acuna, thirty seconds to rally point."

"*Copy that,*" Loki replied. "*I've got you on my sensors. Transmitting AI linkup signal.*"

Alex watched as the navigation computer display flashed the link request warning, prompting her to accept the linkup. It wasn't often that she handed control of her ship to someone else, let alone someone not on board. Border worlds were the only ones that required remote approach control links. Most of their flights since her father's injuries forced her to take command of the Acuna had been well clear of Alliance space, and she preferred it that way. Although she had no negative interactions with the Alliance herself, she recalled many of her grandfather's stories. If they were even half true, she felt it best to steer clear.

Alex pressed the link accept button then confirmed her selection. A moment later, the screen changed to indicate that their AI was now taking flight and navigation directions directly from the AI in Loki's Dragon fighter. "Link accepted and locked in," she reported over comms. "AI's got the helm."

"*Copy that,*" Loki replied.

Alex peered out the forward windows, trying to spot the Dragon fighters that she knew were growing closer to them with each passing second.

"Got a visual on us yet?" Loki asked.

"Negative."

"Eleven o'clock, ten degrees up," a voice instructed from behind.

Alex glanced back over her shoulder, spotting Kit entering her cockpit. She looked back at the spot he had suggested, finally picking out the distant flashing navigation lights of the trailing fighter. Within seconds, the other three fighters appeared as well. "I've got visual," she reported.

"*Excellent. Jumping in thirty seconds.*"

Something felt off. Alex glanced at her nav-com display, realizing that the programmed jump wasn't to the start of the Vernay passage. "Uh, where are we going?"

"*Dencke,*" Loki replied.

A more detailed look revealed the next problem. "Fifty-seven light years?" she exclaimed. "You want to long-jump out of the Vernay? Are you stupid or something?"

"*It'll be fine,*" Loki assured her.

"Not according to the charts!" she argued, reaching for the override controls.

"It's safe," Kit told her, putting his hand on her shoulder in a way that seemed reassuring, yet also served as a warning to leave the controls alone.

"*The charts are wrong,*" Loki promised her.

"I don't care if they *are* wrong," Alex replied. "I'm not risking our family's only way to make a living on some dork in a fancy space-fighter!"

"*Well that just hurt,*" Loki replied, trying to keep his response light.

"How do you think the Seiiki got back so quickly?" Kit told her. "It's safe. There are no gravity wells on this route."

"Alex, I'd never do anything to put your ship or your crew at undue risk," Loki promised her.

"But..."

"Just think of it, Alex," Kit said. "Direct jumps in and out of the Vernay means there's no way the pirates can ambush you along the way."

"Ten seconds," Loki warned. *"What's it going to be?"*

"Are you sure? Have you done this before?"

"No, but if my captain says it's safe, then it's safe."

"How can you be so sure?"

"Because he wouldn't ask us to do it unless he had tried it himself," Loki explained. *"Three seconds..."*

"But..."

"Two..."

"Trust us," Kit urged.

"One..."

"Fuck." Alex leaned back in her chair, dropping her hands to her armrests and closing her eyes.

"Jumping."

Alex tightened up, but when nothing happened, she opened her eyes again.

"Jump complete," Loki reported. *"Dencke, dead ahead."*

"Holy crap," she whispered, looking out the forward window at the approaching planet.

"Transmitting landing coordinates now," Loki reported. *"Go ahead and start your landing sequence. The Aurora will send a remote approach control link request as soon as we are within range."*

"The *Aurora?*" Alex asked. The name seemed like

it should be familiar, but she couldn't place it. "Is that the name of your base?"

"Not exactly," Kit replied with a chuckle.

CHAPTER FIVE

Alex increased the magnification on the Acuna's landing camera until she could make out the object on the surface they were descending toward. "Is that..." She turned to look at Kit, who by now had taken the copilot's seat to her right. "That's an Expedition-class ship. My father took us to see one on Garron when we were little."

"It was my understanding that there weren't any Expedition-class ships left," Kit said.

"None in *service*, if that's what you mean. But there *are* a few on display as museum pieces."

"I had no idea."

"What the hell is one doing all the way out..." More details became visible as they grew closer, and she could make out some of the damage to the ship's outer hull, as well as all the mud caked along her sides. "You guys *found* it out here, didn't you? That's where you got the pristine shuttles. You guys are a bunch of relic hunters, aren't you?"

"Not even close," Kit chuckled.

"What, are you planning on restoring that thing? Are you nuts? It's gotta be at least four hundred years old."

"Five hundred and thirty-five, technically."

Alex breathed a sigh of relief.

"What?" Kit wondered, noticing her relief.

"I was sure you guys were either Alliance covert-ops or a new gang planning on taking over Brodek space," she explained. "But you're just a bunch of antique enthusiasts. Don't get me wrong, I've got nothing against antique hunters, especially considering the other two possibilities." Alex examined the ship on the screen a bit more, panning up and down its length. "What are you going to do, turn it into another hotel or something?"

"Probably better to let the captain explain it to you," Kit decided.

"You know, the one on Garron was found adrift in an asteroid belt in the Targania system. The damn thing was completely intact. Some kind of virus wiped out the entire crew."

"Why didn't the ship's AI fly it home?" Kit wondered.

"I don't know. Some people say its AI decided to stay put to avoid spreading the virus. Others think the AI was infected as well. The official logs say that her captain ordered the AI to keep her isolated."

"Why wouldn't he just blow it up?" Kit said. "They have self-destruct systems."

"They do?"

"Yup."

"Hmm. That's a good question. Is that where you got the Dragon fighters?" she asked. "From inside that wreck?"

"Something like that."

The image of the ship below now filled her camera screen, so Alex reset the magnification level back to zero then began looking out of the windows. The first thing she noticed was that it wasn't sitting at the same incline as the land around it. The second was that there was some sort of excavator working nearby. "Did you guys raise it?"

Kit peered out the window. "Looks like they did," he agreed. "Must've happened while I was gone."

"How long have you guys been working on that thing?"

"A little more than two weeks I believe."

"That's *it?* Must've been in pretty good shape when you found it then. I'm surprised the surveyors missed it. Must've been a lousy survey company."

Kit just smiled as the ship slowed for landing.

* * *

Kit and Mori led Alex, Josi, and Shane into the Aurora's main shuttle bay at the front of her exterior flight deck, where both the Seiiki and the Mirai were parked. Oddly enough, there were no signs of damage to the interior, which told Alex that whatever had brought this ship down centuries ago must have resulted in a landing that everyone had walked away from.

"Something's not right," Josi said under her breath to her sister as they followed Kit and Mori across the bay. "That guy over there is wearing an old Alliance uniform."

Alex noticed the man to their left, who was wearing an Alliance jumpsuit, the same as Loki had worn. "They probably found them on the ship."

"Then they would be too valuable to wear," Josi argued. "Mint condition, original issue uniforms are collectors' items. You could get a few thousand credits easily for that jump suit."

"Maybe they just like to role-play?" Shane suggested.

Alex glanced back over her shoulder. "Not everyone is as big a dork as you, Shane."

Kit and Mori reached the forward hatch, pressing the control to open it. The doors split vertically down the center and slid sideways, disappearing into the walls. Beyond them was a large corridor that looked as if it continued on for at least sixty meters.

They followed the two men into the corridor, encountering an intersection on the other side with corridors leading to the outer edges of the ship. The two men led them to a nearby elevator, stepping inside as the doors opened.

"You've cleaned up her insides pretty nice," Alex commented. "I guess that makes sense. Probably easier to work on her that way. Where's your main ship?"

"The captain will explain everything," Kit replied as he and Mori led them out of the elevator, turning left at the nearby intersection and heading down the short corridor of what appeared to be a much smaller deck than the first.

"Where are we?" Josi wondered.

Kit said nothing, leading them through the doors to the bridge, where Cameron was waiting for them.

"Welcome aboard the Aurora," she greeted.

Alex got a concerned look on her face, noticing that the woman's uniform was nearly perfect.

"I'm Captain Taylor," Cameron continued. "You must be Alex."

"*You're* the captain?" Alex asked.

"I'm the Executive Officer."

"But you just said you were the captain."

"I'm *a* captain, not *the* captain," Cameron explained.

The explanation did little to clear up the confusion in Alex's mind. "What's an executive officer?"

"The simple explanation is that I'm second in command."

"Well if *you're* not the captain, who is?" Alex asked.

Cameron held out her left arm, gesturing toward the hatch to the command briefing room on the starboard side.

"I am."

The three of them turned their heads to the right, spotting Nathan standing in the open hatchway.

"Please have a seat," Nathan urged, gesturing toward the conference table behind him. "We have a lot to discuss."

Alex and her siblings entered the briefing room, taking the first three available seats along the near side. The seats on the opposite side of the table were occupied, and the only person they recognized on that side was Jessica, who sat at the forward end nearest the captain's seat at the head of the table. Alex took the seat opposite Jessica, to Nathan's right, Josi to her right, and Shane in the third chair down, next to the only other person they recognized, Dominic. The other five people on the opposite side of the table were unfamiliar.

"Everyone, this is the crew of the Acuna-Dera. Captain Alex Foruria, her sister and engineer, Josi, and her brother and technician, Shane," Nathan introduced. "You've already met Lieutenant Commander Jessica Nash. Next to her is her brother, Captain Robert Nash, Lieutenant Commander Aiden Walsh, my chief engineer, Commander Vladimir Kamenetskiy, Doctor Abigail Sorenson, and Ensign Laza Soray. The rest you already know."

"What the hell's going on here?" Alex wondered. "What's with all the ranks?"

"They're fucking Alliance," Josi commented. "I *told* you."

"We *were* Alliance," Nathan corrected.

"So, what? You found a ship, and you decided to go AWOL and start your own little para-military organization?" Alex asked. "No thanks," she added as she rose to depart.

"Then I assume you plan to return those two

credit chips our benefactor gave you in exchange for six months of your services?" Jessica stated.

Alex didn't look happy, but she sat back down. "What is it you want from us?"

"Exactly what we told you when we hired you," Nathan assured her. "Run cargo in and out of the Vernay for our associate, Chiqua, and on occasion, run some trips for us."

"What *kind* of trips?" Alex asked. "The last one nearly got us killed."

"I'll do my best to keep the Acuna out of harm's way," Nathan promised. "However, you *do* operate in the most dangerous parts of human-inhabited space after all."

"What if I say no?"

"As long as you refund the credits and pay for the cost of the upgrades and repairs to your ship, you are free to go."

Alex rolled her eyes. "Those upgrades were *your* idea, not mine."

"And the repairs?"

Alex sighed, looking for a way out. "What if I refund you five months' worth and then fly for you for *two* months, but only doing the runs in and out of the Vernay? Will that do it?"

"Yes, but you won't do that," Nathan told her.

"Why wouldn't I?"

"Because you need the money to pay for your father's medical procedures," Nathan explained.

Alex scowled at him. "How did you know about my father?"

"We bugged your intercom system," Jessica told her, smiling.

"You people suck," Alex exclaimed.

"We were risking a lot by trusting you," Nathan told her. "We needed to be sure."

"It seems like *we're* the ones taking the risk by trusting *you*."

"You still haven't told us *who* you are, or *what* you're doing here," Josi stated.

"Very well," Nathan replied. "We'll start with *who* we are." I'm Captain Nathan Scott, commanding officer of the Aurora."

"Okay." Alex looked at their faces, noticing that they seemed to be expecting more of a reaction from her. "Is that supposed to mean something to me?"

Nathan looked at Jessica.

"Told ya," Jessica said under her breath.

Dominic slid his data pad to his left, passing it to Shane, who had it taken from him by Josi. All three of them studied the data pad, which displayed the service history of Nathan Scott and the original Aurora.

"Holy shit," Shane exclaimed.

"I knew there was something wrong here," Josi insisted.

"This isn't *that* ship," Alex said to Nathan. "And according to this, you all died five hundred years ago."

"You're right, this isn't the same Aurora. It's her replacement. The first Expedition-class ship to roll off the Alliance assembly lines back on Earth. But it was five hundred and thirty-five years ago, and we didn't actually die. We were trapped by a Gamazan singularity weapon, and the only way out was to jump through the singularity. We suffered heavy damage and crash-landed here on Dencke eighteen days ago."

"Eighteen days," Alex replied, not believing a word

of it. "What about the other five hundred and thirty-five years? Let me guess...suspended animation?"

"Relativity," Nathan replied.

"You're talking about time dilation," Josi surmised, a curious look coming over her face.

"What?" Alex asked.

"Yeah, what?" Shane seconded.

"The effects of a singularity on jump fields is still theoretical at best," Abby offered. "In this case, we're not sure if it was a matter of time dilation by the singularity or a prolonged decay time on the jump fields themselves that caused them to move five hundred and thirty-five years into the future."

"I thought you were a doctor," Alex said to Abby.

"A doctor of astrophysics," Abby corrected.

"Doctor Sorenson is the *creator* of jump drive technology," Nathan explained.

"*Co*-creator," Abby corrected.

"What, you're five hundred years old as well?" Alex surmised.

"But you said *them,*" Josi insisted.

"I was not with them during their transition."

"Then how the hell did *you* live so long?" Shane wondered.

"That is a long story," Abby replied.

"You people say that a lot," Alex commented.

"If you were all part of the Alliance five hundred years ago, why didn't you just contact them for help when you crashed?" Shane wondered.

"The conditions under which our little *event* occurred were somewhat suspicious," Nathan explained. "Therefore, I decided that we needed more intelligence before determining a course of action."

"And what *course of action* did you decide upon?" Alex wondered.

"To be honest, we're not entirely certain what our future holds. Thus far, it appears that the Alliance has become the very thing it was designed to prevent."

"So, what, you're going to try to bring down the Alliance?"

"That would be foolish," Nathan replied. "But we *are* going to do what we can to protect people such as yourselves from the Korsan and their ilk."

"By protecting the Vernay worlds?" Alex surmised.

"To start with, yes," Nathan confirmed.

Alex shook her head. "The Brodek are one of the most ruthless clans in the Korsan. They'll lay waste to everything then bring in new settlers. Ones who can't afford to settle further out in the frontiers, like us."

"Which is why we'll be establishing a new settlement *deep* in the frontier. Beyond the reach of both the Korsan *and* the Alliance."

There were more than a few surprised faces among those at the table, not including the faces of the Acuna's crew. It was the first time Nathan had clearly delineated their new mission.

Alex's first thought was that they were crazy. A bunch of idealists. She was about to tell them that such an undertaking would cost a fortune, but then remembered the ease with which the man they called Tug had parted with half a million credits. However, that just made them seem crazy *and* rich. Then she thought of the service record she had just skimmed through. Endless accounts of winnable battles, all of which *had* been won. The man at the head of the table had saved Earth...*twice,* at least, along with countless other worlds. And he had always started with *one* ship...a ship named *Aurora*.

Alex looked to her younger sister.

"Don't do it," Josi whispered.

"We don't have a choice," Alex whispered back.

"We're in!" Shane stated with exuberance.

"On one condition," Alex interjected. "You bring our parents *here*, where it's safe."

Nathan looked to Cameron at the opposite end of the table.

"I'll arrange quarters for them all," Cameron stated.

"But I reserve the right to bail in six months," Alex quickly added.

"Of course," Nathan agreed.

* * *

Laza spent most of her time on the Aurora's bridge, sitting at the sensor station analyzing scans. Now that the Aurora was back to full power and had been raised from the mud, she had been able to get all of their recon drones out and into service, increasing the number of areas that she could simultaneously scan.

Laza was determined to prove that her theories about the so-called gravity wells were correct, and the only way she could do so was to gather as much scan data as possible. Unfortunately, the Aurora only carried twelve recon drones, so unless she lived for ten thousand years, she could never gather enough data. The fact that Nathan had already ordered her to send four of her drones to survey possible planets to colonize far out in the frontiers didn't help.

Still, that didn't deter her. For now, she continued concentrating on the corridor between Dencke and the Vernay region, keeping enough drones in play at any moment to monitor the entire fifty-seven-light-year stretch. Of course, this too was impossible. Even that short distance could not be monitored without hundreds, if not thousands, of drones. A string of sensor buoys would be the ideal solution, since they could be stationary, and a single comms drone could be used to collect their data at regular intervals. They would be relatively simple to create, but until the Aurora was fully restored, such a project was unlikely.

Nevertheless, she would be spending most of her time on the bridge either way. She and Ensign Dass were the only ones available to man the bridge on a regular basis. Both comms and sensors needed to be staffed around the clock, but both had been slaved over to the tactical station, since it was the only console on the bridge that had sustained zero damage.

So they took shifts. Eight hours each, with breaks provided by Cameron, Robert, Aiden, Nathan, or whoever was available. Now that the Dragon wing and the Ghatazhak were returning, there would be more officers to rotate through bridge duty, making it a bit easier.

Of course, Abby had been a big help as well. Much of her time was spent on the bridge also, either covering while they took a quick trip to the head or helping Laza analyze data. Proving that the jump drive was not causing damage to the interdimensional barrier was more than personal to Abby. It was a downright obsession. Jump drive technology had been her life's work, as well as her father's. It had cost her a marriage and had driven her daughter away. For more than a century, though, it had been all she had left. And now with her long-lost son back, she was more determined than ever to continue her work.

Ensign Dass entered the bridge five minutes early, as usual. Punctuality was one of the things

Laza liked about her. Consistent performance. It was one of the hallmarks of Jung society. A belief that it was better to set a bar that one could consistently meet than for the quality of one's work to have peaks and valleys.

"Good morning," Ensign Dass greeted as she moved to her communications console on the starboard side of the bridge. "Did you spend the *entire* night crunching data?"

"Of course."

"You really should change tasks once in a while to help break the monotony. Sometimes, I fire up the deep-space array and try to detect distant signals. Maybe something from decades ago...or even centuries."

"Doesn't the atmosphere interfere with reception?"

"To some extent, but it's something different." Sima glanced over toward the ready room to see if the lights were on. "Sometimes," she continued in a low voice, "I watch a vid-flick on a side view screen. But only on night shifts, when everyone's asleep."

"Would that not be a distraction?"

"No comms traffic at night, and the sensor suite has audible alerts. You have to do something to keep from dozing off."

"I prefer not to be distracted from my work," Laza insisted.

"Well you are officially relieved," Sima told her, donning her comm-set.

The contact alert beeped, catching their attention.

"Sensor contact?" Sima questioned.

"Just jumped in. It's on an approach course."

Sima tapped her comm-set, preparing to hail the new contact.

"*Aurora, Bonaventura,*" a voice called over Sima's comm-set.

"Go for Aurora."

"*Aurora, inbound contact is the Montasina. A medium cargo ship owned by House Ta'Akar. Contact has already squawked verification codes, and they are valid.*"

"Appreciate the quick heads up, Taji," Sima replied. "Almost gave me a heart attack."

"*Apologies, Sima, we weren't expecting them to arrive for another day or two, or we would have given you advance notice.*"

"Yeah, that would have been preferable." Sima tapped her comm-set, switching channels. "XO, comms."

"*Go ahead,*" Cameron answered over comm-sets.

"New arrival. A medium cargo ship belonging to House Ta'Akar. The Bonaventura reports the ship has squawked proper verification codes."

"They'll make orbit in five minutes," Laza told Sima.

"They should make orbit in five minutes, sir."

"*Has the Acuna departed yet?*" Cameron asked.

"About an hour ago," Laza said.

"Yes, sir. They left an hour ago," Sima answered.

"*Good. Notify the chief of the boat to prepare for cargo ops.*"

"Aye, sir. Should I notify Chief Ravel?"

"*No need. I'm sure she'll hear Marcus complaining about it.*"

"Yes, sir." Sima looked to Laza. "Looks like we're getting resupplied."

* * *

It had been weeks since all three of their children had been home at the same time, so when Alex, Josi, and Shane all entered the Foruria family home on Estabrook, their mother nearly fainted.

"Oh my God," their mother exclaimed. "What are you all doing here?" A concerned look came over her face. "Who's watching the ship?"

"The ship is being guarded," Alex assured her.

"By whom?" her mother wondered, finding it difficult to believe that anyone on Estabrook could be trusted with their family's only asset.

"The ship is safe, Mom, I promise you."

"Well, what are you all doing here? Can you stay for supper? I can whip up some grien stew with those noodles you all love."

"No time for that, Mom. You need to start packing."

"Packing? Where are we going?"

"Someplace better," Alex said. "Someplace *safe*."

"But what about your father?"

"Trust me, he'll be far better off where we're going," Alex promised.

"But all our stuff?"

"All our stuff is garbage," Alex insisted. "Just pack light and maybe bring a few keepsakes. Just what you need for a few days. We can always come back later and pack more if we need it."

"Why the rush?"

"Mom, this is the opportunity we've been praying for."

"First all those credits, now this...You're scaring me, Alex. Maybe we should talk this over first...as a *family*."

"There's nothing to talk about," Alex insisted. "Estabrook is a shithole. We're only here because it's dirt cheap."

"But where will we go?"

"Someplace beautiful, where neither the Alliance

nor the Korsan will ever bother us, and where we'll have access to everything we need, *including* medical care. And work. *Lots* of work. More runs than we can manage."

"Can the Acuna handle it?"

"The ship is in the best shape it has ever been, Mom. Now start packing."

"I'd really prefer that we talk to your father first."

"Josi and Shane are telling Pop now," Alex assured her.

"*Hot damn!*" her father's voice boomed from the other room.

Alex smiled. She hadn't heard him excited about anything in a very long time. "You see, Pop's on board."

* * *

"There's not much here that will help with repairs," Cameron said as she looked over the cargo manifest on her data pad while picking at her breakfast. "Mostly just basic consumables. According to the Montasina's captain, Jakome wanted to get us *something* to tide us over while he worked on getting the larger stuff that required more finesse to keep off of Alliance shipping logs."

"So just food, water, and such?"

"Cleaning supplies, laundry, a bunch of clothing, bedding, you name it," Cameron explained. "There's enough stuff to keep us going for more than a year, easily. They also sent a lot of medical supplies for you, Doc."

"Any chance they sent one of their diagnostic scanners?"

"No, but the captain did mention that it would be coming in the next load. He also offered to take all your patients back to Takara for care. He suggested that you go with them. Something about doing a quick internship on Takara to help acclimate you with current medical technologies."

"That would leave you without a doctor," Melei said, looking at Nathan.

"The Bonaventura's doctor can back us up if needed," Nathan told her. "And we're not going anywhere soon, so there's not much chance of us taking heavy casualties while you're gone."

"As long as Vlad stays out of the water," Jessica joked.

"Not funny," Vladimir scolded.

"I would prefer to stay with my patients," Doctor Chen admitted. "And I'm sure I'd learn a lot during my stay."

"Then it's decided," Nathan agreed.

"They should finish cargo ops in a few hours," Cameron said. "They plan on departing soon after."

"I'll get my patients ready."

"Anything for me?" Jessica asked Cameron.

"Just a bunch of weapons," Cameron told Jessica.

"Sweet," Jessica exclaimed as she ate.

"What about me?" Vladimir asked with his mouth full, as usual.

"Just a lot of engineering and technical data, in case you want to start incorporating any newer tech as part of our repairs."

"I think we should concentrate on restoring this ship to its original design specs for now," Nathan insisted.

"Party pooper," Vladimir complained.

"Just get us back into space, buddy," Nathan insisted. "Being stuck on the surface makes me nervous."

Nathan watched in surprise as Cameron took a

sausage off his plate. "You know those are not vegan, right?"

"I gave up on vegan," Cameron stated. "According to Tug, veggies have fallen out of favor as a main staple, so they've become a lot more difficult to find."

Nathan laughed.

"What?"

"I'm trying to imagine you chomping on a dollag steak."

"Not a chance," Cameron replied. "These sausages are about all I can handle so far."

"I promise we'll get Robert to plant some veggies for you on our new world," Nathan teased.

"Gee thanks."

* * *

Barris Foruria had spent his entire life aboard the Acuna-Dera. He had inherited it from his father upon his untimely demise. Most of the major renovations to her had been done by his own hands. So when the pirate known as Vodar decided to make an example of him, the pirate took more than just his arm and his health; he had taken his will to live. Had it not been for the efforts of his children and their faith in his eventual recovery and return to full function, he most likely would have faded away long ago.

It had been more than a year since he was forced to leave his beloved ship because of his injuries. However, in their rush to get everyone on their way to a new life, his children had failed to explain just how much had been done to his ship over the last few days. When he finally saw her, he couldn't believe it. "My God." He stared at the ship for several seconds, eyes wide. Finally, his look of disbelief turned to one of joy. "How did you...?"

"It wasn't us," Josi admitted. "I mean, it was a *little* us, but…"

"Who's your client?"

"Some rich guy named Tug," Alex told him.

"Some rich guy?" her father asked. "Is that all you know about him? What does he want you to do?" He studied the ship further as they neared. "Are those gun turrets?"

"Self-powered point-defense cannons," Alex explained, no small measure of pride in her voice. "Eight total. Four on top and four below."

"Shields too," Shane added.

"And an additional jump energy bank," Josi reported.

Their father looked at them, surprised.

"Doubles our one-minute range," Alex added with a grin.

Barris was surprised by his oldest daughter's use of the term. Although she had taken to flying easily enough, she had never had much interest in the details, such as the myriad of terms specific to the task. "What have you three gotten us into?"

"Only the best job this family could ever hope for," Alex insisted as she urged her father to head up the ramp.

Barris looked at her. "Why aren't you telling me everything?" he wondered.

"Because you wouldn't believe me unless you saw it for yourself," Alex explained.

Barris didn't bother looking to his youngest, Shane. Although he was a good man, he wasn't that bright and tended to just agree with his older sisters. But Josephine was different. She had a naturally inquisitive nature and questioned everything. "Josi?"

"She's right, Pop. You have to see it to believe it."

* * *

Vladimir entered the bridge, immediately turning left and entering the captain's ready room, stopping short when he realized the room was empty. He turned back around, looking to Ensign Dass, who was standing at the tactical station.

Sima noticed the look on the commander's face and pointed toward the helm station.

Vladimir moved forward, finding a pair of legs sticking out from under the helmsman's station. "Nathan?"

"Yeah?"

"What are you doing down there?"

"Replacing burnt-out relays."

"Why?"

Nathan slid out from under the console, looking at his friend. "Because they're *burnt-out*."

"That is not captain's work."

Nathan got back to his feet then switched the helmsman's console back on. "I'd rather do something useful than sit in that ready room and stare at progress reports, or worse yet, Laza's latest recon analysis."

"How do you even know how to do this?" Vladimir wondered.

"Pretty simple. Replace red with red, blue with blue, yellow with yellow, and so on."

Vladimir looked unconvinced.

"Okay, Avelles taught me how." Nathan looked at his watch. "It's not dinner time yet. Aren't you supposed to be working on the Dragon launch system?"

"It is already fixed."

"The entire conveyor system is working?"

"Josh tested it. Launch, recovery, and recycle. All went perfectly."

"Really?"

"Why are you so surprised?" Vladimir wondered, taking it personally. "I designed it."

"Yeah, but there was a *lot* of damage."

"Okay, so I had some help from the Bonaventura's engineering teams. But *I* was in charge of the *entire* operation."

"Josh launched from it?"

"And returned through the Dragon recovery deck *instead* of the main flight deck. He did suggest that everyone let their AIs handle their departure. Something about there not being much room to climb out after being launched."

"Maybe we should reduce the acceleration rate on the catapults?" Nathan suggested.

"I have. They will be fine."

"Great," Nathan said, brushing off his hands. "Well you didn't come all the way up here just to tell me that."

"*Nyet*. I wanted to speak with you about something."

"What?"

Vladimir gestured to the captain's ready room.

Nathan took the hint, heading over. Vladimir followed him in, closing the hatch.

Nathan observed his friend's expression, noting his concern. "What happened? You fall in love again?"

"*Nyet*," Vladimir replied. "Did you know that the Bonaventura's chief engineer uses a bio-neural link to monitor his ship?"

"No I did not," Nathan admitted. "How does that work?"

"It gives him instant access to all of the ship's

internal systems' status sensors. He says it is like he *feels* it when something is not right. Like you and I would feel an ache or pain in our bodies."

"Spaceships don't have aches or pains, Vlad."

"No, but they do have hundreds of thousands of sensors built into them. Their AIs monitor all of them, recording every variable, every millisecond. Their AI has a record of performance under all conditions, so it can tell if an anomaly is just that, or an indication of a problem."

"How does that equate to a *feeling?*" Nathan wondered.

"I don't know. Gyandev says it takes time. For some, it even takes years. It's all just data at first, but eventually it turns into an instinct. He just *knows* when something is amiss, without even *looking* at the sensor data that proves him right."

"But our AI isn't even online at the moment."

"Her *consciousness* is not online," Vladimir corrected. "All her monitoring algorithms are still running, and I'd have access to all of them...*in my head*. I would have such a better understanding of this ship's condition, and it would be in *real time*."

Nathan thought for a moment, recalling something from his own past. "I think I know what you mean."

"You do?"

"When I was learning aerobatics, we would do detailed debriefs of my maneuvers afterward. We'd analyze every bit of telemetry from the flight. Airspeed, load forces on the airframe, G-forces, environmental factors like wind, temperature, humidity...you name it. My grandfather would explain to me how each element affected the execution of my maneuvers. It was overwhelming at first, but eventually it began to sink in. I developed a deep understanding of *why* my aircraft did what it did when I gave it a control input. But after a few years, I began to realize that I wasn't paying attention to all those factors as closely as I had been in the beginning. I was afraid that I was becoming complacent, and that my complacency was going to get me killed."

"What did you do?" Vladimir wondered.

"I eventually got the nerve to admit this to my grandfather, and he laughed at me."

"What?"

"He explained that my *instincts* had finally matured to the point where I was no longer consciously *aware* of all the variables I was tracking. He said I had finally become a *real* pilot. Then he scolded me for taking so long. You had the same thing with the original Aurora, and someday you'll have the same thing with *this* Aurora."

"But getting the implant would give me that instinct even sooner," Vladimir said.

"*You* want to get the implant?"

"*Da.*"

"Is it safe?"

"More so for me than for anyone else."

"Why is that?" Nathan wondered.

"Because I'm a clone."

"What's that got to do with it?"

"Apparently, when you get cloned, they rearrange your neurons to reduce the chance of memory loss when they transfer your consciousness over."

"Oh yeah, I remember. I thought it took several cloning cycles to make the necessary changes."

"I guess they've improved the process over the last five centuries."

"Did you talk to Doctor Chen about this?"

"No, but I did talk to Doctor Prokhorov on the Bonaventura. He says it is an easy procedure."

"I thought cloning was illegal within Alliance space?"

"Gyandev is not a clone. It can be done on anyone. It just works *better* on clones. Or more quickly...I'm not sure."

"Neither am I," Nathan admitted. "Seems risky. Are you sure it's worth it?"

"That's the same thing I asked when Gyandev told me about it. He put it like this. Imagine you are a body builder. You exercise every day, using the best training regimen known. But you do not have access to a mirror except for once every month. You can *feel* changes in your body, but you cannot *see* them until you look in that mirror. Only then can you make changes to your exercise regimen. With the implant, it's as if you have mirrors all around you all the time, and you can make adjustments to your regimen anytime you like. It is how Gyandev is able to get *maximum* performance out of the Bonaventura's systems. Because he can *feel* when they are running optimally and keep them that way, rather than only responding when something is wrong."

Nathan sighed. "You seem sold on the idea."

"Considering our situation, I think we need every advantage we can get."

"How much recovery time are we talking about?"

"Just a few hours," Vladimir replied. "Doctor Prokhorov said if I do it in the evening, I'll be ready for work in the morning."

"Assuming nothing goes wrong."

"What could go wrong?"

"You nearly died, Vlad," Nathan reminded him. "If Jakome hadn't illegally cloned you, you *would* have."

"So if something *does* go wrong, he can clone me again."

Nathan leaned back in his chair. "You're going to do this whether I approve or not, aren't you?"

"I would never disobey your *direct* orders, Nathan," Vladimir said, doing his best to sound sincere.

"Bullshit."

* * *

Nathan and Cameron were waiting for Alex and her parents in the main hangar bay when they arrived.

"Captain," Alex greeted as they approached. "These are our parents, Barris and Eloisa Foruria. Mom, Pop, this is Captain Scott, commander of the Aurora, and this is Captain Taylor, the ship's executive officer."

Barris and his wife studied Nathan and Cameron closely.

"An honor to meet you both," Nathan said, reaching out to offer a handshake to Barris. When Barris just kept staring, he asked, "Is something wrong?"

"*Five hundred years?*" Barris asked.

"Uh…Five hundred and thirty-five, technically."

"I've never met someone your age," Barris said, finally shaking Nathan's hand with his left hand. He pulled Nathan closer, looking him sternly in the eyes. "I don't give a fuck about my ship. But I *do* give a fuck about my kids. You get me?"

"I'll do my best to keep them safe, sir," Nathan promised.

"I'm going to want to know about every mission they fly for you *ahead* of time."

"I was hoping you'd allow us to do one better," Nathan replied.

"How do you mean?"

"I assume you noticed the cargo ship in orbit when you arrived?"

"I did," Barris replied. "Makes me wonder why, with *two* modern ships in orbit, you need the *Acuna-Dera*."

"Mainly because her design blends in nicely out here," Nathan explained. "Unlike our Navarro-class shuttles," he added, gesturing toward the Seiiki on his left.

"How are you going to do one better?" Barris asked, still suspicious of this infamous, five-hundred-year-old kid.

"We've secured passage for you on that cargo ship back to Takara, where you will receive whatever medical care you need to return you to flight status."

"What?" Alex exclaimed in disbelief. She had dreamt of the day her father would once again captain the family ship, and now, it was finally going to happen.

"Your daughter is a fine second officer," Nathan assured him. "But the Acuna-Dera *needs* her true captain at her helm."

Barris looked at his wife, unable to believe his good fortune. "I'm not sure I have the right," he said, still looking at his wife. "She's spent a lifetime worrying about me. I was getting used to being around her all the time."

Eloisa touched her husband on the cheek lovingly then turned to Nathan. "I think that would be a wonderful idea," she told him.

"El..." Barris objected.

"I love you, Barri, but having you underfoot all day and night...well you just drive me crazy sometimes."

All three of their children were smiling. After a moment, so was their father.

"Then I guess it's settled," Barris told Nathan. "When do we leave?"

"In the morning," Nathan replied. "Meanwhile, Captain Taylor will get you settled into your new quarters."

"If you'll both follow me," Cameron invited.

Barris and Eloisa followed Cameron toward the forward hatch, with Shane and Josi carrying their bags behind them.

Alex stepped up to Nathan. "Why are you doing this?"

"Because it needs to be done."

"You're going to have to do better than that."

"Your father has a lifetime of experience in this region of space. He's worth far more to us on the Acuna with you than on the Aurora. Nothing personal."

Alex smiled. "You always know the right thing to say, don't you," she commented, continuing on to join her family.

Nathan watched them walk away, Jessica coming over from the Seiiki to join him.

"She's right," Jessica said.

Nathan cast a quizzical look her way.

"You always know the right thing to say...*and* do. It's *really* annoying sometimes."

* * *

Vodar woke, his eyes fluttering as he struggled to open them. Something was wrong. His head was heavy, as were his hands. He couldn't think clearly, and his vision was out of focus. There was something else too. He was no longer in the medical facility.

"The sedative will wear off in a few minutes," a familiar voice stated.

Vodar turned toward the voice, still unable to focus properly. But he was getting a sense of where he was. He was aboard a Brodek shuttle, probably the same one that had brought him to Estabrook. He turned his head forward again, his eyes focusing more quickly on far away objects. He was indeed back on Estabrook. He recognized the landscape and the buildings.

"We're letting you go, to deliver a message to your leaders."

Vodar struggled to force his eyes to focus on the man speaking to him from the copilot's seat. After a moment, he recognized him as the man who had been in command of the ship that had held him prisoner. "And what message would that be?"

"Stay out of the Vernay."

Vodar flashed an evil grin. "You are a fool."

"Probably," Nathan agreed.

"What makes you think I'll even return to the Brodek?"

"Because I set your auto-flight system to take you there and then locked you out of the controls," Nathan replied, glancing at his watch. "You should be launching in about a minute." Nathan rose from his seat. "Have a nice flight," he said as he headed aft.

Vodar turned to watch Nathan leave, spotting Jessica and Kit standing on either side of the cockpit door, smiling.

"Looks like *that* wiped the grin off your ugly mug," Jessica commented as she turned and followed Nathan out.

"I just love how you always have to poke the bear on the way out," Kit told Jessica as he joined them.

Vodar began frantically trying to override the auto-flight system as the shuttle's gravity lift generators began spinning up. "Son of a bitch!"

* * *

Nathan stared at his friend as he stuffed his mouth full of eggs. "A little hungry, are you?"

"No more than usual," Vladimir replied, his mouth full of eggs.

Nathan smiled. "So how does it feel?"

"I think the eggs are a little overcooked," Vladimir commented.

"I was talking about the implant."

"I don't really know," Vladimir replied. "I haven't used it much. The doctor said it is designed to incorporate itself into my consciousness over time... in *phases*."

"Like?"

"First, it is just as a demand-based terminal."

"What does that mean?"

"I think of something I need to know, and the answer is given to me."

"Like what?"

"Like, I can tell you that four hundred and eighteen thousand times Pi is one million three hundred and thirteen thousand, one hundred and eighty-five point seven three."

"Not exactly useful."

"I can access any monitored system parameter in the entire ship just by thinking about it. Did you know there is a small pressure leak in the aft dorsal cargo airlock outer door?"

"No I did not."

"Neither did I until this morning."

"Did you *think* that question?"

"I asked for a list of current anomalies, prioritized by anything that would make the ship not space-worthy."

"That's a long list."

"Yes, so I further sorted it by asking for anomalies that were likely to go unnoticed by human inspections."

"Also a long list."

"*Da.*"

"You could do all of that from a terminal though."

"But I did it while I was taking a shower," Vladimir explained.

"What's the next phase?"

"Steady data flow, but restricted until my consciousness is able to keep it separate from my own self-awareness. So I can tell the difference between the two."

"Are you telling me this ship is *self-aware?*" Nathan asked.

"Not in the same way as you and I, but yes."

"I'm not sure how I feel about that," Nathan admitted.

"It is aware of its existence and of its role. But it has no understanding of free will as a *whole entity.* Only in the sense of making decisions on its own to maintain its ability to fulfill its role."

"And that role is?"

"To protect and serve its captain and crew."

"It has no sense of allegiance to the Alliance itself?"

"Its thought matrix was not designed that way," Vladimir told him. "This was done for multiple reasons, including to make it more difficult for Alliance military power to become too centrally controlled. This ship only cares about itself, its captain, and its crew. *Unless* its captain expands that scope."

"Good to know," Nathan decided. "But I'm assuming that you knew all that *before* you got the implant."

"Of course," Vladimir confirmed. "The implant just reminds me. Sometimes it is like there is another consciousness inside of me. One that is me but is not me."

"Now *that* I can understand. It took me *years* to reconcile Connor *and* Nathan. Honestly, I don't know how covert operatives like Jess can keep such things straight in their heads."

"It's easy," Jessica said, having overheard their conversation as she approached, "once you get the hang of it." Jessica plopped her tray down on the table and took a seat next to them. "How's it going this morning, boys? You all plugged into the ship?" she asked Vladimir as she started eating.

"*Da.*"

"That's gotta be weird."

"It is...*different.*"

"The Montasina get off okay?" Nathan asked.

"She jumped out about an hour ago," Jessica reported. "It'll take her a few days to get home. Apparently, they have to circumvent about a quarter of the Alliance territory before they can enter the gate network, so the Alliance won't know where they *really* went. And they don't have long-jump capabilities."

Nathan shook his head in dismay. "We put everything we had into developing greater single and one-minute jump ranges, only to have them all dialed back for nothing more than wealth and power. It makes you wonder how far out we might have explored had that not happened."

"According to Abby, we'd probably be jumping between galaxies by now," Jessica said.

"When did you talk to Abby?" Nathan wondered.

"This morning," Jessica replied. "I've been helping her train."

"Train for what?" Vladimir wondered.

"She felt like her coordination hasn't been quite up to par since she got her new body. So I've been putting her through Ghatazhak hand-eye drills."

"I remember the feeling," Nathan said, recalling his own experiences after being transferred into his current body. "You would've thought they'd have solved that problem by now."

"I thought she was still in her original body?" Vladimir said.

"Nope. This is her third one. Long-term stasis is accomplished by putting the consciousness into digital storage and a freshly cloned *body* into stasis."

"When did this start?" Nathan asked.

"Abby says it was developed for a crewed, intergalactic exploration mission to the Andromeda galaxy."

"They sent a *crewed* mission to another *galaxy?*" Vladimir asked in disbelief. "*Kashmar!*"

"Don't get too excited," Jessica told him. "Apparently, they lost all telemetry from it a few months after departure."

"Did you get the quick response rotations set up?" Nathan asked Jessica.

"Two teams of four, accompanied by four Dragons," Jessica replied. "Mori is reprogramming the QRF shuttle's AI pilot to be able to jump back and move the backup team in case we have two activations in close order."

"Is it a good idea to split them up?" Nathan wondered.

"Not much of a choice really. The shuttle will drop the team in then circle until it receives clearance to return from the team it just put on the ground. So there would be about a five-minute period where we wouldn't be able to respond to a second alert unless the Mirai or the Seiiki were available."

"I hope that's enough," Nathan commented as he continued eating.

"Don't let Vodar psych you out," Jessica insisted. "From what we've seen so far, these *Brodek* are not that organized. Plus, the Vernay is only a small percentage of the area they control, so they might just decide to cut their losses."

"It would make sense from a business perspective," Vladimir agreed.

"Hopefully you're right," Nathan said. "Still, we're going to be spread pretty thin covering six worlds at once."

"Well when Tug returns, he should be bringing some additional manpower."

"Military?" Vladimir wondered. "I thought Takara didn't have its own military any more."

"They don't," Jessica confirmed. "These are private security types."

"You mean *mercenaries*," Nathan realized.

"I mean private individuals who possess the right training and are available for hire," Jessica corrected.

"Not exactly Ghatazhak," Nathan opined.

"No, but we can do some basic cross-training with them," Jessica suggested. "Kit and I were thinking of creating fireteams composed of two of Tug's men and one of ours."

"I'll leave that decision to you and Kit," Nathan decided. "I've got to start concentrating on finding a suitable planet for us to colonize."

"You're really going through with that crazy plan?" Jessica wondered.

"I think it's a great idea," Vladimir insisted.

"Once we get this ship back into space, we're going to need a place to call home. We can't keep having Tug resupply us. Sooner or later, the Alliance is going to figure out we're alive and that House Ta'Akar is helping us. If that happens, his people are going to need that planet just as much as ours will."

"What if we *can't* get this ship flying again?" Jessica wondered.

"Now why would you say something like that?" Vladimir objected.

"It's a fair question, Vlad," Nathan insisted.

"Nothing personal, dude," Jessica defended. "Jeez, did that implant make you more sensitive or something?"

"If we *can't* get this ship flying again, then we're *really* going to need that planet," Nathan insisted. "Unless you want to be stuck on this rock forever."

"I don't know," Jessica said, smiling. "It's got its charms. Hey, you think boka snakes are good to eat? Maybe grilled or something."

"Very funny," Vladimir griped.

CHAPTER SIX

The leader of the Brodek clan emerged from one of the many holding cells in the basement of his headquarters, displeasure on his face. "I trust you have good news," he grumbled to the man waiting for him in the poorly lit corridor.

"I have *news*," Ottar confirmed. "Whether it is good or not is a matter of interpretation."

Halvor just glared at him.

"I have heard from Shya," Ottar began. "Her intel has been very enlightening."

"Who is it that challenges us?" Halvor demanded, growing impatient.

"A man named Connor Tuplo. He operates an old Navarro-class shuttle that is in mint condition. He also has at least four Dragon fighters at his disposal."

"An odd choice of hardware."

"The Navarro-class shuttles were very versatile, and the Dragons are still considered top-notch fighters by many."

"This idiot says he also has a ship," Halvor said, pointing back over his shoulder at the cell door he had just come through.

"Did he mention the size or type?" Ottar asked.

"He never saw it. Just the inside of their sick bay."

"Then perhaps there is no ship."

"Perhaps is not good enough."

"He has contracted the Acuna-Dera to run cargo to the Vernay worlds."

"Who is his importer?"

"A woman named Chiqua Kimbro."

"Find out where she operates from," Halvor instructed. "I want her taken out."

"What about the Acuna-Dera?"

"Destroy her. We cannot allow these people to get a foothold in our territory. It sends the wrong message to the other privateers."

"I thought we might try to follow the Acuna-Dera. Track her back to this Tuplo person."

"No. We kill *anyone* trying to enter the Vernay. Then this Tuplo character will come to us."

"Destroying every ship entering the Vernay will result in a loss of revenue," Ottar reminded his leader. "And our margins are already tight. If the Korsan leadership notices a drop in productivity in our region, they may become displeased.

"You let me worry about the Korsan leadership," Halvor snapped. "You just get Tuplo to come after us. *That's* where we'll get him. On our home turf."

* * *

Nathan entered the flight operations briefing room, where the crew of the Acuna-Dera, Kit, Mori, Loki, and Robert were all waiting. "Good morning, people," he said as he took the podium. "Going forward, the Acuna-Dera will be conducting flight ops between Hadria and the Vernay worlds at least twice a week. When and where will be determined by Chiqua, who will notify us via jump comm-drone at least twenty-four hours ahead of time."

"How many Vernay worlds will we be visiting on each trip?" Alex asked.

"That, too, will be determined by Chiqua, and is likely to change from flight to flight."

"But we will know ahead of time, right?" Loki asked.

"Yes, you'll know your complete mission itinerary prior to departure," Nathan assured him.

"Will we be direct jumping?" Loki asked.

"The Acuna will jump directly from here to Hadria, load up, then return to Dencke orbit. Once cleared for the Vernay, you'll execute a direct single long-jump to your first stop." Nathan looked to Robert.

"While the Acuna is on Hadria, a three-element flight of Dragons will perform a recon patrol of the destination worlds in the Vernay. Once they have verified there are no threats present, they will send the all-clear signal back to the Aurora, and the Acuna will jump into the Vernay, where the Dragons will be waiting for them."

"What will they be doing while we're on the surface?" Alex wondered.

"They'll continue to fly cover."

"What if the Brodek are waiting for us on the ground?" Josi challenged.

"Mori and I will provide security during surface ops," Kit told her.

"Also, all six Vernay worlds have been issued jump comm-drones in order to warn us of the presence of any Brodek forces," Nathan added.

"And if they're there?" Shane asked.

"Then a Ghatazhak QRF team will sweep the target planet and either isolate or eliminate the threat," Jessica explained.

"Also, during all Acuna operations, either the Seiiki or the Mirai will remain available as backup, should the situation warrant," Nathan added.

"Why not have the Dragons escort us while we're on Hadria?" Josi asked.

"Chiqua is responsible for security while *on* Hadria," Jessica stated. "But you'll still have Kit and Mori, just in case."

"And don't forget, you've got shields and point-defenses now," Nathan reminded them. "And although

Hadria is not the safest place in the fringe, the level of risk there does not warrant fighter escorts."

"And if it does?" Alex challenged.

"Then you jump the hell out of there and return *here* as quickly as possible," Nathan instructed. "That's the recommended course of action for *any* armed encounter. Jump to safety first. Don't stand and fight."

"Who makes that call?" Loki asked.

"The final call is the Acuna's of course," Nathan replied. "But if your fighter escort *tells* you to jump, you jump."

"Understood," Loki acknowledged.

"We expect the Brodek to be closely monitoring the Vernay passage," Jessica told them. "But we have to assume they have spies on *all* of the Vernay worlds, so sooner or later, they will realize the Acuna-Dera is *not* using the passage."

"Won't they be able to use our arrival course to figure out where we're coming from?" Alex suggested.

Nathan was a bit surprised she had even considered that. "Well first off, they'd have to be *in* the destination system, monitoring your arrival. They'd either need a shuttle or some special equipment on the surface to do so, which we'd likely already know about. But, if necessary, we can vary your entry angles to obscure your route. I should point out, however, that it is imperative that we do *not* lead the Brodek to this location. Even with the Bonaventura to protect us, it is a risk we should avoid at all costs. So if you have to jump clear of an engagement, you do *not* jump directly back here. You use the evasion algorithm that was programmed into your jump control systems."

"We'll be conducting regular decoy flights *through*

the Vernay passage using the Seiiki and a few Dragons as escorts," Jessica continued. "This should keep the Brodek focused on the passage. However, it's only a matter of time until they figure out what's going on, so assume you'll be ambushed every time you jump into the Vernay."

"Why do I get the feeling there is something you're not telling us?" Josi asked aloud, shocking her sister.

"Why do you say that?" Nathan wondered.

"Shields and weapons on the Acuna; pre-arrival fighter sweeps and escorts; onboard security...It seems to me you're *expecting* trouble."

"We are," Nathan replied without hesitation.

"Then why even go?"

"Because the people on the Vernay worlds *deserve* better," Nathan explained.

"There are thousands of worlds out there being extorted by pirates," Josi argued.

"And they deserve better as well," Nathan agreed. "But we are *one* ship. We have to start somewhere." Nathan took a breath. "Look, all of life involves risk. I believe we've done what is necessary to mitigate *this* risk."

"For now," Josi stated. "But if the Brodek come in force?"

"Then we'll deal with things differently," Nathan replied. "That's all we can do for now." Nathan surveyed the room, looking for anyone else with questions. "Dismissed."

"Why are you busting his balls?" Shane asked Josi.

"Because it's *our* asses on the line, not his."

"That's where you're wrong," Loki corrected, having overheard the exchange. "If our asses are in danger, he'll be the first one to come to our rescue. All of them will. That's what these people are like. That's why I trust them. They're family."

"Not my family," Josi insisted, turning to leave.

Loki looked to Alex, who just shrugged.

"Give her time," Alex told him.

* * *

Robert and Nathan studied the holographic star chart floating in the air above the center of the command briefing room's conference table.

"According to the charts, most of the frontier settlements are no more than three hundred light years beyond the badlands," Robert explained. "So far, we have sent drones out along these routes." Robert pressed a button on his data pad, and four routes began to extend outward into the edges of the display: two to the left, and two to the right. "On just those four routes, we've already found eight uncharted settlements. The furthest being on Gruvan B-4, just over six hundred light years into what's considered to be the frontier."

"That's not good," Nathan commented.

"According to Laza, there's an eighty-percent chance that this pattern will continue, regardless of which direction we explore."

"It looks like most of the migration has been into the Perseus arm, where we are."

"Of course. It's denser, so more choices. But now it's looking like we'd have to travel beyond the Perseus arm if we want to be the farthest settlement from Sol. The problem is, the further out you go, the fewer hospitable planets, and the greater the chance of gamma ray bursts."

"And the closer to the center you go, the greater

the density and the chance of super nova exposure," Nathan added, remembering his training.

"The Alliance has pretty much swallowed up the Orion spur, and part of the medial side of the Perseus, so I'm betting that most of the settlements are in the Perseus, extending out in either direction."

"What about this area?" Nathan asked, pointing to an area to the right of the chart.

"That's where historians believe the survivors of the Jung civilization headed," Robert replied.

"Maybe we should be looking up here?" Nathan suggested pointing up and left.

"The Sagittarius arm? That's more than forty thousand light years from here. Do you really want to go that far out?"

"Well let's make some assumptions here. We know the Alliance is going to eventually swallow up all of these areas," Nathan began, pointing and encircling the areas in question. "Assume the historians are correct, and the Jung went out here and settled. Their civilian ships probably didn't go far, maybe out here. But their big military ships probably traveled further. Knowing the Jung military caste, they would head for a place far enough away to have plenty of time to rebuild their society and rearm before the Alliance expanded into their new territories. So out here in the Sagittarius arm is the best place for *us* to go. That would put us equal distance from both the Jung Empire and the Alliance."

Robert looked at Nathan. "Planning on creating an empire, are we?"

"Who knows what our descendants will do," Nathan defended. "We may as well give them the best chance possible."

Robert studied the chart a moment, shaking his head in disbelief.

"What is it?" Nathan wondered.

"It's hard to believe that when I started my career, we were only exploring an area of about twenty light years, and it took us *years* to do so. Now we're looking at the *entire galaxy* and thinking that *thirty thousand* light years might be too close to our neighbors."

"We should probably run this by Abby first," Nathan suggested. "Just in case there are some issues about jumping too close to the galactic core."

"If we settle in the Sagittarius arm, you're looking at a two-day trip, one way. Even our drones will take about fourteen hours each way."

"We could multi-jump it in half a day," Nathan said. "But I'm hoping Abby can design us a jump gate to bridge the gap."

"A jump gate to single-jump across *forty thousand light years?*"

"There was a time when a thousand-light-year jump seemed impossible," Nathan reminded him.

Robert sighed. "I don't know. It just feels like we're getting way ahead of ourselves here."

"Sooner or later, the Alliance's lies about long-jumping will get out," Nathan said. "And then you'll be wishing we had gone to another galaxy."

"I'll be long dead by then."

"I don't know," Nathan said, smiling. "Did you ever think you'd still be alive in the fortieth century?"

"I'll send the drones to the Sagittarius arm next," Robert agreed.

* * *

"Jump complete," Loki reported.

"Sure is nice not to have to close our eyes," Alex

commented. "Still not sure how I feel about jumping straight into the Vernay, though."

The sensor display beeped, catching Loki's attention. "Our escorts are here," he announced, spotting two icons on the screen. "They just jumped up from the surface."

"When do we jump to Kataoka?" Alex asked.

"As soon as Josh clears us in." Loki looked at her. "You were at the briefing, right?"

"Don't get cute."

"New contact," Loki announced. "Comm-drone. Incoming message." Loki looked at the comm-screen. "That's the all-clear signal."

"How do you guys time things so precisely?" Alex wondered.

"It's all in the planning," Loki explained. "We know exactly how long each step takes, and we plan when to execute those steps so that it works the way we expect."

"I can't even get up on time," Alex lamented.

"Well it's a different kind of flying, to be sure. It requires discipline."

"Or you can just let your AI execute everything, and just enjoy the ride."

"There's not a fighter pilot alive who would rather let his AI fly their ship," Loki stated. "Not even me. That's why I enjoy flying larger ships. It's not about *flying*, it's about *piloting*."

"What's the difference?"

"Simple. Piloting is working the systems, plotting your flights, entering settings into your flight nav-com, operating your comms, getting clearances. Flying is manually controlling the ship with the flight controls. The best pilots can do both *simultaneously*."

"I prefer telling my AI to take me here and there."

"And what happens if your AI stops working?"

"Then I yell at my sister until she gets it working again."

"You need to learn how to *manually* fly this ship, and you know it."

"Yeah, I just don't want to admit it," Alex said.

Loki chuckled as he calculated the jump parameters on his data pad. "You just did." He handed her his data pad. "Now enter these jump parameters into the jump controller."

"Why not just run the calcs *in* the jump controller?" Alex wondered.

"If your jump controller was on the fritz, this is what you'd have to do."

"But I didn't make these calculations, you did."

"Don't worry, you'll learn how to do that as well."

"Oh God. Does it involve math?"

"Everything in flying involves math," Loki told her. "Now enter those parameters so we can jump to Kataoka."

Alex sighed in resignation, entering the parameters as instructed. "You're taking all the fun out of this."

"You can't just point and jump," Loki told her. "That's known as the Josh Hayes method."

"I thought you said he was a great pilot?"

"He is," Loki admitted. "He's just not great at *piloting*."

"I'm so confused," she mumbled as she finished entering the parameters. "Done."

Loki checked her entries. "Good. Now sync up with our escort and execute."

"We're going to control *their* jumps?" Alex asked in disbelief. "Is that wise?"

"It's in the mission profile."

"That doesn't mean it's wise."

"It'll be fine, trust me."

Alex pressed the sync button and waited for the confirmation signals. "I assume the two green lights mean we're synced?"

"See the icons?" Loki said. "The flashing green outlines indicate *those* contacts are jump-synced with *our* jump controller. So we're good to go."

"If you say so," Alex said, pressing the execute button.

A few seconds later, the subdued jump flash washed over them, and the planet Kataoka appeared before them, closing rapidly.

"You see?" Loki said.

Alex instinctively reached for her plotting screen and zoomed in on the settlement on the surface, touching the point where she wanted to land the ship. "There, we're good to go."

"I'm not going to make you hand-fly the landings yet," Loki stated. "But you are going to hand-fly the takeoffs."

"*That* I can handle."

* * *

Vladimir charged onto the bridge more excitedly than usual. Ever since he had returned as a clone, he had been unusually energetic. It reminded Nathan of the man he had first met fresh out of the academy.

"What's going on?" Cameron asked as Vladimir charged past her, heading straight for the helm station.

"You're not going to believe this," he declared, plopping down into the helmsman's seat and sliding forward. He quickly pressed a few buttons then inched the grav-lift throttles forward ever so slightly.

The entire ship rocked slightly, alarming Cameron,

Nathan and Ensign Dass as the deck shifted under their feet.

"What the hell?" Nathan exclaimed.

"We're hovering!" Vladimir announced proudly.

The ship swayed a bit, seeming to have a hard time balancing itself on the fields of anti-gravity being emitted from under its massive grav-wing.

"Maybe we shouldn't be?" Nathan urged.

Vladimir eased the grav-lift throttles back, allowing the ship to settle back down onto its landing gear.

The bridge shifted again then stopped moving altogether. The internal comm-panel lit up, demanding Ensign Dass's attention as calls came in from all over the ship, wondering what had just happened.

Vladimir slid his seat back again, jumping to his feet and turning around to face Nathan and Cameron, a huge grin on his face. "We can fly!"

"What the hell?" Nathan repeated.

"There's nothing wrong with the grav-lift systems."

"So it's normal to sway about in a hover?" Nathan questioned.

"Well it needs some recalibration, but the point is, we could fly this ship anywhere on the planet that we want!"

"That's great, Vlad, but maybe next time you could just *tell* us the good news instead of demonstrating it unannounced and frightening the entire crew," Cameron stated, nodding toward Ensign Dass who was still dealing with the influx of calls.

"Oh, sorry." Vladimir turned to Ensign Dass. "Sorry." He turned back toward Nathan and Cameron, stepping up out of the shallow well of the helmsman's station. "The main drive is fine as well.

So once we clean all the mud and crap out of the forward maneuvering thrusters, we could even take her back into space."

"We've got about twenty hull breaches, Vlad," Cameron reminded him. "Maybe we should fix those first?"

"Hull repairs are easy," Vladimir argued. "Besides, the integrated pressure shielding will seal any breaches; not to mention, you could seal off all the compromised compartments if you had to."

"I'm probably just being picky, but I'd prefer to wait until our *entire hull* is intact," Nathan insisted.

"Of course, but...aren't you at least a *little* excited?"

"Yes, Vlad, we're all very excited," Cameron replied. "Now how about you return to the hundreds of systems that still need repair."

Vladimir looked disappointed. "You people are no fun," he pouted, heading toward the exit.

Nathan and Cameron watched him exit.

"Maybe Tug should have aged his clone a bit more before transferring him into it," Cameron suggested.

"It *is* exciting though."

Cameron cast a look of disapproval his way.

"I mean, we've only been down for *fifteen days*, and we're nearly able to get back out there."

"You're counting the days?"

"You're not?"

"We're still a long way from getting 'back out there,'" Cameron insisted.

"Yes, but at least we're making progress."

"Captain?" Ensign Dass called from the comm-station.

"Tell the crew everything is fine," Nathan told her.

"I already have. We just received word from the

Bonaventura. Jakome's shuttle has returned and is inbound."

"Just in time for dinner," Nathan stated.

* * *

"Thank you for inviting me, Captain," Hanna stated as she entered the captain's mess. "To be honest, I thought you'd forgotten about me."

"Things have been a little hectic lately," Nathan defended as he escorted her to the table. "I believe you know everyone here."

Hanna nodded to the others at the table as she took her seat.

"Tug has just returned from Takara," Nathan told Hanna.

"*Tug?*" Hanna asked Jakome.

"A long story," Jakome told her.

"*Everyone* aboard this ship has a long story," Hanna commented.

"Yourself included," Jakome replied.

"We weren't expecting you back so soon," Nathan declared as he took his seat at the head of the table.

"You were only gone a week," Jessica added as she sat down at Nathan's right, beside Robert.

"I felt it best to return once I got things in motion back home," Jakome explained. "Besides, we still have much to discuss."

"Such as?" Cameron asked as she sat down to Jakome's left, across from Hanna, who was sitting to his right.

"Such as your recent discovery about the gravity wells." He looked to Laza. "I am curious as to how you came to this conclusion. Alliance scientists have been studying this data for centuries, and their findings have always been the same."

"Not surprising when all the data you're studying was collected *by* the Alliance," Abby remarked.

"Still, your data sample was quite small, was it not?"

"I am adept at seeing patterns where others might not," Laza stated.

"Interesting, but is there any chance that your own biases influenced your conclusions?"

"Most people analyze data with the intent of proving a preconceived notion. This bias does tend to lead them to erroneous conclusions. My talent lies in not only *seeing* the patterns, but in *allowing* that data to lead *me*, rather than *me* leading *it*."

"I see." He looked at Abby. "And the good doctor did not influence your findings?"

"Why would she?" Laza asked.

"Even the best scientists often allow their personal agendas to skew their work," Jakome stated. "No offense intended, Doctor."

"On the contrary," Abby assured him. "I welcome the questioning of any findings that I come to. Being a *true* scientist means accepting our own faults as human beings, biases being one of them."

"Not in my day," Hanna droned.

Everyone at the table looked to her.

"Sorry, it's just that *science* was *power* in my day. *Political* power."

"Which many historians believe contributed to the fall of humanity," Nathan stated.

"Your findings may have reopened deep-space exploration," Jakome stated, getting back to Laza.

"My *findings* are only valid for travel between Dencke and the Vernay worlds," Laza reminded him. "There is no reason to assume that the same findings would be found *everywhere*."

"Perhaps, but it is a good place to start," Jakome insisted.

"To start *what?*" Hanna wondered.

"To start breaking the Alliance's control over humanity," Jakome replied.

"I've heard several people from this time period complaining about the Alliance," Hanna stated. "How exactly do they *control* humanity?"

"*Control* is a relative term," Jakome stated. "Just like *freedom*. One person's definition of *control* is another's definition of *guidance.* Humans no longer make their own decisions, at least not within Alliance space. Instead, they use their AI assistants to help them make the right choices."

"I don't see how that's better," Jessica wondered.

"The belief is that AIs remove human biases from the equation," Jakome explained. "They offer detailed analysis of the likely outcomes of any decision, allowing their human counterparts to make well-informed choices."

"And this works?" Cameron asked.

"Again, that is open to interpretation," Jakome admitted. "One can still make a bad choice despite the advice from its AI. However, the AI negates the effects of misleading propaganda."

"Unless that propaganda comes *from* the Alliance itself," Abby muttered, only partially under her breath.

"There has never been any evidence to show that AIs are used by the Alliance to disseminate propaganda," he reminded Abby.

"Ask an AI if long-range jump drives damage the interdimensional barrier and see what they say?"

"Like with any question, your answer depends on how you phrase it."

"Okay, ask it if there is any solid, irrefutable evidence that long-range jump drives damage the interdimensional barrier," Abby argued.

"I have," Jakome replied.

Nathan got the feeling that Abby had argued this point before.

"And what did your AI say?"

"That there is no irrefutable evidence that supports this claim due to the fact that measurements of this barrier are still beyond our current technology."

"And what else did it say?"

Jakome sighed. "That the popular consensus among experts in theoretical interdimensional astrophysics supports this theory."

"And?" Abby pressed further.

"That considering the potentially catastrophic effects of a complete failure of the interdimensional barrier, all reasonable steps should be taken to prevent such an occurrence."

Abby looked pleased with herself, satisfied that she had made her point.

"Human history is replete with catastrophic predictions that were widely accepted without any real scientific evidence," Nathan stated. "Most of which turned out to be flat-out wrong."

"In other words, they were lies," Abby replied.

"For a statement to be a lie, the one stating it as fact must *know* that it is untrue," Jakome stated.

"A lie, a falsehood, a mistaken assumption; call it whatever you like. It's still equally harmful."

"*Harmful* is also a relative term."

"You just like to argue," Abby insisted.

"Only with truly intelligent people," Jakome said, disarming her.

"So how did this dependence on AIs begin?" Nathan asked.

"The integration of AIs into the decision-making progress in *our* time began during the great war. The Alliance had underestimated the size and strength of the Jung fleet, as well as how many of their ships had been equipped with long-range jump drives. In short, we were losing. Someone in fleet strategic planning got the idea of asking an AI for advice."

"And what did the AI tell them?" Cameron wondered.

"Obvious stuff like increasing production, using more aggressive tactics...that kind of thing. But the one recommendation that they *weren't* expecting was to reduce the *human* component to the absolute minimum," Jakome explained.

"Why?" Cameron wondered.

"The AI postulated that the Jung ships were far more automated, and their AI-controlled weapons systems did not require *human* authorization to fire in either defensive *or* offensive situations. This not only made the Jung ships more difficult to destroy, but it also made Alliance ships easier for the Jung to kill. Humans, no matter how well trained, simply cannot match the reaction speed of automation."

"And the Jung don't care about collateral damage," Cameron realized.

"Another common denominator of conquerors throughout history," Nathan added.

"At first, the Alliance only gave its AIs authority to take defensive action without human authorization."

"The Aurora already *has* that authority," Nathan said.

"Actually, our AI is limited in what sort of defensive actions it can take," Cameron reminded him. "It can take out offensive weapons on an enemy ship, but it cannot *kill* them without human authorization."

"Precisely," Jakome agreed. "And even a few seconds of delay can make all the difference. Fleet immediately experienced a reduction in losses by simply giving its AIs more aggressive standing orders. Over the course of the next ten years, the very nature of fleet operations changed. Dragon fighters were completely AI-flown, and the Expedition-class ships became more automated as well, until they were being operated by skeleton crews of humans augmented by androids to maintain the ship's systems. Because of this, human losses were greatly reduced, which dramatically improved public perception of the war. The tide changed, the Gamaze fell, and the fighting moved out of Alliance space and into *Jung* territory. That's when the real change took place."

"I'm almost afraid to ask," Cameron stated.

"Since the bulk of the Alliance fleet was no longer being used to defend its member worlds, the AI recommended massive strikes against the most populous Jung worlds, *starting* with Nor-Patri."

"Against *civilian* targets?" Nathan asked in disbelief.

"The AI took humanity out of the equation, reducing it to pure numbers. The death of trillions to prevent the death of hundreds of trillions. The AI recommended the use of the very weapon that had started the war...the singularity weapon. But they stepped up its mass and used it against *entire planets*. In a matter of weeks, eighteen planets were erased from existence, and what remained of the Jung people fled for the stars. The Jung fleet continued to fight, but without their industrial base to support them, they did not survive long. They either fell in battle or simply disappeared. Probably heading off into deep space themselves. After that, the use of AI consultations in all governmental decisions became commonplace. Over the decades, it just sort of filtered down into everyday life."

"Which is the main reason why so many people moved out into the fringe after the war," Abby stated.

"They saw the writing on the wall," Jessica concluded.

"This does not make any sense," Vladimir insisted. "AIs are easily controlled. They are just programs. As long as the data they rely upon is accurate, their advice should be sound. There is nothing to fear from them."

"People aren't afraid of the AIs themselves," Jakome explained. "They just don't want to give up control of their lives to them."

"But you said they do not have to follow the AI's advice," Vladimir pointed out.

"Yes, but humans generally take the path of least resistance," Jakome replied. "Following AI advice is more likely to result in a better quality of life. Better careers, better relationships, better health...all of it."

"Most people are willing to give up their freedoms in exchange for peace and security," Nathan commented.

"Many, yes, but not *most*," Jakome argued. "In fact, the tide has recently turned."

"How so?" Nathan asked.

"For the first time since the war ended, more people live *outside* of Alliance space than live *inside*," Jakome explained.

"I guess people care about freedom more than you thought," Hanna commented to Nathan.

"Is the Alliance aware of this?" Robert asked.

"Quite aware," Jakome assured him. "I suspect their AIs predicted this centuries ago. That's why all of this exists."

"All of what?" Aiden wondered.

"The fringe, the badlands, the Korsan, even the lies about the interdimensional barrier," Jakome explained. "Many believe that all of it, directly or indirectly, is controlled by the Alliance."

"To what end?" Vladimir wondered.

"Power, control, profit, you name it."

"I understand how having a monopoly on transportation gives them all of that, but only within Alliance space," Nathan opined.

"To understand, you have to look at statistics," Jakome explained. "Nearly all of the worlds that achieve any level of success do so *because* they are connected to the Alliance transportation network. Either by the gate network, or by short-range, multi-jump cargo ships. The more success they achieve, the more reliant they become until eventually, they have no choice but to join the Alliance in order to maintain the quality of life their citizens have become addicted to."

"And the pirates?" Vladimir asked.

"They prevent worlds *outside* of the Alliance's reach from becoming independent and successful, thus demonstrating the *advantage* of being part of the Alliance."

"So the Alliance wipes out all enemies then creates an enemy to justify their existence," Jessica concluded. "Very nice."

"So you're saying that the pirates *work* for the Alliance?" Aiden surmised.

"No, just that the Alliance chooses to let them operate to the extent that they do because it serves their purposes," Jakome explained. "But their plans go far beyond the badlands."

"The frontiers," Nathan realized.

"Many deep-space settlements originate from within Alliance space," Jakome explained. "That's how they get all their initial equipment and supplies. Even their transportation. Most agree to an ongoing resupply contract in order to save on the cost of their initial settlement package. Sort of an insurance policy to get them through the first few decades. But what it really does is maintain their dependency on Alliance goods and comforts. You see, the resupply contract grants the Alliance the right to decide *how* to transport goods to and from those worlds. The most prosperous worlds, or at least the ones that actually have an export of value to the Alliance, are eventually given a dedicated gate linking them *back* to Alliance space. Now if you look at the distribution of those gates, you begin to see a pattern."

"What kind of pattern?" Laza asked, becoming curious.

Jakome decided that showing them might work better. He touched the device on his wrist and then pointed to the middle of the room. A moment later, a 3D holographic map of the galaxy appeared, floating above the table. "This is the Milky Way galaxy," he said, making a pinching motion with his fingers and causing the display to zoom in. "This is the known human-inhabited portion. The stars circled in red are frontier worlds that have been given Alliance gates."

"I'm not seeing any kind of pattern," Jessica admitted.

"I am," Laza stated. "Does your AI have a

prediction going forward over time based on these gate assignments?"

"It does." Jakome touched the device on his wrist again, and more stars began to be circled in red, first around the perimeter of the frontier, then with new gates appearing closer in, including within the badlands and the fringe.

"What criteria are you using to predict which worlds will be given gates?" Cameron wondered.

"Habitability, environment, beauty, resources, predicted population growth, successful colonization probabilities, all the things that attract migrants," Jakome explained. "As you can see, in about two hundred years, most of what is now considered *outside* of Alliance space will be completely reliant on the Alliance's gate network for their survival. At that point, those worlds, and all the worlds that trade goods with them, will be de facto members of the Alliance, in much the same way that the fringe border worlds are today. The Alliance will see a tenfold increase in size, all without firing a shot. They will be invited in by people addicted to the peaceful, stable lives that Alliance membership provides."

"But not all of those worlds will join," Cameron stated, "at least according to your projections."

"It won't matter," Jakome insisted. "They'll be surrounded by worlds that adhere to Alliance rules whether they are members or not. They may not become *formal* members, but they will still have to behave as if they were in order to continue to trade with their neighbors who *are* member worlds."

"The same thing happened on Earth just before the third world war," Nathan said. "The aligned nations forced the unaligned ones to adhere to their rules or risk economic sanctions. Eventually, some of them grew tired of it and created their own alliances. The result was terrorism, small-scale wars, and eventually another world war."

"I remember reading about that war," Jakome said. "It ended with a limited nuclear exchange. Billions died."

"But that war is what finally got the nations of Earth to begin working together," Hanna pointed out. "It's what led to the Unified Earth government. It was the end of war."

"Apparently not," Jakome replied.

Hanna nodded his point.

"Unfortunately, armed conflict is part of human nature," Nathan said. "That's *why* freedom is so important."

"It's also why people *chose* to live in the badlands, where there *is* no government telling them what they can and cannot do," Dominic pointed out.

"Except for the Korsan," Jessica replied.

"Yes, but only because they *choose* to."

Hanna looked at the faces of those in attendance, feeling as if she were missing something. "You all act is if government is a *bad* thing? I mean, big government usually sucks, yes, but if everybody is healthy, happy, and safe, are the losses of a few freedoms really that bad?"

"They are if the reasons you gave them up for were a lie," Abby insisted.

"But isn't the *result* more *important* than the truth?" Hanna defended.

"Better a happy lie than a miserable truth," Nathan commented. "In short, no."

"Why?" Hanna asked.

"Because we're human," Nathan answered.

Hanna wasn't following.

"Because we *want* to struggle," Nathan explained. "We *want* to achieve. We *want* to look back when we're done and admire what we've created. But more than anything else, we want to choose our own paths, right or wrong, and live with the consequences."

"Again, why?" Hanna demanded.

"Because anything less isn't living, it's just *existing*," Nathan told her. "It's as simple as that."

"Perhaps, but there doesn't appear to be anything you can do about it," Hanna stated. "This Alliance seems way too big to stop, especially with just a single ship."

"She's right about that," Jessica agreed.

"I have no desire to *stop* it," Jakome stated. "If people freely choose to give up their freedoms in exchange for whatever it is they seek, that is their right. I only wish to ensure that choices *exist*, and that they can be made based on *truths*."

"One person's truth is another's propaganda," Nathan stated. "People believe what they *want* to believe."

"Yes, but they should not be punished for not wanting to live in the Alliance," Jakome insisted.

"You're talking about taking on the Korsan," Jessica realized.

"I am," Jakome admitted.

"Granted, we don't know much about them, but isn't that a pretty big task?"

"Yes and no," Jakome replied. "The Korsan *is* a very large organization, but they are not as formidable as most people assume. The truth is, they are a collection of much smaller gangs, most of whom would be unable to hold onto their territories without the *perceived* threat of Korsan retaliation."

"There must be *some* threat, or they wouldn't be able to maintain that perception," Cameron insisted.

"The Korsan have hundreds of ships," Dominic insisted.

"Do you *know* that to be true?" Jakome asked.

"No, but that *is* what everyone says."

"Just like everyone says that long-range jump drives damage the interdimensional barrier," Abby stated.

"Regardless of how many ships the Korsan actually have, we're still going to require more than *two* ships," Nathan pointed out.

"I'm afraid we only have *one* ship," Jakome corrected. "The Bonaventura cannot be involved in any conflict with the Korsan."

"Why not?" Jessica asked. "She's well-enough armed."

"But she has an Alliance registry," Jakome added. "Which means, if she exchanged fire with the Korsan, it would be akin to an Alliance warship doing the same."

"By that logic, the same would hold true with the Aurora," Nathan said.

"Except that the Alliance could not impose any sentence against your vessel since it is not tied to any holdings within Alliance space. The Bonaventura *is*. Were she to become involved in anything short of a purely defensive exchange of fire, House Ta'Akar and all its assets would be seized. That is why it is imperative that we create a world that can support not only the Aurora, but any additional ships we may acquire. And it must be far beyond Alliance reach."

"If you expect to build additional ships, it's going to take a while," Cameron said. "Just the mining, materials processing, and fabricators *alone* will be a challenge, let alone the skilled labor needed to assemble trillions of parts into ships. It took five years to get the first Expedition-class ship built, and that was on a world that already had the necessary industries in place."

"That is why I suggest that we *steal* the additional ships."

Hanna nearly choked on her food.

"*Steal?*" Nathan wondered.

Jakome looked around the room, noticing the surprise on their faces, especially Hanna's. "You've done so before, right?"

Hanna looked toward Nathan. "You have?"

"Extenuating circumstances," Nathan assured her.

"On the contrary," Jakome disagreed. "These circumstances are nearly identical."

"I'm afraid to ask exactly *whom* you're suggesting we steal them *from*," Nathan said.

"From the Alliance of course."

"You want us to steal Alliance warships?" Cameron asked.

"Well technically they are *not* warships, at least not any longer. They're not even *owned* by the Alliance. In fact, the company that *does* own and operate them is planning on scrapping them. I doubt the Alliance would even try to retrieve them."

"If they're in that bad of shape, why would we want them?" Nathan wondered.

"Because they were the second, third, and fourth Expedition-class ships to roll off the assembly line five hundred and thirty-something years ago," Jakome explained.

As expected, Vladimir was the first one to react, his eyes growing wide with excitement. He looked to

Nathan as if he were a child hoping his dad would give him permission to go someplace with his friends. "Nathan…"

"Slow down, Vlad," Nathan replied. "Why are they being scrapped?"

"Because they are no longer profitable," Jakome explained.

"Profitable?" Cameron asked.

"The few Expedition-class ships that survived the war were kept in service for a while but were eventually replaced. Because of their historical value, they were put on display as museum exhibits. Eventually, they were purchased by a private company that turned them into tourist attractions."

"Tourist attractions," Nathan stated, not liking the sound of it.

"Hotel, restaurant, simulation arcades, action re-enactments, gift shops. They would position them on a world for a few months until the locals lost interest then move them to a new world. But interest has waned over the last few years, and they are operating at a loss."

"But wouldn't stealing them further complicate matters?" Cameron asked.

"The corporation that owns them will have to spend millions to have them properly decommissioned and disassembled. Most of the time, older ships are sold to operators outside of Alliance space, where standards do not exist. But they are not interested in such large ships since they are more difficult to maintain. Most likely, they'll just drive them into a star or a gas super giant."

"Is that legal?"

"Not in Alliance space, but…"

"I'm not sure stealing five-hundred-year-old ships is a good idea," Nathan said.

"These ships are extremely over-built and are designed to last a *very* long time," Vladimir insisted.

"I refer you to our long list of repairs," Nathan stated. "And *this* ship is still a baby."

"I'm fairly certain the ships he's talking about weren't jumped through a singularity," Vladimir argued.

"Just out of curiosity, what ships *are* we talking about?" Jessica asked.

"Excuse me?" Jakome replied.

"What are their *names?*" Jessica clarified.

"The Celestia, the Navarro, and the Dayton Scott," Jakome listed.

Everyone in the room looked at Nathan.

Nathan sighed. "Everyone, please excuse us," he said, rising from the table. "I believe Jakome and I need to talk."

CHAPTER SEVEN

Jessica was starting to get the hang of being Nathan's copilot aboard the Seiiki. She had spent a few hours in the simulator with Loki, and it wasn't as if she had zero flight training. She just hadn't flown anything in a long time. Fortunately, most of the Seiiki's operations were automated. Even when being flown manually, her AI had the pilot's back, ensuring the ship remained safe and stable through all phases of flight. It was practically like flying with an instructor in the seat next to you, except the AI didn't remind you when you forgot something or did something poorly. It just made the necessary corrections. Like raising the landing gear after departure or deploying it for you on approach.

Of course, Nathan had his own idiosyncrasies when it came to flying. Fortunately, Loki was aware of them. He had explained that Nathan flew a lot like Josh, but with far more discipline, which was easy since Josh had none. For the most part, Jessica's primary responsibility was to just monitor various displays and alert Nathan of any abnormal conditions he did not immediately notice.

So far, that rarely happened. Nathan, like Josh, was an amazingly instinctive pilot. But Nathan had no problem letting the AI fly the ship under normal conditions, and only flew manually when necessary. Loki explained that Josh flew everything as if it were a fighter, regardless of the situation. Nathan flew each ship the way it was designed to be flown *unless* the situation dictated otherwise.

The thing was, Jessica was not really sure which style she preferred. Josh's style was more in line with the way Jessica approached things, but Nathan's style was less stressful. She eventually had settled for Nathan's more cautious approach. Just knowing that he could fly like Josh when it was necessary was enough for her.

"Two jumps left," Nathan announced. "I expected to see someone by now."

"By someone, you mean the Brodek," Jessica replied. "I doubt they're going to patrol the passage twenty-four seven."

"They don't really have to," Nathan said. "All they'd have to do is put a sentry shuttle at each end and then jump back to alert interceptors if they detected anyone entering the passage. It takes only two ships and a squad of interceptors on standby at their base. So other than the interceptors, they'd only need about six shuttles to maintain a constant watch."

"Makes sense," Jessica agreed.

"Thirty seconds to the next jump."

"So have you decided?" Jessica asked.

"Decided what?"

"To steal those ships?"

Nathan shook his head, sighing. "I told Tug he shouldn't have blurted that out in front of everyone."

"I'm not *everyone*," Jessica defended.

"No, I haven't decided."

"Well I think we should do it," Jessica told him.

"No surprise there."

"You *don't* want to steal them?"

"It's not a matter of *want* Jess."

"Yes it is."

"I've kind of got my hands full just getting *our* ship back in operation. How am I supposed to deal with *four* ships?"

"Better to have them in your hands as a possible option for the future than to let them be flown into a sun. I mean, the *Celestia*, the *Navarro*, and the *Dayton Scott?* Come on, how can you not want to save them?"

"If we were just *buying* them, I would agree with you," Nathan admitted. "But *stealing* them would put a target on our backs."

"We've got a target on our backs now," Jessica argued.

"From the Brodek maybe."

"It's only a matter of time until the Alliance learns that we're alive and kicking," Jessica reminded him. "It seems to me it's better to acquire the additional ships and get them fixed up *now* before the Alliance *really* starts hunting for us."

"They're *tourist attractions*," Nathan argued. "They don't even have jump drives."

"We have jump rescue nets," Jessica replied. "We'd just have to make a couple more of them. And the Aurora has all the plans and fabrication equipment needed to repair anything on board. Hell, she could build an entire ship from the ground up."

Nathan looked over at her. "You've been talking with Vlad, haven't you?"

"And Cameron," Jessica admitted. "She thinks we should steal them as well."

"No she doesn't."

"Okay, she didn't say *that*," Jessica admitted. "But she didn't say we *shouldn't*."

"That's what I thought."

The subdued jump flash washed over the Seiiki's cockpit.

"One jump left," Nathan announced.

Jessica glanced at the sensor display, checking

that their three escorts had jumped with them. "Dragons are still with us."

"I'm with Cam," Nathan said. "I'm *considering* it."

"Well don't *consider* it for so long that we lose the opportunity," Jessica urged.

"Tug said all three ships are booked through the end of the year, so we've got time."

"That's weird," Jessica commented.

"How is *that* weird?"

"No, these readings," Jessica corrected, her attention focused on the sensor display. "It looks like a debris field."

Nathan glanced at the display as the shields status light changed to active. "What the...our shields just snapped on."

"*Heavy debris field ahead,*" the ship's AI announced.

"Any other contacts?" Nathan asked.

"*Negative.*"

"*Fuck!*" Josh exclaimed over comms. "Cap'n, I just had a body bounce off my forward shields!"

"*What the hell did we fly into?*" Nikolas asked.

"I've got a contact dead ahead," Jessica announced.

"A ship?"

"If it is, it's dead in space," Jessica replied. "I'm only picking up tiny amounts of power and no signal emissions at all. No life support, no life signs, no radiation, nothing. Just a big chunk of something. Looks like it's tumbling end over end."

"What's its heading?"

"Same as ours," she replied. She looked up, peering through the forward windows, trying to spot the tumbling wreckage.

"Stay alert," Nathan urged his escorts. "This could be a trap."

"I can't see shit out there," Jessica complained, returning her gaze to her console.

"We're two and a half light years from the nearest star," Nathan told her. "That's why we have lights." He touched his console, activating their forward flood lights. "Fuck."

Nathan and Jessica both stared out their windows at the wreckage. Debris was everywhere, including a few bodies. The forward half of the ship appeared to be intact, but the back half was gone.

"Looks like their drive section blew," Jessica commented. "That doesn't look like a cargo ship."

"It's not," Nathan confirmed. "Are you picking up anything, Josh?"

"*Negative,*" Josh replied. "*My threat board is clear. But this looks like it happened recently.*"

Jessica looked at Nathan. "How recently?"

"Minutes."

"Why take out a passenger ship?"

"To send a message."

"To us?" Jessica asked.

"To everyone," Nathan said. "Send word to the Aurora to set Condition Two. We need to be ready to respond."

"You think they'll strike the Vernay worlds?"

"I'm certain of it," Nathan replied. He pulled on his flight control stick, pitching up as he pushed his throttles forward, steering their shuttle up and over the tumbling wreckage. "No use in hanging around. May as well get to Kataoka and warn them."

* * *

Alex carefully guided the Acuna to a landing that wasn't quite as gentle as she would have liked. She immediately pulled her grav-lift throttles back to zero then manually killed power to the system. She reached up to the center overhead panel, shutting down several more systems but left the main reactor running as planned. After a moment's thought, she relaxed back in her seat then looked to Loki.

"Did you forget anything?" Loki asked.

"I don't think so."

"Are you sure?"

"Uh…no?"

"Why aren't you sure?" Loki asked.

It hit her. "Because I didn't use the checklist," she said, rolling her eyes.

"Exactly. Other than that, you did a great job."

"Then I *didn't* forget anything?"

"*Are we clear to crack the hatch?*" Shane asked over the intercom.

"Just that," Loki said, smiling.

Alex reached for the intercom button. "Clear to unload."

"And that's why you use a checklist," Loki stated.

"Do you *really* use a checklist on *every* flight?" Alex wondered.

"Honestly no, but not by choice. Sometimes things are just happening so fast that even an automated checklist takes too much time."

"Isn't that what AIs are for?" Alex suggested. "To back you up?"

"Not in full manual mode."

"So I'm going to have to use a checklist forever?"

"If you want to be safe, yes."

"Even if my AI is working fine?"

"Especially if your AI is working fine," Loki told her. "AI dependency creates poor pilots. If you consistently use your checklists, you'll be able to handle the situations where there's no time to use them. And those are usually the same situations where you can't *depend* on your AI."

"So Dragon pilots use a checklist?"

"In training, yes. But flying a fighter is a completely different task than flying most ships. Everything you do has to be instinctual. That comes from hours of practice and even more from time studying and reviewing. Fighter pilots spend far more time practicing in the simulator than they spend in actual flight. Some of them practically *live* in the simulator."

"Like Josh?"

"Josh's biggest fault is that he spends *too much* time in the simulator, and not enough time studying procedures."

"But everyone says he's the best they've ever seen," Alex said.

"He is," Loki agreed. "But not because of his training. It's just a gift with him. He just has this innate understanding of *how* things fly. His mind is always several steps ahead. But for the rest of us, it's about practice *and* study. The big advantage *you* have is that you only have to fly this *one ship.* The Aurora's pilots have to know how to fly *all* ships: Dragons, shuttles, and the Aurora herself. Not to mention any number of other ships we may be called upon to fly."

"How do you keep up with all of that?"

"Let's just say that the full-immersion VR sims are invaluable. Most of us fly at least a few missions a day in them."

"Even on the days you're flying *real* missions?"

"*Especially* on those days."

Alex began climbing up out of the pilot's seat.

"By the way, congratulations are in order," Loki added.

"For what?" Alex wondered.

"That was your first fully manual flight from departure to landing."

Alex was surprised she hadn't realized it. "Huh. How about that," she said as she headed aft. "I guess I'm better than I thought."

"Don't get cocky," Loki warned as he climbed up out of his seat to follow her out.

* * *

"Here we go, people," Nathan announced over comms as he initiated the first jump into the Vernay passage. "Sync-jump in ten seconds."

"How many of these decoy flights are we going to make?" Jessica asked as she double-checked her displays at the Seiiki's copilot's seat.

"I'm guessing about a half dozen flights until the Brodek figure out that we're a decoy, and that the Acuna is the real cargo runner."

"But then they'll go after the Acuna," Jessica reminded him.

The jump flash washed over the cockpit.

"The Acuna never jumps in from the same vector twice," Nathan replied as he checked the sensor screen, making sure that the escort fighters had jumped with them.

"They'll figure *that* out eventually as well."

"Maybe, but not any time soon. Chasing old light isn't as easy as some people think."

"Maybe not back in our day, but who knows what tech they've got now."

"If we were talking about the Alliance, I would agree with you. However, based on the Brodek ships we've seen so far, I'm betting they're not exactly stocked with all the latest toys."

"That's a hell of a risk."

"Maybe, but it's the only way we're going to find out for sure."

"So we're doing force recon then. Feeling out the enemy?"

"Yup."

"Isn't that usually *my* idea?" Jessica questioned.

"What can I say? You've rubbed off on me." Nathan called up the next jump in the eight-jump Vernay passage series and loaded it into the jump controller.

"Any reason we're not letting the AI auto-jump us all the way there?" Jessica wondered. "It *would* be a whole lot faster."

"Wouldn't be much of a decoy if we were too fast to intercept, would we?" Nathan looked at her. "But you knew that."

"Just checking to see how *much* of me has rubbed off on you."

"Don't worry," Nathan assured her. "I haven't reached the point where I distrust *everyone* just yet."

"Just everyone I don't know," Jessica muttered as she verified that the jump controller had synced up with those of their escort fighters. "The children are synced."

"*Did you see that?*" Josh called over comms.

"See what?" Jessica replied.

"*An energy spike. Zero two five, up ten and two thousand klicks out,*" Josh explained. "*AI couldn't ID it. Want me to jump out and take a look?*"

"Negative," Jessica instructed.

Nathan looked at her.

"If it's Brodek, better they don't know that we know."

"*Confirming...no intercept?*" Josh asked.

"That's right. Negative on the intercept." Jessica glanced at the jump sequencer. "Ten seconds to jump two. Heads on a swivel, boys and girls."

"If they don't ambush us at the next waypoint, they will at the following one," Nathan said.

"Maybe we can get a little *payback* for that passenger ship?"

"Let's just concentrate on not becoming their next victim," Nathan suggested as the jump flash washed over them.

Jessica's eyes were stuck on the sensor screen, fully expecting Brodek fighters to jump in from all directions. "No sign of them."

Nathan went about setting up the next jump. "Jump three in thirty seconds," he announced over comms.

"*Same rules of engagement?*" Josh asked.

"We *never* shoot first," Nathan replied.

"What kind of a pirate never shoots first?" Jessica muttered to herself.

"We're not pirates," Nathan insisted.

"The hell we're not."

"Pirates steal things. We don't."

"We're stealing the Brodek clan's profits."

"No we're not. We're just interfering with their ability to extort from the people on the Vernay worlds."

"Which means they lose profits," Jessica argued. "In their minds, that's stealing."

Nathan looked at her. "Why are you arguing? You know we're doing the right thing here."

"Are we?" Jessica wondered. "I mean, yeah, we're

stopping bad people from doing bad things, but have you ever wondered if we're going to make things *worse* for the people of the Vernay? I mean, what happens after we're done with them?"

"Define *done with them*."

"You know, when we no longer need the revenue from this little business arrangement we have with Chiqua," Jessica clarified. "We leave, and the Brodek will be right back. And you never know. They might just kill them all."

"No profit in that," Nathan said as the next jump flash washed over them.

The ship rocked suddenly, its port shields flashing red-orange.

"Pretty sure that qualified as 'shooting first'," Josh declared as he rolled his Dragon fighter to port, turning to intercept the attacking pirate snub-fighters. "Lannie, stay on me. Trish, cover the Seiiki."

"*I got your six,*" Lannie confirmed.

"*I've got the Seiiki,*" Tricia acknowledged.

"Seiiki, jump ahead one light second to set these two up for me," Josh advised as he prepared his intercept jump.

"Jumping one light second," Nathan replied over comms as he dialed up a manual jump.

The Seiiki rocked again as more plasma bolts slammed into her port shields, causing them to flash repeatedly.

"I don't think these guys plan to board us to take their cut," Jessica stated as she tried to lock the Seiiki's defensive weapon on the attacking snub-fighters.

"No they don't," Nathan. "Jumping in three...... two...

"*One......*"

A flash of blue-white light appeared ahead and to the right, and the Seiiki disappeared. A split second later, the icon on Josh's tactical display representing the Seiiki also vanished. Then the icons representing the enemy fighters turned to their left in pursuit and disappeared. "Suckers," Josh said with glee. He touched the jump button on his flight control stick, causing both his and his wingman's ships to jump ahead one light minute. The icons reappeared, but now he was looking at the target's superheated thrust gases, giving him excellent heat signatures for his missiles to lock onto. "Two and two," he told his wingman. "You got right."

"*I got right*," Lannie replied over comms.

"Launching two," Josh announced as he pressed the missile launch button.

On the underside of the two Dragon fighters, rectangular doors opened under their wings, and two missiles dropped out, their engines lighting up a second after deployment. The four missiles sped away, accelerating as they steered toward their targets.

Just as the missiles were about to strike, the two snub-fighters jumped away.

"Looks like their fighter pilots are better than their shuttle pilots," Josh said as he turned in toward the Seiiki.

"*We're jumping to the next waypoint,*" Nathan announced over comms.

"Right behind you," Josh replied as he quickly added the distance between his ship and the Seiiki, minus ten meters, to his jump calculation for the next waypoint in the Vernay passage. "I'm jump lead," he told his wingman.

The Seiiki and its escort Dragon disappeared in a flash of blue-white light a few hundred meters ahead of them.

"*Ready when you are,*" Lannie confirmed.

Josh pressed the manual jump button on his flight control stick, leaping ahead just over a light second in an instant. Suddenly, the Seiiki and Tricia's Dragon fighter were right in front of him, about two hundred meters and closing. "Steer right and firewall it," Josh instructed his wingman. "I'll pass to their left."

"*Got it,*" Lannie acknowledged. "*Why?*"

"I've got a hunch," Josh replied as he rolled slightly left and shoved his main drive throttles to full power. "Pitch up two degrees and get ready to jump twenty clicks. Load two jumpers."

"*Got it.*"

Nathan watched out of his side window as Josh sped past them on their port side and his wingman passed to their starboard. "What are you up to, Josh?"

"Anticipating," Josh replied over comms. "*Jump now, Lannie.*"

The Dragons were accelerating so quickly that their jump flashes were almost unnoticeable ahead of them.

A warning alarm sounded.

"Four bogeys, dead ahead. Fifteen klicks and

closing fast," Jessica warned. "They're launching missiles. Four inbound. Twenty seconds to impact."

"Seiiki, point-defenses," Nathan said to their AI.

"I *knew* it," Josh exclaimed as four red icons appeared on his tactical display about five kilometers behind them and headed away. "You take the two on the left. Jumpers with frag-heads," Josh instructed his wingman as he pulled his throttles back to zero thrust and yanked back hard on his flight control stick.

Both Dragons flipped over to face aft, rolling back over as their main drives returned to full power. After a few seconds of maximum thrust, their speed dropped to nearly zero, and two mini jump-missiles dropped from their undersides. The engines on the four missiles lit up, their initial thrust first bringing them back to a dead stop in space then propelling them back in the opposite direction toward the four pirate snub-fighters attacking the Seiiki five kilometers away. As soon as they attained forward momentum, the targeting systems made the calculations and jumped, the missiles disappearing behind four blue-white flashes.

Having launched their missiles, the four pirate snub-fighters began to spread out in anticipation of finishing off their target once the missiles disabled its shields. The far right two fighters changed their minds when they spotted a Dragon fighter racing out from behind their primary target and turning to an intercept course.

What they didn't see were the four blue-white flashes announcing the mini jump-missiles arriving directly behind them. Each of the missiles altered their course slightly to reestablish locks on the casually maneuvering targets.

All four snub-fighters began jinking wildly, trying to both break the missiles' locks as well as get a clear jump line. But they had two problems. First, they believed their nav-charts, which showed rogue gravity wells all around them, which would restrict their jump lines. Second, they didn't know that the weapons chasing them didn't need to actually *hit* them.

The nosecones on the missiles suddenly separated, tiny charges driving them away from the missile's body. Next, one hundred and twenty projectiles were ejected from the fronts of the missiles, spreading out into fields of tiny explosive warheads.

More than half of the warheads missed the pirate snub-fighters, and while the ones that found their targets did not create enough damage to destroy the snub-fighters, it was enough to make them easy to kill.

Two jump flashes appeared behind the snub-fighters, revealing two black Dragon fighters, forward plasma cannons blazing.

"Two down! Five seconds!" Jessica warned.

Nathan fired his port docking thrusters, holding them for two full seconds before pushing the manual jump button on his flight control stick. The jump flash washed over them, and they found themselves about one hundred meters to the right of their original course, and five kilometers downrange.

"Tear' em up, guys!" Josh cried out with glee over comms.

Nathan turned his attention to the tactical

display. The last two inbound missiles were passing harmlessly to their port side and would not have enough propellant to come about. Better yet, the four icons representing the attacking fighters were disappearing one by one. Their escorts took them out with ease now that they had no shields and were having difficulty maneuvering. Within seconds, all red icons were gone.

"*I stand corrected!*" Josh exclaimed. "*They're not that good after all!*"

"Don't get cocky," Nathan replied. "Next jump in thirty seconds."

Jessica looked at him, puzzled. "You think there's more?"

"Not the issue. We're here to keep them thinking we're using the Vernay passage."

Jessica sighed. "I hate being bait."

"*Forming up on you,*" Josh announced.

A few seconds later, there were two jump flashes on either side of them, and the two Dragon fighters appeared, streaking past them in the opposite direction.

Josh pulled back hard on his flight control stick, adding in some roll as his nose came over to point in the same direction the Seiiki and Tricia's Dragon were traveling. He jammed his throttles all the way forward, holding them there for several seconds to reverse his direction of travel and begin closing on Tricia and the Seiiki.

"*Synchronizing,*" Nathan announced over comms.

Josh glanced at his jump control display, noting that it was now being controlled by the Seiiki.

"*Five seconds to jump,*" Nathan added.

"*Should we hold position until after the jump?*" Lannie asked.

"Why?" Josh replied.

The jump flash washed over them. When the flash cleared, the only change in the view outside was a slight, barely noticeable shift in the position of the stars. He was still closing on the Seiiki and Tricia's Dragon trailing behind it. "See. That's the big advantage in sync-jumping. You don't have to reestablish your position and flight attitude in relation to the other elements in your flight. Nothing changes *except* the location you're all flying in."

"*Pretty crazy,*" Lannie commented. "*We didn't have sync-jumping in the Lightnings.*"

"Maybe not, but those things were fun as fuck to fly, especially fast and low."

"*Never had the chance,*" Lannie admitted.

"Yeah, peace makes for boring flying."

Nathan looked back over his shoulder to check on Hanna, who had been silent for some time. "You okay?"

Hanna nodded but didn't look certain.

"Are you sure?"

"No."

Nathan smiled.

"You do this sort of thing often?" Hanna asked.

"Until recently, no. But years ago..."

"Yeah, I just finished reading the summaries of all your past adventures. I'm still trying to figure out how all of you managed to survive."

"One could say the same about you," Nathan pointed out. "You know, you and your friends could actually be the oldest people alive...*anywhere.*"

"I hardly consider that an accomplishment," Hanna said.

"But it does give you a unique perspective."

"Is that why you asked me to chronicle all of this?"

"Partly," Nathan admitted. "But mostly it was because we need an impartial accounting of what we do, for history's sake."

"Because the Alliance that *you* created now blames you for the great war?" Hanna assumed.

Nathan looked back at her. "Exactly."

"Did you?"

"That has yet to be determined," Nathan stated. "Perhaps *you* will figure that out?" he added, with another glance back at her.

"I'll try, but I can't promise a favorable conclusion."

"I'll settle for the truth," Nathan assured her. "Besides, it wouldn't be the first war I've started."

"So you're *admitting* that you've started wars?" Hanna asked, surprised at his statement.

"Sometimes, circumstances leave you no choice."

* * *

Persa was perhaps the most beautiful of the six worlds located at the end of the Vernay passage. Originally settled by the Persan church on Musano, its residents enjoyed a temperate climate, an abundance of water, and vast expanses of arable land.

The Persans were a peaceful people, and their world produced much of the food that made life possible on the other worlds in the region. Ranches and farms dotted the landscape of the Isle of Penna, where the Persan settlement was originally founded.

Persa itself was also the largest settlement in the Vernay region. Sitting on the coast of the island, it hosted a small fishing fleet. Nearly a thousand people lived and worked in the city of Persa, and hundreds more lived and worked in its countryside.

Like most worlds outside of Alliance space, there were no actual laws and very little government. The few services provided by city management were performed by volunteers and were funded by donations from its citizens. The law of the land was the Persan code, which was basically to do unto others as you would have them do unto you.

There was, of course, the occasional dispute, but these rarely resulted in violent confrontation. Most people on Persa owned some sort of weapon, but few actually carried them around. In most cases, others would step in and break up disputes. It was a small, tight-knit community. The last thing anyone wanted was to develop a bad reputation. When that happened, trade became difficult, and offenders quickly found themselves unable to acquire even the most basic goods.

Four flashes of light appeared in the evening sky over the water, followed by the distant thunderous booms resulting from the air being displaced by the suddenly arriving ships. Normally, ships arrived alone. So multiple jump-booms meant trouble for the people of Persa.

Elan Toray was the youngest member of the Persan volunteer corps. Normally, his job entailed unplugging storm drains or repairing streetlights. All the best tasks went to the more senior volunteers. Today, he had gotten lucky. Old man Kelan had called in sick, and no one else had been available to cover for him, so the duty had fallen to Elan.

That task was city watch, and it involved sitting in a booth affixed atop the city center and alerting whomever needed to be alerted if the watcher spotted something amiss. Elan had received pretty clear instructions. If there's a fire, call the volunteer fire brigade. If there's a distress flare on the water, call the water rescue team. And so the list went, the most recent addition being to alert the QRF if the Brodek showed up.

Elan didn't even know what a QRF was. He only knew that if the Brodek did come, he was to push the button marked QRF on the communications console in his booth. So when the pirate shuttles streaked low over the city, he pressed it and pressed it hard.

The shuttles flew fast and low over the rooftops, their intent being to cause fear and panic among the residents. It was their way of reminding the people of Persa that the Brodek did not answer to their code.

That was their first mistake.

* * *

Sima Dass had been on duty for hours. Evenings were generally uneventful. The shuttles and Dragons were all parked, and most of their crews had already had their evening meal and were either resting or practicing in the sims.

At some point, either Captain Scott or Captain Taylor would come in and disappear into the ready room for an hour or so before heading to their quarters for the evening. Occasionally, Captain Nash would come by, as would Jessica, who usually just checked over the ship's weapons and shields, then promptly departed.

Sima actually preferred the graveyard shift, where she was generally alone for most of her shift. She spent most of her time either studying the procedural manuals for other bridge positions, or just watching movies and sipping coffee. It gave her the opportunity to put herself through training drills on the other bridge stations, with them in simulator mode. Unfortunately, some were still not fully repaired, but the tactical and sensor stations were operational, and those were the ones she found the most interesting.

The communications console beeped, and the main screen before her lit up. One of their jump comm-drones appeared and was sending flash traffic. Three letters: 'QRF'. Sima pressed the QRF alert button before she even ID'd the world where the call had originated.

* * *

Life for the Ghatazhak had gotten considerably easier now that they were stationed back on the Aurora again. With Kit and Mori assigned to the Acuna-Dera, Alpha and Bravo teams were now three men each. Each team took four-hour shifts being first up for any call to action. But in the four days they had been back, no such call had come. Most of their time had been spent training and helping out with repair tasks as best they could.

Being currently first up, Alpha Team, led by Sergeant Jokay Deeks in Kit's absence, was restricted to the space just off the main Dragon service bay, which they had converted into their ready room. Now that the Aurora was out of the mud and resting on her landing gear, the Dragons were able to use their dedicated recovery deck and launch tubes instead of the midship main elevator pad. The Ghatazhak QRF shuttle was now permanently located on the elevator pad in order to respond more quickly.

Every shift started the same way. You checked out the shuttle, your gear in the shuttle, and your weapons. Then you read the latest comm-log entries, as well as the daily reports. Every single shift began this way, regardless of the fact that all these things had just been checked eight hours earlier, at the start of your previous shift. Ghatazhak equipment *never* malfunctioned in combat. Not just because it was of the highest quality, but also because it was thoroughly checked so frequently.

The best part about being first up was that you were required to stay ready to respond in less than a minute. That basically meant that once your equipment inspections and report reviews were completed, it was time to sit down and relax. It took less than an hour to do your checks and reports, which left three hours to fill. Some read, some played games, some watched movies. But today would be different.

The alert klaxon sounded once, and the trim lighting changed to red, indicating that they were being called into action. Jokay, Abdur, and Jephen immediately rose from their seats and headed out the door, quickly crossing the massive hangar bay to their shuttle, which was already spinning up for launch.

"*QRF response to Persa,*" Sima announced over the hangar bay loudspeakers.

Jokay led his team across the bay, stepping onto the elevator pad as it began to rise toward the doors sliding open directly above. As they stepped up into the shuttle, the doors closed automatically.

Jokay tapped his comm-set as he stepped up to his gear pad. "Derel, you copy?" he called to Chief Anson.

"*We'll be ready,*" he replied.

CHAPTER EIGHT

Josh was the first of his team to reach the Dragon ready room, where the cockpit modules awaited. By the time he stepped up to his gear pad to start the automated flight gear donning system, Lannie and Tricia had also entered.

The half minute it took for the donning system to clad him in a fully sealed and pressurized flight suit seemed like forever. But soon, Josh was suited up and moving quickly to the nearest available cockpit. He stepped down into the cockpit, plopping into the seat and punching the activation button. His canopy slid forward, sealing him in as his seat locked onto the back of his torso and thighs to hold him in place. As his cockpit quickly descended into the transition tunnel system below, he could see Lannie and Tricia, suited up and heading for their cockpits.

Once onto the track system, the opening in the deck he had just descended through closed up, and his cockpit accelerated backward. The cockpit module itself had no artificial gravity nor any inertial dampeners. All of that was provided by the Dragons themselves. So it was best to just grab the small handholds on either side of the cockpit to keep his arms from flailing about while his cockpit streaked backwards toward the Aurora's aft end.

With all of the Dragons currently aboard, his ride was short. His cockpit came to a stop then slid to the left toward the port-side Dragon ready storage tunnel. A few seconds later, his sideways motion stopped and his cockpit was quickly lowered into his fighter, automatically mating up with the vessel and causing his screens and controls to come to life.

"Hello, Josh," his AI greeted. *"All systems are ready for departure. All weapons systems are charged and ready, and we are carrying maximum armaments."*

"Aurora, Dragon One. What's the scoop?" Josh asked over comms.

"QRF request from Persa," Sima replied. *"Unknown force size."*

"Copy. You in, Lannie?"

"Dropping in now," his wingman answered.

"See you there."

"Shouldn't we all jump in together?" Tricia suggested.

"QRF will be airborne in fifteen seconds," Jokay reported over comms.

"I'll jump in low over the water and do a quick size-up. Lannie, you and Trish jump in together up high, along with the QRF shuttle."

"Copy that," Lannie replied.

"Dragon One, launching," Josh reported as he touched the launch button on his flight control stick. His fighter lurched forward, the mag-rails quickly accelerating his fighter down the tunnel toward the exit. A few seconds later, he reached the exit as his engines went to full power and his wings began unfolding.

Dragon fighters weren't really designed to be launched by catapult while in the atmosphere, and until his wings completely deployed, Josh had very little control over his ship. He was basically a missile. Because of the close proximity of a near-vertical rock face directly in front of the Aurora, his AI managed the launch, pitching his nose up with thrusters until he had a clear jump line, at which point his AI jumped him several hundred kilometers forward, putting him in space where his wings could more easily deploy. Ten seconds after jumping, his wings were fully deployed and locked, and Josh immediately turned toward Persa.

"*QRF, launching,*" the QRF shuttle's AI pilot reported over comms.

"*Dragon Two, launching,*" Lannie announced.

"*Dragon Three, launching,*" Tricia followed.

"*Transition instructions?*" Josh's AI asked.

"Over the water, a few clicks from the city, down low," Josh instructed.

"Persa City is currently on the opposite side of the planet from Dencke," his AI warned. "Two jumps will be required."

"Then make it happen," Josh instructed. "I'll take manual control once in the atmo," he added, taking his hands off the stick.

"*Joshua Hayes is allowing an AI to fly the ship?*" his AI commented. "*I'm honored.*"

"Loki's been playing with your speech algos, hasn't he?"

"*He referred to it as 'pilot specific customizations',*" his AI explained as it initiated the first jump.

Josh smiled as the jump flash washed over his fighter.

Cameron entered the bridge, moving quickly toward Sima at the tactical station. "What's up?"

"QRF alert from Persa, sir," Ensign Dass replied. "No details. Dragons are away, and the QRF shuttle is about to lift off. Dragon One has instructed Dragons Two and Three to jump in high and await his sit-rep."

"Let me guess. Josh plans on jumping in solo and taking a peek," Cameron opined.

"Yes, sir. How did you know?"

"I know Josh."

The QRF shuttle began to lift up off the elevator pad before it even reached the flight deck. As soon as it cleared the deck, it began to rotate to starboard, continuing to climb. Once it was above the top of the nacelles, it pitched up slightly and its main engines lit up, propelling it forward as it jumped away.

Josh's AI guided his Dragon fighter through a tight turn to starboard, pitching down and decelerating at the same time.

"Insertion jump in five seconds," his AI announced. *"Shields are up, and all weapons are online and at full power."*

"Let's do it," Josh instructed, putting his hands back on the flight controls.

The jump flash washed over the cockpit, albeit greatly subdued by its specialized projection canopy.

His fighter rocked slightly as it transitioned from the vacuum of space into the Persan atmosphere, despite the best efforts of its inertial dampening systems. A quick glance outside verified that his AI had done as he had asked. It had jumped him in low over the water on a heading for the spaceport next to Persa's only city.

"Four contacts," his AI reported. *"Brodek attack shuttles. Two of them are firing indiscriminately at the city as they circle. The other two are on the ground at the spaceport. They are deploying armed men."*

"Lock missiles on the two shuttles on the ground," Josh instructed as he pitched up slightly to give the missiles room to deploy without ending up in the water below. Are they shielded?"

"Affirmative. I'm also detecting three cargo shuttles on the ground, all destroyed."

"Two missiles each, please."

"Missiles locked. Two per target."

Josh pressed the weapons activation button on his flight control stick. Three seconds later, four missiles burst out from under him, racing ahead toward the rapidly approaching spaceport.

All four missiles streaked across the water, rising just enough to avoid striking the ground as they sped toward the pirate attack shuttles sitting at the Persan spaceport. Seconds before impact, the first two missiles veered slightly downward, detonating as they reached the point where the target's shields touched the ground, where they would be their weakest.

The explosions opened up craters in the ground which allowed most of the blast energy to travel under the shield edge and into the shuttles, knocking out their near-side shields. Two seconds later, the next two missiles arrived, slamming into the unprotected sides of the shuttles, detonating and blowing them apart, spreading fiery debris flying in all directions, especially downrange toward the edge of the city. The explosions also knocked the eight armed men who had disembarked less than a minute ago to the ground.

Josh glanced at the tactical display, instinctively turning toward the one circling to his left. "Intercept jump, target three, contact range one hundred meters."

"Contact range is not..."

"Shut up and do it," Josh ordered. His AI was still

learning his flight habits, especially his tendency to intercept the enemy at ranges that were considered too close to be safe.

"*Jump ready.*"

Josh touched his jump button and immediately found himself zooming low over the city instead of the water, closing uncomfortably fast on the enemy attack shuttle, which was just a few meters higher in altitude than he was. "Tie bow thrusters into the flight controls," he instructed. He pulled up on his flight control stick and his ventral nose thrusters fired, forcing his nose to rise unnaturally, considering the aerodynamics involved. But it was enough to put his targeting reticle on the shuttle about to pass over him at extremely close range. Without thinking, his index finger flipped the weapons select switch on his flight control stick to plasma cannons, and then moved to the trigger, pressing and holding it.

Streams of red-orange bolts of plasma raced forward from either side of his cockpit, slamming into the underside of the target's ventral shields. A moment later, the target passed over him, and Josh flipped the thrust-reversal levers on his main engine throttles. In a few seconds, his forward speed dropped by fifty percent, just enough to reduce the airflow over his wings so that his next maneuver would be possible. Another yank backward and his nose came up hard. The slipstream kicked in as his nose passed a forty-five-degree angle, causing it to come all the way up and over. He let go of the stick for a split second as his AI adjusted the ship's grav-lift systems to keep him in the air, despite the fact that he was now flying backwards *and* upside-down.

"*Theoretically, this maneuver shouldn't work,*" his AI warned.

"Kinda looks like it does," Josh boasted as he flipped his thrust-reversal levers back to normal and his speed dropped quickly to zero before beginning to increase again, but now in the opposite direction. He pressed and held the trigger again, sending streams of plasma bolts into the aft end of the pirate shuttle's underside, tearing it apart and sending it falling toward the surface.

"Two-click jump," he instructed, touching his jump button a second later.

"Sit-rep?" Nathan requested as he entered the bridge.

"QRF request from Persa, no details," Cameron replied. "Josh has already jumped in. QRF shuttle just jumped up to rendezvous with Lannie and Tricia in orbit. We should have more details shortly."

"Sima, instruct the QRF shuttle to stay on station after deployment. And redirect QRF Two to the hangar bay."

"Aye, sir."

"You taking the Seiiki out?"

"If need be," Nathan replied, tapping his comm-set as he left. "Marcus, load an MCI into the midship bay. I'm on my way down."

Cameron tapped her comm-set. "Jess, report to the Seiiki ASAP."

"*On my way,*" Jessica replied.

"Medical, XO. Grab as many TRKs as you can carry and head for the Seiiki."

"*XO, Medical, aye.*"

"*Jump to orbit complete,*" the QRF shuttle's AI pilot reported. "*Joining up with escort Dragons.*"

"Escort, QRF One-One. Sit-rep," Jokay called over comms.

"Dragon One jumped in ahead to recon. We'll get details when we reach orbit over Persa."

"Understood. Let's move."

"QRF Pilot, Dragon One-Two has jump lead," Lannie announced.

"*Dragon One-Two, QRF Pilot. You have jump lead.*"

"So still no confirmation huh?" Jephen surmised.

"You expected different?"

Three flashes of blue-white light appeared in orbit of Persa, revealing two Dragon fighters and the QRF shuttle.

"*Dragon One-One, Dragon One-Two. QRF in orbit. Waiting for instructions,*" Lannie called over comms. "*Sit-rep?*"

"Two movers down at the spaceport, one down in the city. I'm leading the fourth one away. Eight shooters infilling the city from the spaceport. QRF clear to insert at center of spaceport. You and Trish provide fire support from the city side to keep those assholes from moving deeper into town."

"*One of us can handle that,*" Lannie replied. "*You want someone to back you up?*"

Josh glanced at the screen displaying the rear camera view as he jinked his fighter from side to side and up and down. The dumbass behind him believed Josh was doing his best to shake the guy off his tail. "I can handle this idiot myself."

"*Understood.*"

Nathan entered the main hangar bay, walking quickly toward the Seiiki's aft cargo ramp. The second Ghatazhak QRF team was already on their way up the ramp, fully suited in their flat black, level three combat gear.

"MCI module will be loaded by the time you reach the cockpit," Marcus assured him. "Jess and the med-techs are already inside."

"Great," Nathan said as he reached the ramp.

"Captain!" Hanna called from behind.

Nathan stopped, turning and spotting Hanna and Martina, having just entered the bay.

"I heard something is happening on Persa?" Hanna inquired. "We'd like to go with you."

"We don't even know if we'll be heading out or not," Nathan replied.

"Well if you do…"

"If we do, we'll be jumping into a hot zone."

"I'm not going to be able to tell this ship's story if I don't see it *all* first-hand," Hanna reminded him.

"And I'm a med-tech," Martina added.

"Come on then," Nathan told them, continuing up the ramp.

Talisha's cockpit module came to a halt after sliding sideways for several seconds then dropped down into the Dragon fighter waiting in the starboard fighter launch bay.

The module's descent suddenly slowed, and the cockpit made contact with the fighter, her screens lighting up to confirm the mating.

"*Mating complete,*" her AI announced.

"Aurora, Dragon Two-One, ready for launch."

"*Stand by, Two-One,*" Sima replied over comms. "*We're waiting for an update from QRF One-One.*"

"Copy that." Talisha relaxed, knowing there was a good chance she wasn't going anywhere soon.

"*Dragon Two-Two, ready for launch,*" Evan reported.

"*Copy, Two-Two,*" Sima replied.

"*Dragon Two-Three, in the pipe,*" Meika announced.

"*Copy, Two-Three, in the pipe.*"

"Get comfortable, people," Talisha told them. "We may be here awhile."

Cameron watched as the data relayed back from Josh's Dragon fighter via one of the QRF shuttle's jump comm-drones loaded onto her tactical display. "Patch me in to the Seiiki and the ready Dragons," she instructed Sima.

"Patched in."

"QRF Two, sit-rep from QRF One," she reported over comm-sets. "Four pirate shuttles. Two landed and deployed troops; the other two circled and fired on the city from the air. Dragon One-One took out the two on the ground and one of the circling shuttles, and is now leading the fourth one away while QRF One is inserted."

"*Dragons One-Two and One-Three are providing cover and air support,*" Cameron finished.

"Button her up," Nathan told Jessica. "I'm going to roll us out so we're ready to launch."

"Anson, everyone in?" Jessica asked over the intercom.

"*We're good here. Close her up,*" the leader of the second Ghatazhak QRF team replied.

"Aurora, Seiiki," Nathan called over comms. "Seiiki is rolling out to stage for quick-launch."

"*Copy, Seiiki rolling out.*"

"Sounds like Josh didn't waste any time," Jessica commented as the shuttle began to roll toward the massive exit from the hangar bay onto the flight deck.

"He usually doesn't," Nathan replied.

"That boy's going to end up on the Brodek's most-wanted list."

"I'm sure he'll take it as a compliment."

Eight armed men fired wildly into the city, blasting through windows and doors, mowing down anyone they saw. Their rides home had just been destroyed, and they were determined to make sure no one would be alive to challenge them as they searched for alternate transportation or for someplace to hide until the Brodek came to rescue them.

This was a new era in the badlands. None of them could remember a coordinated, well-armed resistance against the Brodek or any other pirate clan. The only exceptions were when one clan attacked another for control of their territory. But those attacks always came against a clan's home base, not against one of the worlds they controlled. But someone *was* resisting, and they were doing a damn good job of it. So now, per their leader's orders, the beneficiaries of that resistance had to pay the price.

Men, women, and children alike were slaughtered on sight. The attackers ignored any pleas for mercy from those they cornered. But within minutes of their attack, the streets were barren, and they would have to root out additional victims.

Two jump flashes appeared further up the street, revealing two wide, flat, black shapes, hovering just above the rooftops and advancing slowly toward them. At first, no one reacted. The two fighters were too far away for them to make out any details. But that quickly changed, and they could make out the small, double-barreled gun turrets under each ship's nose.

"Cover!" their leader barked, running for the nearest doorway as the approaching fighters began spraying the street with streams of tiny bolts of energy that tore up the fused earth. Two of their men fell to the first pass.

"Those are Dragons!" one of the men yelled after the fighters passed over them.

Their leader stepped back out in the street, opening fire with his rifle, but his bolts of energy simply bounced off the fighter's aft shields. More turrets appeared on the underside of the black fighters' aft ends, opening fire.

This time, all of them managed to find cover. The fighters parted, each of them turning in opposite directions to circle back.

"We have to get back to the landing field," the lead man decided.

"What good will that do us? We destroyed the only two shuttles there."

"There's got to be a shuttle in one of those hangars. We'll blow them all open if we have to, but we're finding a way off this rock."

The remaining six men broke into a dead run back toward the Persan spaceport, wanting to reach new cover before their attackers returned.

"Time to die, dumbass," Josh said to himself as he switched his plasma torpedo selection from his forward tubes to his aft ones. He then put his fighter into straight and level flight, suckering his pursuer into the trap. "Jesus, this guy is *unbelievably* stupid," he muttered as the Brodek shuttle lined up directly behind him and opened fire with everything he had.

Josh imagined how excited the Brodek pilot must be, anticipating his return to base to brag to his friends about single-handedly shooting down a Dragon fighter. An evil grin appeared on Josh's face as he pressed and held the weapons trigger on his flight control stick.

Red-orange balls of plasma energy shot out of the stubby barrels recessed into the sides of the Dragon's fuselage where its wing roots met up. Six balls of plasma leapt out from each side as the Dragon's own shields flashed with each impact from incoming fire. In one and a half seconds, the first of the series of plasma balls slammed into the Brodek shuttle's forward shields, causing them to flash brightly several times, failing completely on the third impact. The fourth pair impacted the shuttle's nose and right forward engine, breaching the hull and disabling the impacted engine. That alone was enough to put the shuttle down, at the very least into a controlled crash-landing, making the next two pairs of plasma energy unnecessary.

As Josh had suspected, the Brodek pilot had spotted the other two Dragons and was keeping all of his shields powered up, fearing they would come to the aid of his target. The result was a forward shield that was not powerful enough to withstand six plasma torpedo impacts at close range and in rapid succession. His suspicions were confirmed on his rear camera view screen, which showed the fourth Brodek shuttle coming apart behind him. "That's right! This dragon shoots fire out its ass!" Josh shook his head, a satisfied grin on his face. "That boy should have studied up on ancient fighters."

He pressed the transmit button on his flight control stick. "We own the skies, people."

The black, unmarked, QRF shuttle appeared low over the water from behind an almost unnoticeable blue-white flash, less than a kilometer offshore of the Persan spaceport. Unfortunately, there was no way to hide the thunderous clap caused by the sudden displacement of air.

The six armed Brodek men running back into the landing field of the spaceport immediately opened fire, lighting up the incoming shuttle's forward shields.

Small, anti-personnel turrets dropped down from the underside of the QRF shuttle, immediately opening fire on the Brodek men on the surface, sending them scattering for cover.

The QRF shuttle settled into a hover a few meters above the surface, extending its shields down to the surface once its forward motion ceased. Its side doors slid open, and three men in flat-black, full-body combat armor dropped down to the surface, immediately opening fire on the Brodek forces once they were on the ground.

Nathan and Jessica scanned their consoles as the Seiiki rolled past the shuttle bay's outer doors onto the flight deck.

"*QRF is on the ground and has engaged the Brodek,*" Cameron reported over comms. "*Initial contact was eight combatants, currently down to six. Josh confirms they have control of the airspace over the Persan colony.*"

Jessica tapped her intercom. "Relax, boys. QRF One will have this wrapped up shortly."

"How can you be so sure?" Hanna wondered from the seat behind Jessica.

"Trust me on this," Jessica replied. "Unless the odds are worse than ten to one, we've got nothing to worry about."

"What if the Brodek drop in more troops?"

"That's why we send Dragons," Nathan added. "If any Brodek shuttles try to put troops on the ground or bombard the colony, they'll take them out."

"But there are only three of them," Hanna said. "What if they send a dozen shuttles in at once?"

"Dragons can engage up to ten targets at a time. They'd have to send more than thirty shuttles," Nathan argued.

"But they have gunships that could bombard it from orbit, right?"

"Yes, but the Dragons could chase them off," Nathan explained. "Don't forget, we've got three more Dragons ready for quick-launch, and five more that can be launched within a few minutes. And these shuttles can be fitted out as full-on gunships in a matter of minutes. I doubt that the Brodek are going to risk their limited assets trying to glass one colony bucking their authority."

"But there are *six* colonies bucking their authority," Hanna pointed out. "Doesn't that complicate things?"

Nathan glanced back at Hanna as the Seiiki came to a stop. "We don't have any idea how much area the Brodek control beyond the Vernay region. If it's ten times as many worlds, then they will be less likely to risk those assets."

"And if the Vernay represents, say, half their area?" Hanna wondered.

"That's what worries me," Nathan admitted.

The three Ghatazhak moved quickly to cover as the QRF shuttle slid forward, continuing to fire as it passed over the enemy.

Jokay reached his firing position first, taking cover behind a damaged service vehicle in the middle of the landing area. He quickly scanned the area then continued pouring energy weapons fire at the various combatants scattered along the edge of the spaceport.

The QRF shuttle rose as it passed over the colony then began to climb sharply, finally disappearing behind a faint blue-white flash as it jumped to its circling altitude, well out of reach of any weapons on the surface.

Lannie continued his hard right turn, still flying low over the Persan colony. "QRF, Dragons One-Two and One-Three are circling back for another run on the bad guys. We'll pass low and slow, from the city center toward you, to draw their fire. ETA to target, twenty seconds."

Jokay spotted one of the Dragons in the distance, coming about over the city center. "Copy that, Dragon One-Two," he replied as he rose up just enough to send more fire toward the enemy positions. "QRF, use the cover fire to flank them. Three-sided attack."

Tricia rolled out of her turn, Lannie on her starboard side. "Good locks on the ground targets," she reported, glancing at her tactical display.

"*They see us*," Lannie called over comms as energy rifle blasts rushed toward them from the surface ahead. "*QRF One, time to move.*"

Out of the corner of her eye, Tricia could see the bolts of red-orange plasma begin spitting out of the double-barreled turret under the nose of Lannie's fighter, and she too pressed her firing button, holding it down as they flew slowly over the rooftops, dumping fire into the enemy positions.

As soon as the approaching Dragons opened fire, Abdur rose from his cover along the left side of the landing field and ran for the hangar, crossing the gap in about ten seconds. Once behind the hangar, he moved around its back side, advancing quickly but cautiously, his rifle held at the ready. He stopped between each building, carefully glancing around each corner before crossing the open ground between them, the roar of the Dragon's cannons, the Brodeks energy rifles, and the exploding ground echoing in the distance.

Once he was about forty-five degrees behind and left of the enemy position, he turned inward, advancing to the next corner of the building to get a clear firing line. At the corner of the building, he glanced out for a moment, just as the Dragons passed over the Brodek positions, the ground troops turning away from him as they followed the black fighters that were now pitching up to start another circle back.

Abdur rolled back behind the corner, not wanting to alert the enemy to his change in position. That's when he noticed the bodies lying near the opening of the next building down, on the opposite side of the street. A woman and two children, their bodies smoldering from their plasma wounds, all of them dead. And they were not the only ones. The further down the street he looked, the more bodies he saw.

The Brodek may not have advanced far into the city, but they had done their best to inflict damage wherever they had gone.

"One-Two, in position," Abdur reported calmly over his helmet comms.

Jephen ran along the far right, ducking between buildings, his rifle at the ready. He was about to peak around the corner at the enemy when a man came running around it, nearly colliding with him.

Jephen grabbed the man's arm and stuck out his foot to trip him, sending him spinning around and onto his back. Now with the business-end of Jephen's assault rifle in his face, the man instinctively pulled his hands to his face in an attempt to shield himself from harm.

Realizing it was a Persan and not a Brodek pirate, Jephen raised his rifle and gestured for the man to keep going, which the terrified Persan quickly obeyed.

Another glance up and down the street revealed more bodies, all smoldering from fresh plasma burns. Some of them were moving, others were not. In the distance, he could see columns of heavy, black smoke marking numerous fires no doubt caused by the minute or two of bombardment that the Persan colony had endured prior to Josh's arrival.

"One-Three, in position," Jephen reported over comms.

Jokay checked the tactical display on the inside of his helmet visor. Dragons One-Two and One-Three had just passed over him and were starting their circle back, but Dragon One-One was not on his display. "Josh, you out there?"

"*Dragon One-One is inbound from the water. Two klicks out at angels four,*" Josh replied. "*How can I help?*"

"I need a distraction so I can move in closer. Wanna play pop-up?"

"*Love to,*" Josh replied. "*Ready when you are.*"

"Go for it."

"*One-One, jumping.*"

Jokay heard a thunderous crack behind him and instinctively ducked as Josh's Dragon fighter slid low overhead, less than two meters off the deck, his deceleration thrusters at full power. When Jokay came back up, the Dragon had already assumed a hovering position about two thirds of the way between him and the enemy, now only a meter off the surface. The Dragon opened fire with its forward nose turret, sending a frightening barrage of energy weapons fire at the enemy positions on the city side of the landing field.

Jokay leapt from his position, running out toward the aft end of the hovering Dragon fighter. "QRF One-One, moving." He continued running until he was as close to the tail end of the hovering Dragon as was safe then dropped to one knee, his rifle at his shoulder. "Pop up...NOW!"

"Popping up," Josh replied over comms as he jammed his grav-lift throttles to full power, causing his fighter to surge upward. A split second later, he jammed his main drive throttles all the way forward, pitching up as he accelerated forward.

Abdur stepped out around the corner, calmly walking toward the six Brodek pirates still cowering behind their cover while firing at the Dragon fighter accelerating away from them. He took aim, ready for their rise.

Jephen also stepped out, walking toward the Brodek. The screaming of the Dragon's main drive suddenly disappeared, the fighter jumping away. The fire from the crouching Brodek men ceased, and their heads began to pop up, one by one.

"*BRODEK!*" Jokay's amplified voice beckoned from behind the band of pirates. In unison, they all turned toward the booming voice, bringing their weapons around to engage the challenger.

Jokay stood in the open, his position revealed by the departure of Josh's Dragon. All six Brodek men immediately opened fire, expecting to cut him down with ease, which they would have, had Jokay's personal shield not been activated.

Jokay raised his own weapon and fired, just as shots from behind the Brodek rang out. He fired twice, placing needle-beam plasma bursts into the foreheads of the two men in the center. As his two targets fell, so did the other four behind him.

Six shots from three Ghatazhak, resulting in six kills.

Jokay picked up his pace, moving quickly to the enemy position, his weapon at the ready. But when he arrived, no one was moving. "That was easier than I thought," he said. "Ground forces neutralized," he announced over comms.

"*We've got a lot of wounded in the streets,*" Abdur reported over comms.

"Copy that," Jokay replied. "You two start helping those you can. I'll secure the Brodek weapons. Josh, update the Aurora."

"Incoming message from QRF One," Sima reported from the Aurora's comm-station. "All Brodek forces have been neutralized, but they are requesting assistance for the wounded."

"Ours?" Cameron asked.

"No, sir. Persans only."

"Number?"

"Unknown."

Cameron tapped her comm-set. "Nathan, Persa is clear."

"They need help with wounded civilians," Cameron finished over comms.

"On our way," Nathan replied as he moved his grav-lift throttles forward and started their lift off.

"Chief, QRF One is contact over, managing civilian wounded," Jessica told the Ghatazhak QRF team in the Seiiki's cargo bay over the intercom. "We're headed there now. ETA, three minutes."

"Call the Mirai's crew to action stations and launch the alert Dragons. I want Josh's flight back here and reupped ASAP," Cameron instructed her comms officer.

"Aye, sir," Sima replied.

"Chief Taggert, XO," Cameron called over her comm-set.

"Taggert," Marcus replied.

"Configure the Mirai for an MCI response. Her crew is on their way."

"Already done," Marcus replied.

Cameron smiled. Their crew might be small, but they were good.

"Alert Two Dragons, you are clear to launch," Sima announced over comms. *"Accompany Seiiki to Persa and relieve Alert One flight to return and re-up."*

"Understood," Talisha replied. "Dragon Two-One, launching," she added, pressing the launch button on her flight control stick and sending her ship accelerating toward the exit of the launch tunnel.

"Sima, get me Captain Elias aboard the Bonaventura," Cameron instructed.

"One moment."

Abby entered the bridge, curious as to all of the activity that the Aurora's crew seemed to be experiencing. "What's going on?" she asked Cameron as she approached.

"Captain Elias on comms, sir," Sima announced.

Cameron held up her hand to signal Abby to give her a moment. "Captain Elias, Captain Taylor. We've just put down a Brodek raid on Persa in the Vernay region. Our forces are reporting Persan casualties, unknown number. We're dispatching both shuttles and another flight of Dragons. How many patients can you handle?"

"One moment, Captain," Captain Elias replied over comms.

"Say no more," Abby told Cameron.

"Captain Taylor, Doctor Prokhorov says he can handle twelve serious, six if they are all critical. We also have six empty cabins that can be used as recovery rooms. But all patients will have to be stabilized first and brought over by our shuttles. Our docking systems are not designed to work with Navarro-class shuttles."

"Understood. Can you send Doctor Prokhorov to us to help with the incoming wounded?"

"*He's already packing.*"

"Thank you, Captain. I'll keep you informed."

"Were we expecting this?" Abby wondered.

"Half expecting, half hoping we were wrong," Cameron replied.

Talisha's fighter bounced slightly as she jumped into the Persan atmosphere. "Dragon One-One, Dragon Two-One," she called over comms as the other two Dragons in her flight jumped in behind her, showing up on her tactical display along with Josh's flight in the distance. "Bearing one five seven, twenty-five clicks, angels twenty. We have orders to relieve you on overwatch while you RTB for re-up."

"*Understood,*" Josh replied. "*Alert One flight, returning to base.*"

Talisha watched the three icons representing Josh and his other two Dragons as they disappeared one by one. "Evan, on me. Meika, jump back up to orbit and take system watch while we fly atmo BARCAP."

The Seiiki's inertial dampeners were much stronger than those of the Dragon fighters. Her much larger mass and far less efficient aerodynamics pretty much required it. Therefore, there was almost no perception of the sudden displacement of air that occurred whenever a ship jumped into the atmosphere of a world, unless it was abnormally thick. The only exception was if you jumped into turbulent weather, but only for a few seconds until the dampeners compensated.

"*Dragon Two-Three, on system overwatch,*" Meika reported over comms.

"Talisha and Evan are taking up atmo BARCAP

positions," Jessica reported, studying the Seiiki's tactical display.

"QRF One, Seiiki," Nathan called over comms. ETA, two minutes. What's your status?"

"Seiiki, QRF One," Jokay replied. "We've got thirty-seven casualties and counting. Unknown deceased, but probably a lot. There are a lot of collapsed buildings with people trapped."

"Confirm area secure?"

"From Brodek, yes, but we could use some help with crowd control. It's getting chaotic down here."

"Copy that. QRF Two will join you in a few. Mirai's on her way, fitted for MCI response. See you in two."

Nathan and Jessica both looked out the forward windows, immediately noticing columns of smoke rising all over the colony.

"Does this qualify as something to worry about?" Hanna wondered, also looking out the forward windows from her seat behind Jessica.

"No!" Jokay yelled at the confused Persans carrying one of their wounded. "All wounded go over *there* first!" he instructed, pointing to the area where Abdur was triaging the Persan wounded and assigning transport priorities.

No longer wearing his helmet, Jokay tapped his comm-set. "Jephen, you gotta tell the Persans that everyone goes to the *triage* area, *not* to the QRF shuttle."

"*I did, but their comms are down, and everyone is shouting over each other,*" Jephen replied. "*We need help.*"

"Seiiki and QRF Two will be here in one minute, and the Mirai should be here in less than five. But you've got to keep the flow directed to triage. I don't want to have to stun people to keep them off our shuttle."

"*Copy that.*"

"QRF Pilot, QRF One-One," Jokay called over his comm-set. "Reconfigure for casualty transport."

"*Understood,*" the QRF shuttle's AI pilot acknowledged.

Inside the QRF shuttle's main bay, the eight equipment lockers currently arranged four abreast, in two rows back-to-back across the center of the bay, rose a few centimeters from the floor. The lockers moved forward and aft, the two rows parting from one another. Then, their bottom halves swung upward on their back hinges, folding in half. All eight lockers rose up into the ceiling, leaving only the bottom few centimeters still extruding.

Next, two columns of rescue litters descended from the ceiling, just fore and aft of the retracted equipment bays, their telescoping arms extending down and locking into the deck. The result was two stacks of three litters oriented crossways and equally spaced fore and aft within the bay, providing adequate space for any med-techs who would be attending to the patients during transport.

Nathan rose from the Seiiki's pilot's seat. "Seiiki, put us down at the spaceport, aft ramp facing the triage area, thirty meters away," he instructed as he headed for the exit.

"*Understood,*" the shuttle's AI acknowledged.

"And dispatch an update to the Aurora," Nathan added as he passed Hanna.

"*Launching comm-drone now.*"

Jessica rose to follow, pausing only for Hanna's question.

"You're not even going to wait for landing?" Hanna asked, looking a little unnerved.

"Wasn't transportation fully automated back in your time?"

"Yes, but…"

Jessica ignored her, continuing past and out the exit.

"I guess not," Hanna said to herself, also rising to follow them out.

"*All hands, prepare for landing,*" the AI announced over the shuttle's intercom system.

"Reconfiguration complete," Marcus reported over comms.

"Thanks, Master Chief," Aiden replied as he looked over the Mirai's systems displays. "All good here."

"All good here," Erica echoed.

"*All systems are ready for departure,*" the Mirai's AI reported.

"Aurora, Mirai, ready for departure," Aiden announced.

"*Mirai, Aurora, clear for departure,*" Sima replied over comms.

"*Mirai, XO. Maintain level one cockpit security as long as you have Persans aboard,*" Cameron instructed. "*There could be Brodek spies among them.*"

"Understood," Aiden replied. He looked at Erica. "It's your flight."

Erica went into action, immediately activating the automated roll-out sequence. "Mirai, confirming that we have the updated approach and landing instructions from the incident commander?"

"*Confirmed,*" their AI replied as the shuttle began rolling out of the bay. "*All jumps required are loaded and ready.*"

Josh's Dragon came out of the jump into Dencke's atmosphere less than a kilometer away from the Aurora, aft and to her starboard. He quickly adjusted course, lining up with the ship's longitudinal axis before turning inbound. "It's all yours," he told his AI.

"*I have control,*" his AI confirmed.

"Aurora, Dragon One-One, on auto-final," Josh reported over comms as he leaned his head back and relaxed, probably for the first time since he had taken off twenty minutes earlier.

"*Dragon One-One, Aurora. Clear for landing. Welcome home,*" Sima replied.

Josh watched through the forward canopy as his fighter descended, slowed, and finally passed into the open bay at the back of the Aurora, between her main drive nacelles. His gear extended, locking into place only two seconds before his AI landed the fighter gently onto the recovery deck. Once down, his ship began rolling toward the open doors to the processing bay just inside, its wings folding up into storage position on the way.

"*Aurora, Dragon One-Two, on auto-final,*" Lannie announced over comms.

Josh's fighter passed through the doors, clearing the recovery deck. Its landing gear rotated ninety degrees, and the ship began rolling sideways to make room for the next Dragon about to land.

"Dragon One-Two, Aurora. Clear for landing. Welcome home."

As Josh's fighter rolled sideways, the apparatus they affectionately referred to as the 'plucker' came down, attached itself to Josh's cockpit, and pulled it up out of the Dragon fighter,tracking sideways even faster. Seconds later, his cockpit reached the port-side Dragon storage tunnel and accelerated forward down the dimly lit corridor.

The Seiiki's aft cargo ramp had begun deployment as the ship descended the last ten meters to the surface. By the time it reached level, the ship was low enough that the Ghatazhak jumped to the surface, weapons at the ready. Once on the ground, the three men scanned the area, checking for any new threats that might have developed unnoticed by Jokay and his team. Seeing none, they placed their assault rifles onto their backs, where they automatically locked into place for storage, and headed for the triage area.

The cargo ramp reached its final position, touching the fused-dirt surface as the shuttle settled onto its landing gear and its grav-lift systems began to wind down. Nathan and Jessica were next, each carrying four medical rescue bags. One in each hand, and the other two slung over their shoulders.

Following them were the Aurora's med-techs, Master Sergeant Baris, and specialist Moss. Each of them was guiding two anti-grav rescue litters, one by each hand, stacked with as many medical rescue kits as they could carry. Behind them followed Martina and Hanna, also carrying as many med-kits as they could manage.

As soon as Jessica saw the chaos ahead, she broke into a jog, leaving Nathan and the others behind as she headed for the triage area to take command. As a trained spec-ops, she had extensive training in mass casualty incident management. Furthermore, her years of training with the Ghatazhak made her intimately aware of their combat medical training. She also knew that, although Nathan was the most senior officer on site, she was infinitely more qualified to run the response on the ground and wasted no time in doing so.

Nathan was taken aback slightly by the number of wounded. Not just the ones already at the triage area, but also the stream of people hobbling or being outright carried toward it. Nathan had seen his fair share of wounded in his career, probably more than most. But there was always that multi-second lag when presented with such massive suffering. To this day, he still marveled at the ability of experienced medical-rescue specialists to ignore that suffering and simply do their jobs. It was a skill he hoped he would never have the opportunity to manage.

Master Sergeant Baris and Specialist Moss moved past Nathan, guiding their gear-laden, floating litters ahead of them, followed by Martina, who was now jogging toward the triage area, her bags bouncing against her as she ran.

"My God," Hanna exclaimed as she stepped up next to Nathan. Despite all she had witnessed during the bio-digital plague fifteen hundred years ago, the site of so many wounded still gave her pause.

Hanna's reaction, although similar to Nathan's, served to snap him out of it as he continued following his team to the triage area.

"Go talk to the Persan leaders and explain to them what we're doing," Jessica instructed Nathan. "They're going to be freaked, so keep them calm.

Above all else, we need order, or we *will* start stunning people."

"I'll take care of it," Nathan assured her, heading toward the city.

With no specific function in the current response, Loki had chosen to go to the wing ready room, where he knew the rest of the pilots would be nervously awaiting orders. But when he arrived, he found only four pilots, which meant that two flights of Dragons were currently operating.

"Anyone know what's going on?" Loki asked the others.

"All we know is a QRF activation on Persa," Allet replied.

"Josh, Lannie, and Tricia were first up," Mick added. "Talisha, Evan, and Meika were second."

"Is Talisha's flight still the ready-up?" Loki wondered.

"They launched a few minutes ago," Allet replied. "We're next up for QRF for a second incident."

"Where's Captain Nash?" Loki asked.

"He went to the bridge," Tika replied. "Said he'd update us when he learned more."

"Did you contact Master Chief Taggert?" Loki wondered.

"Why would we do that?" Nikolas wondered.

Loki tapped his comm-set. "Marcus, Loki."

"Taggert," Marcus replied over comm-sets.

"What's our shuttle status?"

"Both went to Persa," Marcus replied. "Mirai was configured for MCI response."

"Thanks." Loki looked at Nikolas. "That's why."

"Deck chiefs *always* know what's going on," Mick agreed.

"The fact that both shuttles went to Persa, and the Mirai is configured for MCI tells me that the battle is over, and that the mission has switched to rescue and recovery," Loki explained.

"Yeah, but who got injured?" Allet asked.

"Commander Sheehan, XO," Cameron called over comm-sets.

Loki tapped his comm-set. "Commander Sheehan."

"Get the Acuna ready for departure."

"Yes, sir," Loki replied. "Mission?"

"Unknown at the moment. We're still waiting for an update. I'm guessing it will be either to help evac the wounded or to make an emergency run to Hadria for medical supplies. We should know by the time you're spun up and ready for takeoff."

"On our way," Loki said, tapping his comm-set again as he headed for the exit. "Alex, Loki. Get everyone to the Acuna ASAP. I'll meet you there."

Tricia stared out of the front of her canopy as her AI guided her fighter across the threshold into the Dragon recovery bay at the aft end of the Aurora. As she set down, she could see Lannie's fighter inside the processing bay forward of the recovery deck as it began sliding to starboard. In another minute, she would be in the same place, starting her slide to port as the plucker lifted her cockpit out of the fighter and carried it to its next one sitting in the storage tunnel, fueled, armed, and ready to go.

The advantage to the system was that you didn't have to wait around for your ship to be made ready for flight again. The disadvantage was that you didn't get any break time between flights. It reminded her of doing 'touch and gos' during basic flight training back on Earth. Thankfully, the AI took some of the stress off of them. Launch and recovery, by requirement, were handled by the AI, which bought the pilots at least an extra minute of rest.

But the truth was that twenty minutes of flight, only about half of which was spent in actual combat, was not that tiring. And their AIs could tell when they became too fatigued to fly, because their performance would begin to degrade. Luckily, their AIs were able to compensate for that degradation and even take over completely should it become necessary. But in order to fight, a Dragon *required* a pilot in the cockpit. While the AI could take defensive measures, it could not destroy assets or take human life without authorization from its pilot, or in the absence of a pilot, from command authority aboard its home ship, the Aurora.

All these things combined to provide some measure of confidence, even in newly trained pilots, that they had a good chance of getting back alive. The fact was a Dragon fighter was designed to fly on the edge, and doing so was fraught with risks. Without their AIs, very few pilots would be able to successfully complete a mission in a Dragon. Not even Josh, although he would never admit it.

"Where is Elder Seemas?" Nathan asked one of the Persans trying to control the chaos at the edge of the city.

"No one knows," the man admitted. "He may be in one of the collapsed buildings."

"Listen, you have to get your people to follow the orders of my people. The men in the black combat armor."

"We have to get these people to safety," the man argued. "The Brodek may return..."

"If they do, we'll handle them," Nathan assured him.

"Like you handled this?" the man challenged.

"All your wounded will be cared for," Nathan assured him.

"And can you bring back the dead?" the man barked angrily. He looked Nathan in the eyes. "*You* caused this." After a moment, he added, "*You* need to end it."

Nathan stood there as the man turned away, yelling directions at his people again. Something hit him. It wasn't guilt. It was more like a realization. The man was right. He had thought he was *helping* these people, but in reality, it had been more about helping *his* people and about getting the Aurora back in service.

Even more disturbing was that he knew he was doing just that from the very beginning. But like all others who believed they were doing something for the greater good, he had let the strength of that belief justify the risks he had imposed upon the people of the Vernay worlds. He had fully intended to protect them, but he had failed.

Josh's fighter shot out of the launch tube, its AI firing its attitude thrusters and driving its nose up just enough to clear the rapidly approaching, nearly vertical rock face. The fighter's main engines went to full power, and the ship rocketed upward, jumping a split second later.

His canopy now filled with the blackness of space, Josh took control of his fighter again, rolling left and right, yawing and translating, just to verify that the new fighter-body was working properly. He knew his AI wouldn't have allowed the ship to launch if everything wasn't working, but he just felt better checking his ship's responsiveness just after launch. He still didn't quite trust this whole musical-fighters system, although he did appreciate that it got him back into the action more quickly.

This time, however, was different. There was no urgency to get to Persa, so he would wait in orbit for the other two members of his flight group. That gave him about two minutes to eat and pee into a tube.

At least he'd get to eat.

Only moments after the first shuttle from the Bonaventura landed on the Aurora's flight deck, the black QRF shuttle jumped in nearby, swooping in low and landing fast.

Doctor Prokhorov was the first one off the shuttle, two of his own med-techs hot on his heels with rescue gear. He sprinted across the massive flight deck, arriving as the QRF shuttle's side doors slid open.

Inside, all six litters were loaded with the most critically injured, tended to by Specialist Moss and Martina.

While Doctor Prokhorov had no experience in mass casualty incidents, he did know how to treat trauma, and he jumped in and got to work.

It was going to be a long day.

* * *

Nathan returned from the city, heading straight to the triage area where Jessica was barking out instructions to the Aurora's med-techs and to any Persan volunteers with medical training.

The QRF shuttle had already departed with the

first load of critically wounded Persans. By now, the triage area had tripled in size and number. Those who were injured but still ambulatory had gathered to the side to treat themselves as best they could, using the med-kits brought by the Mirai. Patients who were not critical, but needed more advanced care to remain stable until they could be safely transported, were moved to the Mirai, which had landed only a few minutes ago and was configured to handle at least two dozen patients.

But people were still coming in on litters from deep within the Persan colony. And the nature of their injuries had changed from plasma blasts to crush injuries, which were far more difficult to assess *and* treat.

Luckily, none of this seemed to faze Jessica, the Ghatazhak, or the med-techs. Not even Martina, who had suffered a far greater time-shift than the Aurora's crew, seemed affected by the chaos and gore that surrounded them.

"*Persa Command, Dragon One-One is back with a flight of three,*" Josh called over comms. "*Where do you want us?*"

Nathan tapped his comm-set. "Divide your flights into three two-man teams. One pair maintains system integrity while the other two pairs start jumping between Vernay worlds, in case the Brodek decide to strike somewhere else today."

"*Copy that,*" Josh acknowledged. "*Are we still letting them shoot first?*"

"Negative," Nathan replied. "Don't even bother warning them. Just take them out."

"*Works for me.*"

Jessica walked over to Nathan. "You okay?" she asked. "You have that look on your face."

Nathan looked at her. "What look is that?"

"The one that says, 'I'm about to start another war.'"

Nathan sighed. "I guess I am."

CHAPTER NINE

Alex stood at the top of the Acuna's port cargo ramp, staring out at the organized chaos that was the Persan spaceport. They had set down on the south edge of the landing field, with their aft end facing the center of the field to ease with the unloading of the medical supplies they had brought from Hadria.

Alex had grown up in the badlands, and cruelty at the hands of pirates was not unfamiliar to her. But she had never seen them kill so many people so indiscriminately. Her own family's dynamic had been drastically changed by one pirate's depraved act. She was imagining how so many Persan families were now affected in the same way.

The question she could not shake was, *Was it worth it?*

Many had proposed standing up against the Brodek and other pirate clans. Some had even called for war against the Korsan itself. But those people tended to disappear rather quickly. Life in the badlands might be free from taxation and overregulation by governments, but the tributes required by the pirate clans to avoid such punishments were a tax in themselves; one that provided no services other than a much better chance of being allowed to live.

Josi stepped up next to her sister, staring out from the top of the ramp, while Kit and Mori stood guard to prevent the ship from being rushed by panicked Persans. "This is *exactly* why we shouldn't be part of this," she said. "You see those two ships over there?" she added, pointing to the two destroyed cargo shuttles, both of which were only slightly smaller than the Acuna. "That could've been us."

"We have escorts," Alex reminded her. "And shields."

"You know damn well that our shields could be overcome in less than a minute if they hit us with enough firepower. Honestly, one or two blasts from a Brodek gunship would take us out. Are two Dragon fighters going to be able to take *a gunship* out before that happens?"

Alex had no response.

"I'm telling you, Alex, these people don't care about *any* of us. We're all just a means to *their* ends."

"What would you have me do, Jo?" Alex finally asked. "They fixed our ship. They upgraded. We have a *contractual* obligation."

"Which doesn't mean crap if we're dead."

"*Everything* we do has risk. And they're doing all they can to mitigate that risk. Do you really think we'd be any safer on our own?"

"Yes I do."

"I'm pretty sure Pop would disagree with you," Alex stated.

"That's low, Alex, even for you."

"You started it," Alex defended.

Josi turned and walked away without another word.

"That *was* kind of harsh," Loki commented as he stepped up to join Alex at the top of the ramp.

"She's right," Alex stated. "We shouldn't be part of this."

"No one should. Not us, not them," Loki replied, pointing to the chaos outside.

"You've been through this kind of thing before, haven't you?"

"I've seen far worse."

"Worse than this?" Alex asked in disbelief.

"I've seen entire worlds glassed or destroyed completely. I've lost two wives, my child, and my entire family."

Alex looked at him. "How do you deal with that kind of loss?"

"You just do. Everyone has a different way of coping. For me, it's best to just keep working. To keep serving a purpose you believe in."

"What purpose are *you* serving?" she wondered.

Loki took a long, deep breath, letting it out slowly as he pondered her question. "I guess I just try to do what's right."

"And how do you know what's *right?*"

"Sometimes I don't. That's why I follow Captain Scott."

"I don't understand."

After another breath, Loki tried to explain. "For most of us, our decisions, our sense of right and wrong, are skewed by our own needs. Greed, lust, revenge...a desire to provide for and protect our families. Even the socio-economic environment in which we live can influence our decisions. Nathan is the one person I know who is capable of putting his own needs aside and doing what is right for the many rather than for the few or the one."

Alex thought for a moment, unsure that she agreed with everything he was saying. "But didn't he risk everything to try to save his friend Vladimir?"

"Yes, but he didn't do so *just* for himself. He did it for *everyone* on his crew. We are asked to take risks every day. We have to know that our leader will do everything possible to protect us and keep us safe."

"And you trust Captain Scott *that much?*"

"I do."

"I'm not sure I could ever trust someone that

much," Alex admitted, before turning to head back inside.

Loki watched her walk away then headed down the ramp, pushing through the crowd of Persans at the bottom, making his way toward the Seiiki at the other side of the landing field. He didn't know what else to say to Alex. She would have to come to her own conclusions, the same way Loki had.

Loki spotted Nathan speaking with a Persan woman near the Seiiki's aft cargo ramp. As he approached, he looked to his right at the triage and staging areas that had been set up. By now, half of the Aurora's crew was on the surface of Persa, regardless of their lack of emergency medical training. He even noticed several groups of people from other Vernay worlds, evidenced by their lack of Persan fashion, which was quite specific to their culture.

On one side of the triage area, there appeared to be a makeshift clinic that had been set up to provide initial care to those with less severe injuries. The other side was the exact opposite. It was simply a large tent where the bodies of the dead were being collected.

As he approached the Seiiki, the sound of an arriving jump ship came from behind him. He turned, spotting the QRF shuttle as it passed over the shoreline, settling in for a landing about ten meters from the triage area. The moment its grav-lift systems began to spin down to idle, its side doors slid open, and the Aurora's two med-techs jumped out. They began directing local volunteers to unload the rescue litters from the shuttle and move them to the triage area in order to transfer the next group of critically injured Persans back to the Aurora.

"Loki!" Nathan called.

Loki turned and continued to the Seiiki.

"How much were you able to bring?"

"Didn't even halfway fill the Acuna's holds," Loki admitted. "But Chiqua said she'll be able to fill us by this time tomorrow. It was just poor timing."

"You need help unloading?" Nathan asked. "I can get some Persans over there."

"It's already happening," Loki replied. "Kit and Mori had to hold them back so they didn't run off with everything. We should be empty within the hour."

"Good. I want you back at the Aurora as soon as possible," Nathan explained. "I don't want the Acuna on the ground if the Brodek return."

"You think they'd strike again so soon?"

"If you're trying to inflict as much terror and fear as possible, attacking during the relief effort would be a good way to do so."

"Well you've got three Dragons patrolling the system and four more Dragon pilots itching to respond back on the Aurora."

"I'm sure they are."

"Alex seemed a bit shaken by all this," Loki told Nathan. "I think she may be having second thoughts."

"You want me to talk to her?" Nathan wondered.

"I think it's better if you let her come to you, assuming she feels the need. She's under a lot of pressure, what with her entire family depending on her and the Acuna. She sees this arrangement as a way to get her family back to normal."

"And her sister doesn't," Nathan concluded. "Yeah, I noticed the tension between them."

"It's even worse on board. Especially since Shane usually sides with Josi. Alex's only ally is her father, and now he's incommunicado."

Nathan sighed. "Unfortunately, I don't think this is going to get less dangerous any time soon."

"That's what I figured," Loki replied, turning to head back to the Acuna.

Nathan was not happy. This whole arrangement was headed in a direction he had hoped to avoid, and he was only seeing one way out of it.

* * *

Nathan, Jessica, and Hanna walked across the Aurora's shuttle bay, making their way toward the exit. As they neared the hatch, Cameron appeared, coming to greet them.

"You guys look like crap," Cameron declared, shocked by their long faces and bloodied clothing.

"It's been a long day," Nathan replied.

Hanna just kept going, passing by them all without a word and disappearing through the hatch.

"Is she alright?" Cameron asked.

"She will be," Nathan assured her.

"She's tougher than I gave her credit for," Jessica admitted. "She had no idea what she was doing, but she was shoulder to shoulder with us, doing everything she could to help."

"What was the final count?" Cameron asked.

"Three hundred and eighty-seven wounded, two hundred and ninety-five dead, and thirty-two still missing," Jessica replied.

"How are the Persans doing?" Cameron wondered.

"This whole thing may fall apart," Nathan told her. "I need all department heads in the command briefing room ASAP."

Cameron looked them over. "Maybe you should shower and change first?"

"One hour then," Nathan agreed, moving past her.

"He thinks it's his fault, doesn't he," Cameron said after Nathan left.

"Doesn't he always?" Jessica commented, continuing past Cameron.

* * *

A shower and a hot meal had been a welcome respite, though they had done little to distract Nathan from the situation he found himself facing.

"As you were," he said as he entered the command briefing room. He sat down, reviewing the faces of his command staff. "Where's Jess?"

"On her way," Cameron stated.

"She'll have to catch up," Nathan said. "The Persans are threatening to drop out of the trade arrangement if we cannot guarantee their safety."

"Can we?" Cameron questioned.

"*Should* we?" Robert added. When he found everyone staring at him, he decided to add to his statement. "Surely everyone here is asking themselves the same thing. I know what the Brodek and all the other pirate clans are doing to people like the Persans is bad, and in most civilizations would be considered criminal, but it *is* a balance that has worked for these people for more than a century. Then we came along, bypassed it, and upset the system. Are we not at least partially to blame here?"

"Perhaps," Nathan agreed, "but if so, the Brodek should have come after *us*, not the Persans."

"Perhaps that was their intent," Cameron suggested. "They don't know where we are, so they used the Persans as a proxy."

"They're testing us," Jessica opined as she entered. "They have no other way to determine our force strength. They blow the crap out of a few hundred Persans, get them to boot us out, and see what we do," she continued as she took her seat. "If we do nothing, they'll assume we're all bark and no bite. If we respond, they'll find out what we're really made of. Either way, they force us to respond."

"So the ball is in *our* court," Nathan stated.

"You're bypassing my question," Robert insisted.

"I think we can all agree that what the Brodek are doing is *wrong*," Nathan said. "However, Robert makes a good point. *Is* this a fight we should be taking on, especially considering our current situation?"

"We can't make that decision without better intel on their forces," Jessica insisted.

"From what we've seen so far, they pretty much suck," Kit offered.

"But we may not have seen their best just yet," Jessica argued. "How many troops do they actually have? I mean, if we're talking thousands, then it doesn't matter how poorly trained they are as long as they are compliant."

"We need to recon their home system," Nathan stated. "Which is why I'm taking the Seiiki on a cold-coast through the Crowden system immediately after this meeting."

"Why not send a recon drone?" Laza wondered.

"Our drones would tip off the Brodek that we have bigger ships than the Seiiki."

"They already know," Cameron argued. "Vodar had to have told them."

"He told them what we *said* and what he *saw*," Jessica corrected, "which was only a single room in medical. Not exactly solid evidence."

"Exactly," Nathan agreed. "Sending a recon drone would confirm whatever Vodar told them. Plus, for all we know, our drones might be unique to Expedition-class ships, which would be even more revealing. They already know about the Seiiki."

"They already know about our Dragons as well," Cameron argued. "Why not send one of them?"

"We can't spare them," Robert stated. "If we're going to maintain twenty-four seven BARCAPs of the Vernay, we're going to need every ship and every pilot. Even then, they're going to be putting in a lot of flight time."

"Using the Seiiki for the recon flight isn't up for debate," Nathan pointed out. "I'll fly the mission, and Jess will go with me."

"Damn right," Jessica confirmed.

"And if you come under fire?"

"I'll jump out of there so fast it will make their heads spin," Nathan replied.

"Then you're considering a direct attack against the Brodek," Kit surmised.

"Assuming it appears doable, and the risk is not too great," Nathan confirmed. "But knowing what we're up against is only a third of the equation."

"What are the other two?" Aiden wondered.

"Robert covered the second," Nathan said. "But his question can't be answered without knowing the other two variables. That brings us to you, Vlad."

"Why me?"

"Because you're the chief engineer."

"*Da, konyeshna.*"

"A few days ago, you said the Aurora could fly."

"I meant she *technically* could fly," Vladimir clarified. "I did not say it was a good *idea* for her to fly."

"Can she?"

"Grav-lift systems are working, but they still need

to be recalibrated. I would not advise using them to launch."

"They worked well enough to get us up on our gear," Jessica argued.

"Very different than actually climbing up to orbit."

"What about propulsion and maneuvering?" Nathan asked.

"Main propulsion is working. So is maneuvering except for our bow thrusters. They were too heavily damaged to repair. They must be completely replaced, along with most of our bow."

"We still have half a dozen hull breaches," Cameron reminded them.

"All of which can be sealed off until they are repaired," Nathan defended. "Remember, we operated the original Aurora with the entire front quarter of her open to space."

"That's because we had no other choice," Cameron pointed out.

"We can install rescue airlocks on the breached compartments," Vladimir suggested. "That would give us access to those sections as needed, wearing pressure suits of course."

"I'm more worried about weapons and shields," Jessica commented. "I know all our dorsal shields are working, as well as our lateral shields, but what about ventral shielding?"

"Most of the shield emitters were damaged on impact. We were concentrating on replacing the jump emitters, so we haven't even started on shield emitters."

"Which brings us to the big question," Nathan said. "Can this ship jump?"

Vladimir looked to Abby. Nathan took the cue and nodded to her.

"The Aurora's jump drive is fully functional," Abby began. "However, there are some complications. Namely, the lack of an AI."

"What does our AI have to do with our jump drive?" Nathan wondered.

"Everything and nothing," Abby replied. "The Expedition-class ships were designed with what we call 'fluid jump calculations'. Their AIs constantly recalculate thousands of likely next jumps, updating them every nanosecond, in order to provide instant and *highly accurate* jumps."

"And our AI is still down," Nathan surmised.

"Without an AI, jumps would have to be calculated in much the same way that we did in the early days," Abby explained.

"We can pull a backup Dragon AI module and task it to assist with the jump calculations," Vladimir suggested. "But that's all it would be able to do."

"Aren't all the AIs the same?" Nathan asked.

"Because of her greater range, the number of possible jumps being calculated by the Aurora's AI is exponentially greater in number than those by a Dragon's AI," Vladimir explained.

"And jump calculations are *very* complex," Abby added.

"You used to do them manually, didn't you?" Nathan said.

"Yes, but those were short-range jumps, all less than ten light years."

"But you *can* do the jump calculations manually, right?"

"Yes," Abby confirmed. "And with each manually calculated jump that we execute, the more precise my calculations will become. I should be able to create a standard jump table to make the calculations easier."

"There is one other problem," Vladimir stated. "Without our AI, the Aurora must be flown *manually*."

"That's not so bad," Nathan figured.

"You do not understand," Vladimir insisted. "I mean...*manually*."

"You mean like stick-and-rudder manually?" Nathan asked.

Vladimir looked confused. "The Aurora does not have a rudder, Nathan. I mean straight manual flight, without any AI enhancements whatsoever."

"So fly her like a barge and not a fighter," Nathan surmised.

"Like a really slow and not very maneuverable barge," Vladimir corrected.

Nathan sighed. "What about weapons?"

"All four topside fixed guns are fully operational," Vladimir boasted.

"I'm assuming our ventral fixed turrets are not?" Nathan surmised.

"They are not."

"What about our tracked guns?" Jessica wondered.

"Our upper tracks are fine. Our midship tracks are fine, except the bow pass-through is damaged. So guns can only be moved from side to side through the midship transfer tunnel," Vladimir explained.

"What about our ventral track?" Nathan wondered.

"Same as the midship track. The front quarters on both sides are damaged."

"So we can deploy weapons, but we can't shift them from side to side during battle," Nathan concluded. "What about our plasma torpedo tubes?"

"They are fine," Vladimir assured him.

"Well that's good news."

"Not really. Both plasma torpedo generators are only capable of producing sixty-eight percent of their maximum power output. We haven't even started figuring out what's wrong with them."

"Am I missing something?" Dominic, who had thus far remained silent, asked. "If the grav-lift systems are unstable, how do you expect to get this ship through the atmosphere and back into space?"

"Easy," Nathan replied. "We jump her."

"Don't you need forward momentum, first?"

"Only a little," Nathan said, "which the planet's rotation already provides."

Dominic nodded. "I suppose it does."

Nathan noticed Cameron at the far end of the table. "Something on your mind, Cam?"

"I'm wondering what happens if we *do* take out the Brodek. Won't that create a power vacuum?"

"If we *do* take them out, that will make us responsible for *all* the worlds they currently control, not just those in the Vernay region," Robert opined.

"I don't see any other way," Nathan admitted. "At this point, we either take responsibility, or we walk away and let Jakome pay off our debts."

"Is that such a bad thing?" Dominic wondered.

"If this ship isn't here to protect the freedom, peace, and prosperity of humanity, then what is it here for?" Nathan stated. "Why are we even fixing her? If we're just going to find a world and make it our own, we don't need a ship this size. Without a mission, the Aurora is just a ship. With one, she is an ideal. She is hope. Hope for those who left the comfortable embrace of the Alliance for the sake of freedom. They deserve better than to be at the mercy of pirates and organized mafias."

"But how is that *our* responsibility?" Dominic questioned.

"Because we *choose* to make it ours," Nathan replied.

After a moment, Dominic answered. "Fair enough. Count me in."

"I already had," Nathan replied with a slight grin. "Vlad, get this ship ready to fly and, hopefully, ready to fight. The sooner the better."

"I thought that was what I've *been* doing," Vladimir replied.

* * *

Although the battle had lasted mere minutes, management of the wounded had taken hours. But as night fell on Persa, order had been somewhat restored. All the wounded had either been treated on Persa or evacuated to Dencke for more advanced care in the Aurora's or the Bonaventura's medical departments.

The Ghatazhak had chosen to remain on Persa to help maintain order. There was still a lot of destruction to deal with in the city, and many people had lost their homes or businesses. Despite the Persan ethos, times like this sometimes drove people to do things they wouldn't normally do, and the Persans had no security forces. Like any civilization, massive disruption promoted chaos. The Ghatazhak would do their best to prevent that from happening so that the Persans could concentrate on caring for the wounded, rebuilding their colony, and burying their dead.

Jokay and Abdur had chosen to sift through the wreckage of three cargo shuttles that had been unfortunate enough to be on the surface when the attack had begun. One of the ships was just a pile of rubble, but the other two were still somewhat intact, with their cockpits still whole.

The first one had been empty, and the main console in the cockpit was pretty much destroyed. But the second one appeared undamaged from the outside. After pushing a large piece of wreckage aside, he and Abdur gained access and went inside.

The interior was more burned than they had expected. From the look of things, one section of the main console had shorted and blown out, with the pilot taking the full force of it in the face, dying instantly.

Jokay noticed something on the dead man's neck, just above the burnt collar of his jacket. It was the tip of a tattoo, but when he pulled the burnt collar away from the dead man's neck, it pulled the skin off with it.

"What is that?" Abdur wondered.

"The tip of a tattoo, I think," Jokay replied.

"Hold on," Abdur said, pulling his combat data pad out of his thigh pouch. He held it up, calling up the photos they had taken of the dead Brodek men, stopping at one with the top portion of a tattoo showing above his jacket. He held it next to the dead man's burnt neck. "Looks the same, doesn't it?"

"Could be," Jokay agreed. "Did they all have that tat?"

"Yup."

"Interesting."

"Retired Brodek maybe?" Abdur suggested.

"Maybe," Jokay agreed. He moved over to the side of the cockpit to the main computer panel, pulling the data cores from it. "Let's take these back to the QRF shuttle and see if we can figure out who this guy is and where he's been."

"Nav logs, jump logs, comm logs?" Abdur assumed.

"Anything that can tell us something useful." Jokay agreed. "We don't know shit about these fuckers just yet."

"We know they're hardly worth killing," Abdur commented as he grabbed the data cores and headed out.

* * *

"We're jumping direct?" Jessica asked, noticing the jump plot on the Seiiki's navigation display. "Putting a lot of trust in Laza's theories, aren't you?"

"More like Abby's," Nathan corrected. "Are you telling me you don't see a conspiracy in the whole interdimensional barrier damage thing?"

"Of course I do," Jessica admitted. "You're also jumping directly into Crowden's atmo. I thought we were going to cold-coast."

"I just told them that so that Cam wouldn't try to talk me out of it."

"You'll be signaling the Brodek that we know where they are."

"That's my intention," Nathan said as he turned the Seiiki toward the desired heading.

"Kind of ruins any hope of surprise, doesn't it?"

"Yeah, but it will give us excellent intel on their defensive capabilities, and hopefully it will make them think twice about attacking another Vernay world."

"You don't really believe that, do you?"

"No, but I can dream, can't I?"

"Are you at least going to stealth jump?"

"Nope. You got a problem with that?"

"Of course not. I love force recon, but I can already tell you what we're going to learn."

"And what would that be?" Nathan asked, humoring her.

"That the Brodek can't shoot for shit, and they probably can't operate their air defenses any better, assuming they even work at all."

"What makes you think they won't work?" Nathan wondered.

"Pirates aren't generally well disciplined. They're more interested in enjoying themselves than doing preventative maintenance, especially on systems they don't expect to ever use."

"You don't think they expect to use their air defenses?"

"According to Vodar, the Brodek are the strongest clan in the entire sector. Their neighboring clans wouldn't dream of attacking them, and they certainly don't expect any of their *victims* to attack them."

"You do realize that automation is really big in this century, right?"

"When's the last time you saw automation that didn't depend on humans to keep it running?"

"Pretty much everything made by SilTek," Nathan argued.

"Judging by their cobbled-together shuttles and fighters, I doubt the Brodek spent millions of credits on state-of-the-art, SilTek surface defense systems."

"Let's hope you're right about that," Nathan commented as he reached for the jump control console. "Ready?"

"I always am."

Nathan pressed the jump button, and a second later, the cockpit filled with the subdued blue-white flash. The next second, the ship bounced and rocked as it suddenly found itself in the atmosphere of Crowden.

"We got lucky," Nathan declared, noting the darkness outside. "Night *and* a cloud layer."

"We're only ten clicks from the colony," Jessica reported, her eyes fixed on the sensor display. "I'm collecting a butt-load of emissions. Voice comms, data links, automated command and control, even something that looks like some sort of entertainment feed."

"Really?"

"From the number of signals, this colony must have at least ten thousand people in it," Jessica added. "Maybe twenty."

"Well that doesn't sound good."

"Oh crap, we've been detected."

Nathan glanced at the threat display but saw no warning indicators.

"Inbound shuttle, this is Crowden Spaceport Control. You are out of the designated approach corridor. Climb to five zero and turn to heading one five seven to intercept landing beacon."

Jessica laughed. "He sounds pissed."

"Uh, sorry about that," Nathan replied over comms. "We've...uh...we've been having problems with our jump nav-com lately. Turning to one five seven and climbing to five zero."

"Inbound shuttle, we're not picking up your transponder."

"That's because it's not working. We were kinda hoping we could get fixed while we're here."

"Inbound shuttle, identify yourself."

"This is the......Nashica."

"What is your cargo?"

"We're empty. We were hoping to pick up some work on Crowden."

"What is your port of origin?"

"Control......breaking......can......repeat?" Nathan switched off the comms. "That conversation was going nowhere."

"The *Nashica*?"

Nathan shrugged. "Keep an eye out for that landing beacon he was talking about. If we can turn inbound on it as instructed, we might be able to fly right in and get a close look before they realize we're not a privateer looking for work."

"I'm pretty sure they already figured that out," Jessica replied as a threat warning light began flashing. "They're painting us."

"How many?"

"Eight...make that twelve. Various ranges and bearings. Now sixteen."

"Go active," Nathan instructed as he prepared an escape jump.

"Already scanning." The threat warning light began flashing rapidly, an audible alarm sounding at the same time. "Crap. Missile launches. Lots of them. Ten seconds."

"I think that's enough recon, don't you?" Nathan announced as he pressed the jump button.

* * *

Looking her best, as usual, Shya exited her room and headed down the stairs to the main lobby. Her descent was always enough to attract the attention of a few potential customers, although she currently was planning on spending time with only one of her regulars.

Despite the fact that Shya did not care for the old man who controlled her future, she did appreciate that he had never made any sexual advances toward her. Still, he could be scary at times. He had the same stare that all the old pirates had. The look that told you he could kill and not lose a moment's sleep over the act.

On her way down, she did not spot the old man, which was odd. Despite all his faults, he was quite punctual. But after a pause and a second scan of the room, he was nowhere to be found.

Shya continued across the room, headed for the bar. One of the perks of her job was the free booze. A shot before each new meeting and transaction helped considerably, and the fact that she didn't have to pay for it helped even more. The proprietor was already getting thirty percent of her earnings, and the Brodek another fifty, leaving her very little to save toward her dream of escaping. But her family was indebted to the Brodek, and her body was the only way to pay that debt.

That was all about to end.

The bartender placed her usual drink in front of Shya as she stepped up to the bar. She had barely taken a sip when a man stepped up next to her, leaning against the bar and facing her. Like most men, he had a smile on his face. But not the usual, lecherous grin that most had when sizing her up. This man was also quite fit and not bad looking, which also set off some alarms in her head.

Not wanting to interact with the stranger, Shya picked up her drink and turned to her left but was surprised to find a similar-looking man standing on that side as well.

"Hi there," the man on her left said.

Shya turned back right, only to find that the first man had stepped in closer.

"You should probably down that now," the first man told her. "You're going to need it."

It wasn't the first time Shya had felt threatened. In

fact, it was one of the hazards of the job. She signaled the bartender, who under normal circumstances would have signaled the bouncer. Instead, the bartender just shrugged.

Shya looked back at the first man. "Who are you? What do you want?"

"I'm Kit, and that's Mori," the first man replied. "You need to come with us."

"I'm not going anywhere with you," Shya insisted, turning to look for the bouncer herself.

"No one is going to harm you," Kit assured her. "However, we are not opposed to stunning you and dragging your ass out."

"Where are you taking me?" Shya demanded, resigning herself to the situation for now. One thing she had learned over the years was to play along and wait for an opportunity to turn any situation to her advantage.

"To answer some questions," Kit said, slapping a restraint cuff on her right hand and pulling it around behind her back as he turned her toward Mori to connect the cuff to her other hand.

Kit and Mori turned Shya toward the exit and started marching her out. At the same time, the three women who had come to Kataoka with her came down the stairs, accompanied by two more similar-looking men. They too were restrained.

By now, more than a few men in the saloon had taken notice, and some had stepped up, thinking they needed to protect their entertainment.

"That would be a really bad idea," Kit told the first Kataokan who approached.

Just then, four more men entered, each of them carrying heavy assault rifles. The four men fanned out, their weapons held at the ready.

The Kataokan looked back over his shoulder, spotting the four armed men, then back to Kit. "Where are you taking them?"

"You always stick up for Brodek spies?" Kit asked.

It was more of an accusation than a question, and the Kataokan man knew it. Without another word, he stepped aside.

Shya suddenly got a sinking feeling.

* * *

Nathan and Jessica walked through the hatch from the hangar bay into the central corridor just as Cameron was stepping off the port elevator.

"You're back early," Cameron commented as she approached. "I take it you didn't cold-coast through the Crowden system."

"Of course not," Jessica chuckled.

"I knew it."

"You did, huh?" Nathan remarked.

"How much intel did you get?" Cameron asked, not taking his bait.

"A lot more than we would have on a cold-coast," Jessica admitted. "I'll start reviewing the scans."

"You both might want to head down to the brig," Cameron told them. "Seems our Ghatazhak scored some additional intel sources while you were gone."

* * *

The Aurora's brig consisted of four cells clustered around a central guard station and two interview rooms. Designed to house four prisoners, each cell now held six, all of them provocatively dressed.

Nathan and Jessica walked in, immediately heading for the guard station where Jokay sat with a smile on his face.

"What are you smiling about?" Jessica wondered.

"Are you kidding?" Jokay replied. "This is the best duty I've had in weeks."

"Who are all these women?" Nathan wondered.

"Prostitutes," Jokay replied.

"Planning a party?" Nathan joked.

"We found a body in one of the damaged shuttles on Persa. The pilot. He had what looked like a Brodek tattoo on his neck, so we pulled the data cores from his navigation and comm-systems. Turns out he was the handler for all these ladies."

"Handler?" Nathan asked. "You mean *pimp?*"

"These women were put onto each Brodek world to gather intel," Jokay explained. "Probably on *us*. It looks like the dead pilot's job was to visit all six cells once a week to collect the Brodek's cut of the girls' earnings, as well as any intelligence they had picked up from their customers."

"This is exactly why men shouldn't be in charge," Jessica quipped.

"Have we learned anything?" Nathan asked.

"Kit is interviewing one of them now," Jokay replied, pointing to interrogation room one. "We only got them back here about half an hour ago."

Jessica moved over to the door of the interrogation room and tapped on the window. A moment later, the door opened and Kit came out, closing the door behind him.

"Learn anything?" Jessica asked Kit.

"Only that she's scared shitless."

"Of us?" Nathan asked.

"Of the Brodek mostly. Her name's Shya. Best I can tell, she was the leader of the four working girls on Kataoka. I have a feeling there'll be a leader for the other five groups of four as well."

"Is that it?"

"The Brodek take a big cut of her earnings. Something about a family debt."

Nathan thought for a moment. "Mind if I take a crack at her?"

"I think it's better if Kit and I do the interrogations," Jessica insisted. "We've got the training."

"It was a rhetorical question," Nathan said, turning toward the door. Jessica rolled her eyes, stepping in to follow. "Alone," he told Jessica.

Kit and Jessica exchanged glances as Nathan entered the room, both knowing that arguing was not going to change their captain's mind.

Nathan closed the door and stepped up to the table at the center of the room, taking a seat across from the young woman.

Kit had been right. She looked terrified.

"I'm Nathan Scott, captain of the Aurora. What's your name?"

Shya said nothing.

"You can make up a name if you like. I just want to know how to address you properly."

"Shya."

"Do you have a last name, Shya?"

"Leno."

"Excellent." Nathan took a breath, letting it out slowly as he studied the young woman. "I'm not going to beat you or inject you with truth serums or try to trick you. That's for the other guy if needed. I don't have time for any of that. I have six worlds to protect from *your* employer. So I'm just going to be straight with you, in the hopes that you'll be straight with me. I plan to take down the Brodek, and I'd like your help. If you help me, I'll see to it that you and anyone you care about are provided safe haven on a world of your choosing. Refuse, and I'll send you and your friends back to Crowden with traces of truth serum still in your blood for the Brodek to find."

Shya's head fell back slightly. Just as she had feared, a new pirate clan was hoping to take over an existing territory. "What clan are you?"

"What clan?"

"You're planning on taking over the Brodek's area, aren't you?" Shya asked. "So what clan are you with?"

"You misunderstand. I'm not looking to take over the Brodek's extortion racket, I'm looking to shut them down."

Shya's brow furrowed, staring at the man before her. "Why would you do that?"

"Because it's the right thing to do," Nathan replied. "I'm hoping that you and your friends will help."

Shya wasn't sure if she should trust him or laugh at him. No one cared about the people of the badlands. No one ever had. "You can't *take down* the Brodek."

"Not from what I've seen," Nathan insisted. When he saw the puzzled look on her face, he decided to elaborate. "I just flew a shuttle into Crowden, buzzed right over the spaceport. I was close enough that I could have launched a dozen missiles on them before they finally fired at me. And I got away clean. You know what that tells me?"

"No, what?"

"That although the Brodek have lots of weapons and some cobbled-together shuttles and fighters, perhaps even a few gunships, they're missing two key elements. Would you like to know what those are?"

"Why not," Shya replied, feeling like it was better to humor him for now.

"Discipline and purpose," Nathan replied. "Especially the latter."

"Oh, they have purpose," Shya told him. "Power and profit."

"That's not purpose," Nathan argued, "They're character flaws. *Purpose* is something that you do for the benefit of others, not for yourself."

Shya looked confused. "Men only care about themselves," she said with disdain.

"Not all men," Nathan insisted. "As I understand it, you work for the Brodek to pay off your family's debt. Is that correct?" She didn't answer. She didn't have to. He could see the answer in her eyes. "*That's* a *purpose*. You help us, and *your* purpose will be completed, and you'll be free to live your life in peace."

"There's no such thing," she told him. "Not in the badlands."

"Help us, and maybe there will be."

* * *

"I assume you've all read Jessica's intelligence report," Nathan said as he took his seat at the head of the conference table in the command briefing room.

"It looks like a no-win scenario," Cameron stated. "Their entire garrison is knitted into the center of the city. There's no way we can take them out from the air without killing thousands of civilians."

"That was my conclusion as well," Nathan agreed. "What do you think, Jess?"

"If the Brodek are only a hundred strong, like Shya says, then the Ghatazhak should be able to handle them, provided we can flush them out."

Nathan looked at Kit. "Eight against a hundred?"

"One hundred armed men who can't shoot worth shit," Kit added. "My concern is for their citizens. How many of them will pick up arms and join the fight? According to those ladies in our brig, life on Crowden is pretty good as long as you're willing to put up with a tyrannical ruler."

"Maybe we should just announce our intention to attack to the people of Crowden," Jessica suggested.

"And give away the element of surprise?" Cameron asked, surprised that Jessica had made the suggestion.

"We gave that up the moment we jumped into Crowden's atmosphere," Jessica stated. "That Nashica crap sure as hell didn't fool them. If we warn them, the civilians might have a chance to clear out."

"Assuming the Brodek will *let* them," Nathan said.

"I'm betting they won't," Kit offered.

"Some will slip away," Jessica insisted. "That city had at least ten thousand in it. The Brodek can't contain them all with a hundred men."

"It doesn't matter," Nathan said. "We can't take the chance. We're liberating Crowden and all the other Brodek-controlled worlds, not just those of the Vernay. If we slaughter civilians, they'll hate us as much as they hate the Brodek."

"We can take out their surface turrets easily enough," Robert opined, studying the holographic rendering in the center of the table. I count only twenty batteries, a mixture of guns and missile launchers, none of which appear to be shielded."

"Or they didn't bother raising their shields because we weren't attacking," Jessica argued.

"That is a possibility," Robert agreed. "I'd suggest

a probing strike with Dragons, and maybe even the Seiiki, to get a better feel for their defenses."

"Why the Seiiki?" Nathan wondered.

"As far as they know, the Seiiki and the Acuna are the only ships we have," Robert explained. "If they *do* have three gunships, our handful of fighters and a shuttle, no matter how well armed, probably won't worry them much. That might work in our favor."

"Your scans didn't verify the gunboats," Cameron said.

"Shya confirmed them," Nathan replied. "She said they're housed in some caves a few hundred kilometers from the city. Apparently, the Brodek regularly sent her and others out there to entertain the crews."

"Was she able to give you their actual location?" Robert wondered.

"Unfortunately no."

"The city is surrounded by mountains," Jessica added. "All of which are a few hundred kilometers away. They could be anywhere."

"And the mountains probably shield them from sensors," Laza said.

"There is one other option," Nathan told them.

"No there isn't," Jessica scolded.

"According to Korsan law, anyone can challenge a clan leader to personal combat for control of their territory."

"I thought we discarded that idea," Jessica reminded him.

"No, *you* decided to discard it," Nathan corrected.

"Don't be ridiculous," Cameron said, taking Jessica's side. "We don't know anything *about* the leader of the Brodek."

"She's probably lying," Jessica insisted. "It's

possible she was *supposed* to be captured, so that she would tell you about this duel to the death crap and get you to walk into a trap."

"Duel?" Cameron asked.

"With swords no less," Jessica added.

"Did we go forward or backward in time?" Cameron wondered.

"You could always put me in command," Kit suggested. "I'll take the guy down."

"Shya said he's an old guy with a pot belly," Nathan defended.

"She also said he's got arms like a gorilla and is a master swordsman," Jessica argued, "*and* that he's killed more than a dozen challengers. Two in the last year."

"I thought *you* thought she was lying," Nathan replied.

Jessica just shook her head in disgust.

"I'm not saying it's a good idea," Nathan admitted. "I'm just putting all our options on the table for discussion. Trust me, I have no desire to get into a saber duel with *anyone*."

"I still think at least one or two pre-strikes are warranted," Robert insisted. "We target their air defenses in the first raid and then attack again a week later to see if they were able to replace them. Then we'd get a really good read on their defensive capabilities."

"It might also get some people to move away from the city center," Jessica suggested.

"Well I haven't committed to anything just yet," Nathan stated. "We've only had *one* attack against a Vernay world thus far. For all we know, it was put down so effectively that there may not be another."

"And if there is?" Cameron asked.

"Then we start with Robert's idea," Nathan said. "Maybe a few direct attacks against their home base will make them reconsider whether the Vernay worlds are worth dying for. In the meantime, we maintain Dragon patrols of the Vernay worlds, and we maintain the same level of readiness with our QRF." Nathan looked around. "Any questions?"

"Just one," Cameron said. "Is this all worth it?"

"How do you mean?" Nathan asked.

"I get that these people are being extorted, and I want to help them, but perhaps we should face the reality that we are in no shape to take on this kind of fight, not to mention the responsibility we might be taking on should we win."

"That's a fair question," Nathan admitted. "Trust me when I tell you that I have my doubts. But this ship was designed *precisely* for this purpose. We *formed* the Alliance to protect the freedom, maintain the peace, and promote the prosperity of the human race...*regardless* of alliances or lack thereof. The Alliance we once knew may no longer exist, but *we* do. I, for one, cannot turn my back on my oath to its original principals, and I'm fairly certain that none of you can either." Nathan paused, scanning the faces of his senior staff, looking for any signs of disagreement. As expected, he found none. "That is all." Nathan remained seated as the others rose to depart. "Vlad, a word?" Nathan said as Vladimir was about to pass by. As soon as everyone left, he said, "Take a seat."

Vladimir sat at the seat on Nathan's left. "What happened?" he asked.

Nathan looked at his friend. "No bullshit, no bravado...How soon can you get this ship into space and ready to take on those Brodek gunships?"

Vladimir studied Nathan a moment. "One week," he finally replied. "But she won't be pretty."

"Define 'pretty'."

"She won't be performing to design specs," Vladimir explained. "Not even close."

"All I need her to do is to get us to Crowden orbit and destroy those gunships."

"And get away if something goes wrong," Vladimir recommended.

"That option would be nice," Nathan agreed.

"It would be a lot easier if we could use our tech droids."

"That requires our full AI to be online, doesn't it?"

"*Da.*"

"You know we can't take that chance, not until we're certain we can trust her."

"We can," Vladimir assured him. "I *know* it."

"Can you honestly tell me there is no back door in her code that the Alliance or worse, the Brodek, could use to seize control of this ship?"

"Nathan, there are millions of lines of code which would have to be analyzed…"

"The fact that you said *that* gives me my answer. You have a week."

Vladimir sighed. "I never should have taken this job."

"And miss all this fun?"

* * *

"I thought I'd find you here," Nathan said to Neli as he entered the main galley. "Working kind of late, aren't you?"

"The crew is working night and day, so there's got to be food available around the clock."

"How are the Grunites working out?" Nathan

asked, noticing a few of the locals working further back in the kitchen.

"Pretty well actually. Most of them don't know much about cooking our usual staples, but they've taught me how to use some of the local roots and berries. Hard workers too."

"I know you're busy, but I've got a job for you."

"What is it?" Neli wondered.

Nathan pulled the Alliance patch off his left shoulder then pulled the Aurora patch off his right. "I need you to find a way to combine these into a single patch. Something to symbolize our new mission."

"What, survival?"

"Funny," Nathan replied. "Same mission as before, except we're no longer *part* of the Alliance. Our oath is now to *all* of humanity, not just members."

Neli studied the two patches for a moment. "I'll see what I can come up with," she promised. "There's fresh dollag stew on the line."

"Thanks." Nathan exited the galley into the mess hall, going straight to the food line and dishing himself up a bowl. He then turned to exit, planning on taking the stew to his quarters, but spotted Hanna sitting by herself.

"Mind if I join you?" Nathan asked as he stepped up to her table.

"Please," Hanna replied politely. The truth was, she didn't feel much like talking, but at the same time, she didn't feel much like being alone either.

"Not hungry?" Nathan asked as he sat, noticing that she had barely touched her stew.

"I guess not," she admitted.

Nathan dug in, having not eaten since morning. "Not bad," he said after his first bite.

"I'm not sure what kind of meat it is," Hanna admitted.

"Dollag. It's like beef."

"Not like the beef I remember."

"A lot of people don't realize that dollag actually *is* beef. The Takarans brought a small starter herd with them when they left Earth. They eventually modified their genetics to better adapt them to their new world. A little more gamey, and the texture is different, but you get used to it. I actually prefer it to regular beef now."

"I was always more of a seafood person, myself," Hanna admitted.

"Then you should visit Rakuen someday. It's ninety percent ocean. Hard to find a bigger variety of seafood anywhere in the known galaxy."

Hanna had no response.

"Something wrong?" Nathan wondered.

"I guess I just wasn't really ready for today," Hanna replied.

"No one ever is."

"The Ghatazhak seem to be. Nothing seems to faze them."

"The Ghatazhak are unique. They see the same things you and I do, and they feel the same way about what they see. They're just able to put it aside and do their job."

"Doesn't it catch up with them eventually?"

"You'd think so," Nathan agreed. "But I've never seen it. Their leader, General Lucias Telles, explained it to me once. He said that the Ghatazhak are trained to convert such emotions into ones that enhance their performance rather than hinder it."

"How?"

"By constant training," Nathan explained.

"They're fanatical about it. They barely sleep. I've seen them go days on end without rest. Everything is a challenge to them. A challenge to do better than before. If they're not improving, they're not happy."

"Sounds like a difficult way to live."

"I suppose so, but it seems to work for them. I actually tried applying that principal to my own life recently."

"How so?" Hanna wondered, becoming curious.

"I had a year off. After a month, I was bored out of my skull, so I joined a local hockey league."

"Hockey as in *ice* hockey?"

"Yup."

"They still play hockey these days?"

"I don't know about now, but they did back in my time."

"So did it help?"

"It did. After the first scrimmage, I identified several areas I was weak in," Nathan explained. "Which was pretty much *all* areas. So I started skating for a couple hours every morning, concentrating on a different skill each session."

"Did it help?"

"It did," Nathan replied. "In fact, it felt pretty good to set goals and accomplish them, even if they were little ones."

"So did you end up scoring a lot of goals?" Hanna teased.

"A few," Nathan replied. "Mostly, I was just happy not to embarrass myself too much. But it made me understand why the Ghatazhak train so hard. Improvement inspires confidence. Lack of confidence inhibits performance when performance is needed most."

"Well I'm not sure how I'd train for what I saw today," Hanna said.

"I'm sure you've seen worse," Nathan insisted. "I mean, you were there during the bio-digital plague. You had to have witnessed an incredible amount of suffering."

"It was different."

"How so?"

"The people I saw today were brutally attacked. They couldn't even defend themselves. Women, children...it didn't matter to the Brodek."

"Didn't the same thing happen on Earth during the plague?"

"Yes, but those people were just trying to survive," Hanna argued. "Besides, that was fifteen hundred years ago. I thought the human race would have matured by now."

"The one thing I've found to be true is that humans are the same now as they were thousands of years ago. As a species, we are programmed to survive. Unfortunately, that makes us able to commit truly barbaric acts. But it's also why we're still around, despite all the ways we've invented to destroy ourselves."

"You paint a bleak picture of the future, don't you," Hanna commented.

"I just try to accept what is and do what I can to make things better. That's all any of us can do."

"How can you possibly make things better in an entire galaxy of chaos and suffering?"

"You start with yourself then your own little world. My father used to say, you have to get your own house in order before you can help others with theirs."

"Maybe that's my problem," Hanna concluded. "I don't have any control over my *own* house."

"But you do have control over yourself."

"I suppose. I just wish I could help more."

"Just keeping journaling what you see," Nathan urged. "Someday, it *will* make a difference."

* * *

There were many places on the Aurora that Nathan had not yet visited, and its gun range was one he hadn't even known existed until recently.

All four lanes were populated with Ghatazhak. Not surprising, since they were known for being precise marksmen with just about any weapon known to man. These men started and ended each day shooting. It was the only way to stay proficient.

Nathan moved along the back of the range until he found Kit at the last station. But he wasn't shooting, or so Nathan thought. Suddenly, the sidearm that was in his side holster was out, tiny bolts of plasma energy spitting out and flying downrange a split second after the barrel had cleared the edge of the holster and leveled toward the distant target. Four shots later, and his weapon was back in its holster just as fast as it had been drawn.

Nathan looked downrange as the scoring computer projected highlights around the impact points on the virtual target. "Impressive," Nathan congratulated. "Heart, lungs, and head."

"Actually, the one on the left would open up the victim's right lung and liver," Kit corrected.

"Don't plasma bolts cauterize their own wounds?"

"Only at higher power settings," Kit replied. "If the head shot missed, the other wounds would kill him."

"I did not know that."

"Also, lower power settings don't cause the target to jerk as much when hit, making it easier to land the other shots where you intend."

"You guys put a lot of thought into the science of shooting," Nathan commented.

"The Ghatazhak put a lot of thought into everything we do," Kit said. He smiled then added, "We just do it more quickly." Kit drew again, this time putting a single shot into each of the three targets that appeared downrange. Again, every shot landed exactly where he intended, and his sidearm was back in its holster before any of the targets would have hit the ground had they been real. The system reset, and the targets disappeared. A second later, two more virtual targets appeared, the one on the right reaching for a boomer hanging from his shoulder, while the one on the left raised his weapon to open fire.

Kit drew his weapon, but despite there being two virtual adversaries, he only fired a single shot. That single shot hit the man in the left shoulder, causing him to rotate to his left as he squeezed his own trigger, sending a blast into his cohort to his left. One shot, two targets down.

"You knew that would happen, didn't you?" Nathan said.

"I upped the power setting to full as I drew," Kit explained. "The higher setting has greater kinetic energy on impact, which causes him to rotate more. The additional energy also causes his peripheral nerves to fire wildly, which causes his fingers to flinch and pull the trigger."

"Why not just shoot them both?"

"If it were only two of them, I probably would have. But if there were more, then it's better to kill more quickly. Reduces the chance of any of them getting a shot off before they fall."

"But you have personal shields."

"Yes, but what if we don't?"

"Train for the worst scenario," Nathan surmised.

"Train for *every* scenario," Kit corrected. "Just train for the worst ones more often." Kit turned to face Nathan, stepping aside and revealing the collection of weapons laid out on the counter before him. "When's the last time you shot?"

"It's been a while," Nathan admitted.

"How long?"

"A few months at least."

Kit shook his head. "If you don't shoot daily, you've got no business carrying a sidearm."

"I *don't* carry a sidearm," Nathan reminded him. "At least not usually."

"You should. You're operating in the world of pirates after all. And you should be practicing."

"How do you know I didn't come down here to do precisely that?"

"Because you didn't bring your sidearm." Kit gestured to the array of weapons on the counter. "Care to show me what you've got?"

Nathan stepped up, looking over the weapons, none of which he recognized. He then looked at Kit, holding out his hand. "I'd like to try yours."

Kit pulled his sidearm, albeit slowly, and laid it on the counter along with the others.

Nathan picked up the sidearm and stepped onto the shooter's pad, indicating to the target system that he was ready. A single target appeared. A man with a gun pointed Nathan's way. Nathan raised his gun and fired twice, first striking the target's gun hand then his chest. He then stepped back off the pad, placing the weapon back on the counter.

"Not bad," Kit congratulated. "Took out his gun first then him." Kit removed his gun belt and handed it to Nathan. "Now try a fast draw and aim for his head."

Nathan donned the gun belt and placed the weapon in its holster.

"Whenever you're ready," Kit told him.

Nathan took a breath then stepped onto the pad. A man appeared downrange, his hands at his side, his right hand hovering over the butt of his own sidearm. The man drew his weapon, as did Nathan, both of them firing at the same time. The light over him turned red, indicating that Nathan had not been fast enough.

Kit looked downrange, noting that Nathan's shot, though too late to prevent his own demise, had indeed landed on the virtual man's forehead, but slightly high and left of center. "Nice shot. Better than I expected actually, but you played it wrong."

"How so?"

"To start with, you know you haven't shot in a while, which means you definitely haven't practiced your quick-draw," Kit explained. "So relying on being faster was stupid. Second, your opponent was nice and still, like someone who has faced men down many times before. He was calm and confident. The inexperienced ones are twitchy. Their eyes are usually focused on your gun hand instead of your eyes. The *really* inexperienced ones can't make up their mind where to look and are constantly shifting back and forth between your gun hand and your face."

"So what should I have done?" Nathan asked.

"Your opponent was right-handed and had quick-draw experience."

"So?"

"That means he would probably shoot from the hip, which he did. It also means his shot is more likely to hit you on your left side than center or even right. So you should have leaned *and* twisted into your draw. If you had, he probably would have missed, and that light would be green instead of red."

"Perhaps you can demonstrate?" Nathan invited, removing the gun belt.

"Gladly," Kit replied, taking the belt from Nathan and donning it again. He picked up the weapon and holstered it. "Computer, same scenario, and increase the shooter's draw speed to match my own." Kit stepped onto the pad, taking a far more casual stance than one would expect. A few seconds later, his virtual opponent drew his weapon, this time far more quickly than before. Kit drew his weapon as well, but did exactly as he had described, leaning to his right as he drew his own weapon, twisting at the same time to reduce his target profile. Just like his opponent, Kit fired from his hip, his shot landing between his opponent's eyes. A split second later, Kit was standing normally again, his weapon in its holster and his hands hanging at his sides. He stepped back off the pad, turning to face Nathan again.

"Impressive," Nathan admitted.

"Not really. We practice those kinds of moves all the time."

"I wasn't aware the Ghatazhak got into many quick-draw duels."

"Generally no. But it's still a nice skill to have.

And it's fun too. Isn't that why you learned to quick-draw?"

"Actually I had an unhealthy obsession with old post-plague movies when I was a kid. I wanted to be Dylan West, traveling the post-plague landscape and taking down the gangs that plagued the tribes."

"So *that's* where you get it from," Kit realized. "I always wondered why you always seem bent on saving the galaxy."

"Don't tell anyone," Nathan said.

Kit smiled. "You start now."

"Start what?"

"Training," Kit replied. "That is why you came here. To ask me to train you to fight the leader of the Brodek."

"How did you know?"

Kit smiled again. "I'm a Ghatazhak," he replied. "I can tell what you had for dinner by the smell of your fart."

"Of course. So what do you want me to shoot?"

"No shooting. Not yet," Kit replied. "Go to the gym and do an hour on the variable treadmill."

"Actually I was planning on hitting my rack," Nathan replied. "It's been a long, fucking day."

"Which is exactly why you should get in a little exercise now. We'll start your real training at zero six hundred. So you have to be there at zero five hundred."

"Why?"

"So you can do another hour on the treadmill before we start."

"Understood."

"You know, no one would fault you if you pulled us out of the Vernay tomorrow."

"No one but me," Nathan replied as he turned to exit. "See you in the morning."

CHAPTER TEN

Nathan awoke that morning feeling as exhausted as when he had gone to bed the night before. The additional hour on the treadmill first thing in the morning hadn't helped. He was just thankful that he had been skating every morning for the few months leading up to his taking command of the new Aurora.

When Nathan entered the training gym, the change in gravity hit him like a ton of bricks. "Jesus, what do you have it set at?" he asked Kit, who was waiting for him.

"One point five," Kit replied. "I was going to go with two Gs, but I decided to take it easy on you."

"Crowden has only point eight you know."

"Then you'll be a superman on that world." Kit tossed him his sword.

Nathan caught the sword but nearly dropped it, finding it far heavier than he had expected. "You sure it's not at two?" he asked, feeling the surprising heft of his sword.

"It's a training blade," Kit explained. "Five times heavier."

"Are you trying to convince me that I'm in over my head or something?"

"Nope. Just trying to get you as strong and capable as possible. Train with that monster for a few weeks, and a standard blade will be nothing."

"Couldn't we just work on my arm strength?"

"It's not about strength, it's about endurance. Swinging a sword around can get tiring more quickly than you might imagine. If the guy you're thinking of fighting is an experienced swordsman, superior endurance is your best hope of beating him."

"I feel like I can barely move," Nathan complained as he walked into the center of the training area, blade in hand.

"According to our prisoners, the Brodek have been based on Crowden for nearly a decade, and in all that time, the Brodek leader has never left Crowden. That means that his body has gotten accustomed to a lower gravity. Training with a weighted blade in a high-G environment will give you an edge."

"I'm assuming that's why the air feels so thin in here?"

"Lower air pressure on Crowden," Kit explained. "Not to mention a lower level of oxygen."

Nathan took a deep breath, feeling as if he wasn't getting enough oxygen. Even breathing seemed difficult in the higher gravity. He swung the saber about a bit, finding it far more difficult than he thought. "This is going to be fun," he remarked.

"You have no idea," Kit replied. He moved into the training area, swinging his own sword around him with incredible speed and accuracy, even though he was probably just warming up. "The trick to sword fighting, just like any other type of combat, is to determine your opponent's style, find their weaknesses, and then exploit them. You're already adept at noticing tiny details and realizing their importance, and doing so faster than most. For the Ghatazhak, this is the result of decades of training. For you, it came from being cloned a few times."

"I'd like to think I had *some* skill in that area to begin with," Nathan said.

"Computer, activate holo-training program Scott one," Kit stated.

An image of a man holding a saber identical to Nathan's appeared in the middle of the training area.

"What's this?" Nathan wondered.

"Your instructor. Mimic his moves. Once you do it correctly, he will move on to the next move automatically. When you can go through the entire series without having to repeat a move, the program will begin giving you combinations to practice and so on." Kit walked over to the side, placing his sword on the floor.

"Where are you going?" Nathan wondered.

"I've got more important things to do than walk you through the basics," Kit said. "I've got my own training and a supply flight this afternoon."

"How long do I do this?" Nathan asked.

"Until you can barely hold up your sword any longer," Kit said as he headed for the exit. "Then you pick up my sword and continue."

"Why? Is it lighter?"

"Nope, heavier," Kit replied. He paused at the door, looked back at Nathan, and smiled. "*Much* heavier." Kit headed through the exit, calling out, "Be back here at twenty hundred!" as he disappeared into the corridor.

Nathan took a deep breath, raising up his heavy sword. "Computer, begin program," he instructed.

"*Difficulty level?*" the computer inquired.

"Beginner," Nathan replied.

The holographic man assumed the first position, raising his sword to a horizontal position in front of him at shoulder level while stepping back slightly with his left foot. Nathan performed the same move but with far more difficulty than his holographic training partner exhibited.

It was going to be a long morning.

* * *

Nathan walked down the corridor, headed back

to his quarters for a shower. If the artificial gravity on the Aurora had been set any higher than normal, he doubted he would make it. His arms and legs were weak, and he was covered with sweat. All he wanted to do was to get clean, eat something, and take a nap.

Nathan rounded the corner, running into Vladimir and several technicians busy installing an emergency rescue airlock.

"What happened to you?" Vladimir asked, noticing Nathan's condition.

"I got my ass kicked by a hologram," Nathan replied.

"What?"

"Long story. How's it going with the airlocks?"

"They're not designed for long-term usage, so we had to fabricate an extra metal ring on the seal-skirt so that we could weld them onto the bulkheads."

"Are they going to hold?" Nathan wondered.

"They should," Vladimir replied. "As long as you don't crash us again."

"I'll do my best," Nathan promised, continuing on his way.

* * *

Cameron had spent most of the day managing Grunite volunteers, who seemed to be showing up in droves after hearing about the attack on Persa. It was already approaching noon, and this was the first time she had managed to get to the bridge, despite the fact that she had the watch for most of the day.

When she entered, she found both Laza and Sima, as well as Abby, working at the starboard auxiliary station. "Abby?" she said, going over to her. "I thought you usually worked in your quarters."

"I was, but I needed to set up my station," Abby replied.

"Your *station?*"

"Manual jumps?"

"Ah yes," Cameron remembered. "I've been so busy with Grunite volunteers, I completely forgot. How's it going?"

"Well I wrote some specialized algorithms to do quick calculations for jumps less than half a light year. Anything longer than that means I'll have to do the entire calculation manually just to be sure. The hard part is configuring this console to control everything and to tie the sequencer into the sensor array, so we know we have a clear jump line at the moment of execution. It's like I'm trying to reengineer the same setup that we had on the old Aurora back in the Pentaurus cluster. Never thought I'd being doing that again."

"It is kind of strange. We've traveled five hundred years into the future, but our jump system has slid fourteen years into our past."

"To be honest, this is exactly what I feared when the Alliance began pushing the barrier-damage theory."

"Huh?"

"Not *this* per se, but that jump technology would cease to progress and begin to *regress* instead. This ship was built over five hundred years ago, yet she has a far greater jump range than anything in operation today. Just for the sake of power and profit."

"All science is for the sake of power and profit," Cameron stated. "It always has been."

"Not for everyone," Abby argued. "It wasn't for us."

"Unfortunately, people like you and your father are the exception rather than the rule. Try to see the bright side."

"What bright side," Abby wondered, still staring at her screen as she worked.

"Since we can out-jump everyone, we've got a hell of an advantage over the rest of the galaxy."

Abby cast a dubious look Cameron's way.

"Sorry, that's all I could think of," Cameron apologized, continuing on to the captain's ready room on the opposite side of the bridge.

To Cameron's surprise, Nathan was lying on the sofa in the ready room. "What are you doing here?"

"I came to get my data pad," Nathan said, not moving.

Cameron looked at the desk, spotting the data pad in question. "It's right here."

"I know."

"You're not on duty for two more hours you know."

"I know."

"Maybe you should rest? You look like shit."

"I am resting," Nathan said. "Or at least I was until you came in."

"That bad huh?"

Nathan looked at her curiously.

"The combat training?"

"How did you know?"

"I'm the XO," Cameron replied. "I know *everything* that happens on this ship."

"Jess told you, didn't she?"

"Kit told Jess, Jess told me."

"Can't keep a secret on this ship, can I."

"Everyone's just looking out for you, Nathan. That *is* our job after all. Both as your senior staff *and* as your friends."

Nathan sighed. "I know."

"If it weren't for us, you'd have died several times over by now."

"I know."

"I'll work in the briefing room," Cameron said, laying the data pad on Nathan's chest and heading out.

"Thanks."

Cameron went to the exit and turned out the lights. She paused a moment, looking back at Nathan. She was certain it was a mistake for him to challenge the Brodek leader to a duel to the death, but she also knew that when Nathan decided to do something, there would be no talking him out of it, especially if the only other choice was to walk away.

* * *

Kit watched Nathan sparring with Mori on the view screen in the QRF ready room.

Jessica entered, immediately noticing the display. "How's he doing?" she asked, taking a seat as she watched.

"Better than I expected," Kit admitted. "It's only his third session and his first time with an actual sparring partner."

Jessica studied the view screen a bit more. "He moves pretty well," she said. Then Mori tricked him, pulling his guard open and jabbing him with the training sword. Nathan reacted as if he were shocked. "Are those charged training swords?"

"Mori's is charged," Kit replied. "Nathan's is just weighted...a *lot*."

"You're mean."

"Fear of pain makes you try harder."

"How much time has he been putting in?"

"Four hours a day on the treadmill and four hours

training. Then he goes to the range and shoots for an hour."

"Why?"

"I don't know. I didn't tell him to."

"You think he's got a chance?"

"If this Brodek guy is an old, fat slob, sure. Otherwise, he's fucked."

"I don't know, he doesn't look so bad at the moment. And it's only been two days."

"Trust me, Mori's going *really* easy on him."

"Why?"

"The best thing we can do right now is to give him a little confidence. But as soon as he starts to get cocky, Mori stabs him to remind him he still sucks."

"Just don't over-train him," Jessica warned as she rose again. "He's still got his own job to do."

"Don't worry, I've been giving him some of our nanites to help him heal faster."

"And he agreed to that?"

"I put them in his water," Kit replied.

Jessica smiled and headed for the door.

* * *

Once the darkness fell on Kataoka, most people went inside and stayed there. The lush landscape was home to a variety of wildlife, several of which found humans quite tasty.

The city center was the only place with any signs of life at night. Indigenous creatures rarely ventured that deep into the colony, and people who were still moving about at night generally lived nearby.

Four flashes of blue-white light appeared in the night sky over the Kataoka colony, with four cracks of thunder sounding seconds later. The few people who were outside looked to the skies in the direction of the sound but saw nothing at first. In fact, most of them continued about their business.

Less than a minute after the thunderous claps, the terrifying sound of diving attack fighters was heard. Suddenly, out of the distant dark horizon, streams of red-orange plasma lashed out toward the unsuspecting colony. The energy bolts tore through buildings, causing some to collapse, and setting ablaze nearly everything they touched.

Since the streets were nearly empty, there was very little chaos. Only a few people were running in different directions as they rushed to help those trapped inside damaged buildings.

But after the four fighters streaked overhead, they peeled off, climbed, and jumped away.

* * *

Breden was the smallest of the colonies located near the end of the Vernay passage. Having only been established a decade ago, its population was still well under a thousand.

Being such a young colony, Breden was also far more reliant on trade to survive. The sudden influx of goods provided by regular visits by the Acuna had been a blessing. Their world was not the best place to grow crops or raise livestock, although it was rich in other resources, many of which were needed by other worlds in the Vernay region and beyond. It was for this reason that Artur Breden had originally left Kataoka and settled the little world.

Most people took their meals in Breden's central cafeteria. Few homes had cooking facilities of their own, and the scarcity of game made centralized food production and distribution much more efficient. Hunting parties brought back massive gorons from their sorties into the highlands around the colony on a daily basis, providing enough food for the colony's small population.

The hunting parties left at sunrise and generally did not return until late afternoon. Today, their return would be a somber event.

Standing on the crest of the final hill before descending toward the settlement, the hunting party could see their modest village below. It was ablaze, with columns of smoke billowing from multiple fires, all of them coalescing into a massive cloud casting a haze over the entire valley. And there were no indications of what had started the fires.

* * *

There were times when Josh did not mind letting his AI pilot his Dragon fighter. Patrols were definitely one of them. Jump, scan, and jump again…for hours on end. If it wasn't for the vid-flicks on his data pad and the makeshift mounting bracket he had fabricated for it, he doubted he'd be able to stay awake for the entire four-hour patrols.

Splitting the Dragons up into two-ship patrol elements instead of three helped. It took about thirty-eight minutes to patrol all six Vernay worlds, which left a hell of an attack window for the Brodek, assuming they were paying attention. The two-ship configuration allowed them to overlap their patrols, decreasing those attack windows to half that time.

The truth was that, until the Vernay worlds were equipped with some sort of surface-based air defenses, they would be vulnerable to attack. Brodek snub-fighters could easily jump in, perform a single strafing run, and then jump out, all before the Dragons could respond. Even if they flew single-ship patrols, there would still be a five-minute gap.

Even with AIs, pilots could only fly so much before their performance degraded to unacceptable levels.

Between movies and catnaps, Josh could go all day without a problem. The snacks and the thermos of coffee that he always brought along also helped. But even with the entertainment, the boredom would hit about halfway through their four-hour patrol.

"Hey, Remo," Josh called over comms. "How about we have a little fun?"

"*What did you have in mind?*" Nikolas asked.

"How about you jump in ten seconds ahead of me, and then I'll jump in on your six and pretend to attack you."

"Why?"

"Practice, why else?"

"I thought we were on patrol," Nikolas reminded him.

"Are you saying you don't need practice shaking off an attacker?" Josh wondered.

"We have rear-facing guns and plasma torpedoes," Nikolas replied.

"Pretend we don't," Josh suggested. "Nothing but forward-facing cannons. Straight up dogfighting. Whattaya say?"

"I say it's a bad idea," Nikolas admitted. "However, since I know you'll just pull rank on me, what the hell."

The latest scans completed, and Josh's threat display showed no contacts in the Persa system. "Okay, you jump directly into Willingham's atmo… say angels five, and I'll jump in ten seconds after you."

"Copy that," Nikolas agreed. "Jumping to Willingham atmo, angels five, two miles east of the colony."

"See ya there," Josh replied, excited to finally do something besides sit on his ass.

* * *

"New contact," Laza reported from the Aurora's sensor station. "Comm-drone." She turned to her auxiliary screen which she had configured as a communications station since Sima was currently on break. "Flash traffic. Kataoka was just attacked."

"By the Brodek?" Cameron asked.

"Based on the description, probably Brodek snub-fighters," Laza replied. "They report a single attack pass, and then they jumped away. No word on damage or injuries."

"Launch the next Dragon patrol now and get a second pair on the cats and ready to launch if needed," Cameron instructed as she tapped the intercom panel on the tactical station where she was standing. "Captain Walsh, get the Mirai ready for launch for possible MCI response." She pressed another button. "Medical, XO. Report to the Mirai for possible MCI response."

Nathan entered the bridge, expecting to relieve Cameron for the afternoon watch. "What's going on?"

"Looks like the Brodek may have attacked Kataoka," Cameron replied. "We're scrambling a pair of Dragons now."

"Where's the current patrol located?"

"They should be jumping to Willingham about now," Cameron replied, referencing the patrol schedule on her display.

"Better dispatch an alert to them as well," Nathan suggested.

"I'm on it," Laza assured him.

* * *

As expected, Nikolas came out of his jump to

Willingham exactly where he had planned. Every system patrol started with buzzing the colony to let the people know they were there. But their initial jump into the system was usually to orbit rather than directly to the atmosphere. However, Dragons were far more fun to fly in the atmosphere than in space.

In space, it was all thrust vectors, delta-v, and attitude vs. course. Dogfighting was a completely different animal in space, and in most engagements, your target was too far away to see. In the atmosphere, however, dogfighting was about circles. Each pilot trying to out-turn the other in order to get behind them for a kill shot.

Of course Dragons had numerous cannon turrets and could fire in any direction at any time. However, those cannons required quite a few hits to take down an opponent's shields, while their forward and rear-facing plasma torpedo cannons could do the job with a single hit in most cases.

As planned, the Willingham colony was due west, about five kilometers and closing. Nikolas was cruising along at five thousand meters above the surface.

The alert light flashed just above the threat display, just as expected. But the expected icon was in front of him, not behind him, and was only fifty meters in altitude. Suddenly, there were two icons, and they both switched from orange to red, indicating that his AI had identified them as hostile contacts.

"Oh shit," Nikolas muttered to himself. He selected the two targets now four kilometers away and armed his missiles, but then two more icons appeared directly behind and above him. And they were close in, diving at him.

Another alarm sounded, and two flashing red icons appeared behind him. *Missiles.* Nikolas quickly changed course, pulling hard left and climbing, looking for a clear jump path. He flipped his jump-range selector to micro and selected a single kilometer as his range. A glance at the threat display told him he had only a few seconds until the two incoming weapons would reach him, so he didn't wait. He pushed the jump button.

* * *

Josh pressed his jump button, transitioning to Willingham's atmosphere, expecting to arrive directly behind Nikolas in the kill position. Nothing was more fun than atmo dogfighting.

But Nikolas wasn't there. Instead, there were four hostile contacts, two of them over the colony and coming about, and the other two close behind him, slightly above.

Two missiles streaked past to his left, both of them turning hard right as they tried to come about and acquire their new target.

"What the fuck," Josh exclaimed as he instinctively took evasive action. He immediately turned into the missiles, knowing they wouldn't be able to turn sharp enough to get their targeting cones onto him. But that also gave the two fighters that had launched those missiles a much bigger target as his course came around to be perpendicular to theirs.

Another icon appeared on his threat display, but this one was a few kilometers away, higher, and more importantly, it was green. "Remo! Lock on these two, and I'll lead them to you!"

"*Copy that!*" Nikolas replied. "*Popping alert drone!*" he added, indicating that he was notifying the Aurora of the situation.

With the immediate missile threat now avoided, Josh turned back right, hoping that the two snub-fighters now targeting him would assume he had turned into the missiles' path being unaware of the position of the fighters that had launched them. So the natural reaction, once the real threat was discovered, would be that right turn and a climb for a clear jump path, which is precisely what Josh was doing.

Two more icons appeared, moving quickly toward him. Another pair of missiles. "You ready?" Josh asked Nikolas over comms.

"*Ready!*"

"Three, two, one..." Josh pushed his flight control stick all the way forward. "...jump!"

At the same time, Josh pulled his throttles back to idle, his nose coming down quickly. A blue-white flash appeared less than a few meters away, and Nikolas's Dragon fighter streaked past, having jumped to the very position Josh's fighter had been only a few seconds ago.

* * *

Nikolas's eyes widened as Josh's fighter passed close under him. It was a move they had practiced in the simulator, but he had never actually executed it in real life. The fact that he had jumped in so close to him was at the very least frightening if not overwhelming.

His AI immediately locked missiles on both of the rapidly approaching targets, neither of which had realized the change in their situation. Nikolas pressed the launch button on his flight control stick, switching to plasma torpedoes as four missiles streaked out from either side of his fighter. He rolled left, pulling his nose over at the same time, expecting the two fighters to split up, and his angle in relation to the pair was better suited to a left-angled intercept.

The right icon flashed, and Nikolas spotted a fireball to his right. A second later, the icon disappeared.

"*Target Two, destroyed,*" his AI reported.

Nikolas's targeting reticle flashed as it centered over the fighter turning away to his left, and he pressed the trigger. Red-orange balls of plasma shot forward from either side of his nose, but the distant target disappeared behind a blue-white flash of light before his plasma torpedoes reached him.

"One down, one got away!" Niko reported.

* * *

As Josh's nose came down, it lined up nicely with the colony now three kilometers away. A quick range selection, and Josh initiated a jump to get down and over to the colony as quickly as possible.

A blue-white flash, and Josh was passing over the colony only a few meters above the rooftops. The two Brodek snub-fighters strafing the city were dead ahead, only a few hundred meters away. Josh didn't wait for a weapons lock, pressing the trigger on his flight control stick and sending balls of red-orange plasma streaking toward the enemy fighters. He knew he wouldn't hit them, but it would likely scare them into breaking off their attack on the defenseless colony below.

It worked. The two fighters broke in opposite directions, both of them jumping away a few seconds later. Josh glanced at his threat display, spotting only his wingman. "Remo. Join up, one four two, angels four, due south."

* * *

Talisha was probably the only pilot aboard the

Aurora who was accustomed to flying with an AI. For as long as she could remember, utilizing your AI was just part of being a pilot. In her mind, it was all about striking a balance. Yes, you had to practice manually operating your ship in all situations, but you also needed to practice utilizing your automation in such a way as to improve the efficiency of operation and give your mission the greatest chance of success.

"*Dragon Two-One, cleared for launch.*"

"Dragon Two-One, launching," Talisha replied. The next moment, she was pushed back in her seat as her fighter accelerated rapidly down the launch tunnel.

In three seconds, she reached the exit end, and her bow thrusters fired, pushing the nose of her Dragon fighter up forty-five degrees. At the same time, her AI pushed her throttles all the way forward, raising her main propulsion to full power and sending her rocketing skyward.

A glance out the forward window as she cleared the nearby ridgeline showed nothing but open sky in front of her. Now ballistic, her AI jumped her from the lower atmosphere of Dencke into space. The sky was gone, replaced by the star-filled blackness of space.

Talisha glanced to her right and slightly aft, spotting her wingman, Tika, about one hundred meters away, his wings finishing their unfolding cycle and locking into place. "Good and green, Tika?"

"*Good and green, lead the way,*" Tika replied.

* * *

Sima sat down at the comm-station, having returned from her break the moment the alert was sounded. "More flash traffic," she announced. "From

Breden. They were just attacked. Two fighters strafed the city then jumped away."

"What the hell's going on here?" Cameron wondered.

"New contact," Laza announced. "Another comm-drone."

"Flash traffic," Sima quickly followed.

"Let me guess," Nathan commented. "Another attack?"

"Dragon One-Two reports they have engaged four over Willingham," Sima reported.

"Launch another flight of Dragons," Nathan instructed. "Send them directly to Estabrook."

"Not Vicari?" Sima wondered.

"If these are the same fighters jumping world to world, then Vicari's already under attack, and Estabrook is next."

"What about Persa?" Cameron asked.

"They're trying to scare the rest of the Vernay," Nathan insisted. "Persa's already scared, and they know it."

"Should we just launch everyone?" Cameron suggested.

"We don't have enough fighters to cover all six worlds, not unless one of them goes solo," Nathan reminded her. "Besides, I have a feeling Josh has already figured out what the Brodek are up to and is on his way to Vicari as we speak."

"I think we should launch the Mirai now and get her in the Vernay just in case," Cameron suggested.

"Agreed," Nathan replied. "Launch the rest of the Dragons and QRF One, and have them position in the Kataoka system. "Send QRF Two to the Seiiki for deployment," he added as he turned and headed for the exit.

Cameron looked to Sima. "You heard him."

"What the hell is going on?" Abby asked from her workstation.

"I'm not sure, but I don't like where this is heading," Cameron replied.

* * *

"Dropping a comm-buoy," Josh reported.

"*Why?*" Nikolas wondered.

"We're jumping to Vicari," he explained as he called up a new jump.

"*Why?*"

"Jesus, Remo, do I have to explain everything to you?" Josh snapped. "I've got sync-lead. You ready? And if you say 'why' again, so help me..."

"*I'm ready,*" Nikolas assured him. "*Just so you know, I really wanted to say 'why' just now.*"

"Smartass," Josh commented, smiling as he activated his jump sequencer. His AI took over flight controls and guided his Dragon fighter onto the proper course then executed the jump.

Josh's fighter barely appeared to move. The only indication that he had jumped, other than the jump flash, was that the sky was now dark, as it was the middle of the night on Vicari. It also took on a deep purplish hue due to its different atmospheric composition. But none of that interested him at the moment.

Three red icons showed on his threat display. On the one hand, he was happy to have been right. On the other, Vicarians were under attack. "*That's why!*" he yelled triumphantly.

"*How did you know?*"

"Don't question genius, kid," Josh declared as he turned his fighter toward the contacts. "Let's go shake things up." He pressed his jump button, transitioning to less than a kilometer away from the Vicari settlement and the three Brodek snub-fighters that were currently attacking it.

"*Shouldn't we shoot them down?*" Nikolas asked, having jumped in right behind him.

"They'll just jump," Josh insisted, opening fire with his forward-facing plasma torpedo cannons.

Four pairs of red-orange balls of plasma streaked out, slamming into the aft shields of the nearest snub-fighter. Josh fully expected him to jump away, along with his two friends. Instead, all three ships pitched up and fanned out, each turning in a different direction. "What the hell are they up to?" Josh wondered as he pitched up to follow the snub-fighter he had just fired upon. "Still with me, Remo?" Josh asked, already knowing the answer.

"*I've got your wing,*" Nikolas assured him.

"Lock a seeker on the one to the right, just to keep him busy,"

"*Locking.*"

Josh rolled right, staying with the snub-fighter as it tried to outmaneuver him. Then the small fighter jumped.

"Son of a bitch," Josh cursed, quickly dialing up another jump. "I'm lead again," he announced as the other two fighters also jumped away.

"*Now where are we going?*"

"Right where they're leading us," Josh replied.

* * *

Allet's cockpit module dropped into its Dragon fighter, and his console lit up, its displays now connected to the spacecraft it was about to control. Two seconds later, his fighter accelerated down the launch tunnel, its nose pitching up as it exited the end of the tunnel. A few more seconds, and his cockpit filled with blue-white light, and he found himself in space, high above Dencke, his wingman, Mick, on his right.

"Dragon Three-One is away," he announced.

"*Dragon Three-Two is away,*" his wingman followed.

"*Dragon Three-One, Aurora. Combat jump to Estabrook.*"

"Dragon Three-One, copy," Allet replied. "Ready, Mick?"

"*Lead the way, Kusya.*"

* * *

Talisha was the first to jump into Kataoka's atmosphere. From a few kilometers away, she could see columns of thick black smoke rising from the colony.

Not again.

"*Dragon Two-One, QRF One. Are you seeing this?*" Kit asked.

"Affirmative," Talisha replied. She glanced at her threat display, only seeing icons for her wingman and the QRF shuttle, both only a few hundred meters behind her. "Threat board is clear."

"Leta, low pass for a sensor scan. I need to know the casualty count."

"*Understood,*" her AI acknowledged.

"Maintain position while I make a sensor pass on the colony," Talisha instructed.

"*I've got the overwatch,*" Tika confirmed.

Talisha's Dragon fighter dipped, and the ship accelerated sharply, settling into an altitude one kilometer above the surface. She watched as the sensor scan of the surface began, the results reading out on her displays. "Damn. QRF One, Dragon Two-One. No bandits on the surface. Send word back to the Aurora. We're going to need an MCI response here."

* * *

It was early morning at the colony on Estabrook, and the dawn sky was its usual pinkish hue due to the vissian gas constantly seeping out of the planet's porous surface.

Three small flashes of light appeared a few kilometers from the colony, revealing tiny dots that descended toward the distant horizon. A few seconds later, there were two more flashes.

"I knew it," Josh exclaimed, immediately spotting the three red icons on his threat display. "Let's shut'em down before they can do any damage, Remo."

"I'm with you," Nikolas assured him.

Josh pushed his nose down. "Tandem intercept jump, fifty meters behind them," he instructed his AI.

"Jump ready and synced," his AI confirmed.

"Execute."

His AI took control, adjusting the heading and descent angles of both Dragon fighters before initiating the synchronized jump. The cockpit was momentarily awash with their jump flash, and Josh took the controls again, his AI sensing his pilot's hands on the flight control stick and releasing it to him.

"Popping three, one each," Josh announced.

By now, the Dragon's AI had spent enough time with Josh to understand his unique brand of shorthand commands and immediately locked a single missile on each of the three enemy ships, launching them a split second later.

"Three away."

Josh held his course just long enough for the missiles to clear his nose on their way to their targets then pulled up slightly as he gave his next command. "Jump us just above them, ventral guns down."

"*Jumping forward, ventral guns down,*" his AI confirmed.

Again the jump flash washed over their cockpits as the two Dragon fighters jumped forward.

Nikolas glanced at his threat display, noting that the three icons that were just ahead of them a second ago were now directly below, barely a meter ahead. But then, four more icons appeared, above and behind them. At first they were orange, but a second later, they changed to red, and his weapons lock alert light began flashing.

"Four bandits just jumped in, six o'clock high!"

The alert light became steady red, and four tiny icons split off, one from each of the newly arrived bandits, moving quickly across the display screen toward the center.

"Four inbounds!" Nikolas warned. "Two seconds!"

Before he could take control, his AI snap-rolled his fighter fifty degrees to port, pitched up slightly, and jumped his ship ahead five kilometers, beginning a turn to come about as soon as it came out of the jump.

"Damn I love that feature," Nikolas exclaimed, thankful that his AI had jumped him out of immediate danger.

Josh's AI had also taken control and initiated a similar escape jump.

"I fucking hate it!" Josh complained, rolling his ship over to force control back from his AI.

"*Protocols dictate that I take emergency action to protect the ship and its crew whenever there is an immediate threat of destruction,*" his AI defended.

"I could've shaken those missiles," Josh insisted.

"*I calculated only a two percent chance of successful threat avoidance,*" his AI replied. "*Even for you.*"

"Well since you put it that way."

"*I'm afraid there has been a catastrophic explosion at the Estabrook colony,*" his AI reported.

"Oh fuck," Nikolas exclaimed over comms. "*Josh, are you seeing this?*"

Josh continued to bring his nose around, rolling out of his turn as he lined back up with the colony in the distance. A few kilometers ahead, a massive fireball, one large enough to encompass the entire colony, including the surrounding countryside, was growing in size. "Oh fuck is right."

The fireball was expanding rapidly, threatening to envelope them as well.

"Mind if I jump both ships clear?" his AI asked, a hint of sarcasm in her voice.

"Please," Josh replied, his gaze transfixed on the growing fireball ahead.

The fireball sank downward as his AI pitched the ship up just enough to get a clear jump line. A moment later, they were back in space, high over the planet.

Josh took control again, rolling over and pitching back so that he was upside down, flying backwards. Behind them, he could see the fireball on the surface, still growing larger as more and more vissian gas was ignited. "How big will that thing get?"

"*The concentration of vissian gas in the atmosphere is not high enough to sustain its growth for much longer,"* his AI explained. *"It is in the area of the colony where the concentration is highest due to the disturbance of the soil. The gas is also more dense at night when the temperatures are lower."* After a pause, his AI added. *"The fireball should dissipate in a few more minutes. Unfortunately, it will have encompassed eighty-three percent of the population by that time."*

"How many people on Estabrook?" Josh asked.

"Eight thousand two hundred and eighty-seven. However, many of their buildings have auto-seal capabilities, just in case of an accidental ignition event such as this."

"I'm not picking up any bandits," Nikolas reported. *"Do you think they were taken out by the blast?"*

"Doubtful," Josh replied solemnly. "I'm pretty sure they expected this to happen."

After a moment, Nikolas said, *"I really want to kill these fuckers."*

"We will, Remo. We will."

* * *

Nathan entered the main hangar bay, heading straight for the Aurora as the Mirai rolled out onto the flight deck.

"She's still loaded for combat, with a med-bay in the middle," Marcus reported as Nathan approached. "I can reload her for MCI, but it will take a few minutes."

"Get your ass up here," Jessica called over Nathan's comm-set. "QRF Two is aboard, and we're ready for takeoff."

"No time," Nathan said, heading toward the Seiiki's boarding hatch. "But have them in the queue just in case."

"Just so you know, you can drop all your modules

in place and come back empty if you want to speed up the swap out," Marcus told him.

Nathan paused a moment. "Really?"

"Yup. They can still be used as stand-alone units too. Got their own power source and everything."

"Why didn't you tell me this before?" Nathan wondered.

"I just found out."

* * *

Four flashes of light appeared in the night sky above the Kataokan colony, followed by two more slightly larger ones. Moments later, four Brodek snub-fighters streaked over the surface, firing indiscriminately as they passed.

Two pirate shuttles came next, jumping from their arrival point to a hovering position over the center of the colony. The shuttles descended to a meter above the surface, and eight armed men jumped out of each ship, fanning out with weapons firing as they landed.

"Shit!" Talisha exclaimed, rolling her fighter into a tight turn as the six red icons appeared on her threat display. A second later, sixteen smaller icons representing armed men on the surface appeared, clustered around the two icons in the middle of the colony itself. "Troops on the ground! Troops on the ground! Sixteen count! Two shuttles with four snubs flying cover!"

"*QRF One is going in,*" Kit announced.

"Tika, cover their insertion. I'll engage those snubs."

Kit and his team were already suited up, but now all four of them stepped back onto their donning pads.

Their donning systems activated and added large modules onto their standard combat backpacks, as well as additional components on their chest. "Heavied up, going in," Kit announced.

"*Insertion jump...now,*" the QRF AI pilot reported.

The side doors slid open, the shuttle now hovering two meters over the center of the colony. Blasts of red-orange plasma-rifle fire streaked up at them from all directions as the Brodek on the ground opened up on them, their shields flashing brightly as the incoming bolts of energy struck.

"Full power, quick and dirty, boys," Kit instructed.

Four Ghatazhak clad in heavy, black combat armor dropped from the sides of the hovering shuttle, the shuttle disappearing in a blue-white flash as soon as they stepped out. The men landed in a semi-crouch, their personal shields immediately taking fire and flashing with the impacts.

"*Personal shield power falling,*" Kit's AI warned.

Kit wasted no time. "Free to fire," he instructed his AI as he raised both hands and began firing his wrist-mounted blasters.

Two small blasters popped up from each of Kit's shoulders, flipping over and taking aim on the enemy spreading out around the Ghatazhak. The blasters opened fire, laying down suppression fire rather than trying for a kill.

Kit and his men stood their ground, all of them walking in different directions toward the incoming fire, trusting their rapidly draining personal shields to keep them from harm. Their shoulder blasters peppered the area with fire, forcing the enemy to duck for cover, thereby decreasing their ability to return fire.

Kit looked at four different targets displayed on the inside of his tactical visor, sending mental lock orders on each one. "Flechettes, please."

"Firing," his AI replied.

An opening appeared on the back of Kit's assault pack, and eight tiny rockets about the length of a man's hand were ejected about half a meter up into the air. The engines on the back of the rockets lit up, and they streaked out, each of them turning toward different targets.

The same thing occurred with the other three Ghatazhak, a total of twenty-four flechette rockets streaking out from the gang of four at the center of the city. The rockets found their targets a split second later, creating a flurry of explosions and destruction.

Kit ceased fire, standing motionless as red icons began rapidly disappearing from his tactical visor. Two seconds later, his visor was clear.

"Status?" he asked his AI.

"No targets remaining. Personal shields down to forty percent and increasing."

"Dragon Two-One, QRF One-One. Surface threat eliminated. Sit-rep?"

"All airborne targets have jumped away," Talisha replied. "Shall we pursue?"

"Negative," Kit instructed. "Hold position."

"Copy that."

Another jump flash appeared in the distance.

"Mirai, entering the airspace," Aiden reported over comms.

"Mirai, QRF One-One," Kit replied. "Land in the colony center. I suspect we're looking at quite a few civilian casualties here."

* * *

"So far they've attacked every world *except* Persa," Ensign Dass exclaimed.

"Are these attacks all being conducted by the same forces, or are we looking at multiple elements?" Cameron asked Laza.

"I've only received sensor data from two of the engagements so far," Laza replied. "Best I can tell, they were by the same snub-fighters."

"New flash-traffic from QRF One," Sima announced. "The Brodek just put sixteen armed men into the middle of Kataoka. They're going in now."

"The Mirai went to Kataoka, right?"

"Yes, sir," Sima confirmed.

Cameron tapped her comm-set. "Nathan, go to Persa."

"*Why?*" Nathan asked.

"No time to explain."

"*On my way.*"

"Josh reported all clear on Estabrook?" Cameron asked Sima.

"Yes, sir."

"Send them to Persa."

"Aye, sir."

* * *

Josh jumped into Persa's atmosphere, fully expecting to find the entire city ablaze. Instead, he was met with an overwhelming assault of energy weapons fire plowing into his forward shields, rocking his ship violently.

"Fuck!" Josh exclaimed, pitching up sharply to get a clear jump line.

The incoming barrage suddenly ceased.

"What the hell?" Josh glanced down at his tactical display, spotting a single large, red icon. He looked back up just as the clouds cleared, and a Brodek gunship appeared before him, hovering low over the Persan colony. "Oh shit."

The jump flash washed over the Seiiki's cockpit, and their threat warning light began to flash, accompanied by an audible alarm.

"Crap! Something big, directly over the colony," Jessica warned. "About three times our size, with lots of guns."

"Attention, forces of Captain Tuplo," an ominous voice called over comms. *"Cease all operations within the Vernay, or all its worlds will be destroyed. This is your only warning."*

Nathan looked out the forward windows as they punched through the cloud layer, just in time to see the formidable gunship begin its departure ascent. "I guess that confirms at least *one* of their gunships."

A blue-white flash filled their forward windows, and the gunship was gone.

"Tell me you heard that," Josh called over comms.

"I did," Nathan replied.

"I guess we've just been warned," Jessica stated.

"More like challenged," Nathan corrected.

"I figured you would say that."

CHAPTER ELEVEN

"The Brodek just told us to put up or shut up," Jessica declared to everyone seated at the table in the Aurora's command briefing room.

"I've studied the sensor data from your brief contact with the Brodek gunship," Laza stated. "In our current state, we have a very good chance of defeating them as long as there are no more than three. If we include the Seiiki and the Mirai in full combat configuration, in that calculation, the odds become even better. I should point out, however, that I have no data on their shield strength."

"Our shuttles will have to take out their surface defenses as well as provide cover for the Ghatazhak," Robert insisted.

"Agreed." Nathan looked to Kit. "What's your assessment?"

"Put all eight of us in heavy assault configuration and place us around the center of the city. Then we should be able to draw them into the spaceport landing field at the center."

"Why put their spaceport at the center?" Abby wondered.

"Crowden's entire economy is based on the Brodek's import/export business," Cameron explained. "So it kind of makes sense. Pretty much everything they need to exist is imported."

"Then what do they export?" Abby asked.

"Whatever stolen loot they don't need," Jessica commented.

"I should note that my assessment is based on an assumed force strength of up to one hundred armed combatants," Kit cautioned. "More than that, and we're going to need to start blowing up buildings, which means more collateral damage."

"I'd prefer that we avoid that," Nathan admitted. "However, the people of Crowden are well aware of who the Brodek are and what they do. So they bear some of the responsibility for the Brodek's actions." He looked at Kit. "If more men than expected join the fight, we'll lay waste to every building they come out of. If necessary, we'll pull you out and lay waste to the entire colony."

That surprised everyone.

"Are you sure you want to do that?" Cameron asked.

"It's not a matter of want," Nathan explained. "The people of the Vernay do not deserve what the Brodek does to them, nor does anyone else. If we do this, we're not just taking down a single pirate clan. We're sending a message to all the pirate clans out there. We may as well make it clear that hiding among the sheep isn't going to work."

"So rather than poking the hornet's nest, you plan on whacking the hell out of it," Jessica surmised.

"I plan on breaking it wide open," Nathan declared.

"And what if the Korsan come looking for retribution?" Cameron wondered.

"I'm betting it will take more than the loss of a single clan for the Korsan to react."

"That's a pretty big bet," Robert stated.

"Maybe, but they're going to have to find us first."

"Something tells me that sometime soon, that's not going to be very hard," Cameron opined. "For the sake of argument, what if they do?"

"That's why we're going to steal the last three Expedition-class ships," Nathan replied. "After we deal with the Brodek and establish a new world as a base of operations."

Jessica laughed. "Nothing grand about *that* plan, is there?"

"You didn't honestly expect me to turn tail and run, did you?" Nathan asked.

"Hell no," Jessica replied. "And for the record, I wouldn't have let you."

Nathan looked to Cameron at the other end of the table. "This is too big a call for me to make on my own."

Cameron sighed. "I think it's a *horrible* idea. But it isn't the *worst* plan you've ever come up with. And it is the *right* thing to do."

"It's settled then," Nathan decided. "Robert, you and Loki will fly the Seiiki. Aiden, you and Erica will fly the Mirai. Josh, you'll lead the Dragons."

"Who's gonna fly the Aurora?" Josh wondered.

"I will," Nathan replied, "with Cameron at ops, and Jessica at tactical." He looked to Abby next. "I'm assuming you'll operate the jump drive for us?"

"Where else would I be?" Abby answered.

"Vlad, do you have enough people to keep this ship together?"

"Of course," Vladimir replied. "I think. Probably. Well probably not, but if you can just avoid *crashing* her again, then yes...I think."

"Nice, definitive answer there, Vlad," Jessica teased.

"Very well," Nathan stated. "Josh, your Dragons will conduct the initial attack on their air defense batteries on the surface, softening it up for the Ghatazhak insertions. The Seiiki will follow close behind, targeting the Brodek's main building near the center of the colony. After your initial pass, you'll insert your pair of Ghatazhak to the surface while the Mirai and the Ghatazhak QRF shuttle inserts the other three pairs. That should stir up the hornet's nest pretty well."

"What's the Aurora going to be doing?" Robert wondered.

"We're going to stay out of immediate sensor range for as long as possible," Nathan explained. "The Brodek still can't be certain that we even *have* a ship, so we don't want to tip them off from the start. We don't know exactly *where* their gunships are based, just their relative distance from the colony. I'm hoping that the initial attacks will force them to call out their gunships. That's when we'll jump in and join the fray."

"Is there a retreat plan?" Cameron inquired.

"We don't need a retreat plan," Kit boasted.

"If it starts to look like we're going to lose or that winning will cost us too much, then I will order all forces to retreat," Nathan promised. "This is not the hill I plan for us to die on."

"Not going to happen," Kit insisted. "As long as our air cover keeps the fighters off our backs, we'll mow their ground forces down. All you have to worry about are those gunships."

"Let's hope you're right," Nathan agreed. "Loki, where is Alex right now?"

"They're all on the Acuna, waiting to hear from me," Loki replied.

"Good, we'll tell them together." Nathan looked at the others. "That's it, everyone. We launch in one hour."

"Uh, can you make it two?" Vladimir asked. "There are still just a *few* tiny things I'd like to finish first."

"Very well, two hours," Nathan agreed.

* * *

"We need to ditch these people," Josi insisted as she nervously paced the Acuna's port cargo bay.

"Need I remind you that *these people* are fixing Pop's medical problems?" Alex argued. "If we leave now, how are we ever going to hook up with them again?"

"They'll go back to Estabrook."

"Estabrook is burnt over," Alex reminded her.

"They'll rebuild," Josi insisted. "It's not the first time they've experienced a vissian flash-over."

"We're not going anywhere until Mom and Pop get back, and that's the end of it," Alex insisted.

"I don't know, Alex," Shane chimed in, standing by the exit. He turned away from the exit toward his older sisters. "We won't do Mom and Pop any good if we're all dead and the Acuna is destroyed."

"That's not going to happen," Nathan said as he and Loki came up the ramp.

Josi looked around. "Are you still bugging us?"

"No, I just have really good hearing," Nathan replied.

"And you guys were arguing rather loudly," Loki added.

Josi stepped forward, bound and determined to get her way. "No disrespect, Captain, but this thing with the Brodek…"

"Is ending today," Nathan insisted. "We're taking them out. *Completely* out."

"With two shuttles and eleven fighters?" Josi laughed.

"And the Aurora," Nathan added.

That got their attention.

"She can fly?" Josi asked, finding the idea a bit hard to believe.

"And fight," Nathan replied.

"She's still full of holes," Shane commented.

"We are well aware of her condition," Nathan assured him.

"What about us?" Alex wondered.

"The Acuna stays put. Take her over to Gruner and wait for us to return."

"And if you don't?" Josi asked.

"Then you'll be free of your contract, with no debts owed," Nathan replied.

"Just like that?"

"Just like that."

"What about our parents?" Alex asked.

"If you don't hear from us by the end of the day, then it's a pretty safe bet you never will. Wait at Gruner until your parents return. At that point, you can go wherever you like."

"Wherever we like," Josi said. "Where are we supposed to go? You've made us a target for every pirate gang out there."

"Your ship is in good enough condition that you can fly jobs between the fringe and the border worlds, where you won't have to worry about pirates."

"But we're still tagged in the Alliance system," Alex reminded him.

"Tug promised to use his contacts to clear the tag," Nathan told her. "You should already be back in good standing with the Alliance."

"You can probably even pass one of their mechanical inspections," Loki pointed out.

"What about you?" Alex asked Loki.

"I'll be flying the Seiiki in the attack," Loki replied. "With any luck, I should see you all in a few hours."

Alex stared at Loki a moment then rose and

walked over to him. "Make sure you do." She kissed him on the cheek and added, "For luck."

"Thanks," Loki replied.

Nathan turned and headed back out, with Loki following him. As they reached the bottom of the ramp and headed back across the flight deck toward the opening to the shuttle bay, he looked at Loki, smiling. "For luck huh?"

* * *

Nathan entered the bridge just as engineers from the Bonaventura finished up their repairs on the last of the damaged consoles. "How are we looking?" Nathan asked as he entered.

"All consoles should be working," the lead Takaran engineer reported. He pressed a button on his data pad, and the last few consoles lit up. "And we have a surprise for you." He pressed another button, and the forward windows began to glow softly, the outside view becoming slightly opaque, as if they were looking through sheer curtains.

Nathan watched as the opaqueness faded and the outside images returned to normal. "What just happened?" he asked, turning to look at the Takaran engineer. "Did you..."

"We did," the man boasted. "All of them are fully operational again, though the bow cameras are still down. But all your tactical overlays and interior holographic reference projections should work."

"Outstanding," Nathan congratulated.

As the men headed for the exit, Vladimir arrived.

"What are you doing here?" Cameron asked.

"I'll be running things from the port auxiliary console," Vladimir explained.

"Shouldn't you be in engineering?" Nathan asked.

"The Aurora's AI does more than fly and fight the

ship," Vladimir explained. "She manages all systems, reroutes around damaged relays, redistributes power, and constantly optimizes performance to fit the situation. With her consciousness offline, someone must perform these tasks."

"And since you're tied into the ship's network of systems monitoring sensors via your bio-neural interface, that would be you," Nathan surmised. "But wouldn't you do that better from engineering?"

"If I'm *here,* I will be constantly aware of the ever-changing situation. If I'm in engineering, I would have to wait for you to inform me of the situation."

"We could keep an open line for you," Ensign Dass suggested.

"Not the same," Vladimir insisted as he took his seat at the port auxiliary station.

"What if something needs *hands on*?" Nathan asked.

"Dominic and his team can handle it," Vladimir replied as he configured his station for the upcoming task. He turned to look at Nathan and the others. "Do you not *want* me here?"

"We're just not *used* to you being here," Nathan assured him. "But if you think it's best, then by all means."

"Good." Vladimir turned back to his console, tapping away as he called up final checks on all the Aurora's flight systems.

Nathan watched, slightly amazed at the speed at which Vladimir worked, system status lists appearing and disappearing so quickly he could barely read them. "You always work that quickly?" Nathan wondered, noticing how fast Vladimir's fingers seemed to move across the console's inputs.

"I know, it's amazing, isn't it?"

"When did this start?"

"A few days after the interface was implanted," Vladimir told him. "I can't explain it. I just type really fast now."

"Apparently you can *read* really fast as well."

"That?" Vladimir waved the screens off. "I'm not even reading that to be honest. I'm seeing it all in here," he added, pointing at his head before returning to his inputs.

"So are we ready?"

"In a few minutes," Vladimir replied. "I'm bringing the grav-lift systems up to just a hair less power than needed to raise the ship, in an effort to do a little pre-calibration."

"Is that necessary?" Cameron wondered.

"If you don't want to lose control on ascent and possibly slam into the canyon walls, then *da*, it is *very* necessary."

"Then please, take your time," Nathan told him. "Let's get everyone else in the air," he told Ensign Dass. "Just in case."

"Aye, sir," Sima acknowledged.

"I heard that," Vladimir barked, still furiously typing away.

* * *

"How are we looking, Master Chief?" Robert asked as he and Loki walked up to Marcus, Aiden, and Erica.

"Both shuttles are loaded for bear," Marcus boasted. "Fore and aft-facing torpedo cannons in the side bays, air-to-ground fire support module in the midship bay, and a full missile module in the rear."

"Damn," Erica stated, surprised. "I knew you could put weapons into them, but I didn't realize how *many* weapons."

"Are you sure you're up for this?" Robert asked Erica.

"Honestly?"

"She'll be fine," Aiden assured him.

"I'm sure she will," Robert agreed, turning to head for the Seiiki.

"Good luck," Loki remarked, turning to follow Robert.

Aiden turned back to Erica.

"Are you sure?" Erica asked.

"About what?"

"About me," Erica replied. "I have *zero* combat training."

"Yes, but you do know the ship and its systems."

"Not its *weapons* systems," Erica pointed out.

"But the ship's AI does, and she'll be doing most of the firing."

"Most?"

"Pretty much all of it actually." Aiden gestured toward the Mirai. "Shall we?"

Erica took a deep breath and headed for their ship. "This is probably the most insane thing I've ever done."

* * *

One by one, Dragon fighters shot out of the Aurora's launch tubes on either side, spaced only a few seconds apart. As each one left the tube, their bow thrusters fired, pushing their noses up as their main drives went to full power, jumping away a few seconds later as they rocketed skyward.

* * *

Alex watched through the Acuna's forward windows as the Mirai lifted off the flight deck in front of her, with the Seiiki rolling out and departing after her.

"They're not coming back," Josi said from behind.

"You don't know that," Alex replied as she prepared for liftoff.

"They're going up against the Brodek *and* the Korsan."

"We don't know *that* either."

"Even if by some miracle they *do* manage to defeat the Brodek, how long until the Korsan send in another clan to fill the void?" Josi asked.

"I'm sure they've thought of that," Alex said.

"You put too much faith in them," Josi insisted. "Especially Loki."

Alex ignored her.

"*Acuna-Dera, Aurora. You're clear for takeoff.*"

"Aurora, Acuna-Dera copies." Alex activated the liftoff sequence, adding, "Good hunting."

"*See you soon, Acuna,*" Sima replied.

"See you soon," Alex said to herself as her ship began to rise from the Aurora's flight deck.

* * *

"Shuttles and Dragons are away and circling at a safe distance," Sima announced. "The Acuna is also aloft."

"Very well," Nathan replied, turning slowly around in his command chair until he was facing Vladimir at the back auxiliary station on the port side of the bridge.

At first, Vladimir did not notice him, but soon, he felt everyone's gaze upon him, and he looked up. "What?"

"We're waiting on you," Nathan told him.

"I am ready."

Nathan rose from his command chair and stepped over to the helm station, stepping down into the recessed slot and taking a seat. "Comms, broadcast to all ships, the Aurora is taking off."

"Aye, sir."

Cameron took her place at the ops station to Nathan's left. "We hope."

"Your faith in me is overwhelming," Vladimir complained.

The Seiiki settled into a hover next to the Mirai, about a kilometer away from the Aurora's original crash site.

"Attention all ships. The Aurora is about to lift off," Ensign Dass broadcast over comms.

"Hold it here," Robert instructed.

"Holding hover position," the Seiiki's AI confirmed.

"We don't want to miss this," he commented to Loki as both men gazed out the forward windows.

"Message from the Bonaventura," Ensign Dass announced from the comm-station. "They wish us 'fair winds and following seas.'"

"Wouldn't 'clear skies and tailwinds' be more appropriate?" Cameron suggested as her fingers skimmed over her operations console, checking that everything was ready.

"I'll take any kind of luck I can get right now," Nathan insisted.

"Tactical is ready," Jessica stated from the tactical console. "Not that it matters at this point."

"Jump systems?" Nathan asked, his question directed to Abby, who was behind him and to his right.

"I've got an escape jump loaded and ready," Abby replied. "All I need is a clear jump line and a few meters per minute of forward momentum."

"I thought we could jump just using the planet's rotational speed as our momentum?" Nathan questioned.

"*Theoretically*, which I assume you'd prefer not to test at this particular moment."

"Agreed," Nathan replied. "Alright, people. Here we go."

"Remember, just ease her up and hold," Vladimir reminded.

"Got it," Nathan replied as he eased the grav-lift throttles forward gently.

Aiden and Erica watched through the Mirai's forward windows as they hovered nearby next to the Seiiki. In the distance, they could see the Aurora begin to rise slowly from the ground, her massive landing gear hanging below. As soon as her landing skids lifted from the dirt, the ship began to slide sideways, tipping slightly in the process, her nose also beginning to yaw to starboard.

"Is she supposed to do that?" Erica wondered.

"Uh...no."

"Vlad?" Nathan asked, struggling to control the undesired motion of the ship.

"I've got this!" Vladimir insisted as his hands danced across his console.

"This valley isn't wide enough for more than thirty degrees of yaw," Cameron warned.

"I know," Nathan assured her. "I'm working on it."

"Ten degrees," Cameron announced. "Fifteen..."

"Vlad, I've got no bow thrusters, and the docking thrusters are already burning at full power," Nathan reminded him.

"I'm calibrating the starboard grav-lift emitters now!" Vladimir replied.

"Twenty degrees…"

"I've almost got it!"

"Twenty-*five* degrees!" Cameron warned.

Nathan glanced out the side windows, seeing the ridge line moving toward them. "Screw this, I'm going to full grav-lift power."

"No!" Vladimir yelled. "Not yet!"

"Oh…my…God," Alex exclaimed as she, Josi, and Shane all stared out the windows of the Acuna's cockpit, watching the Aurora begin to roll over to her starboard.

"She's going over," Josi warned.

"I can't watch this," Alex decided, covering up her eyes with both hands.

Nathan glanced to his right again. He could practically reach out and touch the canyon wall outside. "Vlad!"

"Twenty-eight degrees!" Cameron warned. "Impact in five seconds!"

Abby's hand went to the jump button, her index finger hovering over it. Despite the fact that she had zero scientific evidence that a ship could *not* jump through solid matter, Loki's successful passage through the tip of a mountain made her ready to give it a try rather than allowing the ship to crash yet again.

The ship suddenly stopped yawing and rolling to starboard, leveling off.

"I got it!" Vladimir cried out. "You can start climbing!"

Nathan eased the grav-lift throttles forward and

the canyon walls outside began to fall away as the Aurora climbed for clear skies.

All ten Dragon fighters were lined up along the Aurora's port side, about a kilometer away. Not one of them wanted to miss this moment, good or bad.

Josh watched confidently from his cockpit as his fighter hovered a few meters off the ground, his broad smile growing as he watched the mighty Aurora climb up above the canyon walls and begin moving forward, her landing gear retracting into her hull. "She's flying!" he exclaimed over comms as he pushed his throttles forward slightly to pursue their home ship.

Nathan and Cameron's gazes danced back and forth between the windows in front of them and their own consoles as the Aurora continued climbing and accelerating forward.

"Gear is coming up," Cameron reported happily.

Nathan had his left hand on the flight control stick and his right hand moving back and forth between the grav-lift throttles and those for the Aurora's main engines. His attention was mostly on his flight dynamics display, but he could not resist a glance outside every few seconds.

"Pressure is holding in all sealed compartments," Vladimir reported. "Artificial gravity is a little shaky in some areas but still within tolerances. "We're looking good for orbit."

"Climbing out," Nathan announced. He moved his hands from the grav-lift throttles back to the main propulsion throttles, pushing them forward until he felt the fifty percent indent. "Mains at half."

"Accelerating nicely," Cameron reported. "We'll clear the atmosphere in twenty seconds."

"Unbelievable," Josi gasped as she watched the Aurora climb away and disappear. "That ship can really move out."

"No kidding," Shane agreed. "It takes us like five minutes to reach orbit."

Alex just smiled as she turned the ship toward Gruner. "Good luck, everyone," she broadcast over comms as the Dragons and shuttles climbed away in pursuit of the Aurora.

Nathan couldn't look away from the windows as the Aurora reached Dencke's Kármán line. The planet's lavender skies faded quickly to black, the stars filling the sky ahead.

"That's my girl," Nathan crooned to himself. He glanced over to Sima at the comm-station to his right. "Ship-wide."

Sima nodded to him.

"Attention all hands. The Aurora is back in space. Nicely done, everyone. Nicely done."

"I have your jump to the Crowden system ready," Abby told Nathan. "It's a series of four jumps, each progressively longer than the last. Sort of a test, if you don't mind."

"Your call, Abby."

"Turn to three two seven, up eighteen relative, and accelerate to five hundred thousand kilometers per hour."

"Turning to three two seven by plus eighteen and accelerating to five hundred thousand," Nathan confirmed, pushing his throttles forward a bit more and adjusting course. "So long, Dencke."

CHAPTER TWELVE

Things had been tense on Crowden for the past few weeks, but the recent raids on the Vernay worlds had given the Brodek cause to celebrate. And when the Brodek celebrated, all of Crowden joined in. The streets were packed with revelers dancing to music, drinking, eating, and carousing with one another in a myriad of forms.

Halvor Brodek sat on his balcony in the center of Crowden, observing the raucous festivities in the streets below. As usual, a bevy of attractive, suggestively dressed women stood ready to cater to his needs.

His trusted subordinate, Ottar, sat nearby, although his mood was not as festive.

"Why the foul mood?" the Brodek leader asked.

"You know as well as I that this was not a victory."

"All six Vernay worlds have sent word that they will not accept any trade that has not passed through our hands. If that's not a victory, I don't know what is."

"You said you wanted Captain Tuplo's head," Ottar reminded his leader.

"You don't get to lead a clan by force and swordsmanship alone," Halvor stated. "It also requires patience. I doubt this Tuplo fellow will give up that easily. He will try to convince the Vernay worlds to stay the course. He will appeal to their sense of freedom, but the people know that it is the pirate clans who keep them safe *and* supplied. And there are costs in providing such services. Our brutality gets the job done, and the people in the badlands understand this. If not for us, there would be a dozen independents stealing from them, jacking every ship that passed through the passage."

"But they did not run their cargo *through* the Vernay passage," Ottar reminded his leader.

"They either found another safe route, or they are taking their chances dead-heading. *That* is why I had our forces strike the Vernay. To show them the price of disloyalty. We will increase the frequencies of our patrols of the *destinations* and ignore the passage. I have every confidence that you will find him and bring me his head."

"Of course," Ottar replied. There was more he felt he needed to tell his leader, like the fact that he had not heard from his spy handler since the last Vernay raids. That would have to wait. His leader was famous for his short temper and had on more than one drunken occasion removed the heads of subordinates with a single stroke of the saber that always hung opposite his gun holster. Besides, there was still a chance the handler was simply lying low, maintaining his cover. After all, the second raid was less than a day old, and the Vernay worlds had only capitulated in the last few hours. The Brodek empire would still be around come morning, and by noon, his leader would be wide awake and sober once more.

* * *

"Jump four, complete," Abby reported as the Aurora's jump flash faded.

"We're at the rally point," Cameron reported from the ops station to Nathan's left. "One light year outside of the Crowden system."

"Threat board is clear," Jessica announced.

"All ten Dragons, the QRF shuttle, the Seiiki, and the Mirai have arrived," Laza announced.

Nathan tapped his comm-set. "Neli, status?"

"Ordering a snack?" Cameron joked.

"*Distribution complete,*" Neli replied. "*I'm on my way to you now.*"

"Comms, broadcast to all units and ship-wide," Nathan instructed.

"Aye, sir," Sima acknowledged. "Ready."

"Attention all hands," Nathan began. "This is your captain. Over the years, we have taken many oaths. First, to protect and defend Earth, then to do the same for the people of Corinair, and after that, the people of the entire Pentaurus cluster. Like so many of us, I too gave my life to protect others. But thanks to my crew…my *friends*…I was reborn."

Neli entered, carrying a small box full of envelopes that she began passing out to the bridge staff.

Vladimir was the first to receive an envelope. On it were handwritten words. 'Do not open until instructed.'

"And like an idiot," Nathan continued, "I did the same thing again, leading the crusade against the Dusahn Empire, and finally coming back to defend Earth yet again, if only from herself. In that time, I have learned one thing above all else: that all of us *deserve* to be free." Nathan paused a moment. "The Alliance was formed to protect freedom but has somehow become more concerned with its own perpetuity than the people it was formed to protect. Therefore, I have chosen to cast aside my oath to that Alliance and instead will take it upon myself to adhere to the common principles of every oath I have ever taken."

Neli finally reached Nathan but handed him two patches instead of an envelope.

Nathan looked at the patch then smiled, looking back at Neli. He studied the patch again, reading aloud the words written above and below the image of the Aurora. "Liberty and truth, peace and prosperity. That is what this ship will stand and *fight* for. Not for a select few, but for *all*. We will not answer to any authority other than ourselves, and anyone who threatens these ideals shall become our adversaries. Unfortunately, there will always be those who use force to threaten these rights, just as the Brodek have done. And while we may stand for peace, there is a reason this ship has weapons."

Robert and Loki listened intently to Nathan's speech over comms as they prepared the Seiiki for battle. *"All of you have received a small envelope. I invite you to open it now. Inside, you will find new shoulder patches."*

Josh scanned his display, ensuring that his Dragon was ready for combat as he listened.
"Use them to replace the two you currently wear."
Josh glanced down at his left shoulder, having already opened the envelope and placed the patches on his shoulders. "Oops."

"We are one ship. We are one mission," Nathan's voice continued over the intercom speaker in the Mirai's forward boarding bay, where Chief Anson and Corporal Teece stood waiting, each outfitted in Ghatazhak heavy assault armor. *"We are one family. This patch symbolizes this and all that we stand for."*

"Liberty and truth, peace and prosperity...for all of humanity. Henceforth, this will be our mission."
Kit exchanged glances with Mori, Jokay, and

Abdur, all of them in their heavy assault armor. All men nodded.

"Always good to know what you're fighting for," Mori said.

"We already knew," Kit replied.

Nathan pulled the patches off his shoulders then stuck the new ones on in their place. "That is all."

Cameron also donned her new patches. "Nice speech."

"What are the four stars for?" Jessica wondered as she stared at her patches.

"The four ideals that we stand for," Neli explained.

"I was hoping it was for *this* ship and the three we're planning on stealing," Jessica said.

"That too," Nathan admitted. "But let's take care of the Brodek first, shall we? Abby?"

"Insertion jump plotted and ready," Abby confirmed.

"Very well. General quarters. Comms, signal all ships to start the battle clock."

* * *

Ottar made his way through the crowds of revelers. He had little interest in celebrations, since he was certain this Captain Tuplo would not give up so easily. Men with such resources rarely did. Even his own leader was constantly looking for new opportunities, even though the Brodek clan had virtually everything they needed.

But in the last few years, Halvor Brodek's age had begun to catch up with him. He spent more time cavorting with servants and enjoying the fruits of his exploits than he did practicing the skills that had gotten him there. He was still a formidable man but was not the same man he had once been.

As much as Ottar hated to see his leader's greatness fading, it was also an opportunity. He was already one of Halvor Brodek's most trusted subordinates. If he did manage to capture Captain Tuplo and bring him to Halvor, it would cement his place as the heir to the Brodek clan.

Two flashes of light in the southern night sky caught Ottar's attention. A second later, he heard several distant claps of thunder. He wasn't certain how many, but it was more than two.

Explosions rocked the city, coming from all directions. The celebration stopped, the revelers frozen in shock until the warning klaxons began to sound.

Ottar grabbed his comm-unit from his pocket as he pushed his way through the fleeing crowd. "Gelan! What is happening!"

"*We are under attack!*" Gelan replied. "*The same fighters that we encountered in the Vernay! We count eight so far...wait...make that ten I think. They're targeting our air defense batteries!*"

"Scramble everyone, including our gunships!" Ottar instructed. "I'm heading for my ship now!"

* * *

Immediately after jumping out at the end of his first attack pass, Josh rolled left and pulled his Dragon fighter into a sharp left turn to come about.

"*I didn't see a single shot coming from the surface!*" Lannie reported over comms. "*Did you?*"

"I guess they don't have any early warning systems," Josh replied. "Don't count on it being that easy on the second pass." He glanced down at his tactical display, examining the remaining surface defenses. "They've still got plenty of batteries down there, so be ready to make a quick escape jump if they lock and launch on you."

"*Copy that*," his wingman confirmed.

Another glance at his tactical display, and Josh saw that his AI had selected the targets for their next pass. "This swarm target management shit is slick as hell. Sure beats calling your shots over comms."

"*I know! Zero thinking. Just fly.*"

Josh chuckled. "I never did much thinking anyway," he said as he rolled out of his turn and pressed the jump button on his flight control stick.

The jump flash washed over him, and he suddenly found himself low over the city of Crowden, rapidly approaching his designated targets.

"*Targets acquired,*" his AI announced.

"Firing four," Josh announced as he pressed the missile launch button on his flight control stick. Four short missiles raced out from underneath and on either side of his fighter, fanning out as they raced toward their respective targets. He immediately pulled back on his flight control stick and gunned his throttles. He was so close to his targets that it would only take six seconds for them to reach their targets, and he didn't want to be caught in the blast.

A few energy bolts lashed out at him from the surface, most from handheld energy rifles. Josh's nose rose up sharply, and the city rapidly fell away as all four of his missiles found their targets and exploded. A second later, his wingman's missiles also hit their targets, adding four more explosions to the chaos below.

A quick tap of his jump button, and he was now ten kilometers higher in the atmosphere and just as many downrange. This time, he rolled right to come about. "A few more passes and we'll own them."

Talisha and Nikolas jumped in for their second attack pass just as Josh's second wave of missiles exploded. Her targets were already chosen and acquired, so all she had to do was press the launch button then turn onto her designated escape course. By the time her missiles detonated below, she was already jumping clear.

"How are you doing, Remo?" Talisha asked over comms.

"*So far, so good,*" Nikolas replied.

"Coming onto heading for pass three," Talisha announced as she rolled out of her turn.

Allet's ship shook violently as he came out of the jump and started his next attack run. "A lot more fire coming at us."

"*I am detecting multiple surface-to-air defense turrets now in operation,*" his AI announced.

"No kidding." His targets lit up on his tactical screen, and Allet pressed the launch button, sending four more missiles streaking out from under him toward the surface. He immediately rolled left and pulled back on his flight control stick, pressing his jump button as more energy weapons fire slammed into his shields.

A second later, he and his wingman were high in the sky again, far from Crowden and the guns that defended it.

"*It took them three passes to get their defenses spun up,*" Mick commented over comms. "*That's pretty lousy combat readiness if you ask me.*"

"I don't mind."

Nikolas followed Talisha out of her turn, his fighter jumping ahead simultaneously with hers.

Now over the city again, his tactical display lit up with targets popping up all over the place. And not just surface batteries. "Uh..."

"Launching four," Talisha reported.

Nikolas glanced at his tactical display again, noting that his targets were locked in. He pressed his own missile launch button, sending four streaking ahead. "Launching four."

Nikolas glanced at his tactical display again, first four, then four more icons representing the surface defense batteries they were targeting disappeared as expected, but several others were appearing... and they were moving. "Fighters!" he realized. "They must have them stashed all over the city!"

"*I've got 'em,*" Talisha acknowledged. "All Dragons, Dragon Two-One. Fighters launching from all over the surface. Go to attack plan Bravo."

"Dragon Two-One is reporting Brodek snub-fighters launching from all over the city," Loki reported from the Seiiki's copilot's seat.

"They've got them spread out so we can't target them as easily," Robert commented. "That's why we didn't see them on Nathan's recon pass."

"How nice. A snub-fighter in every garage." Loki tapped his intercom panel. "Be ready, guys. Snub-fighters in the air."

"Seiiki," Robert called to the shuttle's AI. "Weapons free on all enemy snub-fighters and combat shuttles. Maximum force is authorized."

"*Understood,*" their AI confirmed.

Robert glanced at Loki. "Here we go."

"*Surface defenses have been eliminated,*" the QRF shuttle AI pilot announced over the Ghatazhak's helmet comms. "*However, there are numerous Brodek snub-fighters launching from all over the city. Dragons are going to attack plan Bravo. Prepare for first insertion jump.*"

"See you all down there," Kit announced as he leaned forward, causing his heavy assault pack to disengage from the locker face. He moved over to the port door as their AI pilot opened it.

The doors slid open on either side, exposing the interior of the QRF shuttle to the Crowden atmosphere. It was dark outside and cloudy.

As Kit and Mori stepped up to the open port hatch, the shuttle's jump flash washed over them. Now the clouds were gone, and they were in a near hover, barely sliding forward over the city about fifty meters below them.

Weapons fire lashed out from the surface, striking the shuttle's ventral shields and causing them to flash brightly. Kit was first, turning to face forward as he stepped out the door and began his fall to the surface. His suit immediately flashed, jumping him to a meter above the surface before he could gain too much momentum.

Kit landed in a semi-crouch, breaking into a jog with both arms held high, firing his wrist-mounted energy cannons at anyone that his tactical visor tagged as a threat.

Mori landed two-steps behind him, also firing as he followed Kit forward.

The moment Mori had stepped out, the QRF shuttle jumped again, but only enough to transition to the opposite side of the city center, where Jokay and Abdur also stepped out and jumped to the surface, wrist-cannons blazing.

The Mirai jumped in on the west side of the city center, hovering fifty meters above the surface. Her port forward boarding hatch popped open, and two Ghatazhak in heavy combat armor stepped out, each disappearing in a flash of blue-white light, reappearing a split second later on the surface, their weapons firing.

"Where do you think you're going?" Josh said as he launched the last of his missiles at the Brodek surface batteries. He pulled his fighter into a tight left turn, coming over hard to get on the tail of a snub-fighter that had just taken off. He quickly switched his weapons selection to plasma cannons, bringing his nose onto the rising target. He pressed the trigger, sending several balls of red-orange plasma streaking toward the unprepared snub-fighter, blowing it apart and sending its remains crashing to the surface below.

"*Mirai, operators away,*" Aiden announced over comms.

"Weapons free!" he told his AI. "Splash any Brodek ships that try to get off the ground!"

"*QRF, operators away.*"

"*Maximum force?*" Josh's AI inquired.

"You guessed it," Josh replied as he rolled to the right to target another fighter.

"*Seiiki, operators away,*" Loki reported over comms.

"Stay with me, Lannie," Josh said. "Don't let anyone get in behind me."

"*I've got your back,*" Lannie promised.

"What are you doing?" Loki wondered, noticing that Robert wasn't turning to their escape heading.

"I thought we might take out a few targets before we jump clear," Robert replied.

Loki couldn't help but smile. "It's like flying with Josh again."

"Except I'm better looking," Robert joked. "Feel free to target whatever you like."

"All over it," Loki assured him as he began selecting targets on the tactical screen.

Talisha rolled right, pushing her nose down, then pressed and held her weapons trigger, sending a series of red-orange balls of plasma racing out and slamming into the Brodek snub-fighter attempting to turn away from her. The target exploded in a ball of fire, raining down and igniting several fires in the process.

"This is going to get out of hand," she exclaimed.

"*Nothing we can do about that,*" Josh replied over comms. "*We keep the fighters off the shuttles, and the shuttles cover the Ghatazhak.*"

"I know, I'm just saying."

"*Slider! Two on your six!*" Tricia warned. "*They just jumped in! Break right! Break right!*"

Talisha rolled right and pulled back hard on her flight control stick, forcing her fighter to come about hard. Dragons could easily out-turn Brodek snub-fighters, which weren't very maneuverable to begin with. "Where the hell are you at, Remo!" she called as blasts of energy streaked past on her left, barely missing her.

Erica did her best to keep on top of the tactical

display, trying to ensure their AI wasn't missing any opportunities. As expected, it wasn't. "Our AI is dropping their shuttles like flies."

A blue-white flash high and to their left caught Aiden's eye. "It's not the shuttles I'm worried about."

Kit and Mori advanced slowly, their personal shields flashing brilliantly with each impact from Brodek energy weapons. With sweeping motions of their arms, their wrist-mounted energy cannons sent streams of yellow balls of energy the size of a man's fist in waves across the cityscape in front of them, stunning anyone unlucky enough to get in their way.

Meanwhile, their suit AIs controlled their shoulder-mounted cannons, targeting only those they identified as threats, firing balls of plasma that killed on impact.

As needed, guided rockets about the length of a man's hand popped up out of the Ghatazhak combat backpacks, their drives kicking in and sending them racing to their targets: any heavily armed combatants nearby.

Two men were dropping the enemy and stunning civilians by the hundreds. And there were three more pairs of soldiers doing the same thing around the city.

"I'm on them!" Nikolas assured his leader as he rolled out of his turn, coming up directly behind the two snub-fighters that had just jumped in behind Talisha. Before he could even think about it, his AI locked missiles on the two snub-fighters. Nikolas pressed his launch button, sending the missiles streaking forward. Both found their targets, breaking them apart in two roaring detonations that sent debris flying in all directions.

"*Yeah!*" Nikolas exclaimed. "*Your six is clear, boss!*"

"Nice shooting, Remo," Talisha replied.

Josh's threat alert indicator began flashing rapidly. "What the..." His eyes went wide. "Is that what I think it is?"

"*Brodek gunships,*" his AI reported.

"We've got trouble, people!"

Two more flashes of light appeared in the same part of the sky as the first.

"Three gunships," Erica announced. She looked at Aiden. "That's bad, right?"

"It sure ain't good," Aiden agreed. "Pop a comm-drone with word to the Aurora."

"On it."

"Attention all ships," Aiden called over comms. "Three gunships at one five seven, angels ten, five clicks out. Mirai is turning to engage."

"We are?" Erica asked.

"*Seiiki, engaging,*" Robert added.

"We need them to think we're all there is," Aiden reminded her.

"Oh yeah."

* * *

Ottar was able to avoid the black-clad men assaulting the city by taking back alleys and passages not known to most. By now, most of the Brodek combat shuttles and snub-fighters had been launched, and more than half of them had been shot down. The Brodek were losing, and he knew it.

He also knew what would happen to Crowden once Halvor Brodek realized his demise was inescapable. The only thing that could save them was their gunships. And their arrival would give him the cover he needed to get his own combat shuttle airborne and into the fight without getting shot down as soon as it took off.

Ottar could have taken any shuttle in the city, but he preferred his own. It was better armed and shielded than most, and he knew it well. Like most ships in the badlands, the Brodek shuttles were cobbled together from the parts of multiple ships, making each unique. Thanks to a few well-paid mechanics, his shuttle was faster and more maneuverable than most, and with the ease with which Captain Tuplo's Dragon fighters were picking off the Brodek forces, he was going to need it.

Ottar reached the building that shielded his shuttle from detection and quickly entered. As expected, his ship was waiting for him, having already responded to the activation signal he had transmitted the moment Crowden was attacked. He boarded, closing the hatch, and headed straight to the cockpit. A flip of a switch and the press of a button, and the roof above parted, his shuttle rising skyward. In seconds, he would join the fight for his clan.

As soon as he cleared the building, he accelerated forward and pitched up, jumping away almost instantly, transitioning to the upper atmosphere in the blink of an eye. He brought his ship around as his weapons and shields charged. A quick scan of the city below revealed that the situation was about to turn in their favor. All three of their gunships had arrived and were taking positions over the city, forcing the two shuttles providing air cover for Tuplo's ground forces to break off and engage the gunships. But their Dragon fighters were still having their way with the Brodek snub-fighters, and if the gunships didn't put down those two shuttles quickly, there would be no snub-fighters left, leaving them severely weakened.

Luckily, neither the ancient Navarro-class shuttles nor the Dragon fighters were significant threats to the heavily shielded gunships. It would take dozens of direct hits to even weaken them, let alone bring them down completely. Even then, the gunships were armored and compartmentalized, designed to take considerable punishment and still get their crews home safely. They were a reward from the Korsan for more than a decade of membership, and they all but guaranteed that none of the lesser, unaffiliated clans would make a play for Brodek territory.

But Tuplo was something different, and Ottar knew it. He was obviously not another clan leader seeking entry by conquering another. And he wasn't a well-funded privateer looking to make a quick fortune and then move on to the next region of the badlands once the Vernay worlds realized they were better off with the Brodek protecting them. This Tuplo character had a different agenda, and if he was to be taken down, Ottar would have to figure out what that agenda was.

Ottar selected the two enemy shuttles as his targets then turned his ship toward them, jumping back down to join the battle.

* * *

Waiting while others were engaged in battle had never been Nathan's strong suit. The fact that the Aurora's current lack of a fully functional AI required him to be in the pilot's seat was the only thing keeping him from pacing the bridge.

"New contact," Laza reported. "Comm-drone."

"It's from the Mirai," Sima added. "Three gunships have joined the fight over Crowden. The Mirai and the Seiiki are engaging."

"Did they include any sensor data?" Nathan asked.

"I've got it," Jessica announced from the tactical station. "It looks like they've neutralized most of the surface batteries, and the Ghatazhak are wreaking havoc in the city. There are still about fifty snub-fighters and about a dozen shuttles in the air. The Mirai and the Seiiki aren't going to be able to do much attacking with that many ships gunning for them, even with the Dragons flying cover."

"My analysis of the sensor data on the gunships indicates that our shuttles would not be effective deterrents, even without the Brodek forces to deal with."

"Comms, message to all forces. Be ready to break contact with the gunships," Nathan instructed. "We're going in."

"Aye, sir."

"Just avoid low-altitude passes if you can," Vladimir suggested. "The grav-lift systems may still need a little work."

"No promises," Nathan replied.

"Sending you course and speed data for insertion jump," Abby reported.

Nathan glanced at the jump data as it came across his displays. "Is that the closest you can get us?"

"No, but it's the closest I'm *comfortable* getting us."

"Hopefully, those gunships will be watching the skies," Cameron stated.

"Jess, the moment we're in range, you light them up," Nathan instructed.

"My pleasure."

* * *

"First wave of missiles failed to penetrate their shields," Loki reported as the Seiiki rocked from incoming energy weapons fire from the Brodek gunship.

"Let's see how they handle plasma torpedoes," Robert said as he lined up his ship on the target. A press of the trigger and three red-orange balls of plasma shot out from either side, slamming into the gunship's forward shields less than a kilometer away.

"Barely a one percent drop in their shield strength," Loki reported. "Their guns may not be that powerful, but their shields are rock solid."

The shuttle lurched violently, her tail kicking to port without warning.

"Damn!" Robert exclaimed. "Not that powerful?"

"Relatively speaking," Loki admitted.

"All Dragon leads, ignore the snub-fighters and leave them to your wingmen," Josh instructed as he rolled his fighter out of its turn. "Leads attack the gunships. Wingmen, only attack targets that are attacking our ground forces."

"*What if their fighters are attacking us?*" Tika wondered.

"Let them pound you. Lead them away from the colony," Josh instructed. "Your shields can take it. And don't wuss out and jump away just because your teeth are gettin' rattled! The moment you do, they'll turn around and strafe the Ghatazhak!"

"*There's no way we're bringing down those gunships,*" Talisha insisted.

"We don't have to," Josh replied. "All we have to do is make them believe we're all there is…right up to the moment the Aurora arrives."

"*Lovely.*"

"Sometimes we're the predators, and sometimes we're the prey," Josh mused as he jumped forward and opened up on one of the gunships with his plasma cannons.

The Mirai passed close underneath the first gunship, both ship's shields lighting up as they scraped past.

The shuttle lurched downward sharply, forcing Aiden to compensate with additional grav-lift power to avoiding slamming into the tops of the buildings passing beneath them.

"Our weapons are doing nothing!" Erica exclaimed. "Maybe we should get out of here while we can!"

"Not yet," Aiden insisted.

"Our shields are down to fifty percent!"

"We'll last a few more minutes at least," Aiden told her.

Erica shook her head as the ship took more incoming fire, bouncing about wildly. "I prefer flying cargo ships."

Aiden smiled. "Don't worry, you get used to it."

"You shouldn't *have* to!"

Kit's eyes constantly shifted between the position of Brodek combatants and the status of his personal shield. Even though he was neutralizing dozens of men every minute, all the Ghatazhak were still taking heavy fire.

"*Shields have fallen below fifty percent,*" his suit AI warned. "*Recommend cover to allow partial recharge to occur.*"

"Evens take cover!" Kit ordered over comms. "Odds, keep pounding them until you're down to twenty percent, then we swap!"

Kit glanced at the tactical display in the inside of his helmet visor, noting that half of his team was moving to cover positions as instructed. He quickly looked at several targets, all of which were the most direct threats to himself and the other three Ghatazhak remaining in the open, causing his AI to automatically select them.

"*Launching anti-personnel seekers,*" his AI reported.

Four projectiles, not much bigger than a man's finger, fired straight up from Kit's combat backpack, arcing over smoothly as each steered toward a different Brodek soldier currently firing at him.

Kit focused his wrist cannon fire on combatants not currently targeted by any of the Ghatazhak, so as to maximize his efficiency of fire.

A squad of six Brodek men, all armed with heavy assault energy rifles, appeared from between the buildings behind him, taking aim as they deployed.

The two small cannons mounted to the shoulders of his combat pack spun around and opened fire, dropping all six of the men about to ambush Kit from behind.

At the same time, the four seekers found their targets, embedding themselves in the torsos of their unsuspecting victims, exploding a second after impact, sending bits and pieces of flesh and blood flying.

"Enemy fire is becoming more concentrated," his AI reported. "Shields down to forty percent."

The bridge of the Aurora lurched violently as it came out of the jump, its windows full of swirling, dark gray clouds outside.

"What the hell?" Nathan exclaimed.

"We're in the atmosphere," Cameron reported, urgency in her tone. "Five kilometers above the surface and falling fast, about two hundred kilometers east of the Crowden colony."

"What the hell, Abby?" Nathan said as he advanced the grav-lift throttles to arrest their rapid descent.

"I'm not sure what happened," Abby replied. "Maybe some kind of a power surge..."

"Don't blame me," Vladimir defended.

"Multiple contacts!" Laza warned. "Three gunships, thirty-eight snub-fighters, and eight shuttles."

"What about our forces?" Nathan asked.

"Hard to tell, they're jumping around so much. One moment."

"The gunships are pounding the hell out of our shuttles," Jessica reported from the tactical station. "But the Dragons are jumping around so much they can barely be tracked."

Nathan struggled to keep the ship level. "I could use a little help, Vlad."

"I'm working on it!" Vladimir insisted. "I told you to avoid low passes!"

"Not my idea," Nathan reminded him.

"Locking jump missiles on the gunships," Jessica reported.

"Good idea," Nathan agreed.

"Descent is slowing," Cameron reported. "Two point five clicks, two point two five...two clicks...... and holding! Nice work."

Nathan accepted the compliment while trying to balance the ship on their constantly fluctuating grav-lift emitters. "This is no way to fly, Vlad."

"Maybe you should consider climbing?"

"Good locks," Jessica reported.

"Fire away," Nathan instructed.

Ottar jumped in behind one of the antique Navarro-class shuttles attacking a gunship, opening fire on the unsuspecting vessel. The enemy's stern shields flashed with each impact, and Ottar watched with satisfaction as his sensors displayed the target's rapidly falling shield strength. His more powerful weapons had been money well spent.

Twelve missiles shot out of the Aurora from either side as she plowed through the swirling gray clouds, jumping away as soon as they cleared the hull.

The Seiiki rocked and jolted from side to side.

"We've got a combat shuttle on our six," Loki warned.

"*Attention all shuttles and Dragons,*" Sima called over comms. "*Break engagement and clear the area.*"

"Sounds like an excellent idea," Robert decided, pulling his flight control stick up and his throttles forward.

A sinister smile crept onto Ottar's face. He was certain that he had the ship dead to rights. He pitched up hard, keeping his guns on the fleeing shuttle, continuing to batter its stern shields. In a few more seconds, their shields would fail, and...

Flashes of blue-white light coming from all around him suddenly lit up his cockpit, followed by detonations, four of which were on the gunship directly ahead of him. Another flash of blue-white light, and the shuttle that he was about to destroy was gone.

Ottar instinctively rolled right and turned, activating his own jump drive to get clear before it was too late.

"Oh crap!" Aiden exclaimed, pulling up hard as detonations began going off all around the gunships before him. He touched his jump button, transitioning his shuttle five clicks ahead and several thousand meters higher. "I think the Aurora just arrived."

The Aurora streaked over the top of the three gunships that had just been struck with a dozen of its jump missiles, their ventral guns firing with both their plasma cannon barrels and their rail guns. The shields of the Brodek gunships, now weakened by the multiple impacts of the Aurora's more powerful missiles, flashed and sputtered, struggling to stay energized and effective.

Kit looked up as the Aurora passed overhead, hammering both gunships with her massive quad-barreled ventral guns, and the Brodek troops on the surface with the smaller point-defense cannons along her sides.

She passed over them with a thunderous roar, kicking up dust, her grav-lift systems humming loudly.

Kit glanced back at the enemy, seeing them being taken out right and left by the Aurora's guns. Their plan had worked. He and his men had drawn the Brodek out, and the Aurora was picking them off with ease.

"Now *that's* an entrance!" he exclaimed, opening fire on the few combatants still standing.

One of the gunships leaned right, looking as if it was losing balance and about to roll over, but it managed to level itself and turn away.

The second gunship barely avoided colliding with the first, its pilot quickly climbing to pass over the other.

The third gunship, having now lost all shields, and with smoke pouring out of its dorsal stern aspect, turned left and tried to accelerate but found its engines not cooperating.

"Are you targeting their gunships?" Nathan asked as he struggled to keep the Aurora under control while they passed over the city.

"I'm targeting *everyone!*" Jessica replied.

"Target three has lost all shields, and its port engine is offline," Laze reported. "The other two still have partial shields and are attempting to maneuver to higher altitudes."

"Coming about," Nathan reported as he began a slow turn to port. "Jess, put another round of missiles on targets one and two, and put our big guns on target three as we come about."

"All over it," Jessica assured him.

"Maybe we should climb as well?" Vladimir suggested as he found himself constantly adjusting the output of the Aurora's grav-lift emitters to keep them from flipping over.

"I don't know, I think we're doing pretty well," Nathan insisted, knowing it would irritate his friend.

"Let me rephrase," Vladimir suggested. "Climb now before I lose complete control over the grav-lift emitters, and we roll over and crash."

Ottar brought his shuttle around to jump back into the fray but suddenly found a Dragon jumping in directly in front of him. There was a bright, red-orange flash, and his ship shook violently, warning lights and alarms flashing all over his console.

The Dragon fighter passed low over him, pounding his ship.

More alarms sounded, and Ottar quickly pressed his jump button, transitioning into high orbit. He glanced at his sensors, noticing that one of the gunships had just broken up and was crashing down into the city. The other two were moving away, but in haphazard fashion, while the much larger ship that had just arrived was making a casual turn to reengage, confident in its superiority over the Brodek gunships.

The third gunship broke in half as the Aurora's plasma cannons ripped her open, and the entire ship came crashing down, pulverizing several buildings.

The other two gunships were coming about, trying to get in behind the Aurora, their still-functional guns blazing.

Loki studied his tactical display in the Seiiki, watching as red icons disappeared. "Brodek ships are dropping like flies," he reported.

"Kind of makes you wonder why we didn't just lead with the Aurora, doesn't it?" Robert remarked.

Ottar was also watching icons dropping off his sensor display. His clan was losing and quickly, and there was nothing he could do to prevent it. So he dialed up a jump out of the system and activated it.

It was time to move on.

Multiple jump missiles suddenly appeared directly in the path of the two Brodek gunships attempting to maneuver into optimum firing positions on the Aurora. One of their shields failed with the first impact, allowing the other three missiles to find the target's unprotected hull. The resulting detonations blew the gunship apart, raining debris onto the city below.

"Hell yeah!" Josh exclaimed, seeing that more than half of the Brodek's airborne forces had been taken out by the Aurora. "All Dragons, jump up to intercept runners!"

"*Shields at twenty-two percent,*" Kit's AI warned.

Incoming weapons fire from Brodek troops suddenly eased to only a few shots here and there. There was a loud explosion behind him, and a few seconds later, the resistance stopped completely.

Kit glanced back, seeing the last gunship limping away, looking as if it would be lucky to stay aloft much longer. He looked back, spotting men emerging from cover, their weapons held up to indicate surrender. One by one, they placed their weapons on the ground, their hands held high, and the icons on the inside of his tactical visor started changing from red to orange.

"Last gunship is losing power," Laza reported from the Aurora's sensor station. "She appears to be headed for a controlled crash-landing outside the city."

"Keep an eye on them," Nathan told Jessica. "If they manage to recover, hit them again."

"I've got another round of missiles locked on her," Jessica replied.

"Ghatazhak report remaining ground forces are surrendering," Sima reported.

"Remaining snub-fighters and combat shuttles are fleeing," Laza added.

"What are you doing?" Vladimir asked Nathan.

"I'm putting us into a hover," Nathan replied.

"Why?"

"Psychological impact."

"Could you maybe get the same impact from a higher altitude?"

"Just keep her in the air, Vlad."

* * *

It took only minutes for the Ghatazhak to round up the last of the Brodek's forces, including accessing their headquarters and retrieving their leader, Halvor Brodek.

Chief Anson and Corporal Teece brought Halvor to Kit, who was standing before the group of prisoners now being guarded by his men.

"You must be Halvor Brodek," Kit greeted.

"Are you Captain Tuplo?" Halvor growled.

"Not exactly," Kit replied. "He's up there," Kit added, pointing over his shoulder to the Aurora hovering about one hundred meters above the city behind him.

"I should have known," Halvor sneered. "Tell your captain that I challenge him to face me and fight me to the death."

Kit tapped his comm-set. "Captain? Halvor Brodek is challenging you to a fight to the death."

"*I'm on my way,*" Nathan replied.

Kit smiled at Halvor. "Enjoy the night air while you still can, old man."

* * *

"This is a really bad idea," Cameron said as Nathan rose from his seat at the Aurora's helm station.

"Take over the helm," Nathan told her, not wanting to discuss his decision any further. "Maintain position," he added as he headed for the exit.

Cameron was not happy about Nathan's plan but took the helm anyway.

Jessica didn't like it either and followed Nathan out. "Nathan," she called as she entered the corridor outside of the bridge.

"Are you going to try to talk me out of this as well?" Nathan snapped.

"Stop a moment and listen," Jessica demanded, grabbing his shoulder and turning him to face her. "You have no idea what you're about to face," Jessica began.

"I have to put an end to this."

"Agreed."

"Then what?"

Jessica paused a moment, thinking. "Don't play by someone else's rules."

"What?"

"Make *them* play by *your* rules," she explained. "That's how you win."

"By cheating?"

"No such thing when it comes to life and death." She stared him in the eyes then said, "These people don't need to see a diplomat. They need to see a badass. So go *be* that badass."

* * *

A single Dragon fighter shot out of the Aurora's port launch tube as she hovered above the Crowden colony, just south of the center spaceport where the Brodek prisoners were being detained. The fighter's wings unfolded and it rolled sharply to the right, coming around the Aurora's bow as it descended rapidly toward the surface. In less than a minute, the sleek black fighter's landing gear extended, and it set down about ten meters from Kit, Mori, and Halvor Brodek. The canopy slid back, and Nathan climbed out, immediately dismounting and heading toward Kit and the Brodek leader.

By now, a crowd had begun to gather. Colonists were coming out of their hiding places and had nearly surrounded the open spaceport field that encircled the Brodek headquarters at its center. All wanted to witness the fall of the Brodek, as well as discover who would now rule their world in their place.

Nathan strolled confidently toward them, coming to a stop near Kit.

"Captain, Halvor Brodek," Kit said, introducing the pirate leader.

Halvor looked like an angry bull, ready to charge at any moment. When he saw Nathan and realized the significant size advantage he had over his adversary, a sinister smile came across his face. He could practically taste his victory, and nothing was more satisfying than snatching victory from the jaws of defeat.

Nathan noticed the saber hanging from the Brodek leader's hip.

"Someone give this man a blade, so that I may kill him," Halvor seethed.

"I don't need one," Nathan replied.

Although he didn't show it, Kit became more alert. Nathan was up to something, and he needed to be ready to back whatever play his leader made, just as every one of his men would.

"I challenge you to mortal combat," Halvor demanded, making sure that everyone watching heard his challenge.

"I don't recognize your right to challenge me to anything," Nathan declared.

"I will have your head!" Halvor exclaimed, drawing his saber and pointing it at Nathan's face.

In the blink of an eye, Nathan drew his sidearm and fired a single shot, striking the Brodek leader in the right shoulder.

Kit and the rest of the Ghatazhak immediately went to combat stances, their arms up and their wrist cannons charging while their shoulder-mounted mini-cannons deployed and took aim at the prisoners.

The Brodek prisoners were stunned, by both the actions of this rogue captain as well as the speed at which his men were ready to strike them all down.

Halvor Brodek fell to his knees. The pain in his shoulder was horrific, and it caused him to lose his grip on his saber, dropping it as he fell. He looked up at Nathan, the young captain's gun hand dangling at his side.

Kit stepped closer, whispering, "Nice shot."

"I was aiming for his head," Nathan whispered back.

Halvor could not believe what had just happened. "That is not the pirate way!" he exclaimed with great fury.

"I'm not a fucking pirate," Nathan declared as he stepped closer. He then raised his gun again and shot Halvor in the face, killing him instantly.

Gasps from the crowd had met the first shot, but silence met the second.

Nathan looked down at the dead Brodek leader. "Why is it always *one man* who causes so much pain?" he said, mostly to himself. He then looked up, scanning the faces of the stunned prisoners, and then those of the equally stunned colonists. "This world, and all the worlds the Brodek once controlled, are now free!" he shouted for all to hear. "Do with them what you will! Run them how you see fit! But know this! Anyone who uses force over others to get their way will have to deal with us!"

After a moment, one of the prisoners in front spoke up. "Who the *fuck* are you?"

Nathan glared at the man for a moment. "I am Nathan Scott!" he barked. He then pointed back at the Aurora hovering nearby. "And *that* is the Aurora!"

Thank you for reading this story.
(*A review would be greatly appreciated!*)

Visit us online at
frontierssaga.com
or on Facebook

Want to be notified when
new episodes are published?
Want access to additional scenes and more?
Join our mailing list!

frontierssaga.com/mailinglist/

Manufactured by Amazon.ca
Bolton, ON